HEAVEN'S
WAR

David S. Goyer &
Michael Cassutt

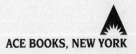

ACE BOOKS, NEW YORK

THE BERKLEY PUBLISHING GROUP
Published by the Penguin Group
Penguin Group (USA) Inc.
375 Hudson Street, New York, New York 10014, USA

USA | Canada | UK | Ireland | Australia | New Zealand | India | South Africa | China

Penguin Books Ltd., Registered Offices: 80 Strand, London WC2R 0RL, England
For more information about the Penguin Group, visit penguin.com.

HEAVEN'S WAR

An Ace Book / published by arrangement with the authors

Ace Books are published by The Berkley Publishing Group.
ACE and the "A" design are trademarks of Penguin Group (USA) Inc.

For information, address: The Berkley Publishing Group,
a division of Penguin Group (USA) Inc.,
375 Hudson Street, New York, New York 10014.

ISBN: 978-0-425-25619-0

PUBLISHING HISTORY
Ace hardcover edition / July 2012
Ace premium edition / July 2013

PRINTED IN THE UNITED STATES OF AMERICA

10 9 8 7 6 5 4 3 2 1

Cover art by James Paick.
Cover design by Lesley Worrell.
Interior illustration by Steve Karp.

This is a work of fiction. Names, characters, places, and incidents either are the product
of the authors' imaginations or are used fictitiously, and any resemblance to actual persons,
living or dead, business establishments, events, or locales is entirely coincidental.
The publisher does not have any control over and does not assume any responsibility for
author or third-party websites or their content.

ALWAYS LEARNING   PEARSON

PRAISE FOR

Heaven's War

"This is the best kind of hard science fiction: the kind that creates a world that feels plausible. This is a universe where cause and effect still applies. The blending of science fiction and suspense is absolutely superb. This book is definitely its own story while still fitting into the big picture. It's the sort of work that can hold its own among the genre's greats: the Clarkes and the Nivens and the Heinleins."   *—The Maine Edge*

PRAISE FOR

Heaven's Shadow

"David Goyer always delivers thoroughly imagined, minutely researched worlds, spun around the most outlandish premises; Goyer acknowledges and understands the genre while turning it over its head."

—Guillermo del Toro, creator of *Pan's Labyrinth* and *New York Times* bestselling coauthor of *The Night Eternal*

"A terrific SF novel from two of the hottest scriptwriters in Hollywood. With *Heaven's Shadow*, Cassutt and Goyer give Arthur C. Clarke a run for his money. Prepare to have your world rocked."

—Robert J. Sawyer, Hugo and Nebula award–winning author of *Red Planet Blues*

"In a fast-paced blending of *Rendezvous with Rama* and *The Right Stuff*, Goyer and Cassutt offer a compelling yarn about first contact in the near future. Nobody 'does NASA' better."

—David Brin, Hugo and Nebula award–winning author of *Existence*

continued . . .

"*Heaven's Shadow* is a big, sprawling epic that recalls Arthur C. Clarke at his heights. It moves steadily through surprising twists, reverses, revelations, and a big finish. Better still, there's more to come!"

—**Gregory Benford, Nebula Award–winning coauthor of *Bowl of Heaven***

"Reading this book is like riding a roller coaster—full of unexpected twists and turns that lead to a thrilling conclusion. For those who like a good dose of science with their fiction, enjoy challenging their theological beliefs, and perhaps once wished to become an astronaut themselves, this book will be a great read."
—***Booklist***

"*Heaven's Shadow* is a faster-than-the-speed-of-light science fiction [novel] that targets readers who prefer action to the *n*th degree . . . Fans who relish an outer space . . . disaster thriller along the lines of movies like *Armageddon* will appreciate this exciting tale of first contact."
—***Alternative Worlds***

"A fast-paced SF trilogy opener that features a varied cast and an intriguing plot . . . A cinematic style and action-filled plot make this a good choice for readers who enjoy the multivolume space sagas of Kevin J. Anderson and David Drake."
—***Library Journal***

"[A] slick space opera trilogy starter."
—***Publishers Weekly***

"*Heaven's Shadow* is worth the price of admission, delivering a blockbuster novel full of pulse-pounding thrills and epic fun. Throw in popcorn, soda, and 3-D glasses, and it's almost like being at the movies . . . Crisp pacing, characters with engaging personalities and distinctive traits, accessible prose, and skillfully handled plotting highlighted by nearly nonstop tension and excitement . . . *Heaven's Shadow* is one of the most entertaining novels I've read this year, offering more bang for your buck than most big-budget movies that will be released this summer."
—***Fantasy Book Critic***

**Ace Books by David S. Goyer
and Michael Cassutt**

Dedicated to all our Architects, especially
Jack Vance
Gene Wolfe
Jack McDevitt
Allen Steele
and
Connie Willis

NEO "Keanu" Interior

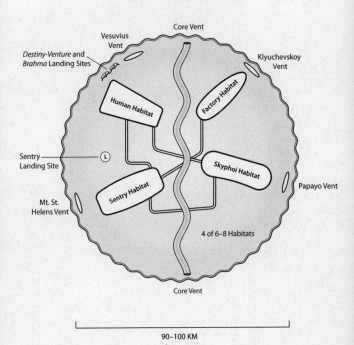

Core Vent

Vesuvius Vent

Destiny-Venture and *Brahma* Landing Sites

Klyuchevskoy Vent

Human Habitat

Factory Habitat

Sentry Landing Site

Skyphoi Habitat

Papayo Vent

Mt. St. Helens Vent

Sentry Habitat

4 of 6–8 Habitats

Core Vent

90–100 KM

Dramatis Personae

Present on Keanu

ZACK STEWART, astronomer and astronaut, former commander of *Destiny-7*

CAMILLA MUNARETTO, 9, Revenant

YVONNE HALL, astronaut Revenant

COWBOY, dog, formerly the property of Shane Weldon

DASH, Sentry

Houston Group

RACHEL STEWART, 14, Zack's daughter

SHANE WELDON, *Destiny-7* mission director

HARLEY DRAKE, former astronaut

SASHA BLAINE, astronomer

GABRIEL JONES, former director of the NASA Johnson Space Center

BRENT BYNUM, White House deputy

XAVIER TOUTANT, Katrina refugee, drug dealer

Bangalore Group

VIKRAM NAYAR, *Brahma* mission director

ZHAO BUOMING, Chinese intelligence agent

PAVAK RADHAKRISHNAN, 16, son of *Brahma* commander Taj

MAKALI PILLAY, exobiologist

VALENTINA MAKAROVA, exolinguist

DALE SCOTT, disgraced former astronaut

CHITRAN RANHOTRA, refugee and mother

JAIDEV MAHABALA, enterprising engineer

DAKSHA SAIKUMAR, engineer

HEAVEN'S
WAR

DESTINY-7 LANDING

NASA's *Destiny-7* multipurpose crew vehicle successfully splashed down today in the Pacific Ocean near San Clemente Island, California, at 9:45 A.M. PDT.

The combined crew of acting mission commander Tea Nowinski and *Brahma* spacecraft crew members Taj Radhakrishnan, Natalia Yorkina, and Lucas Munaretto were taken aboard the recovery vessel *Liberty* within an hour and are undergoing physical examinations at Vandenberg Air Force Base.

Nowinski is expected to return to Houston this evening.

The landing ended a ten-day mission filled with anomalies, including unplanned events aboard the Near-Earth Object Keanu that resulted in the deaths of *Destiny-7* astronauts Patrick Downey and Yvonne Hall as well as *Brahma* cosmonaut Dennis Chertok and the apparent loss of mission commander Zack Stewart. The Coalition spacecraft *Brahma* was also destroyed, resulting in a combined return crew.

NASA mission control continues its attempts to contact Stewart. Meanwhile, Keanu has departed Earth orbit at a speed of over 40,000 kilometers an hour.

Those seeking information regarding the impacts near Houston and Bangalore are referred to the U.S. Department of Homeland Security. NASA PRESS RELEASE

Just came out of the presser—amazing in its uselessness. Dear God, "anomalies"? *Destiny-7* made it back, yeah, but no one is talking about the two UFOs and 200 MISSING PEO-PLE!!!!

POSTER ALMAZ AT NEOMISSION.COM

Part One

No one's going to read this, I guess. Not even me. But it has to be done.

Slate battery power is better than it used to be. If I'm careful, I might have two days with it. (It'll last longer because I'm not using the Net, ever again.)

Anyway, here's what I know: I'm Pav Radhakrishnan, and I'm 16.

Last week two spacecraft, one from NASA commanded by Zack Stewart, and the other from the Coalition of India-Brazil-Russia commanded by my father, Taj, landed on the Near-Earth Object named Keanu . . . and everything went to shit. First, it turned out that there were aliens living on Keanu as well as human beings. And these human beings were people who were killed on Earth—including Stewart's wife, Megan, and a girl named Camilla. Pretty fucking weird.

Then two of the NASA astronauts got killed and one of the Brahmans. No one's quite sure how or why, but they're gone.

Brahma got blown up.

Eventually four of the survivors, including my father, managed to get aboard the *Destiny* spacecraft and head back to Earth.

Two days ago me and about a hundred other people from Bangalore got abducted from Earth by a big white balloon thing, some kind of spaceship sent by the Near-Earth Object Keanu. Wrong place, wrong time, story of my young life. About eighty other people got collected from Houston, Texas, too.

We're all here now, trying to figure out what the hell we do now—how do we eat, sleep, live? Oh, yeah: Who grabbed us and why?

And how do we get away from them?

It's weird to think I'm never going to see my father again, and that we were really just passing each other in space.

I'm going to call this the Keanu-pedia.

Correction: No one HUMAN is ever going to read this.

KEANU-PEDIA BY PAV, ENTRY #1

THE PRISONER

The days no longer had meaning. Even in the space beyond the barrier between the Prisoner and its former habitat, the cycle of light/lesser light/lesser dark/full dark/light had been irregular. The Keepers had almost certainly been manipulating it.

But now even that false rhythm was missing. Here one could rely only on the subtle gradations of the barrier's temperatures. Touch warm: light. Touch cold: dark.

A poor method of keeping time, especially when keeping time was the only activity available.

There was food—barely enough to sustain life, nowhere near sufficient to give one energy for action. Waste simply drained away.

It was almost certainly another stratagem by the Keepers: to keep a being alive indefinitely, but useless, able only to measure the dimensions of the living space, to create fantastical scenarios of revenge, then to sleep and dream.

Then, somewhere in the next cycle, to repeat.

Even the revenge fantasies had long grown old and too familiar. Lately, in the past six cycles, they had given way to reconciliation dreams!

To consider reconciliation with the Keepers—that was a

sure sign of madness, and a cause for terror. . . . What came after that? Complete mental collapse?

Fortunately, there had been an interruption . . . sharp vibrations through the floor and walls that allowed the Prisoner to reconnect with the physical universe, no matter how limited.

Revenge scenarios were once again dominant. There was much touching of the walls, in search of temperature data and now more vibrations.

Something was happening beyond the chamber. Whether bad or good, it was welcome . . . if only because it meant change.

ZACK

Where was it?

The question played in Zack Stewart's mind like an annoying ad jingle. And those three words had been present all through the past seventy-odd hours . . . hours that were very odd indeed, if, in fact, they even numbered seventy . . .

Formerly a typical middle-aged American male of less than average height and weight, often dressed in khakis and polo shirts, he had become a haggard-looking man in stained and soiled long johns. Designed to be worn under a NASA EVA suit, said long johns were actually a garment filled with small plastic tubes through which water circulated. The outfit was now the only tangible reminder of Zack's former life as an astronaut. Or as an inhabitant of planet Earth.

His life before Keanu.

Lacking a mirror and able to feel the ragged stubble on his face, he suspected that he now looked like a cartoon castaway, which, come to think of it, was exactly his state. Stranded on the interplanetary equivalent of a desert island—

Steady, he told himself. *You've been running on fumes for a week. You're stranded on a runaway planetoid. Your choices are . . . find the exit from this habitat while still breathing.*

Or lie down and die.

Even that decision wasn't simple: Death on Keanu, anywhere around Keanu, didn't seem to be permanent, or not immediately permanent.

Maybe that whole life-death-what-have-you business was why he kept looking for the way out.

Because of Megan. The last he'd seen of his wife, she had been swallowed up by a rogue Sentry and carried off to certain death. An hour later, Zack had had to fight a Sentry . . . The same one? He'd thought so at the time.

Now . . . he wasn't so sure.

Of course now, he was five days more exhausted, five days less fed. Five days more distracted.

Because two days after losing Megan, after killing that Sentry, 187 people had arrived on Keanu. According to them, they had been literally scooped from the surface of the Earth and carried across almost half a million kilometers in a pair of giant Objects that resembled soap bubbles—

"Great number," Harley Drake had said. "One eighty-seven is the section of the California Penal Code for murder." Harley was Zack's best friend, a fellow astronaut who had been crippled in the auto accident that killed Megan Stewart (for the first time, he had to remind himself, two years before the *Destiny* mission), only to somehow wind up on Keanu, too.

It was clear from the moment the 187 arrived that, beyond what they wore or carried, they had no clothing, few tools, no shelter, not even a common language. There *was* food on Keanu—the habitat had obviously been designed for creatures from Earth, but which era? There were edible plants, but few that Zack recognized. And how long would those supplies last? What nasty parasites or Keanu-specific bacteria were waiting to strike humans living on the Keanu diet of fruits and vegetables?

There was also a lack of organization and leadership. Plenty of candidates, but to what end? Questions like "Can we go home?" or "Are we stuck here forever?" couldn't be answered.

Zack was the human race's expert on Keanu—a title he would gladly have relinquished, given the shallowness of his expertise.

Not that it stopped everyone, including Harley, from bombarding him with questions, questions, questions.

Maybe that was another reason to go walkabout: for the sweet moment of silence.

There was also shame and nagging responsibility; the castaways' presence here was largely due to Zack's actions as commander of *Destiny-7*. Zack had seen the anger in more than a few of their faces. How long before someone picked up a rock and clubbed him to death, just for the sheer catharsis?

So, yes, Zack had wanted to get away from them.

Even from his own daughter, one of the miraculously improbable new immigrants. Well, not so improbable: Harley Drake had been her guardian. If Harley got himself nabbed, Rachel couldn't have been far away. And Zack had since learned that the reality was the opposite: It was actually *Rachel's* fault that the pair had wound up in the not-so-magic 187.

But, much as he cherished the contact with his daughter, Zack feared the road ahead. Rachel's life—just like the lives of all humans on Keanu—might turn out to be nasty, brutish, and short.

Wouldn't it have been better to leave his daughter to a full life on Earth? She'd have been an orphan . . . but she'd have learned to deal with it.

Another reason to beat himself up.

He needed to think. He needed to take stock.

He needed to explore.

During the horrible end game of the First Contact on Keanu, in which his crewmates had been forced to leave him, in which Megan had been killed a second time . . . Zack had seen what he could only call Keanu's "Factory." He had walked the broad "streets" of this second habitat, marveled at its mysterious but somehow functional structures.

He knew that answers to their situation, and tools to improve it, were likely to be found there.

If only he could reach it.

So, as one of the vaguely defined Keanu days ended (the light in the habitat did not change much), Zack had simply slipped away and headed back toward the tunnel to the Factory . . . a distance surely less than a couple of kilometers.

And now here he was, as alone as any human being in history, and as vulnerable . . . painfully and slowly working his way along one wall of the habitat . . . its farthest reach almost misty in the distance, surely ten or more kilometers away, at the end of the chamber.

In best Boy Scout fashion, Zack had managed to find traces of his earlier passage, when carrying Camilla in that frantic escape. The ground surface was a nanotech-based regolith, but it acted like hard-packed dirt.

And, in places, not so hard-packed. Here were their tracks, unmistakable.

But as far as he could determine, the tunnel he had used to reach the Factory was simply gone! It was like a scene from some episode of the Arabian Nights—as if a giant stone door now blocked his escape.

Had there actually been a door, Zack might have been able to locate the spot where the passage used to be . . . some fine crack or edge.

One thing he had been able to do with his spare time was to create a three-dimensional image of Keanu in his head . . . the Near-Earth Object was a sphere more than a hundred kilometers in diameter. Zack's crew and the competing Coalition *Brahma* team had landed near Vesuvius Vent, one of many craters on Keanu's icy-rocky surface. Vesuvius had been located near Keanu's equator; both teams had descended through the vent, then traversed subterranean tunnels that had given them access to this habitat.

Zack pictured a fat cylinder running from surface to core . . . but that could be wrong: The habitat might just as easily lie at angles to the core.

No matter. He and the others were inside it, until they figured some way out. They couldn't go back the way they had come—Zack's team had entered through a passage that was exposed to the vacuum of Keanu's surface.

And while the information from the 187 new arrivals was still jumbled, it appeared that they, too, had come to the habitat via a one-way system.

Well, Keanu's environment had changed twice in the week Zack had been part of it. Plant growth, sky, temperatures, everything seemed variable, as if programmed by a machine somewhere (likely the case) or, a more horrible thought, entirely at random.

There was no reason to think Keanu's environment would stay the same. A passage that had been open five days ago was now closed, as if the habitat were some kind of Rubik's Cube. Bad news for Zack.

But who was to say it might not open again?

Besides, Zack was so unsure of his directional abilities and perceptions that he made a second, broader sweep of the area near the wall. With his back to it, he ranged a couple of hundred meters to his left, back toward the Temple and the other humans . . . and found no opening or, indeed, anything but more wall.

So he retraced his steps and marched forward, deeper into the habitat. It was as if his mood sank with every ten meters. It wasn't distance from the other survivors that caused it . . . it was the realization that his moment of freedom, adventure, and exploration was about to end.

He was going to have to go back, to resume his unwanted post as titular "leader."

And father.

And he felt completely unequipped for either role—

He stopped. The light inside the Keanu habitat was never as bright as noon on Earth; at its best, it was equivalent to a cloudy morning.

So Zack couldn't be sure what he was seeing . . . some kind of object not far ahead, up against the wall, that was not a plant or tree, and not shaped like the rocks here, either.

He began to run, the tubes in his long johns making clicking and zipping sounds, like corduroy pants—

Then he stopped, because he suddenly knew what he was seeing less than five meters away.

It was the body of a human female so mangled it appeared to have almost been torn in two. It reminded Zack of some classic crime photo—California again, the Blue . . . or was it the Black Dahlia?

Only this wasn't some stranger unlucky enough to be the victim of a crime.

This was Megan, his reborn wife . . . killed a second time by a Sentry. She had sacrificed herself so that Zack and Camilla could live.

He knelt, noting with some relief—the only relief he could summon—that her eyes were closed and her features seemed peaceful.

Zack had already gone through the horror of seeing Megan dead once before, after the auto accident in Florida. That time she—her body—had been intact. But her expression had been different; colder, deader somehow.

This face was more . . . resigned? Accepting? Knowing?

Stop it. He was projecting. He needed to be practical. He couldn't leave her like this—

Not far from the wall he found a stand of trees with giant, fanlike leaves. There were similar trees near the Temple, and one of the survivors had already dubbed them "ginkgos."

Zack stripped off several leaves and several lengths of vine.

He returned to Megan's body and set about the heart-breaking task of rearranging the remains . . . then gently wrapping them for transport.

Zack might not have found the passage, but he'd found closure.

RACHEL

Shortly after dawn, the rain stopped.

At least, that was how Rachel Stewart would have described it: "Dawn" inside the Keanu human habitat meant that after nine or so hours of low light, the squiggly shaped glowtubes in the ceiling warmed up and grew somewhat brighter. A day? It was a lot like one of the few phrases Rachel remembered from the Bible—"the light followed the dark," something like that. There was no sunrise or noon . . . only the glowtubes coming on, then fourteen hours later, fading out to twilight.

The rain wasn't much like the precipitation Rachel had known growing up in Texas, either. It was more like a heavy mist that rolled out of hidden crevices in the habitat walls, filling in the lower areas first, then expanding to a dense wet cloud that coated vegetation, buildings, and people with enough moisture to cause discomfort and even leave puddles.

After two "days" of "rain," three days after her arrival on Keanu, Rachel finally discovered something to do. Something, that is, besides feel dirty and hungry and so constantly terrified she was numb.

"We're going to bury your mother," Zack told her.

He had found Rachel before she'd even rubbed the

sleep out of her eyes—before she'd had any breakfast—
not that any of the almost two hundred humans huddled
in or around this weird Temple structure were eating
much.

Her father had simply touched her on the shoulder,
where she lay atop a bed of leaves, not far from the
strange Brazilian girl, Camilla—nine years old, and a
reborn human, also known as a Revenant—who had
attached herself to Rachel.

Camilla woke up, too, and made it clear she was coming along, whether Rachel wanted her or not.

"How did you find Mom, Daddy?" Even as she said it,
Rachel knew it was a stupid question. How else but by
wandering around in this big stupid tube? And, really,
what difference did it make?

Fortunately, her father recognized her question for
what it was: nervous chatter. He simply took Rachel by
the hand and—with Camilla following several steps
behind—led her away from the Temple to the nearest
rocks, to a bundle of ginkgo leaves that looked more like
a giant seed pod than a human being.

This was the body of Megan Stewart? Her mother? In
Rachel's mind, she had knelt by her mother's Texas grave
as recently as a week ago . . . the same day she had had
the terrifying and bizarre experience of talking with her
via NASA television.

Rachel's back had been aching the moment she woke
up. Last year she'd gotten what should have been a cute
tattoo on her lower back. Now that yellow butterfly felt
swollen and sore.

"I found her this morning," her father said.

"Where?"

"Back that way," he said, pointing farther down the habitat . . . which in Rachel's mind was the northern or lower end, not that direction had any meaning.

The habitat was roughly cylindrical, or half-cylindrical. There was a floor, and a ceiling that, at its greatest, was at least a few hundred meters high. The floor was rolling, actual earth and rocklike terrain covered with various kinds of plant life, including some good-sized trees. The sloping walls looked like cliff faces. Rachel and those who had been scooped from Earth and shipped across four hundred thousand kilometers of space had emerged into the habitat at one end . . . what she now thought of as "south."

The Temple building, a good-sized pile of material that stood three stories tall and covered as much area as a baseball diamond, sat near that southern end. Although Rachel hadn't explored more than a few hundred meters beyond the Temple, she had already decided that the Temple rested on high ground . . . everything farther north was "lower."

Around them people were stirring. It reminded Rachel of the ragged wake-up at the only Girl Scout camp she'd attended, when she was twelve. No one had seemed happy or healthy then, and this morning on Keanu was no different.

Rachel had gone through the insane emotional roller coaster of seeing her mother killed in a car crash in Florida two years ago, then alive again via television here on Keanu . . . only to learn upon arrival that she had died a second time.

"How did she die again?" Zack had told her, but it was that first hour, a very confusing time.

"A Sentry killed her."

"A Sentry?" Rachel hadn't spent nearly as much time with her father as she wanted—of course, given their situation and her mental state, the right amount of contact would have been constant. She had wanted to cling to her father and not let go.

"One of the other inhabitants," he said, clearly too tired to offer much more.

"You mean, like, alien inhabitant." Zack nodded. "Is it still around?" If this Sentry killed her mother, clearly it was a creature to be avoided.

"I don't think so. I stabbed it," Zack said. "Camilla helped." Rachel noticed that the littler girl was still lurking a few meters away. Hearing her name, she smiled and moved closer, to Rachel's intense annoyance.

"Was that the only one?" Rachel asked.

Zack shrugged. "Can't say. There was a passageway between here and the Factory. But I think it's closed now."

Rachel had no idea what that meant, and no chance to ask, because Harley Drake and Sasha Blaine were approaching. Harley was going slowly, using his arms to power his wheelchair across the bumpy ground.

Rachel felt a rush of pity for the man. God, it was so easy to forget what he was like before the accident . . . a pilot, a jock, a total womanizer—or so her mother, Megan, had said once. Now look at him.

Then there was Sasha Blaine, the Valkyrie astronomer and math whiz, eternally perky. Even she looked pale and worn out.

Rachel realized that her father had told the couple about her mother's body—before he'd told her! She didn't much like that.

They exchanged grim good mornings and equally uncomfortable hugs. Sasha said a hello to the Brazilian girl in German—one of Camilla's two languages— earning a smile for her efforts. Then she produced a small shovel. "I rescued this from one of the other teams," Sasha said.

"It'll have to do," Zack said. "Let's get this over with."

Even though Zack had discouraged Rachel from a final "viewing," he needed her to carry the body. Seeing Zack struggle to lift the bundle—which probably weighed forty kilograms, since gravity in the habitat was close to that of Earth—and stagger with it, Sasha had offered to help. But Rachel moved quickly. This was her mother— or so it seemed. And her poor father.

It was her job.

They made their way slowly to the south, a little uphill, into the deep dark recesses of a corner of the habi- tat Rachel had not visited. She quickly grew tired and then frustrated by the distance. "Why are we going all this way?" she snapped. "Didn't we bury the others—" Two people had died during the awful first arrival day.

"We don't have a cemetery, kiddo," Harley Drake said. "Your dad has his reasons."

"We're here," Zack said.

They had reached a cavernous opening, inside which

Rachel could see strange cell-like structures lining the walls. "We called this the Beehive," Zack said, gesturing with alarming weakness. "It's where we came through from the vent. It's where . . . Megan . . . your mother . . . came from."

Camilla stepped forward, as if eager to explore. Sasha held her back.

Harley jabbed the shovel into the ground. "Got any particular place in mind?" he asked Zack.

Zack looked around, then stepped out into the open. "Right here, I think." He turned to Rachel and offered the first smile she had seen from her father in days. "This is a little like St. Bernadette's, right?" That was the name of Megan Stewart's earthly resting place, a cemetery near the space center.

Harley rolled his wheelchair toward the spot, but Sasha took the shovel. "Let me."

Harley began to protest, but Zack said, "Hey, Harls, why don't you grab some of those melons?" He pointed to a nearby tree laden with large red fruit of some kind.

Rachel knew Harley's expressions, and what flashed across his face was fury—less at Zack or Sasha than his situation. But he accepted the assignment, though not without a final grumble: "Maybe I should volunteer to taste-test them, too."

Sasha quickly and efficiently scratched out the borders of a grave, then dug the shovel into the earth. "Oh, thank God," she said. "It's loose. I was afraid it would be hard."

The tall woman from Yale worked methodically as Zack simply watched, hands folded over his chest.

Camilla wandered all around them, careful never to go any closer to the Beehive. Eventually she joined Harley, helping to carry a handful of the red melons back to the gravesite.

After several minutes, Sasha stopped, clearly exhausted. "Uh, how deep?" she said.

"Tradition suggests two meters," Harley said.

"This is hardly a traditional environment," Zack said. "Keanu will . . . absorb her, I think." He took the shovel from Sasha then, jumped into the grave, which by then was close to a meter deep, and furiously continued the digging.

Emerging, hands and arms trembling from effort, Sasha patted Rachel on the shoulder. "Almost over," she said.

As promised, moments later Zack slid the shovel toward Harley. "That's it," he said.

Sasha reached the bundle that held Megan's body before Zack did. Rachel did, too. It seemed to her that Zack hesitated . . . as if relishing this last moment of contact, no matter how bizarre.

Finally, moving carefully, the three gently lowered the remains into the grave. Zack stepped back. Sasha looked so drained that Rachel picked up the shovel and began covering the body.

Zack took over, and then it was all done.

Except for the words. "Do you want to say something?" Harley said. His voice was so gentle he didn't sound like Harley Drake.

Zack took a big breath, his chest swelling, and said, "I don't think I can." And then he simply broke down.

Which triggered unstoppable tears in Rachel, too. In her head, she was hearing Megan's voice again . . . not the weird way it had sounded during their last exchange via NASA TV, or the sharp tones of a mother-to-teen-daughter, but the voice Rachel had heard as a child, being rocked to sleep or comforted after a nightmare. "There, there, baby girl."

Zack pulled her to him, and there they stood . . . two sobbing wrecks.

"I'll say something." It was Harley Drake. "'Ashes to ashes, dust to dust' . . . it's not just words, it's a commandment. Rest in peace, Megan Doyle Stewart. You've earned it."

Almost on command, the group of five turned and began walking or rolling away. Only Camilla lingered, staring at the grave, making a sad little gesture with her hands.

Rachel shook her head, trying to stop weeping. And found herself laughing.

"What's that?" Zack said, his eyes red.

"Don't you think it's funny, Daddy?"

"Funny?"

"You've buried Mom twice now, on two different planets."

Her father stared at her. His eyes went wide, an expression Rachel had rarely seen, and always feared. But in an instant the scary face was gone, replaced by something more benign. He simply hugged her—

Suddenly they heard a terrifying sound—a raspy screech, like the cry of a demented eagle. Only there couldn't be eagles here . . . certainly nothing was flying.

"Jesus Christ!" Harley said. "What was that?"

Sasha pointed, just as, quicker than any human had ever moved, a creature shot out of the trees and snatched one of the red melons from Camilla's hands. It ran toward the Beehive.

"Come on," Zack said. He was going to follow it.

Harley snapped, "Why do we care? Let it eat the thing!"

"I want to know what that animal is," Zack said. "And whether or not that melon is poisonous." He headed off, showing more energy than Rachel had yet seen. She and the others followed, an increasing distance behind.

"Not to be argumentative," Sasha said, "but that animal might be able to eat all kinds of things that would kill us."

"Not if it's a monkey," Rachel said. She had spotted it again . . . the creature was perched atop a good-sized boulder near the Beehive entrance, banging the melon until it broke open.

"I don't know if that's a monkey," Zack said. "Its skin looked too smooth . . . oh."

Now they all had a good view of the creature on the rock, which was greedily stuffing melon guts into its monkey face.

"It's a vervet monkey," Sasha said. She turned to Rachel. "Good eyes."

Rachel couldn't have named the creature, but something about its head shape, hands, tail, and running posture had just said "monkey."

"Don't they have fur?" Harley said.

"It's probably got fur under that harder second skin," Zack said. "When things come out of the Beehive, that's what they wear . . . at least a couple of layers, like diving suits."

"How do we know it came from the Beehive?" Harley said.

Sasha pointed at relatively fresh tracks that led back into the Beehive. "Look for yourself."

"Does that mean this little guy was resurrected?" Harley said.

"It might," Zack said. He turned to Rachel. "Where on Earth are vervet monkeys found?"

Now she was embarrassed, because she didn't know. But Sasha rescued her. "They're found in the Far East, particularly India."

Harley and Zack exchanged looks. "That sort of fits," Zack said. He nodded to Camilla. "So far we've only seen humans being brought back, and every one of those had a direct personal link to one of the humans here."

Harley snorted. "So, if I get this . . . we're wondering which of the Bangalore people is hot for a monkey?"

Sasha slapped Harley on the shoulder. Meanwhile, Rachel was keeping an eye on the monkey . . . which was busy devouring the melon while staying vigilant.

Zack was heading deeper into the Beehive. "I wonder what else is in here?" Rachel found the whole place creepy in the extreme, but she wasn't going to let her father out of her sight.

She followed. So did Camilla, closely, then Harley and Sasha.

The Beehive was dark, except for light from the large opening into the habitat itself, and from a weird glow emanating from the hexagonal things along the walls.

Camilla made a sound and clutched Rachel's hand. "Daddy, what are these things?"

"We called them cells," Zack said. "They're some kind of incubators."

"And Mom was in one of these?"

Zack nodded. The whole idea made Rachel shudder. "You know, Daddy—"

She and the others heard another strange sound. But this wasn't the screeching of a reborn vervet monkey . . . this was a pitiful yowl.

"God, there wouldn't be a baby *here*?" Sasha said.

Harley rolled forward and around a corner. "No, I think we've got that covered elsewhere." Rachel knew that the Bangalore Object had brought a mother and newborn child to Keanu. "Zack!"

Zack had been searching down another alley in the Beehive. Now he ran to Harley. Rachel wasn't in a hurry, however; she wasn't sure she wanted to see what was making that awful sound.

It was coming from a cell a meter off the ground . . . there was light inside as well as the shadow of a creature— another animal, Rachel thought—thrashing in agony. "Let's get it out of there," Zack said, chipping away at the cell's membrane with the shovel.

As soon as he'd created a tear, he and Sasha peeled back the membrane and reached inside.

They pulled out a *dog*.

Or what looked and sounded like a dog that had lost

its master. The creature had a snout and four legs but was encased in the same leathery second skin as the monkey, coated in slime from the cell. Which the dog immediately showered on Rachel and the others as it thrashed and shook itself. With Sasha pinning the animal, Zack managed to peel the second skin away from its face.

Able to breathe and see, the animal calmed down. "Anybody here a dog person?" Zack said.

"I grew up with a border collie," Sasha said. She was making soothing sounds as she gently peeled away more of the covering.

"I was actually wondering what breed this was."

"Looks like a golden-Lab mix," Harley said. "Not that I'm an expert."

Just then the dog wrestled itself out of Zack's and Sasha's grasps and performed a violent shiver, obviously trying to free itself of what remained of the second skin.

"Poor thing," Rachel said. Not that she was a dog fan.

"I wonder who this guy belongs to," Sasha said.

The dog looked right at Rachel . . . tongue hanging out. *Here he comes,* she thought, ready to back away.

But the dog only took a step toward Rachel. And she couldn't help reaching out to pat his head. The dog responded by licking her hand.

"Well," Zack said, "we know who he belongs to for the *moment*."

"Rachel, you ought to give your dog a name," Harley said.

"He's not my dog!" The only dog Rachel had ever liked had been in some old television show. "All right, call him 'Cowboy.'"

Suddenly Cowboy barked. He had smelled or seen something off in the reaches of the Beehive.

Rachel and the others instinctively clustered together. "God, what now?" Sasha said.

Zack hefted the shovel just as another creature emerged from the shadows. Like Cowboy, this one was four-legged and of earthly design. "Is that a *cow*?" Rachel said.

Harley laughed out loud. "What do you suppose our barbecue-loving Texas friends are going to say to that?"

"Actually," Sasha said, "I'll be more interested in what our friends from Bangalore will say to what our Texas friends will say."

Rachel thought that was pretty darn funny, but Zack only grunted.

There's another thing we won't have on Keanu, she realized.

Fun.

Part Two

I can't believe they're having me do this.

Hi, Rachel, it's Amy . . . Amy Meyer. I hope you can see this . . . your dad's friends thought we should send messages to everyone who went away in those things. I guess they have the idea you'll receive signals. Everyone thinks you're still, you know, alive.

God, that's stupid, I mean . . . hello, we're all still thinking about you and praying for you and hoping you're doing okay. It's a little weird here, that's for sure, but nothing like . . . whatever's going on with you.

Sorry, can I stop now?

BROADCAST FROM HOUSTON MISSION CONTROL TO KEANU
BY AMY MEYER, AUGUST 31, 2019

Okay, who do I know here? Some of the people from Bangalore. There's Mr. Vikram Nayar, who was my father's mission director and my mother's—well, let that slide for now. Mr. Nayar is tall and grim and usually unhappy.

There's Dale Scott, who's this American astronaut who was working for Nayar and my father because he was kind of a dick and NASA got rid of him. His girlfriend is here, too. Valentina is her name. She's Russian and looks unhappy, too.

There's another ISRO engineer named Jaidev who's maybe 28, and creepy.

I also know Rachel Stewart, Zack's daughter, who is 14 and from the Houston group.

There's no one I actually like.

Which makes sense, because there's nothing about Keanu that I like, either.

KEANU-PEDIA BY PAV, UNNUMBERED ENTRY, ARRIVAL DAY

ARRIVAL DAY: VALYA

Valya Makarova would remember several things about the trip from Earth to Keanu inside a giant bubble.

First there was the fear. *Can I breathe?* (Yes, as it turned out.) *Am I trapped?* (She remembered having nightmares about the sinking of the Russian submarine *Kursk* fifteen years back, and the horror of finding yourself in a cold dark tube from which there was no escape. And yes, she was trapped . . . but the bubble was translucent . . . and the temperatures stayed Bangalore-high.)

She noted that she was still holding on to her purse. It was a large black bag, a Hermès Birkin knockoff she had bought in Moscow, and filled with such necessities as her phone, makeup, bits of candy and tissues, and her growing collection of key cards and security passes. Her right arm was through the strap; the purse rode high on her shoulder.

Reassured by that, at least, she commenced a brief, urgent search for Dale Scott. They had been standing right next to each other in the shattered parking lot of the Bangalore Control Center when the looming bubble had expanded.

Tumbled upside down into darkness, she had lost sight of Dale in seconds . . . she wasn't even sure whether he had been scooped up, or left behind, or, horrid thought, sliced in half.

What is happening? She hadn't been able to make a count, but it was obvious that something like a hundred people had been scooped up by this bubble. . . . As it rose into the sky, then beyond the sky into space, some floated in zero g, screaming, while others tried to swim. Several people collided, fighting like panicky drowners. One encounter was so violent it left a cloud of blood floating in air.

And with blood, there came the inevitable discharges of vomitus. At least a third of the hundred people looked either green or pale, each suffering from motion sickness.

Some simply closed their eyes and attempted yoga positions, or sleep. After thrashing around and finding the actions useless—and exhausting—Valya had selected the last option, relaxing to the inevitable, folding her hands across her chest and finding that, after a while, she floated toward the bubble's wall.

For a moment, she was afraid she might sail through it—or slam into it. Or be electrocuted at a touch.

Fortunately, none of that happened. She simply . . . bounced . . . and found herself gently but definitely sliding toward one end of the bubble along with several dozen others. (Just as many seemed to be sliding toward the other "pole.") The Object must be spinning, imparting some motion to its contents.

And now all Valya could do was take in the spectacle of a group of people floating inside a giant bubble, an image that looked as though it were more suited to some demented ride at an American amusement park.

For the longest time, the bubble was filled with screams, complaints, prayers in a polyglot stew of Hindi, Urdu, even Chinese, Portuguese, and Russian.

As for the other, nastier aspects of existence inside the bubble, Valya noted that, quite separate from the water and food dispensers, a different machine was sucking in the blood, urine, and other debris.

She found this reassuring. It told her that the builders of the bubble had deliberately collected them and, for whatever reasons, planned to support them.

Somewhat comforted, Valya had spent much of the next half day, in rotation, sleeping—the worst airplane sleep was better than the best she was able to get in the bubble—and then taking inventory of her purse (There seemed to be fewer items every time! Where had the roll of Dyno-Mints gone?) and speculating on who had grabbed her mints, why, and what for.

Mostly, however, what she remembered was feeling as though she were falling.

Intellectually, she knew it was no different from what cosmonauts had experienced for sixty years: zero g or microgravity or, yes, free fall.

But knowing that . . . even knowing that Dale, her most recent lover, had lived it . . . nothing had prepared her for the unsettling experience.

She passed the journey without significant interaction with her fellow voyagers. Yes, there was an occasional nod, a shared grimace. At one point, a sobbing young woman floated within reach and Valya grabbed her, saying soothing things in Hindi that she half-believed herself. "Don't worry. We're being taken somewhere. If they wanted us dead, they wouldn't be giving us food and water."

One thing that Valya couldn't help noticing: the surprise on the woman's face when Valya spoke. True, she'd been a real outsider in Bangalore. Although she was of average height and weighed more than she wanted (at age fifty-three she was finding it depressingly easy to put on pounds), she had blue eyes and blond hair and spoke Hindi with a Russian accent.

Russians had never been popular in India.

In spite of her linguistic skills, her isolation from the other bubble victims was no surprise. Valya had gotten to know very few of the team at Bangalore. To this point, all her *Brahma*-related work had taken place in Moscow.

As well it should have. She was a linguist, not a space person. Yes, she had grown up on the fringes of the space program—her father, Anton Makarov, worked in the Energiya factory, where spacecraft were built; he was essentially a plumber. Valya's mother was a secretary in one of Energiya's sister organizations.

From both parents their daughter had learned about the overwhelming and unproductive role of the Communist Party—never dealing with ideology, but only with bonuses and perks—and the inside politics of any organization larger than a football team.

Rather than follow her family, and her contemporaries, into aerospace engineering and a sure job at Energiya, Valya had chosen to study languages at Moscow University.

Part of it was her desire to make money as a translator. In the 1980s, the Soviet Union threw itself open to

European and American business interests in a desperate attempt to remain Communist. The effort had failed; by 1992 the Soviet Union had fallen apart.

But the market for translators never slackened. Valya had made a better than decent living—in hard, non-Russian currency—by knowing not only English, but French, German, Spanish, and Portuguese. Over the years she had added some Arabic and Hindi and had a reading knowledge of Chinese (she spoke the Cantonese version).

It was this broad-based knowledge that had brought her to work for the Indian Space Research Organization, to help translate strange signals. Her skill had likely made it easier for her to fall into a relationship with Dale Scott.

On balance, then, she would have to conclude that language had ruined her life.

After a few hours, however, with the bubble clearly in space, the bodies no longer flailing, the long wave of panic having receded, Valya was able to hear.

Somewhere inside the bubble, machines were at work. There was a definite hum, and occasional insane series of mechanical clicks.

Turning her head, she saw dark rectangular shapes at the nearest "pole" of the bubble. They seemed to be the source of the noises.

No matter. By this point, perhaps two hours into the situation, Valya's overriding thought became . . . *Now I need to urinate.*

Before it became an emergency, however, she found

herself joining a collection of humans—none of whom she recognized—at the south pole of the bubble, where it became apparent that the Object was equipped with life support mechanisms. One unit displayed obvious nipplelike structures, and some desperately thirsty people were lapping away, happily wiping their mouths. "Water!" one of them proclaimed.

Water. Good.

Valya surmised that a similar unit next to it dispensed food of some kind. At the moment, a pair of Indian men in the standard white shirts and slacks were examining the device, fingers probing, hands tapping around the edges. A heavyset young Chinese man joined them for a few moments, too, before giving up.

Thank God for engineers, she thought.

Then a different man joined them—American, in his fifties, a bit stocky, yet looking somehow less rumpled than the others. He conversed briefly with the two Indians, seemed to reassure himself of something important, then saw Valya . . . and smiled. "Hey, baby! Happy to see me?"

When the Bangalore Object struck, Valya had just reached Dale's car in the parking lot. Like most of the several thousand employees of Bangalore Control Center, Valya commuted by bus, a trip that often took an hour, one way, from the city center.

But Dale Scott was American. His belief in private transportation bordered on the religious. He was proud of the fact that he had bullied ISRO into leasing a car for him. "Driving it is still a bitch," he said. "What they need is what they used to have in Russia . . . a lane right down the middle of the fricking road for VIPs."

Valya remembered such a road, running near Energiya. "What makes you think you'd be a VIP here?" she teased.

"I've spent four years teaching these folks how to operate in space, and now they're on their way to Keanu. Without me, Vikram Nayar would be just another space wannabe instead of the rajah of *Brahma*." One of the things Valya had liked about Dale, his good looks aside, was his confidence, which, now and then, slipped into arrogance.

It had hurt him with NASA, she knew. His astronaut career had stalled seven years back. But, for some reason, it had endeared him to the Indians Valya had met. Certainly her stock had risen considerably when they learned she was dating Dale, the unspoken observation being, *He could have all the younger women he wanted!*

The same thought had occurred to Valya, of course, who assumed that, in fact, Dale likely *was* having all the younger women he wanted. They had only met two weeks before the *Brahma* launch, hardly time enough to develop a real relationship. She had been flattered by his attention and certainly enjoyed making love with him but wondered how much of the shared attraction was transient—or fueled by a common language.

No matter. Barring a miracle, they had both left behind a world in which relationships existed. Now their goal was day-to-day survival.

She realized, however, that the affair with Dale had

probably saved her life. When the shocking news came that a pair of Objects had been fired from Keanu toward Earth, and that one of them was targeting Bangalore Control Center, Valya had not known what to do, where to run.

Valya had spent the last two days at the center, working frantically and not productively, trying to translate some of the signs, symbols, and signals received from Keanu. The new imagery from the *Brahma* crew on the NEO had not been shared with the linguistic team dealing with the earlier radio signals. Valya knew there was additional material, but in true ISRO fashion, it wasn't being shared.

In fact, she was close to leaving the center when Dale appeared in her tiny office and said, "We're going, now."

"What about the mission?" she heard herself saying, though she was already in motion down the hallway.

"Fuck the mission, it's over, anyway."

They had run for the parking lot, a cramped collection of multicolored automobiles behind the control center. Seeing the jammed vehicles—Indians were worse than Russians when it came to respecting the rights of other cars in a parking lot, and Russians would happily block you in for a day if it suited them—Valya had said, "We're never going to get out!"

But Dale had simply grinned his crooked grin. "Oh, we'll get out if I have to steal a car."

They had barely reached his Mercedes, however, when they realized they weren't going to get away. They could see and hear the approaching Object.

Dale reached for her—to shield her, she thought—but the blinding impact slammed both of them to the pavement. A blast of heat washed over them—it wasn't hot enough to melt metal, or flesh. Either that, or it didn't last long enough. It was possible that the jammed vehicles sheltered them.

When Valya was able to stand . . . helping a stunned Dale to his feet . . . she was confronted by the most bizarre thing she had ever seen.

A giant white sphere rotated where the main control building had stood. The ground story looked largely intact . . . Valya thought she could actually see people in those windows, trying to get out of the destroyed building. A couple of them jumped—not as far or as horrifying as footage from 9/11, but bad enough.

"Don't look," Dale had said.

"I'm not a child," she had snapped.

"Point taken. The plan still holds, though. Let's get out of here."

"We'll never move these cars—" Several vehicles had been jammed together by the shock wave, fused into a giant flat mass of battered automobile.

"Let's just move ourselves."

They had managed to cross a hundred meters, beyond the parking lot to a park that was now a collection of windblown debris and shattered trees, when the light around them changed.

Neither of them could help turning. They saw the bubble expanding toward them, scooping them up.

During the next several hours in the bubble, perhaps a day, they never clung to each other. Dale would park her in some new spot along the wall, then go swimming off. "Nayar is here," he said during one of his departures.

Valya didn't care. She barely knew the man. And, like most Indian men of his generation, Vikram Nayar, the *Brahma* mission director, was unused to working with women in a professional capacity. He showed it by ignoring her.

After Dale's fifth or eighth return from errands, Valya finally said, "Why don't you stay put? What can you possibly be trying to accomplish?"

"Actually, some of us are trying to organize these people, find out what they're carrying."

"You haven't asked me."

He smiled that crooked smile. "I know what you're carrying."

Valya immediately sensed something different. Granted, their circumstances had changed radically. And their relationship was only weeks old. But that voice, that posture, meant a kiss, a touch, a pat on her behind.

But now, here? Nothing. Valya touched his arm. "You're through with me."

She knew him well enough to see that her blind shot had struck home. "What the hell are you talking about?"

"You won't touch me. You won't spend time with me. If it weren't a little crazy, I'd think that you'd found someone else—"

Naturally he seized on that. "Given the circumstances, that is indeed a little crazy—"

"Don't deny it."

He didn't. He floated for a moment, then shook his head. "I'm married."

It took Valya a moment to register this information. Then, to deal with her own irrational surprise. She had never considered it! She knew he'd been married before— her one moment of due diligence had been to access Dale's official NASA biography, which called him "married." But that was years out of date, untouched since Dale's unceremonious exit from the American agency.

Then there were the snickering glances from co-workers about Dale's other, younger, prior women. Somehow it had all lulled her into . . . well, not asking the question.

She started laughing.

"Oh, for Christ's sake . . . it's not as though—" He wisely left that sentence unfinished. "Why is this funny?"

"*Now* you tell me? *Here?*"

He couldn't resist joking. "Well, there's never a good time—"

"Shut up! Leave me alone!" Her anger was as shocking as her surprise at the revelation. Clearly she was hungry, exhausted, frightened . . . at the edge of sanity, most likely. Or over it, because it was very unlikely that Dale Scott's being married made any difference. None of them would be seeing Earth again.

She swam away, taking up a perch a few meters away, beyond the cluster of life support machines. After a few moments, Dale launched himself clear across the forty-meter-wide bubble to the opposite side.

Sometime during the second day, Valya returned from an unquiet doze to note a change in the background noise of the bubble. She clutched at her purse as she realized that the clicking and thumping had ramped up.

Dale, apparently feeling that her anger had subsided, was swimming toward her. "Don't freak out," he said, making her feel a lot like freaking out.

Through the milky walls, one thing became clear:

Keanu was closer! She and Dale and a hundred others . . . they were all falling toward it!

ARRIVAL DAY: XAVIER

"Hey, kid."

Xavier Toutant was startled by the harsh voice behind him. After an hour of tugging and sweating, he had managed to pry open one of the jammed cabinets inside the back two thirds of the big diesel Fleetwood Freightliner 2020—not that he would have known the name, but it was plastered on the side of the recreational vehicle. It was dark; this whole weightless thing made you feel like an idiot even trying to open a door. Every time you pushed, you were the object that gave.

Now there was some other fool floating in here . . . white, thin, balding, midthirties, wearing a pair of slacks and a dress shirt that had suffered some major distressing. Even in the shadowy interior, Xavier could see that his face was red and his eyes small and mean. "Ass eyes" was what his uncle Clare would have called them.

"What are you doing in here?"

There were several possible responses, ranging from *None of your fucking business* to his usual noncommittal shrug. But Xavier had been upside down and dizzy and hungry for two days.

And he had watched this particular cracker lurking

around the RV for the better part of a day. So he said, "Same thing you are."

"Oh really. And what's that?"

"Checking things out."

"Like, what, you're in a goddamned library?"

So far, in fact, Xavier had found nothing worth having in this wreck. Unless you counted a pair of battered lawn chairs, and in the weightless world of the bubble, he did not.

"So, then, what if I told you it was closing time?"

Xavier was getting tired of this clown. "Is this your ride?"

"What if I said yes?"

Xavier had to smile. "If this was yours, you wouldn't have said that. So . . . I'm just scrounging, man. Don't know what's here . . . might be useful to find out."

The cracker had wedged himself into the open front, which had gotten squished down either by the initial scoop or by being slammed into the walls of the big bubble afterward. Either way, it was a tight fit . . . which was one of the reasons little Xavier Toutant was one of the few people, if not the only one, to wriggle inside to see what was what.

He wasn't worried that the cracker would try to tackle him. He would have to swim at him, allowing plenty of time for Xavier to wedge himself and either take a swing at him, or even rip off the open cabinet door and swat him like a big old bug.

"Not the worst idea I've heard," the cracker said, confirming what Xavier had immediately suspected: This guy was a spiritual cousin, which is to say, he was a scrounger, a runner of errands. No matter now nicely he dressed back on Earth.

Or, to be more accurate, he was just another low-level criminal. "Find anything useful?"

"Not yet. Just started."

For Xavier Toutant—formerly of New Orleans, Louisiana, but for the past fourteen years, an unhappy resident of Houston, Texas—the big white scoop came just in time.

Following that afternoon's rain, he had gone out to the secret spot near the inlet to check on his plants. He had nine different sites, including the one up near La Porte. That and seven others were on slightly higher ground, less prone to flooding.

But not the one down near the new park. (Funny how everyone kept calling it "new," since it was already in existence the day Xavier and his mother and sister arrived from New Orleans.)

So he'd put on his galoshes and the big raincoat, grabbed a flashlight, and climbed into his Chevy. As always, Momma had asked him where he was going. As always, he had simply said, "Out! Back in an hour!"

They had a good understanding. Momma didn't pry into Xavier's outings, and he didn't pry into the collection of Chardonnay bottles that grew by one each day throughout the week, dropping to zero on Tuesday, when trash was picked up.

Not that he blamed her. They had lost everything in the Ninth Ward back in August 2005, and they hadn't had much to begin with. Momma had worked as a waitress at Cajun Sam's, which got flooded and never reopened.

Same thing for their ground-floor apartment on Florida Street, or so Aunt Marie had told them; they had evacuated ahead of the surge and had never been back.

And to this day, Momma never knew what happened to her brother Clare, who had been seen in or around the Superdome during all that mess, but never after.

They wound up here in La Porte, Texas, among the oil workers and righteous Texans who, at first, seemed quite happy to show their charity and take in those displaced by the hurricane and flooding.

The First AME Church had been great; no complaints there. They'd found Xavier and Momma a motel room and some clothing and meals, then vouchers for the same as things calmed down.

They'd hooked Momma up with a job at a Cajun barbecue place named Le Roi's over toward some airport, all with the understanding that it was temporary, that one day soon they would go back to New Orleans.

But that day had never come. Xavier had been put into the second grade at Bayshore Elementary, and it turned out to be a better school than the one he'd attended in New Orleans, or so Momma told him.

And her job paid better than the one at Cajun Sam's, too. Eventually—with help from the church—they'd moved out of the motel to the place they had now, and Xavier had gone through grade school and junior high and well into high school.

Maybe it was hanging around the kitchen at Le Roi's that gave him the idea—or, more likely, gave other people the idea that this was his idea—but Xavier was on the way to becoming a cook, if not exactly a chef. He started out washing dishes and busing tables, then graduated to chopping vegetables.

But around that time, Momma was diagnosed with cancer, and they simply needed money. Hanging around Le Roi's, Xavier had gotten to know a few of the boys who, in addition to cooking meals, sold other things people wanted.

Eventually Xavier had started doing favors for them, running out at all hours to pick up or drop off or collect.

When he was eighteen and had been running errands for only a year, he'd gotten caught. Because of the amount of material he was carrying, and the fact that he was no longer a juvenile, he'd been sentenced to six months in the misnamed Harris County Leadership Academy.

It hadn't been that tough—though it was surely one of those experiences that looked better in the rearview mirror—but it had pretty much screwed him with the folks at Le Roi's.

And when he got out, why, he found that the knowledge he had picked up running errands made it possible for him to go into business for himself.

Low level. He was never going to get rich. He would be living with Momma until she died (her cancer had gone into remission, but Xavier knew that meant she wouldn't die today, but don't look for her to celebrate, say, New Year's 2022).

His errand work—basically growing and dealing pot—had been so low-level that he'd had to pick up some part-time jobs, mostly construction, but a little plumbing (there was always a market for small men who were willing to climb through shit under people's houses) and some electrical work.

The electrical work had led to one strange summer where Xavier had helped wire and set up a computer network at an office building. He started thinking that if he enrolled at Remington and got a certificate, he might have a career in IT.

He was looking into it. He'd gone online to check the price and the application dates as recently as last week, right around the time *Destiny-7* got launched toward Keanu.

Now he was a fucking refugee again. Wasn't once enough for a lifetime?

"Shit!" The cracker had started in on a storage place under the seats of the tiny RV dinette. The cushions were still in place, held there by a jagged shard of RV body that had been poked into the interior by some nasty slam on the exterior. Xavier had started his RV search there and quickly given it up.

But the cracker was more persistent. He had tugged the torn cushion out of the way, then managed to push the lid open.

Xavier decided that was worth a look. He tugged himself over there using the former ceiling of the RV for handholds. "Need help?"

The cracker was straining to open the lid far enough to reach inside. His feet kept slipping. "Here," Xavier said. He braced himself against the opposite wall, back against a stove and an empty refrigerator (at least, it had been emptied by the time Xavier got to it), feet on the cracker's back.

The cracker was so intent on his work that he didn't object. And, thus braced, he was able to leverage the lid open. "All right!" The first things he pulled out were two pillows, then a blanket.

"Now you can sleep in comfort," Xavier said. More useless crap.

The cracker kept reaching in, feeling for something. Out came a first-aid kit, which he shoved at Xavier. "Now we're talking," Xavier said. He would have killed for a Tylenol that first day. But he could see that the dusty kit hadn't been used in a while. Still, even if medications were past their sell-by date, bandages and tape didn't go bad with time.

The cracker was sweaty, giving up. "That's it."

"Got something, at least." Xavier went back to his work, which hadn't progressed.

But now the cracker came with him. "Let me." And he just slid right past him to the cabinet, which Xavier had judged to be permanently immovable . . . and with a savage kick, broke the fiberglass piece in two.

Which gave both of them enough room to start scrabbling for the goodies inside.

Which turned out to be worth the effort. There was a backpack, a bottle of Lone Star, a half-inflated football and a Frisbee, a bikini top, a half-squashed box of candy bars . . .

And a shiny Colt .45 pistol.

The cracker let everything go to grab the weapon. Xavier made no move to fight it; hell, it might not even have any bullets. "Now, that makes you wonder," Xavier said.

"What?"

Xavier indicated the mixed-up pile of goods, twirling the bikini top. "What kind of party did these guys have?"

The cracker laughed but jammed the gun in his waistband. "So, how we going to divide this stuff up?"

"Is that the deal? We're dividing it?"

"Think that's fair, don't you? We helped each other, right?"

"I get a blanket and you get the gun?"

"You want the gun?"

Xavier weighed this. The cracker wasn't going to give it up. And, really, what the hell was he going to do with it? "The gun is yours." Xavier looked over the rest of the gear. "I want those candy bars," he said, grabbing the box. Snickers, good choice.

"Why don't we just take turns now?"

The cracker smiled, obviously thinking he'd won. "I'll take the blanket then."

Xavier took the backpack, though he looked longingly at the Lone Star. Told himself it was flat.

In a minute they were done. "Hey," the cracker said, "one thing."

Here it comes, Xavier thought, braced for an argument. But the cracker just indicated the pistol. "Do me a favor and keep this quiet, okay?"

"Got no reason to tell anyone. I don't know anybody."

"Good." The cracker stared at him. "What's your name?"

"Xavier."

"Brent."

The cracker jammed his bundle of loot—gun, beer

bottle, first-aid kit, and pillow, all wrapped in a blanket—under his arm and began the tricky business of extricating himself from the squashed RV.

Xavier wasn't quite ready to leave. He had a few useful items, especially the backpack, but one more search couldn't hurt.

Staying inside the RV gave him sufficient privacy to unwrap one of the Snickers bars and eat it without drawing attention.

In spite of his heritage and familiarity with Cajun cooking, Xavier was not a sophisticated eater. But at that moment he was sure the biggest fan of the most experimental restaurants on Earth would have agreed with him:

A Snickers bar was food of the gods.

It was torture to limit himself to one, but he had only another ten left in the box. He carefully removed them and zipped them into various pockets of the backpack.

Because Xavier knew one other thing. In an environment where food was something you sucked out of an alien tube, a Snickers bar was going to be better than gold. Maybe better than that gun.

ARRIVAL DAY: HARLEY

"Harls, what the fuck are we going to do now?"

Shane Weldon crouched beside Harley's battered wheelchair. Rachel Stewart was off to one side; she and Sasha Blaine were surveying the bizarre landscape of this habitat chamber.

It was too hot and sticky for Harley's taste; of course, he'd grown up in the mountains of New Mexico and never for a moment liked Houston or Florida's humidity.

There were ominous clouds of something—gnats?—drifting across the landscape like gauzy Predator drones.

Everything smelled vaguely of burned plastic, never one of Harley's favorite odors.

Shane Weldon didn't seem to be much happier, though Harley knew that thanks to three tours in Afghanistan a decade or so back, the former Army officer had a greater tolerance for unpleasant conditions.

According to Harley's watch, they had been on Keanu for a little more than three hours. During that time they had managed to translate (a lovely old NASA term for covering distance by walking or other means, which Harley liked to use to describe his chair-bound locomotion) perhaps four kilometers from the entrance into the habitat to this . . . big weird building that Zack Stewart called the Temple.

They had joined and mixed up with the larger group from Bangalore. This uber-group had immediately splintered into (A) those who knew each other, (B) those who immediately got busy working on such matters as shelter and sustenance (with a good deal of overlap between groups A and B), (C) a larger group that had a litany of complaints requiring Immediate Action from Somebody, (D) an even larger group that moved in stunned silence, like the victims of a natural disaster, and (E) a small but disturbing group that seemed too paralyzed by shock to move at all.

In group E was a young woman who had lapsed into catatonia. Which was bad enough, but what was worse was that she seemed to be the mother of an infant—said child had ceased wailing in justifiable complaint and probably hunger through exhaustion. (Harley sympathized; with a bit more provocation, he was prepared to engage in a screaming duel with the kid.)

They had met Zack Stewart in the company of a nine-year-old Brazilian girl. Strange, certainly, but hardly a blip on Harley's recent scale of strange experiences.

Now all of them were gathered, more or less, around the Temple, listening to Zack, former NASA astronaut, former commander of *Destiny-7*, former astronomer, former inhabitant of Earth, answering questions. *What is this place? Who built it? How did they get us here? Can we go home?*

Or, rather, trying to answer. It was obvious to Harley that his friend Zack was getting into deep water with the larger questions. Harley offered a change of subject: "Hey, Zack . . . any thoughts on food and water?"

"Oh, right," Zack said. "Water—there are at least two springs within walking distance. We have food, too. So far I've found fruits and vegetables. No meat, though."

"That is no problem for most of us," a tall, middle-aged Indian man said, to at least some laughter. He was Vikram Nayar, the lead Indian flight director for the *Brahma* mission. Harley suspected that most of those transported humans were either space professionals or people working at one of the two control centers.

Hardly a cross section of humanity. But then, what sort of talent pool was required? Were they going to be stuck here for days, weeks, years? In that case, Harley would prefer a dozen Boy Scouts, or farmers.

Or were they going to find a way to go home? In that case, the space geeks were what you wanted.

Responding to another question, Zack turned, allowing Harley to see his face, and it wasn't pretty. The man was exhausted, filthy, and on the verge of collapse. That much was obvious to Harley, who had known Zack for fifteen years, and to Shane Weldon.

It was even troubling to Rachel, Zack's daughter. "God, Harley, can't we get someone else to do this?" she said.

"Who else knows anything?" Sasha said.

Harley turned to Weldon. "What happened to your inventory?" That had been one small task he and Weldon had worked on during the trip, if for no other reason than to keep them from going batshit crazy.

Weldon waved a piece of paper, the backside of a

wrinkled printout salvaged from someone's backpack. "Right here. I still don't think we've got everything out of the RV."

Among the seventy-nine humans with whatever they wore and carried, the Houston Object had sucked up half of a recreational vehicle as well as a small boat, complete with two life jackets and oars; several coolers and lawn chairs; dozens of personal data devices (phones, laptops, BlackBerrys); various medications; several six-packs of beer; and even a couple of bottles of spirits.

Just glancing at the items carried by the Bangalore crowd, Harley could add a food vendor's cart—"Now *there's* a useful item"—several bicycles, and a dozen colorful umbrellas. Actually, these were more flimsy: call them parasols.

If Harley ever returned to Earth again, he would never make assumptions about what his fellow man or woman might be carrying on, say, the Day of Rapture.

If nothing else, they'd be armed, too. "What about the weapons?" he asked Weldon.

Weldon showed him the list of six handguns and a shotgun. When Harley made a groaning sound, Zack said, "Come on, Harls, what do you expect? It's Texas, and it looked as though we were being invaded!"

Harley Drake had made some strange trips in his life. But emerging from a tunnel on an alien planet into a regular damned Garden of Eden . . . with his old buddy Zack Stewart waiting to greet him?

Then there was the image of half the RV floating

around inside the Object. That had struck Harley as simply terrifying; any space traveler knew that just because a module didn't have weight didn't mean it didn't have mass. A couple of people had slammed into the vehicle, and while the injuries turned out to be bumps and bruises, it could have been much worse, had the thing not eventually slithered to the bottom of the Object and stayed there.

Coming in at third place: becoming foxhole buddies with Gabriel Jones.

For years Harley had dismissed the Johnson Space Center director—an African American astronomer—as an affirmative-action hire, a pleasant face and voice not backed up with leadership skills.

He had been happy to be proven wrong, as very soon after the "scoop," Jones had rallied the troops, taking roll, conducting, in essence, a town meeting.

Not that there'd been much leading he could do. As the Earth receded from view and Keanu grew larger, it became clear that the Houston group—seventy-nine of them; Jones had confirmed the number through several head counts—was on a voyage likely to last two days. (Calculations courtesy of one of the retired JSC engineers swept up by the Object.)

Two days of confusion, hunger, thirst, deteriorating hygiene, and general panic that eventually died out from lack of energy.

But Jones had proven himself to be as capable as anyone could be, given the strangeness factor, offering reassurance where needed, a bit of cheerleading at other times, and even a sharp correction when warranted.

It was quite remarkable, considering that Jones's

daughter, Yvonne Hall, had been one of the astronauts killed on Zack Stewart's snakebit *Destiny-7* mission.

Then there was what Harley later called the "Close Encounter."

It happened midway through their second day. Harley had been half-dozing when Sasha nudged him.

"Did you see that?" Sasha said. The large, flamboyant redheaded woman had become Harley's closest friend throughout this mad adventure. With her highly irregular human interactions, she seemed highly suited to this new environment.

"Don't tell me you saw something weird." He couldn't keep the sarcasm out of his voice.

She slapped him on the shoulder. "Out that side . . . I thought I saw another blob." The Houston Object—or, as most of them referred to it, "the blob"—was essentially a giant stiff-sided balloon . . . its skin was white and it was possible to see through it . . . though, given that the only visible features were the Earth, the Sun, and the Moon, Harley saw little point in doing any observations.

"'Plotting an intercept course, Mr. Data?'" That earned him another slap.

"Actually, flying in formation," she said. Harley and Sasha had begun to act like a bickering couple from a bad romantic comedy. It seemed inevitable that they would wind up together, if they could just overcome the immediate obstacles.

In their case, of course, the obstacles were possible death by impact on a strange planetoid, or suffocation or any of the dozen ways one could die in spaceflight.

One of the other passengers, a short African American

kid named Xavier, agreed with Sasha that "something" was out there. But when Harley had dutifully looked where Sasha had indicated, he had seen nothing.

Which didn't mean there was nothing to see. He knew, of course, that Bangalore had been struck by an Object before Houston had. Maybe that had turned into a scoop, too.

Finally, there was the landing itself. *Fascinating* was the best word Harley could come up with. He had already made the assumption, and confirmed it with Jones and Brent Bynum, the disturbed White House guy, and Weldon and even Rachel Stewart—everyone else he knew who had been scooped up—that the Keanu people weren't going to send an Object to bring them across space only to smash them on the surface.

So, mentally, he had treated it like a landing, the kind of maneuver he had once hoped he would perform on the surface of the Moon.

And, sure enough, during what a *Venture* lander crew would have called the *terminal phase*, as the half-moon of Keanu became the single biggest thing in Harley's universe, something inside the Object had gone online, some kind of deceleration engine.

Everyone had begun to feel it, too, as they started to slide toward the bottom of the spherical Object. The terminal phase had dragged on, in Harley's semiprofessional judgment. Of course, if you had unlimited propellant or a magic engine, you would go slow. Harley had flown a shuttle docking at the International Space Station, and the final closing rate was usually a meter per second. At that velocity, a bump wasn't going to do too much damage.

Which seemed to be the idea behind the Object's touchdown on Keanu.

Or, to be precise, touchdown *inside* Keanu. During the last fifteen minutes of the descent, Harley had spotted a crater growing prominent through the cloudy surface of the Object. No matter what maneuvers the blob made—and it was making occasional adjustments, each of which caused Harley's stomach to turn over—the crater stayed square in the center of the field of view.

And kept growing until it was a target so obvious, no one could mistake it.

All Harley knew was that this wasn't Vesuvius Vent, the large crater that had served as the landing site for both Zack Stewart's crew and the *Brahma* team.

Trying to think ahead, Harley latched on to his wheelchair. (The only truly nice thing about the trip inside the Object had been the lack of gravity. . . . Harley had been able to float just like everyone else.) He wanted support if gravity built up, as he expected it to.

With Sasha's help, he got positioned in the chair. "First time I've felt like I needed to be *strapped* down," he said.

Harley had begun hearing a few "Oh my Gods" and other alarmed whimpers. Before he could say anything, however, Gabriel Jones had spoken up. "People, please! Remember what I said about the voyage itself! Somebody *wants* us on Keanu! They'll land us safely!"

Harley hoped that Jones was right, and not just enthusiastic. He had lost perspective, lost any thoughts of the second Object; the only thing he could do was watch the crater grow until it literally filled the field of view.

Whoosh!

The dark walls of the crater enclosed them with very little clearance, for a moment shaking Harley's confidence that this would all end with a soft landing.

Then, with no more g-forces than you'd experience in the ground-floor stoppage of an elevator, they were down . . . somewhere inside Keanu, all seventy-nine of them. Since they were now subject to gravity, they slid toward the lower fifth of the Object, collecting around the bent RV.

"Now what do we do?" Bynum said. The man from the White House staff—the most unlikely refugee in the whole unlikely group—looked more alive than at any time in the past two days.

"Look for the door marked *EXIT*," Sasha said.

"How do we know we can go outside?" someone asked. That was another one of Harley's associates, Wade Williams, the famous—though not as famous as he thought— sci-fi writer. For all his farseeing intellect, Williams was a cranky, half-deaf geezer wearing an Astros cap he had managed to find somewhere in the cloud of flotsam.

"For the same reason we knew we would live through this," Jones shouted. "Because someone *wants* us here!"

Still nothing happened for at least a minute, maybe two.

Then the entire Object rotated and turned slightly. It was just enough to unsettle everyone and nearly throw Harley from his chair.

Something wasn't right. "Sasha," he said, "do you feel anything really unusual?"

She started to say no, but stopped in midsyllable. "Shit, what's happening?"

The curved surface of the Object was beginning to

soften. It retained its by-now-familiar milky translucency . . . but it also appeared to be melting. Harley sensed the wheels of his chair sinking in. The sensation was not pleasant.

"It's getting gooey," Sasha said.

The voices of those sharing the space with them began to rise, too. There were a couple of moans; someone started weeping.

"Look at the life support gear!" Weldon said.

At their backs, at the very base of the Object, the machines that had provided air, water, and food as well as cleanup service were beginning to melt, too. Harley could smell a nasty odor, like burning plastic. "I hope that's not toxic."

The process seemed to accelerate. . . . The machines were now just puddles of goo, and the surface of the bubble actually writhed and wrinkled, as if losing tensile strength.

"Oh my God, Harley—" Sasha was literally sunk to her knees. She reached for Harley's chair, but it, too, was sinking . . .

At that moment the bubblelike skin of the Object simply collapsed, covering them all in a substance that felt like fabric, but also like liquid.

Which dissolved, leaving only a thin film of powder that quickly, gently wafted away, like ashes from an old campfire.

The entire group, along with every piece of equipment including the RV (lying on its side), was sitting on the floor of a chamber at least five or six stories tall, and substantially wider.

"My ears popped," Sasha said.

Harley's had, too. "I hope that's increasing pressure, not decreasing." He took a deep breath . . . the air actually smelled and tasted fresh, like a spring morning. Of course, any air would be an improvement over the fetid stew he and the others had lived in for the past two days.

"Friends," Gabriel Jones announced, "I think we have arrived."

"In what?" Weldon asked. It seemed to Harley as though the former flight director and chief astronaut got angry every time Jones opened his mouth. He realized he would have to watch Weldon; he wasn't handling the situation very well.

"In a docking bay?" Bynum said. "Isn't that what you NASA people would call it?"

"It's as good a name as any," Harley said. He turned to Sasha, who was staring up, openmouthed. "What?"

"Just . . . looking," she said.

On the "ceiling" Harley saw what appeared to be squiggly luminous tubes growing brighter.

"I think there's a door," Bynum said. He was pointing behind them to a glowing rectangular opening.

"I, for one, am heartily sick of waiting," Harley said. He turned to Sasha. "Could I trouble you for a little help? I want to be first, as in, 'one small roll for Harley Drake, one giant push for Sasha Blaine.'"

She smiled, took a moment to run her fingers through her hair, then settled her hands on the handles.

They were joined by the others now, all crowding behind them as they moved en masse toward the "door."

ARRIVAL DAY: GABRIEL

Their arms filled with whatever they could carry, the Houston group had trudged several hundred meters down a broad, rock-lined tunnel. "Better bring everything," Jones had said. "We may not be coming back this way!"

And while she no doubt meant it to be an aside—this chamber had amazing acoustics—Gabriel heard what Sasha said to Rachel next: "Why does he think we aren't coming back? Does he know where we're going?"

Harley couldn't let that pass. Nor could he let them continue complaining, believing that they couldn't be heard.

"Ladies," he said over his shoulder, "right now we are forced to *look* good rather than *be* good."

Gabriel knew that was how many NASA people—and some outside the agency—would describe his entire career. *He's slick and superficial, no substance. He's affirmative action all the way.*

While acknowledging that he had, indeed, benefited from affirmative action—hell, if it worked for Obama's career, it could work for his—he also knew what he knew. He'd literally done his homework since junior high in Baltimore. He'd managed to balance a promising baseball career with solid academics, enough to get him noticed by scouts for the Ivies, who wouldn't offer money but rather a hell of a lot of prestige and connections.

But a lucky visit to Rice University had given him his first exposure to Houston and the great state of Texas, neither of which were high on his go-see list. And the aero engineering team he'd met there seemed far more experienced and practical than their equivalents at Princeton and Dartmouth.

Then there was the weather. Houston wasn't anyone's garden spot, but at least it didn't have snow on the ground for several months of the year.

So he'd graduated from Rice, then gone to MIT for grad school. A taste of the commercial space world with Lockheed had convinced him he was not cut out for that type of pressure, even with the potential rewards. (Besides, in technical circles, it was still just a bit tougher for an African American to rise than, say, for an Asian. That was another thing the folks who snickered "affirmative action" tended to forget.)

He had joined NASA Goddard outside Washington. Working on NASA's uncrewed programs was not the road to space program glory—until Gabriel found that he was being repeatedly asked to be Morris the Explainer when TV programs deigned to cover Mars landers or Mercury orbiters or asteroid encounters.

He'd wound up at headquarters, and when NASA turned its attention beyond Earth orbit, why, who better to lead the agency's premier operations hub, the Johnson Space Center?

If pressed, Gabriel would admit that his tenure at JSC

had been troubled. He had not been eager to spend the hours required to immerse himself in JSC's unique culture, which looked like the rest of NASA, but was to, say, Goddard what the culture of suburban Maryland was to, say, Saudi Arabia.

He had made mistakes. Hell, maybe he had been lazy, too used to the magic created by his own words and personality.

And his daughter, Yvonne—one of two astronauts killed on the *Destiny-7* mission—had paid the price. Gabriel had had ample hours to consider the reckless decisions that led to her death, the way he had been swayed by "national security" concerns to allow Yvonne to carry a nuclear weapon aboard a "peaceful" mission.

Sure, no one in Houston or Washington had known what the crew and controllers would face on Keanu, but Gabriel had found it too easy to listen to the consensus, to be America- or Earth-first.

There was another issue, too. Thirteen days before the *Destiny-7* launch—a date that, to his amazement, was still less than a month in the past—Gabriel Jones had been given news that forced him to change the way he thought about the future. His original path was to use the JSC directorship as a stepping-stone to deputy administrator, or even the top agency job . . . and then to . . . the Senate, perhaps? Or president of a university. That was now Future I.

The news put him on a radically different track, Future II: manage his health.

Now, even more strangely, he was facing Future III.

He had been dumped into an environment a hundred times stranger than JSC had been to him, and considerably more dangerous than even Future II.

To ensure his future survival, he had days—not weeks, days—to:

One: get off Keanu and back to Earth, or—

Two: find twenty-first-century medical technology on Keanu.

He did not want to calculate the odds that he would be successful at either.

As they headed toward an opening up ahead, Gabriel slowed down so that Harley Drake and his new friend, Sasha, and Zack Stewart's daughter, Rachel, could keep pace with him.

Gabriel noted that Sasha kept reaching out to brush the tunnel wall with her fingers. "Tell me why you're doing that. Are you a geologist?"

"I'm trying to keep reminding myself that I'm no longer on Earth," she said.

Gabriel laughed, then turned to Harley Drake. He knew the crippled former astronaut more by reputation than contact. He admired the way that, following the accident in Florida, Harley had chosen not to crawl into a hole, instead reinventing himself as a planetary scientist . . . while remaining a bit of a trash-talking horndog. Given his own news, Gabriel hoped he possessed similar force of character. "You, too, Harls?"

"Hell, no! I keep hoping this is just the nightmare of all time and that any moment I'm going to wake up."

"Oh, come on," Gabriel said, making sure to smile at Rachel Stewart. *Keep her included*. "Aren't you just a little bit . . . fascinated? I mean, I keep wanting to see one of those Markers the crews found."

"I keep wanting to see a whole set of *Venture* landers waiting to take us home."

"Harley, for an astronaut, you really don't have much pioneer spirit."

Gabriel realized that the exodus was losing steam as it neared the opening. Those in front of them were bunching up, shoving and beginning to make noise.

Brent Bynum sprinted past them, shouting, "Hurry it up, everyone!"

Gabriel looked at Harley and Weldon. "Who woke up and made him cheerleader?"

"Brent?" Weldon said. "He's been acting weird since we got scooped."

"Before that," Harley said.

Harley grinned. "Maybe he thinks that running around flapping his arms will restore his authority."

"What authority?" Gabriel said.

"Exactly."

As they reached the cluster, they saw the cause of the problem.

It was a human female, likely Indian, perhaps thirty years old, wearing khakis and a faded sky-blue shirt. Her long hair was sun-streaked, and she wore an expression of puzzled annoyance, as if she had been interrupted at some important work. In fact, she was engaged in what appeared to be an argument with Bynum, and with another of the Houston group, a sleepy-eyed young

African American Gabriel Jones recognized from the trip. He had been one of the few who kept poking his nose—and entire body—into the RV.

"She says we can't go past her!" the young man said. Xavier was his name; Gabriel was good with names, eventually.

"I said no such thing!" the woman said, as the crowd pressed around her. "I only said you should be careful, that there are a lot of other people right outside—"

Gabriel realized that he ought to take the lead. Before Bynum could open his mouth, he said, "Excuse me, I'm Gabriel Jones of the NASA Johnson Space Center."

"I'm Makali Pillay. Welcome to Keanu." More startling than her surfer girl manner . . . Pillay had an Aussie accent.

Everyone soon saw what the problem was: Just beyond the opening was another opening, off to the right, and out of it an even larger group of humans had emerged . . . and this group had not dispersed. They were collapsed in a collective heap, sick, frightened, paralyzed.

"Who are these people?" Rachel said.

"Folks from Bangalore, I'm guessing," Harley said. He turned to Sasha. "Your other Object."

In this half-lit space, crowded with unwashed, uncounted bodies, it was impossible for Gabriel to see beyond the few people in front of him. He had to concentrate on Miss Pillay. "Are you in charge? Is there someone I can talk to?"

"Come on," Pillay said. She seemed unusually serene

for the circumstances. Gabriel wondered if that was her nature or some Eastern meditative state.

Or drugs. Gabriel would have happily accepted the last two.

She led him through the crowd, few of whom bothered to move.

ARRIVAL DAY: RACHEL

Rachel noted that several members of the new group were eyeing Weldon's cooler, which he'd set down. "You might want to keep that thing closed," she said.

Weldon looked up. "Good point." He sat on the cooler. "You're awfully suspicious for your age."

"Yeah." For once in her life, she had no smart reply. Well, she didn't know Shane Weldon; he was just one of her father's space friends.

For another . . . nothing seemed funny right now. Whatever compulsion she had felt to go to the Object, then stay put as it expanded to absorb them all . . . that was long gone.

She had insisted on being taken to the Object because she believed that she would be seeing her resurrected mother. She had even been silly enough to think Megan Stewart might be aboard the Object when it landed. Why else would it have set down where it did, within walking distance of the Johnson Space Center?

Why else would her mother have told her—not in exact words, but still—to go to it?

These past two days, the worst in her life aside from the day her mother was killed, had forced Rachel to question everything.

It was probably natural, once you spent forty-eight hours in a space bubble, being hungry when you weren't throwing up, feeling filthy (she'd had to simply find a relatively private area of the Object and pee, which was unbelievably gross even if all the other women were doing it!), and basically keeping close to Harley and Sasha.

Now . . . Rachel had reached another planet. She felt as happy about that as she had on the family trip to Mexico, which was not very much.

At least Keanu was quieter than Mexico, though it seemed, right here, just as crowded.

And maybe, just maybe, she would find her mother again.

Or her father. The last she'd heard, and what she believed, was that he was here, alive.

Sasha took her hand. "Come on, everyone's going out."

They were all headed toward an opening a lot like something you'd find in a sports arena . . . a big passage twenty meters wide and almost as tall. For the first time, Rachel examined the walls of the passage, which didn't look like any tunnel she'd ever known from trips or movies or pictures. Mine shafts were dug out of rock and earth, then braced with timbers. There was this cool archive in Pennsylvania where the walls had been carved out of rock by some kind of machine . . . those walls looked ground down, like a tooth before the placement of a crown.

These walls looked poured and smoothed, like the cement of a new sidewalk . . . but with no grain at all. In fact, visually, they appeared to have been painted, they were so even. The "floor" did look a bit machined . . . it was certainly more metallic than stone—

"Whoa, check out the stash."

Harley had interrupted her examination of the passage. The procession had reached the final opening. Just outside it sat a pile of electronic gear: PDAs, BlackBerrys, Tik-Talks, Slates—there must have been two dozen different devices—being examined by several Indian men.

"What the hell?" she said.

"I guess everyone got tired of carrying dead weight," Harley said. "Hey, though, check this out."

The creep from the White House, Brent Bynum, was pawing through them like a hobo in a restaurant Dumpster.

"Brent," Harley said. "What are you doing?"

"One of these things has to work."

Harley glanced sideways at Sasha and Rachel, as if to say, *Stupid son of a bitch.* "I'm sure they all *work*. Even if everyone left their little machines running during the trip, they're still good for days yet. But, Brent, think this through: Where's the fucking network?"

"I know, I know," the White House man said. "But we're not that far away! If we could get to the surface, we could see Houston and Washington!" Harley was pretty sure you couldn't—you could barely make out the shape of North and South America. "How far does line of sight work?"

"Not that far," Shane Weldon said. Rachel had thought so, too, but suddenly she wasn't so sure. Who knew what kind of magical, state-of-the-art PDA a White House staffer carried or knew about? Everyone was talking about the Tik-Talk, which had a walkie-talkie capability, but that item had been too expensive for Rachel; she had no idea what it could do. Maybe a Tik-Talk *was* capable of picking up signals at this distance—especially if some unit of the U.S. government kept an antenna pointed at Keanu.

For that matter, maybe they'd kept it pointed at the Object as it shrank in the sky.

Gabriel Jones returned. "We've all had the same experience . . . scooped up and brought here. Their bubble thing dissolved, too. They know nothing that we don't. . . . Pillay says we should just keep going, and I agree."

The combined group surged forward, reminding Rachel of refugees fleeing a natural disaster like a volcano or maybe a tsunami. Which, of course, they were. Jones and Pillay took the lead, with Bynum at their heels.

Harley seemed tired and overwhelmed; Rachel couldn't believe he would pass up the chance to take a verbal shot at Bynum, who, to Rachel, was moving *exactly* like a golden retriever.

Then she realized that Harley wasn't exhausted . . . he was taking in the breathtaking vista.

They had entered a space that reminded Rachel of the time her parents had taken her to the old Astrodome . . . multiplied by a hundred. It was a roofed enclosure, longer than it was wide. "This is big enough to hold a city," Sasha said.

"Big enough to hold a war," Weldon added. He was growing increasingly pessimistic.

Rachel hoped that Shane Weldon would cheer up. Certainly she was feeling a little better, now that she realized she was entering a parklike landscape. There was soil, there were rocks, there were greenish growing things not far off. Smallish trees . . . or given the odd perspective, maybe not so smallish.

The roof was hundreds of meters high, likely higher, and covered with the same squiggly tubes that had given light in the tunnel, but many more of them.

Harley squeezed Sasha's hand, then Rachel's. "In spite of our differences, I think we all have one thing in common," he said. "Look!"

Every one of the humans, Houston and Bangalore, was staring up, openmouthed, in exactly the same way.

As they marched over a low rise, they gained improved perspective. Not only did the habitat stretch at least ten kilometers in front of them . . . so far that Rachel could not see the other side . . . but one structure was in clear view, looking like an Aztec temple rising above a jungle.

Rachel's appreciation of the alien building was short-lived, however. She heard a growing clamor off to the right, where most of the Bangalores were bunched up and breaking like a wave around a rock.

Two humans were approaching . . . one was a young girl Rachel had never seen before. "How the hell did those people get ahead of us?" Sasha said.

"They don't look Indian," Weldon said.

"They're not," Harley said.

No, they were not. Rachel recognized that walk, that oh-so-typical posture! It was her father.

She screamed and pushed through the crowd, heading for him.

ARRIVAL DAY: JAIDEV

The fighting had stopped.

At least for now, and for Jaidev Mahabala, good. One side of his face was swollen and sore; he had a split lip; his left eye was half-closed. He looked awful, and for a man who took pride in his appearance—said pride already hit hard by the awful stench and misery of the flight from Earth to Keanu—it was emotionally as well as physically painful.

Not that there was ever likely to be a reason to restore his prior appearance: slim, dark-eyed, the carefully cultivated stubble, the close-fitting shirt and tailored trousers. Jaidev's life had effectively ended when he was enclosed in the Bangalore Object.

But he had hoped that getting into a scuffle over food would have paid off with *something*. A Power Bar or even a drink of warm American beer.

Nothing . . . except bruises.

His participation in what began as a mad scramble for rations—one of dozens Jaidev had witnessed—had ended with a nasty punch delivered by Daksha Saikumar, a fellow *Brahma* enviro systems engineer. Daksha was a decade older than Jaidev's twenty-nine, so hairy and slow that unfriendly colleagues dubbed him "the Gorilla."

Jaidev had never considered Daksha a friend, but he had never expected him to shove him aside, then complete the maneuver by striking him in the face.

Jaidev had been left to wander the fringe of the refugee crowd in search of something potentially edible.

All he—and several other members of the Bangalore group—had found was a large, shallow pool of muddy (looking) water, which everyone drank from even as Daksha sniffed in disdain, naming it "Lake Ganges."

It was the latest in a series of humiliations. Jaidev couldn't even blame the worst of them on the Bangalore Object.

He was from an IT family; everyone—his father, mother, an older brother, and two older sisters—all worked in the Corridor in Chennai, though on a lower level. (One brother ran a call center.)

Jaidev had built on the family experience and earned a position at nearby Sathyabama University, a lucky move, since it allowed him to get out of his father's house and into the hostel.

(The school had a fleet of buses available to students, too. Odd how those crowded, hot vehicles reminded him of the Object. . . .)

The other bit of luck was that his specialty at Sathyabama was mechanical and production engineering rather than telecommunications or computing.

What struck his parents and sibs as an unproductive career detour turned out to be a direct route to study in the United States at Cornell, where he was first exposed to computational synthesis and advanced 3-D printing—processes that promised to revolutionize manufacturing. He had taken part in the development of so-called gray goo . . . material designed to serve as the building blocks of any substance or structure, mechanical or biological. They called this stuff *plasm*, *p*reliminary *l*ithographic *as*sembly *m*aterial.

It was Jaidev Mahabala the plasm specialist who was able to work briefly for the U.S. space program, then his country's.

Right up to the week of the *Brahma* mission.

For the last readiness meeting in advance of the launch, thirty members of the Bangalore team flew to Rio de Janeiro.

Jaidev had done his work at the Brazilian Space Agency well; his team had been responsible for crew equipment and consumables. All of the final reports were accepted.

Leaving them all free to play. Leaving Jaidev, alas, free to get drunk in a gay bar on the Avenue Viera Santo near Ipanema Beach.

And to be arrested with a male prostitute.

Jaidev had embraced his homosexuality once out of his family's home, making full use of the Internet to find other friends in Chennai, and especially visitors to the tech zone.

It had been fun—and continued to be fun during his time in the United States. He kept hoping to find someone special, someone he could commit to . . . and had decided to make that his number one personal goal at the conclusion of the *Brahma* mission.

The arrest had destroyed that plan. Rather, he was free to pursue personal goals, because the day the Object struck, he had been called into Vikram Nayar's office and informed that he was being "transferred" away from the control center to an ISRO office in Ladakh, or someplace equally remote.

He'd been fired.

Word of the scuffle must have reached the new "leaders," since a group of them came running to Lake Ganges. Most of them were Americans: people such as Gabriel Jones, Shane Weldon, and even Zack Stewart, all known to Jaidev from *Brahma*.

Stewart, Weldon, and Jones saw that there were no Houston types in the group and drifted off to consider the uses of the water supply.

Nayar was left to chastise the rest, all of them quieter. Even Daksha's temper had cooled and he was now subdued, possibly shamed. It didn't stop Nayar. "Look at you! Have you forgotten where you came from? Everything you learned? Two days and you've become beasts!"

"We need food," one of the men said.

"You'll get whatever any of us gets," Nayar said. "Try to act as though you deserve it. Better yet—be proactive and start searching. Do something useful instead of lying around like this!"

"Vikram!" It was Shane Weldon calling from across the lake. "We need to get back!"

Nayar had turned away from the Bangalores in disgust, finding himself directly in front of Jaidev.

The *Brahma* mission director was surprised. "I didn't know you'd been taken, too."

"Bad luck," he said. "If only you'd fired me an hour earlier."

Nayar grunted; he was not noted for having any sense of humor. But his criticism had suggested something to Jaidev, who had been hearing stories of Keanu's changing environment, of Revenants, of mysterious "goo" or soil that seemed to have the ability to transform itself. "Sir—"

"What do you want?"

"The materials in this place seem to be a very advanced form of plasm—nanotech assembly material," he added, seeing that Nayar, like many his age, was unfamiliar with the term. "I've got some hands-on experience with it. Why not let me see what I can do with it?"

"What do you honestly think you can do?" Nayar said. "This is an alien environment, designed by beings thousands of years more advanced than we are!"

"Designed *for us*," a voice said to Jaidev's right. Daksha.

"You said we should make ourselves useful. I think I can be useful."

Daksha joined them. "Me, too."

"Into the Temple, then," Nayar said. "Both of you."

The director turned away, clearly expecting nothing.

Nevertheless, Jaidev felt better. He had taken one step toward improving everyone's lot . . . and redeeming himself.

But first . . . Daksha. "What do you know about plasm?"

"Beyond the name itself? Nothing."

Jaidev stared at the man. To think that fifteen minutes earlier, Daksha had struck him. "Will you work for me?"

"You're the expert."

"Come on, then." Jaidev Mahabala didn't expect to find lithographic molecular knowledge in this group, so one pair of helping hands was as good as the next.

Besides . . . what better way to plot a bit of revenge than to have his assailant at his mercy?

ARRIVAL DAY: HARLEY

The hours after landing and "merger" of the two groups were consumed by greetings, shouts, jostling, complaints, and what Harley soon judged to be unreasonable joy.

How had their situation changed? There were now two more human refugees, since Zack had no tools and damned little useful information that the Houston and Bangalore groups didn't already possess.

Brent Bynum said as much to Weldon and Jones. "Don't get me wrong," he said as they trudged toward the Temple, Harley wheeling with help from Sasha and feeling every meter in his shoulders. "I'm sick happy that Stewart survived. He's the only one who knows what happened here.

"But unless he's got an alien spacecraft gassed up and ready to go, he's in the same damn fix we are."

Harley had more important things to consider. He had not intruded on the painful reunion between Rachel and Zack. Given Megan Stewart's death in an accident that was Harley's responsibility . . . throw in this mysterious rebirth . . . well, there was nothing he could offer. Best to stay away.

Especially when Harley heard Zack tell Rachel that

Megan was dead . . . *again*. The girl had collapsed, understandably. Harley wondered how Zack could be on his feet, much less coherent.

Then he wondered what had gone wrong. He realized he had a growing list of questions.

But now Rachel was on her feet, wiping her eyes, nodding, forcing a smile, in every way proving her strength and resilience.

And Zack was patting Harley on the shoulder. "What are the odds?"

"Of what?"

"You and Rachel winding up here." He blinked, looking tired but happy. "Everybody else, too."

There was no possible way Harley could avoid asking the next question, though he did lower his voice: "What happened with Megan?"

Zack stared at the earthen floor of the habitat, unspeaking, his shoulders heaving with barely suppressed sobs, his eyes suddenly filling with tears. "I wish I knew what to tell you. She was . . . here," he said. "For two days, Harls, I had her *back*. I heard her. I saw her. I . . . touched her. It was like . . . every damn song about loss. That one last look." He raised his face and smiled bitterly. "You know what? That's a pretty fucking overrated idea. Take it from one who knows. The second separation is worse than the first."

Harley considered that thought, and realized he could not address it or even express it. "Did she die somehow, or . . ."

"A Sentry took her," he said, a phrase that meant

nothing to Harley. Then Zack added, "It was the same kind of beast that killed Pogo."

Harley raised his head slightly and was startled and horrified to see that behind Zack, dozens of people had gathered. It was not only Sasha, who was at the front of the throng, her arm around Rachel . . . and Weldon, Jones, and even Bynum. It was Pillay, the Indian woman, and Vikram Nayar . . . and several Americans and Indians he had no way of knowing.

Their faces were alight, reminding Harley of a classic Bible movie . . . the Israelites waiting for Moses to give them the Ten Commandments.

"Okay, you saw the landing. We pulled some orbital shenanigans and got down ahead of *Brahma*. The moment we landed, Keanu pulled its own maneuver and put itself in orbit around Earth. So we knew we were into strangeness.

"Yvonne and I did the EVA, the vent blew, and she got hurt; Taj and his crew came to the rescue.

"We went down into the vent together, Pogo Downey and me, Lucas and Natalia. We found ramps and a Marker and the membrane, all these signs that we weren't exploring a NEO, we were entering an alien starship . . . which we'd known from the time Keanu maneuvered."

He closed his eyes. To Harley, Zack seemed to be reading another man's after-action report rather than giving testimony.

"Right off the bat, we met . . . something. A big alien; it carried this . . . vest with tools and some kind of layer of fluid. Strong. Faster. Bam—Pogo got killed. And we retreated."

"What was this creature?" Harley said.

"The Sentry; that's what we called it, anyway."

"What happened to it?"

"Oh, it died. I don't know whether we did something to kill it, or it was in the wrong environment." He thought again. "Then, those of us who were left, we began meeting others . . . Natalia, Lucas, me.

"That was where we found Megan. The machines or systems here had rebuilt her or had her reborn." His voice grew thick and ragged. "So we had two days together . . ."

"Do you have any idea how it happened?" Shane Weldon said. "How this . . . resurrection worked?"

Zack was struggling, but he, too, had stepped back from the emotional precipice in order to deal with the mechanics. "They told us a few things—"

"'They'?" Harley suddenly felt like the Grand Inquisitor but couldn't help it. He was also aware that Sasha, Rachel, Weldon, and likely Bynum were listening.

"The Architect, the builder or operator of the NEO."

"You *talked* to one?"

"Sort of." Just to one side, Harley saw Sasha Blaine slipping an arm around Rachel, holding her closely. "I only communicated through Megan."

"So she was, what, channeling this Architect?"

"A good way to put it. Anyway, it has to do with the properties of space . . . the way information, which would be everything from sound to images to the atoms in our blood and muscles to whatever tiny bit of electrical sparks make up a human personality, is never actually lost. It just takes different forms. And these guys are able to access it."

"I think I said this once before," Harley said. "But that's one serious fucking search engine."

Zack merely blinked. The concept would have been overwhelming at the best of times, and these were far from that.

Harley turned to Weldon. "Are you expecting me to shed some light on this?" the former mission manager asked.

Harley looked to Zack. "You're a systems guy. Is this plausible?"

"Harley, I'm also a propulsion guy and a communications guy and a life support guy, too, and I have no idea how these Architects managed to make those things work . . . and I interfaced with them. So when you start talking about—what were you guys on the Home Team calling it? 'Morphogenetic fields' and stuff like that—I'm as dumb as the next person."

Harley didn't know what to say and didn't have to respond, because Gabriel Jones showed up looking agitated.

"Zack, I hate to do this to you," Jones said. "But the, uh, rest of the natives are restless. Can you talk to them?"

Zack forced a smile and aimed it at Rachel. "I don't think I have any choice."

ARRIVAL DAY: ZACK

With Jones and Weldon flanking him, and Harley, Sasha, and Rachel trailing, Zack walked to the front of the Temple and up the wide ramp that led to its entrance. With no special call to attention, the nearly two hundred refugees grew quiet even before Jones could ask for quiet.

"Friends from Houston—Dr. Pillay, Vikram Nayar, and friends from Bangalore—we've been through a lot. To help us know more about where we've wound up, and how we might go forward . . . Zachary Stewart, commander of *Destiny-7*."

He had no outline in mind. All he could say was, "Thank you, hello, everyone."

Then he had begun to speak, as clearly as he could, though nowhere near as forcefully as he would have liked, about the basic facts of their situation. Jones acted as moderator, making sure to elicit questions from Pillay and Nayar in particular.

It seemed that Zack's ordeal was about to end, with the groups breaking off to start their basic tasks, when a voice shouted:

"You haven't explained why you did this to us!"

In the last few minutes, Zack had sensed a steady rise in the general grumbling. The shared elation—*We lived through the trip!*—was fast wearing off, driven away by thirst, hunger, and exhaustion.

Nevertheless, that question—based on the accent, shouted by one of the Bangalore group—was shocking, for both its vehemence and content.

"My wife," he said. His voice was weak; he doubted he'd be heard by half the crowd. He took a breath. "My wife learned from the Architects that they needed us, that we had a purpose—"

"We weren't asked!"

"Neither was I," he said. He noticed a young man—Chinese, likely—stepping out of the mass of people and edging his way toward the front.

"But you were here!" a different voice said, overlapping with the first speaker. "You and your crew started a war!"

Jones leaned over to him, trying not to be obvious. "One of the Bangalore flight controllers." That was helpful information; who else would have known about the nuke?

Zack tried to say something: "No one really knows what happened—" Well, *he* knew about the Sentry attacking Pogo Downey. Had it been unprovoked? Hard to tell. This was humans encountering aliens, for Christ's sake! It had gone badly, no question. The attack had led to the detonation of a nuke, no doubt about that. (A nuke Zack had not known about and, if asked, would not have accepted.)

But the crowd was getting out of control, with lots of yelling and finger-pointing. Most of the Houston people who knew what had happened were up here with Zack.

But Zack could see advocates, of a sort, Texans arguing with Bangalores.

"Oh, shit," Harley said. Zack suddenly thought of Rachel and turned; she was a few meters behind him, standing with Sasha, both looking alarmed, but both safe. "What is it, Harley?"

"I just saw Dale Scott."

Dale Scott? He was a former NASA astronaut that Zack knew from his first International Space Station tour . . . where Zack, as a new arrival, had realized that Scott was not performing well and recommended his early return to Earth. "I heard he was working with Taj's team." Taj had been the commander of the Indian *Brahma* spacecraft—the other set of human explorers who had landed on Keanu.

"Yeah, well, now he's here."

Zack found Scott; the man was standing off to one side next to what had to be a Russian woman. (Where had she come from?) But he wasn't agitating . . . he stood with arms crossed, a smirk on his face.

"Harls, we've got to get a handle on this."

Gabriel Jones was doing his best, trying to shout above the crowd, "People! People, calm down! This isn't doing anyone any good—"

That seemed to work. The volume dropped noticeably. The shoving stopped.

Just then, however, Zack heard a voice not from the crowd in front of him, but from his left.

"Zack Stewart should not be leading you!"

That voice was American.

"Oh, Christ, it's Bynum," Weldon said.

Zack had no idea who "Bynum" was, which Harley knew. "He's the prick the White House sent to spy on us," Harley said.

Before anyone could stop him, this tall, thin, balding, agitated fellow in white shirt and dark slacks—the only American who dressed like the Bangalores—had reached where Zack stood with Gabriel Jones.

"Dr. Jones, may I say something?"

Before Jones could say no, Bynum turned to the crowd. "Almost none of you know who I am, so let me introduce myself. I'm Brent Bynum, and I'm the deputy national security adviser. At the time of the, uh, incident, I was at the Johnson Space Center."

The crowd responded with feeble murmuring—clearly they were all hungry, worn down—but Bynum acted as if the lukewarm response were equal to the roar of the party faithful at a political convention. "Those of you who can, please translate this for our friends from India.

"You've heard talk about leadership here, and responsibility. It's all well and good, but everyone is overlooking one major point: I am the only government official here."

He paused, spreading his hands. "Unless there's someone out there, someone from the government of India, perhaps? No?"

Weldon turned to Harley. "What does he think he's doing?"

"Next thing you know, he'll break into a chorus from *Evita*."

"Come on, Brent," Gabriel Jones was saying. "We can talk about the rights of man once we've had some food and water. And you should know, Zack was not responsible—"

"I was in mission control, Dr. Jones. I saw how badly First Contact went. And Stewart was the commander. If he's not responsible, who is?"

Zack couldn't take it anymore. He got in Bynum's face. "You're right. I was the commander. I *am* responsible for what happened, good and bad. What do you propose to do with me? Confine me? Execute me?"

Bynum seemed surprised by Zack's willingness to confront him. *Typical horse-holder,* Zack thought. *He has no idea what it's like to make decisions that you can't take back.*

"No one's suggesting that," Bynum said, his voice suddenly pleasant and conciliatory. "My point, however, is that the fact that you were commander of *Destiny* and *Venture* doesn't necessarily make you the leader now." He gestured at Jones and Weldon. "Which is what people seemed to be saying."

"Don't worry," Zack said. "I'm the original 'if elected, I will not serve' type."

"You're still not getting it," Bynum said. He turned to the others. "None of you are getting it."

He pointed at Zack again. "You aren't the leader because we aren't going to have leaders anymore."

He dropped his arm and turned to the crowd. He scanned it for a moment, then fixated on a young black man standing near the front with a backpack in his arms. "You there," he said. "Is that yours?"

"What?" the kid said.

"That backpack and what's inside it. Does it belong to you?"

Allowing for the time it took non-English speakers to absorb that statement, the crowd quickly fell silent. "I found it," the young man said. "And you know where, too."

"That's my point. I do know; I know that you have no more right to that backpack than anyone else here. You just picked it up." He smiled. "Maybe you should just give it to your neighbor. It's just as much his as it is yours."

"Maybe you should kiss my ass."

The crowd was growing agitated again. Zack wanted to take Rachel and slip out the back door, leaving this all behind.

Too bad there was no back door.

Bynum stepped forward. "Listen, it's very likely we are here for the rest of our lives. Which means we will have to find ways to work together. Our society can and should be a clean sheet of paper! We can't survive doing things the bad old way. We can't afford 'personal property'! There is no 'mine'—everything here belongs to everyone. Share and share alike!"

Zack looked at Harley, who smirked and said, "That boy sounds like a dang Communist to me."

Weldon shrugged. "No surprise there, given where he worked. . . ."

The young man was charging toward Bynum. "Then why don't you give back the gun?" Zack realized that he was American; surely his accent suggested Louisiana. Before he reached the White House man, the younger one turned and said to the crowd, "He didn't tell you that, did he? How many of you have guns?"

There was a long moment. Bynum smiled and slowly reached behind him . . . drawing a shiny Colt pistol from his waistband.

"He's right. I have a gun. I found it, just like Xavier here found his backpack filled with goodies. Does that give me authority? Does this gun make me more right? On Earth it did. Is that how we're going to live here? Is that how we're going to present ourselves to the beings that made this place, that brought us here? How is that working for us so far?"

Bynum was talking about nonviolence, but to Zack he looked crazy, on the edge of something terrible. If nothing else, he looked like a man who really wasn't familiar with weapons, the way he kept waving the Colt around.

Zack stepped back, wanting to put himself between Bynum and Rachel. As he moved, his peripheral vision picked up a man moving parallel, but the opposite direction . . . toward the front of the crowd. Zack took a closer look, saw that the man was Asian, short, chubby—

"Daddy!" Rachel said.

Zack turned at her voice and saw the muzzle of Bynum's pistol aimed directly at him.

Before he could react, behind him there was a pop, then a second.

Brent Bynum was standing with his arms stretched out, like Christ on the cross. He sank to his knees.

The Asian man moved out from behind Zack. He had shot Bynum.

Suddenly many people were yelling, and three or four started pointing and fighting.

"Get him!" Weldon was shouting.

Within seconds the Asian man had been gang-wrestled. Dale Scott took the gun away from him.

But it was too late for Brent Bynum. He bled out and was dead within ten minutes.

ARRIVAL DAY: ZHAO

Zhao had not wanted to shoot the American. In fact, he had not wanted to hold a gun in his hand; he had spent far too much time on shooting ranges performing urban assaults and mock assassinations to feel relaxed when armed.

And, in spite of his colorful background and training, he had never killed a man. Never shot *at* one. Had he been given time to reflect, he would surely have wondered if his training had made the shooting too automatic, too easy. Fortunately, there had been no time to think back—

When he picked up a weapon, he intended to use it.

And he had picked up this weapon, a 9-mm Glock 39, from the debris floating inside the Bangalore Object. He recognized it as the type worn by the Black Cats, the Indian National Security Guards at Bangalore Control.

He had not seen a Black Cat, though he had come across the bruised, blood-clotted lower half of a human body clad in the same gray trousers worn by members of that organization.

For two days he had held on to the Glock, an easy thing to do in spite of the horrific circumstances. He was the only citizen of China among the Bangalore refugees, and while he knew a good many of the survivors, including Nayar and Pillay, he had actually been introduced to only a few. He had been left alone to contemplate the unlikely events that had put him in this place.

The gun? After the Houston and Bangalore groups merged, Zhao had quickly separated himself from his former Indian colleagues and begun walking with the Texans. His English was better than his Hindi would ever be, for one thing. For another, it appeared that the Texans were carrying a wider variety of items that might be useful for survival.

Among those items . . . a shotgun and at least one handgun.

Zhao was familiar with weapons, of course. Soon after he had been recruited by the Chinese intelligence service Guoanbu from a factory in Foshan (where he had been caught in some amateurish hacking—trying to access nude photos, of all the obvious activities), he had been trained to shoot. He expected to work in the agency's First Bureau as a glorified border guard, with hopes of becoming a police officer hounding corrupt businessmen.

For a brief period, his physical fitness earned him training in special operations. He became a marksman; he learned to swim and scuba dive; he even qualified as a parachutist.

But his intelligence and aptitude scores—and hacking background—quickly put him on a different track with the Tenth Bureau, which specialized in science and technology.

The Tenth Bureau had sent him to CUC, the Communications University of China.

Maybe it was the memory of those seven-day work-weeks, or the smell of plastic being poured into molds for toys that would eventually amuse children in the United States; whatever the motivation, Zhao had finished at the top of his class, even though he had collateral studies at Guoanbu's Intelligence School. It wasn't as though he studied every waking hour—but he made sure he knew his facts before giving answers, unlike many of his fellow students, party princes who were getting a communications degree before going into the business world.

Or maybe it was the fact that of all the male students Zhao knew, he was the only one with a sibling—his older brother, Chongfu, who had been content to do only what was asked of him . . . and who had grown fat and lazy and unhappy as the permanent deputy manager of a shipping firm in Foshan.

Still. Bangalore. August.

Zhao hadn't wanted the assignment to India at any season. Not that his bosses in the Tenth Bureau were in the habit of allowing bids on stations; no one outside the upper reaches of the agency had any notion of where the next cadres would be deployed.

But during his tour at headquarters brushing up his technical skills, Zhao had spoken openly about his fascination with "colder places"—the Scandinavian countries, especially. He mentioned Scotland. He talked of a lifelong dream of visiting Patagonia.

Major Xin, one of his instructors, heard him and, smiling, said, "Careful. You'll wind up at the South Pole."

China had three small stations in Antarctica. Zhao

would have been happier at any one of them than he was in Bangalore, trying not only to be the world's expert on China's relay satellite system—which was being "lent" to ISRO in exchange for access to propulsion technology—but also to cultivate sources all through Bangalore Control Center, against the day when the China National Space Agency would make its own Great Leap Forward beyond Earth orbit.

He had learned enough Hindi to be functional in an engineering situation but was nowhere near fluent enough to be sociable.

He had tried to combat the heat, the humidity, the smells, the bugs, the culture by keeping to himself, in the dark, in air-conditioned buildings.

It wasn't that he especially hated India or Indians; he just loathed tropical climates. His native Guangdong had been bad enough.

It was this . . . well, now he had to label it a weakness, that had allowed him to be scooped up by the Bangalore Object. He had traded shifts with his partner, Lu, in order to avoid travel during the heat of the August day, or he would have been safe in a distant hotel instead of here, inside some kind of alien vessel, his hands bound behind him, squatting on the dirt, surrounded by angry men and women.

Accused of murder. And on display, like a zoo creature, with haggard men, some women, and even a few children pushing for a view. There were shouts, though little that struck Zhao as understandable.

All things considered—and those things included the undeniable fact that he might have acted in haste—Zhao felt serene. Even his posture, back pressed against a rugged stonelike wall, butt on the dirt, legs extended, was easily endured.

Agents of the Guoanbu, China's national intelligence agency, were put through worse physical tortures during their first months as candidates.

"What's your name?" Weldon asked him.

"Zhao Buoming. I was born in Foshan, Guangdong Province, in 1988 and educated at the University of California School of Engineering," he said. "To save you a few questions."

Gabriel Jones returned at that moment. With him was a man in a wheelchair—Harley Drake, Zhao realized, the crippled former astronaut. Both men looked grim and, catching the eyes of their fellows, confirmed what Zhao already knew.

He had not only shot the man, he had killed him.

"Why did you do it?"

His questioner was Shane Weldon, a rangy, gray-haired man whose looks suggested he might be happier as a rancher, an image that was even more apt given the way he cradled the Glock he had taken from Zhao. Not that Weldon's career had taken him anywhere near ranching—Zhao knew that he was a former U.S. Army helicopter pilot and engineer who had lately served as the *Destiny* mission director in Houston, Vikram Nayar's NASA counterpart. Labeling him "rancher," however, was one of the many mnemonic tricks Zhao used in his work.

"I believed he was going to shoot Stewart or someone else."

"You couldn't have shouted?" Zack Stewart said.

Zhao turned to look directly into Stewart's face. "He was waving the gun. If I'd shouted, you'd very likely be dead."

Vikram Nayar and a pair of Bangalores arrived, looking aged and wary. Nayar did not speak but stared at Zhao, as if trying to place him.

"What's your background, Mr. Zhao?" Weldon said.

"I'm an engineer with China National Space."

"American leaders are lawyers; Chinese leaders are engineers," Weldon said. This was a quip Zhao had come to loathe, as much for its persistence as for its inaccuracy. He chose to ignore it, nodding instead toward Nayar and his associates. "You probably know that we leased our tracking network to the *Brahma* mission."

"Yes," Gabriel Jones said. "Complete with state-of-the-art encryption."

Zhao had no fear of the former Johnson Space Center director. "I wasn't aware that all of NASA's links were open to the world."

Weldon laughed. "He's got you there, Gabriel."

Now Nayar spoke. "Where did you get the gun?"

"It was in the debris that traveled with us."

"Ah, so you just *happened* to find it." Nayar was clearly skeptical, but Zhao expected that.

"Yes," he said. "I don't go around armed."

Weldon held up the Glock. "But you are a pretty good shot."

"He's been well trained," Nayar said.

"What's that supposed to mean?" Stewart said.

Nayar waved a contemptuous hand toward Zhao. "He's a *Chinese spy*. All of them were."

"All of whom?" Weldon said.

"All the Chinese sent to support *Brahma*."

Weldon turned to Zhao. "Is that true, Mr. Zhao?"

Zhao knew that whatever he said would be suspect. His training, however, required him to stick to his cover story—which had the supreme advantage of any good lie: It happened to be true. "I'm a network specialist and deputy program manager with China National Space. I can bore you to death talking about ITU allocations and super hydrophobic Lotus effect coatings, if you'd like."

"You didn't say no," Stewart said.

Before leaving Beijing, Zhao had been given a briefing on the *Brahma* and *Destiny* crews. *Brahma* was no longer relevant, of course, and neither were three of the four American *Destiny* astronauts.

But here was Zack Stewart. *"Intellectually brilliant,"* the Guoanbu analyst had written. *"Possesses a rare talent for social adaptability, which allowed him to make a successful transition from an academic scientific career to the operational NASA universe.*

"His flaw is hesitation. He will weigh all options five times before acting."

Zhao had recalled those words when watching Stewart reacting to Bynum's performance. A man who was prone to quick action would have put a stop to that long before Zhao was forced to act.

And now the American was focusing on Zhao. "You're a man of the world, Dr. Stewart. Whenever NASA engineers visit another country, they're debriefed. It's the same in China."

Weldon stood up. "You *still* didn't say no."

"What difference does it make?" Nayar snapped. "China, India, the U.S., who cares now? We are two groups that need to be one."

Gabriel Jones intoned, "He still murdered a man."

Zhao stirred at this. "I *killed* a man who was a serious threat." Now, to use time-honored techniques from his years of training, he went on the offensive. "And what, in all seriousness, are the options here?" He nodded at Weldon, still cradling the Glock. "There are at least four rounds left in the magazine. But you aren't going to execute me."

"Don't be too sure about that," Weldon said, "and I won't need a gun to do it." But Zhao knew he was bluffing and decided to press that point in front of everyone.

"If we're going to survive here, we need every available pair of hands. And in spite of what Mr. Nayar knows, or thinks he knows . . . I'm technically trained. That may be useful."

Weldon looked to Jones, Drake, and Stewart. None of the three called for Zhao's execution. Then Weldon turned to Nayar. "Any suggestions?"

Nayar was shaking his head. "Do whatever you want with him," he said. He seemed tired and distracted. Zhao decided the *Brahma* director was no longer a factor.

But Zack Stewart was smirking at him. "Mr. Zhao, you seem to have a keen sense of the world and its workings. Suppose the situation were reversed. What would *you* do with a captive like you?"

"Social norms require some kind of punishment. I should be confined for several days and limited to a strict diet of bread and water."

Now Stewart laughed out loud. "I'd *pay* for some real bread and water right now."

"I'm aware of the ironies," Zhao said. "Obviously some adjustments will be required."

At that moment a baby screamed nearby, and the whole issue of Zhao's punishment was tabled, leaving him, finally, with a moment to reflect.

For a man who didn't want to be in India, who hadn't wanted to be swept up by the Object, who was reluctant to call attention to himself—

And who didn't want to shoot the American—

Zhao had sure stepped in it.

ARRIVAL DAY: ZACK

"She's just hungry," Sasha Blaine said.

Zack and Harley had gone around to the front of the Temple at the sound of the baby's wail. There, at the edge of the sprawled, exhausted crowd, they had found Sasha Blaine walking the infant like a new mother. Zack recognized the familiar posture, carry, and rocking motion . . . he had done it enough with a colicky Rachel fourteen or so years in the past. "You've done this before," Zack said.

"Two older sisters and four nieces and nephews. And I worked my way through MIT doing childcare."

Sasha was even letting the baby suck on her finger.

"Couldn't someone nurse her?" That was Wade Williams, speaking from the shadows. "Maybe we need a little pioneer spirit," he said.

"After you, Wade," Sasha snapped.

"Where's her mother?" Zack asked.

"Not good," Sasha said quietly, nodding to the far end of the crowd. "She's over there somewhere, in a crouch, almost catatonic. Can't say I blame her. It's tough enough when you're facing this yourself. . . . I can't imagine what I'd do if I felt responsible for a baby."

She made a face and cooed at the child, who was blessedly subdued for the moment.

Harley said, "Who is the mom? Bangalore or Houston?"

"What difference does that make?" Sasha said.

"I don't know. Maybe it will make it easier to find out
where her head is at if she speaks English."

"Got it, but right now the priority is to get this child
some nourishment."

"Daddy, what about all these fruits and veggies you
were talking about?" Rachel said, trying to be helpful.

"People are out gathering right now," Williams said,
pointing back the way they had come, and forward, indicating the range of scouting parties. "It's pretty funny
when you think about all this."

"How so?" Zack said. Zack only knew the sci-fi
writer Wade Williams from his books, and from infrequent appearances on television. He had long-ago out-
grown his affection for the man's work, and if his
suggestion that Sasha Blaine should become a wet nurse
was typical—

"Here we are, transported from the Earth to a small
moon by advanced alien technology, being sustained in
some kind of habitat . . . yet we're reduced to life as our
ancestors lived it before the invention of cities or even
language. We're hunter-gatherers."

"I think we're only gatherers, Wade," said Harley
Drake, who didn't bother to conceal his scorn. "Unless
you've spotted a Keanu wildebeest."

"Have not, and do not expect to," the older man said.
"I doubt we could do much in the way of hunting, in any

case. I see nothing we could use for spears or flints, just to be nearly Paleolithic for a moment."

"There are tree branches," Zack said. He had used one to spear the Sentry that killed Megan.

"Fine. That's half of what we need."

Harley looked at the Temple. "Maybe we can chip off bits of that thing and get useful flints."

"I love optimism," Williams said. "I often sneer at it, but I do so love it."

"A far cry from the *Neolithic Trilogy*, aren't we, Mr. Williams?"

Williams blinked and looked every bit of what had to be seventy-five years of age. "I wrote that series a long time ago. I was younger then."

"So were your readers," Zack said. At one time he had been a committed consumer of sci-fi and fantasy books and graphic novels, and he had read several of Williams's books, which he'd found entertaining and provocative. Williams offered devastating critiques of modern technological society—heavy on the idea that children were being "softened" by a life of ease—in contrast to the benefits of pioneer life on habitable alien worlds or adventures in a different terrestrial past. "We must have some baby-friendly food around here."

"Power bars and Red Bull?" Sasha said. "I got hold of a packet of Pop Tarts. God knows how long they've been sitting, or where."

"Hell," Williams said. "Those things contain enough preservative to make them edible for a century."

"Going into Wade Williams mode, Sasha, how about this," Zack said. "Think like a mama bird."

Sasha stared. It took Rachel a moment to understand what Zack was suggesting. Rachel said, "Oh, Daddy, gross!"

But Sasha nodded. "That might be the only option." She smiled. "Feel free to do some prechewing, too. Given the circumstances, I don't think it's going to make a huge difference to the baby."

She ripped open the Pop Tart and bit off a corner.

Zack took one, too.

The sad thing was that Zack hadn't wanted to share the mulched-up plastic pastry with the baby . . . he had wanted to eat it all himself.

As he forced himself to chew gently, and not swallow, he grinned at Harley Drake. "I wonder what the poor people are doing this summer afternoon?"

Some time later the baby had been fed, after a fashion, and burped, and carried off to sleep.

Somebody on the Bangalore team had performed the miraculous function of locating water . . . it turned out there was a pond of sorts a third of a kilometer up-habitat from the Temple. Open water, seemingly spring-fed, and cleanish.

It wasn't pure, but it was wet.

Another refugee had completed the second most vital chore for a group of humans in circumstances like this—siting and digging a latrine. Weldon had approved the location, down-habitat from the Temple, far enough from the pond, which was already known as Lake Gan-

ges. "I think the trench is far enough downwind to mini-
mize the odor."

"Assuming the wind ever blows here," Zack said. He
and several of the men had just paid an inaugural visit to
the trench. Dozens of women were clustered not far
away, impatiently waiting their turn. "I do think we're
going to need a ladies'. Remember what happens at
sporting events."

"Already on it," Weldon said. He smiled. "I put our
Chinese spy to work with the shovel."

"Excellent. When he's done with the ladies', he can
dig new ones farther away, because this ain't gonna be
good for long."

"You think we're going to be here forever?" Weldon
said.

Zack was about to tell him, *I'm afraid so*, but he collided instead with a tall young Hindu. "Sorry," Zack
said, suddenly feeling old and tired—especially when the
young man glared and shook his head, and edged past
with energy and attitude.

There was something about the young man that bothered Zack—not the rudeness, but a sense that he had
seen him before. But where? Or was it just déjà vu triggered by extreme fatigue?

As they reached the leading edge of the gaggle of
waiting women, Rachel approached Zack. "What happened with Pav?" she said.

"Who?"

"Pavak Radhakrishnan. You just slammed into him."

Shit! No wonder the boy had looked familiar! He was

the son of Taj Radhakrishnan, commander of the *Brahma* mission, Zack's closest friend among the international astronaut community.

"I didn't recognize him."

"Do you ever recognize anybody?"

"Come on! Last time I saw him he was two years younger. And he had a different haircut and no piercings or tattoos." He wanted to laugh, or shout with relief; this was the first normal father-daughter conversation he had had with Rachel in weeks. "But your point is taken."

"Sorry." She moved off.

"Tempers are frayed," he said, as he and Weldon resumed their trek back to the Temple.

"It's not going to get better, not until people have been fed and given some rest."

"And we start all over the next day."

"We need to get organized now," Weldon said.

"Agreed. We need to elect a leader and the equivalent of a city council to assign tasks and referee arguments—"

Weldon smiled and clapped him on the shoulder. "I nominate you." They had caught up to another clutch of male urinators, including Harley Drake, Gabriel Jones, Vikram Nayar, and several men Zack didn't know. You could tell they were engineers and astronauts, Zack realized; they didn't just piss against the nearest wall, but rather waited patiently. Zack had not been present when his wheelchair-equipped friend performed whatever maneuvers were required to urinate. He could only imagine—

"Hey, Harls," Weldon said. "I've just told Zack that he should be Supreme Leader."

Gabriel Jones perked up. This was his area of expertise. "Sorry, Vikram," he said to the *Brahma* mission director. "What Shane means is, he's proposing Zack as a *candidate* for . . . mayor of our combined community. The job should also be open to someone from Bangalore, too. In fact," Jones continued, with enthusiasm so genuine that Zack actually believed he was sincere, "you would be an excellent candidate yourself. Assuming that you agree that we need some kind of structure if we're going to avoid slipping into chaos here."

But Nayar threw up his hands. "I know nothing about this place. I have no more business leading these people than that baby. Make Stewart the mayor. He was *Destiny* commander. He has been here longer than any of us."

Zack didn't like where this political process was going. "Listen," he said, "you guys have been through two days of hell, but I've been on the wire for the last ten. Right now, my judgment is seriously for shit."

"All the more reason to ignore your protests," Harley said.

Zack turned to Jones. "Gabe, this is right in your wheelhouse. You've got the experience and you even know some of the Bangalore folks." Zack realized that he had never called the JSC director anything but "Dr. Jones." *And so our circumstances degrade courtesy.*

But Gabriel Jones was just as reluctant. "I'm a bureaucrat, Zack. What we need here is more like an operational military leader. Some kind of . . . genius."

"Fine, then." Zack was growing tired of the debate. He was tired of everything. "Vote for Mr. Zhao. Look at what he's managed to accomplish."

"Well," Harley said, "he's our only known criminal. That certainly qualifies him for a political job." Tired as they were, some of them laughed at this. "Okay, to be real, if Zack can't or won't do it, Shane's already been acting mayor—"

Then Nayar spoke. "What do you think, Dale? You bridge these worlds."

The beefy, red-faced man stepped forward. He looked and sounded American but was dressed in garb more suited to Bangalore, with a fat gold medallion hanging around his neck like an Olympic medal.

Dale Scott, the former astronaut who had been exiled first to Russia, then, when that nation licensed its spacecraft technology, to India.

"Maybe we ought to have an actual election," Scott said. "Could just be a show of hands, or, hell, do a voice vote and pick whoever you want. But it will make people feel as though they had a say."

He turned to Jones and Weldon, and you didn't need to know the history to know how much he despised both men. "You guys ought to run. And I'll run against you. We'll all have a good time."

"Before we get too pleased with ourselves," Zack said, "we should remember that half of our population is women, none of whom are part of this discussion, and some of whom might be worthwhile candidates."

"Listen to Mr. Politically Correct," Scott said, directing his gaze at Zack. "Of course, that was always your style, wasn't it?" Because, of all the people on Earth, there was one Dale Scott disliked more than Gabriel Jones and Shane Weldon, and that was Zack Stewart.

"Shut up, Dale," Jones said. "He's right. We can't exclude the women from this."

"Exclude the women from what, exactly?" Sasha Blaine said. Zack hadn't seen them, but Sasha, Rachel, and several other women had returned from the women's lavatory event. Sasha cradled the sleeping baby. "Some important decision? I hope not. I hope this men-only discussion was about something really male, like growth on your nuts."

All of them, Houston and Bangalore, assumed varying degrees of shame and sheepishness, even Dale Scott. Finally Zack said, "That's exactly what we were talking about."

Eventually the matter was settled: The Houston group under Jones would put forward one candidate, and the Bangalore group its own. The top vote-getter would become "mayor" and the runner-up would chair a council of seven. The council would be elected directly after that, three from whichever group won the mayoral job, four from the other. "That should give us some kind of balance," Jones said. He was the one who had proposed the winning formula.

"In spite of the fact that there are more Bangalores than Houston folks," Scott said.

Makali Pillay stood up. "We can't re-create representative democracy here, and we don't need to. I believe you have a saying at NASA. '*Perfect* is the enemy of *good enough*.' This formula is good enough."

Everyone would get one vote, including Rachel but

minus Camilla and the baby. Zack searched out the girl, who had been his only companion for two days. She was sitting by herself . . . not truly apart from the Houston or Bangalore groups, but in her own world.

He could hear far-off barking. The dog . . .

Everyone broke to search for food. Zack assumed the "weather" would stay the way it was—a permanent hazy overcast, much like the famed California marine layer— meaning they would not have to scramble for shelter.

True, most or all could fit into the giant ground-floor chamber that had been the domain of the Architect, the outsized alien being Zack and Megan had followed into the Factory habitat, to their great regret. But it would be tight and nasty.

Just pondering that made him think of Megan, and Keanu's brand of life, death, a sort of life again. He went searching for Rachel, just for the mere sight and touch of her.

ARRIVAL DAY: HARLEY

Not that it was the kind of activity Harley Drake sought, or even considered, but exhaustion, immobility, and hunger combined to make him an observer at the group meal near the wall of the Temple.

The impromptu foraging parties had produced a decent feast—food enough for everyone, it seemed. Not that Zack Stewart was much cheered by the accomplishment. "Two hundred people eat, what?" he said. "Two, two and a half kilograms of food a day?"

"Sounds about right," Harley said. He had some memory of the figures, since they had been relevant to planning for long-term space missions. At the moment, however, he was too busy gnawing at one of the purple "vege-fruits," to use Sasha's handy term, to think about logistics.

"That's half a metric ton of food every day. Throw in four liters of water . . . I mean, we've got some kind of big pond not far from here. Don't know what feeds it, though—"

"You're saying we need a lot of food and water every day."

"I'm saying we managed to find enough nearby for one day. It was handy."

"'Low-hanging fruit'?"

"Literally. What about tomorrow?"

"Excellent question," Harley said. He had been doing rough measurements of the habitat, which seemed to be about ten kilometers long, a third as many wide. Call it thirty square kilometers. Even if every square meter was used to grow food—and there was no way even half of the area would be suitable—how much could be produced? This was far outside Harley's comfort zone; he had vague memories of the amount of acreage needed to support, say, an American farm family of the early twentieth century. . . . How did the conversion from acres to kilometers go again? What other factors affected things?

Zack was doing the same calculations, likely with more precision. He said, "The numbers aren't promising."

"Not for human technology or agriculture," Harley said. "But look at the bright side: Your Architects must have designed this to support humans, and you've got to believe they wouldn't scoop up two hundred if they didn't want that many."

"I really, really want to agree with that. But, look, I'm telling you this, but don't repeat it: I'm not sure all the systems here are working right."

"Oh, come on—"

Zack reminded him of how the Sentry seemed ill-suited to the environment or its mission, about the lack of night in a human habitat, about strange shifts in weather . . . about Megan. "What I'm saying is, this is an old, old vehicle. . . . We shouldn't be surprised if it's got its share of malfunctions."

Before Harley could press him further, Rachel arrived, redirecting Zack's attention.

Harley was relieved. There were times when a man just needed to sit back, enjoy what was on the plate before him—or, in this case, in his messy hands.

Which was how he came to observe Rachel and the strange Brazilian girl, Camilla, in their different approaches to Keanu dining. Both were dealing with one of the purple vege-fruits, but whereas Camilla was happily chomping away, juice running down her chin as she chattered with a Russian woman, Rachel was struggling to peel each morsel, clearly forcing herself to eat. Camilla seemed to have found someone—likely the only person in the group—who spoke Portuguese. That would make anyone happier, especially a lonely nine-year-old girl. Her conversational companion was a middle-aged woman Harley had seen talking with Dale Scott not long before—a person she obviously knew.

He was curious about this girl. But Rachel's voice was commanding his attention now. "Tell me we're going to find something else to eat," she was saying to Zack.

"We'll get through this," Zack said. "Whenever one door closes, another opens."

"You sound like Mom." Although Rachel's tone was typically flip, Zack detected a quaver that could, with very little encouragement, lead to a meltdown. She turned to Harley. "Doesn't he sound like my mom?"

This was dangerous conversational territory for a variety of reasons—Harley would no more get between a daughter and father than he would between wife and husband.

And the whole idea of Megan, and Harley's role in her death . . . well, no, do not go there. "Harley wants to stay out of our argument," Zack told Rachel.

Then he glanced at Harley, as if to say, *I'm going in . . . save yourself.* He told Rachel, "Look, you always said not to B.S. you."

"Since when did you start listening to what I wanted?"

"I always listened, kiddo." He smiled. "Sometimes I just didn't do what you asked."

"Sometimes?"

Zack elected to change the subject by using a physical prop. "Here, try this instead." He offered Rachel a differ-ent vege-fruit, this one more barklike. "I've been gnaw-ing on this for a whole day and it hasn't killed me yet."

"Ha-ha."

But she tried it. "It's like . . . what is that, herky jerky?"

"Beef jerky. But *herky jerky* might be a good name for it. You like it?"

"Better than that purple crap."

"Hunger does wonders for the appetite."

"Now you sound like Grandma." And so the latest emotional crisis passed. Rachel brought Harley back into the discussion. "Both of you keep watching her," Rachel said. "Camilla."

"Because they brought her back, right?" Harley said. He hesitated only a moment. This was too important a matter to be put aside just to spare feelings.

"Exactly," Zack said. He lowered his voice. "And because they brought her back, and she's the only one that's still alive. Megan and the others . . . didn't last more than a couple of days."

"Who's 'they'?" Rachel said, too loudly.

"The Architects," Zack said. "That seems to be the

name for the aliens that run the place, or rather, ran it. We only met one, and he's dead."

Harley watched Rachel as she took in this information. To any child born in the last fifty years, this was just some familiar sci-fi story.

But it was also real. And involved her parents. Harley could only liken it to the way in which real combat—something he had played at as a kid, and studied for years—suddenly became real.

It had not been pleasant for him. This could not be pleasant for Rachel.

"How do you know there aren't others still here?" she said slowly, as if trying to dip a conceptual toe into this strange water.

"I don't," Zack said. "Though Megan seemed to be saying—channeling this thing—that he was the only one."

"Of his kind," Harley said.

Zack looked at him, blinking, as if suddenly struck by a notion. "Yes, of his kind."

"Wait," Rachel was saying. "This Architect *spoke to Mom?*"

"Through her, yes."

"Oh, shit—" Now she seemed truly upset.

Zack slid his arms around her. "It . . . didn't hurt her, honey. She said it was just like . . . being on stage with an earbud, getting a prompt—"

"It's not that. It's just that . . . I barely had a chance to talk to her for more than a minute, but some big dumb alien had her for hours!"

Zack looked at Harley. Rachel's point was inarguable.

"I know," he said gently. "It was unfair. Nothing about this whole business has been fair."

Now it was Harley's turn to change the subject. "You said Camilla's 'the only one still alive.' I know they brought back Megan and Pogo, but . . ."

"There was at least one more," Zack said. "A man from Natalia's life, one of her athletic trainers. Konstantin was his name."

"How did he die?"

Zack's pained expression gave Harley most of the answer. *Killed*, was what it said. "He had an accident."

"So, there were four Revenants," Harley said. "Megan, Pogo, Camilla, this Konstantin. Three died in accidents. Why are you so curious about Camilla's survival?"

"Because Megan said—channeling the Architect— that there was a . . . limit."

Rachel rejoined the discussion. "What?"

"They were only brought back for a couple of days. Their job was to communicate with us." Zack looked at Harley: *Save me*, his expression said. "That's why the Revenants were all people we had known in our lives . . . so that we could communicate with them. Camilla for Lucas, Konstantin for Natalia." He paused. "Megan for me."

"Pogo Downey doesn't fit," Harley said. He was going to get this information even if the extraction and circumstances were painful for Zack. They all needed to know this.

"Well, he died here. He was brought back after Konstantin was killed. Maybe he was . . . I don't know, an easier retrieval? Some kind of automatic response?"

"So, if we die here, we might come back?"

"Maybe. For a few days, at least."

"Hardly seems worth it," Harley said. "I'm not entirely convinced we've got this worked out."

Now it was Rachel's turn to stare at Camilla, who was up and around. She and the Russian woman seemed to be getting ready to go somewhere. "So if the Revenants only come back for a couple of days, why is she still here?" she almost hissed.

Zack looked tired. "Honey, I just don't know."

And then, whether newly energized by food, or just out of teen restlessness, Rachel suddenly arose. "I'll be back in a few."

"Where are you going?"

"For a walk."

"I don't think so—"

"Daddy! Come on, I'm not going far. It's not dark yet." Now she was directly challenging him. "There isn't anything dangerous here . . . that's what you told us."

Zack looked at his daughter. Then he smiled the tightest smile Harley had ever seen. "Yes. That's what I told you."

"Don't worry. I'm the one who's always screaming at people in horror movies not to split up, right?"

"Right. Do I need to tell you not to get out of sight and hearing?"

"Probably not." She smiled. "Daddy?"

"What?"

"*Now* you sound like yourself." Victorious for now, Rachel smiled at Harley and walked away. A few moments later, Camilla and the Russian woman headed off in the same direction.

Zack waited until she had disappeared around the corner of the Temple. "Maybe Camilla survived because she's younger, stronger," Zack said. "Being the receiver . . . I think it was a real strain on Megan. Camilla didn't have to do that."

"Not yet," Harley said.

"Nope, not yet, as far as we know." With Rachel gone, Zack was more willing to let his anger and frustration show. "You don't seem to be buying anything I'm telling you."

"I'm just trying to figure out the difference between what we know and what we think."

"Okay." But now Harley wondered. Was he motivated by pure curiosity? Or by a vague resentment that somehow, something Zack had done had brought him here. . . . "Look," Zack was saying. "I'm not hitting on all eight here. I can hardly believe what happened or the fact that I'm still here, and what's really shaking me is that you and Rachel and a hundred and eighty other people are here, too."

"I know."

Zack was leaning back now, eyes closed. "I wonder where Tea and the others are right now? I still don't see how they could really make it home. . . ."

Harley Drake still wore his watch. It was a typical fighter jock's toy, a Chase-Durer Warhawk Chronograph that had cost him seven hundred dollars. It would run for months on its battery, though Harley wondered how useful it would be in a world without a true night. "How long has it been since Bynum's shooting?"

He knew that Zack was one of those people who

carried a fairly accurate internal clock—he rarely needed to set an alarm—whereas Harley never went anywhere on time no matter how connected he was.

Zack shrugged. "Six hours," he said, then, as was often the case, added, "and forty-five minutes."

Harley just shook his head. "Fuck you," and held out the watch. "Six hours and fifty minutes, and, frankly, I'm not sure my watch isn't wrong."

"Chase-Durer has been claiming for years that its watches can stand the stress of launch. Given that *you* came through it, I think the watch is okay."

"That I came through it? Is there something about my physical condition that strikes you as nonoptimal?"

It was the first normal conversation he'd had in . . . what, ten days? Two weeks?

Two years?

"Maybe it will come in useful."

"Like so much of what I know."

"Sarcasm, darling. The children are listening." Harley did some calculations. It was painful to put himself back in Houston mission control, even as a mental exercise.

But it allowed him to remember the last status report on the *Destiny* spacecraft that had carried NASA's Tea Nowinski and three members of the *Brahma* crew—Taj Radhakrishnan, Natalia Yorkina, and Lucas—off the surface of Keanu and onto an Earth-return trajectory.

That flight would have taken fifty hours, not much different from the two-day journey the Objects had taken to carry Harley and the Houston group and the Bangalores to Keanu. (Harley wondered briefly if the vehicles had all passed each other. . . .)

"Tea and the others were off Keanu safely, systems were working. They had enough prop to make the right burns. They should be down," Harley said. "Sometime in the last two hours."

He could barely imagine what kind of media freak show that landing was. "Four surviving astronauts splash down after insane adventures!" It was like *Apollo 13* crossed with aliens.

"You miss Tea?" After Megan's death, Zack had developed a relationship with fellow astronaut and *Destiny-7* crewmember Tea Nowinski. What must it have been like to deal with his current lover and his late, now resurrected, wife . . . Harley had heard of, and been involved in, tricky love triangles, but this one was so unusual it stressed that word to the breaking point.

"Yeah. Given what happened, I'm not sure she misses me too much." He suddenly sat forward. "These Objects that brought you. What was Nayar calling them? 'Vesicles'?"

"What about them?"

"Where are they?"

"Back at the north end of the habitat, through a couple of tunnels, one for each of us."

"I want to go there first thing tomorrow."

"Why?"

"They got you guys here. Maybe they can get us home."

ARRIVAL DAY: DALE

Dale Scott had lingered at the edge of the "picnic" crowd, eating his fill of vege-fruit while watching Valya Makarova and her new little friend.

He had learned that the girl's name was Camilla, and she had not come to Keanu on either Object. She had been . . . grown here.

She was, in Dale's mind, a fucking alien.

And it appeared that the only person here who could communicate with the fucking alien was his psychotic ex, Valya. Well, if exes could manage to work together on matters like child custody or division of property in the blessedly benign environment of planet Earth, Dale and Valya ought to be able to submerge their bad feelings in face of the common challenges of survival on a fucking alien planet.

Especially if Valya's linguistic skills opened up an inside track. And who better to help her . . . distribute and possibly exploit her hard-earned knowledge than the man with whom she had spent so many hours in bed?

Dale Scott loved having the inside track. The idea of it, anyway. He had rarely been able to get it.

So, from a distance, he watched, waiting for an opportunity to slide over to Valya and Camilla.

Meanwhile, from a different angle, he could watch Zack Stewart and Harley Drake at the far edge of an arm of the sullen crowd—Houston people, mostly, with a few Bangalores thrown in. They were talking about something important.

But what? And why wouldn't they share it?

Well, he knew the answer to that.

Dale Scott had come to NASA in the same astronaut candidate class as Harley Drake, but from the Navy. He had flown F/A-18s off carriers and was a solid aviator and even a test pilot, but not a spectacular one.

Nevertheless, he had not only made it into NASA, but snagged an assignment as a pilot on one of the last shuttle missions. Then he had been faced with this decision: Go back to the Navy, or become a space station astronaut.

Scott was already forty-three the day *Atlantis* made its final touchdown. He had a master's in aero engineering, but had never attended other schools; he was never going to get back on the fast track to admiral, not that the Navy would ever promote an astronaut to flag rank. The Navy wasn't going to let him stay in a cockpit, either; hell, with all the uncrewed vehicles coming on line, even for carrier ops, the service was actively pushing pilots into jobs where the only flying was done with a video game joystick from some bunker in Virginia.

NASA not only still let him fly jets, it *required* him to log twenty hours a month!

No, going back to the Navy was a quick ticket to oblivion. (A casual inquiry to the Pentagon confirmed it: The best job he could hope for was "war-fighting staff" at some base in Afghanistan while waiting for retirement.)

So, stay at NASA. Problem with that was, the only choice was to qualify for space station duty. Which meant (a) more time learning to operate the station's remote manipulator arms; (b) hours of work in the Neutral Buoyancy Lab's water tank qualifying for EVA; and, worst of all, (c) getting conversational, if not actually fluent, in Russian.

Oh, yeah, and committing to almost three years of mission-specific training in such garden spots as Moscow; Tsukuba, Japan; and West Germany.

It was the most miserable time of his life, worse than when his parents split up; worse than his second operational tour flying F/A-18s off the USS *America*, where he'd had to fly a whole shitload of post-9/11 intercepts and at one point was convinced he was going to have to bring down an American airliner; worse than his first marriage; even worse than his association with AGC Engineering.

For example, NASA had told him that of his two-and-a-half-year ISS assignment, he would be spending twelve percent of his time in airports. He had misunderstood; he had believed that to mean "in transit." No, flying time was separate! He spent hundreds of hours just *sitting* in fucking airports!

Which meant he was exhausted whenever he moved from Houston—where he began to have zero life, losing a succession of girlfriends—to Moscow, where he found himself drinking a bit too heavily.

In the old days, he would have essentially flunked out;

some trainer would have tattled to management. One of his colleagues would have dropped the right word in the right ear—bang. Dale Scott would have developed a "medical condition," likely good old "cumulative radiation exposure," and been quietly moved out of the ISS flow into a less stressful job.

But that hadn't happened. Maybe it was due to the fact that NASA was having a tough time finding volunteers for ISS missions—two dozen astronauts left around 2011 rather than make the transition.

In any case, Dale got his training done. He had great hand-eye coordination and was a fast learner, and better yet, had mastered the art of smiling when what he really wanted was to punch someone in the face.

Which was his first impulse when he learned that he'd been assigned to serve under a thirty-five-year-old Russian who wasn't even a fucking pilot.

Dale had been launched to ISS on a *Soyuz* with his Russian commander and an engineer from Japan. They joined another crew of three—two Russians and a NASA astronaut named Zack Stewart—to form what was known as Expedition 31/32.

Shit—literally and figuratively—immediately began to go wrong. First of all, the toilet in the American segment of the station failed, forcing Dale to work with Zack on tedious, smelly repairs.

No sooner had they finished that project than an ammonia line on the outside of the station sprung a leak, meaning that Zack and Dale had to do repairs on that, too.

Dale had proven himself in the EVA pool and did a creditable job on the work, which required three space walks over the course of ten days and left him exhausted, his hands clutched like an old lady's.

And in a bad mood. He noticed that, as Zack's Expedition 31 was winding down, preparing to give way to a new crew and Expedition 33 and then go home, no one was talking to him.

Now, life aboard the ISS was a bit like what Dale imagined life aboard a Navy vessel might be, allowing for a smaller crew. There was scheduled work, some of it science, most of it station "operations," which generally meant maintenance.

There was mandatory exercise, over an hour per day for each crew member.

There was the lack of female companionship. Dale had not realized what a challenge that would be—hell, he had soldiered through two longish stretches in Russia living the life of a monk, and together they almost added up to the ISS tour. (He had not been celibate during his first visit to Russia; for his pleasures he had had to worry about disease and missing money.) There had been some slight chance that one of his crewmates might be female—not that he had any expectation of enrollment in the Hundred-Mile-High Club with a female astronaut or cosmonaut; he only hoped to find a whiff of estrogen in the dull ISS atmosphere.

There was damned little privacy, with each crew member allotted a coffin-sized "stateroom."

Then there was the noise, the constant drone of fans and motors. In the Russian segment the decibel level was frankly unacceptable; it would have earned NASA a fine from OSHA.

It all made him uncomfortable, unhappy, unproductive.

ISS crews worked on the "job jar" method . . . the various control centers in Houston, Korolev, Europe, and Japan would uplink daily lists of activities that contained, in addition to the usual operational tasks, a good number of mundane chores that usually got divided up by the crew.

Dale quit volunteering for those. He decided he was going to do his work; if Houston wanted him to handle something else, Houston could tell him.

The larger problem was that he lacked motivation. He didn't care about the mission. He would have happily piloted the shuttle through half a dozen missions, or landed on the Moon. But six months in orbit? It was nothing but looking at stars, pissing in jars.

Still, he had been shocked and angered when Kondratko, the formerly jolly Russian commander, took him into the noisiest part of the Zvezda module for a private conversation the week before the arrival of Expedition 33 and Zack Stewart's departure. "They don't think you're happy here."

"Happy? Who's happy here, Valery?"

"Your health is affecting your work."

"What the hell are you talking about? When did this come up?"

During years of training, Dale had found Kondratko's expressions and gestures hard to read. In microgravity, even faint clues vanished. The stocky Russian just floated a meter away, face blank, eyes dead. "It was reported to me last week. Today I received orders."

"Orders for what?"

"Talk to Houston."

An hour later Dale was on the radio with Bettyjane

Handler, the chief of the astronaut office, who confirmed the news: "Your EKG has been out of family for the past three weeks."

"And you're telling me *now*?"

"It's fine-line time, Dale. If it were just the EKG, we wouldn't be having this conversation. We had you adjust your diet, remember?" True, two weeks earlier Dale had been advised to temporarily eliminate some of the saltier foods from his intake. "But even with that, your tracings are more erratic and your operational errors are rising."

"What does Stewart say?"

There was a long pause on the link. "He's only responded to questions from here."

He had noticed Zack growing more distant, but assumed that was because his colleague was packing for his return to Earth.

"Okay, fine. What do you want me to do?"

"We want you to take Stewart's place on 30S." 30S was the *Soyuz* scheduled to carry Zack and his two colleagues home in two weeks' time.

"You're aborting my mission?"

"Not just us. All the international partners."

"Fuck that, B.J. They don't do anything without checking with Houston."

"Dale, I'm sorry. Tell me . . . wouldn't you rather button it up and come home now, rather than press on for another three months?"

"Shit, yes."

"We're in agreement, then."

Dale Scott had been happy to come home early. But while they worked cordially and politely for the next two weeks, replacing Zack's gear on *Soyuz* 30S with Dale's, the two never discussed the matter.

Even after Zack returned and they crossed paths in debriefs or Monday morning astronaut meetings, they never had a private conversation about what Dale had done wrong.

From one of his Russian colleagues, he heard what he had always suspected, that Zack Stewart had informed Houston about Dale Scott's unwillingness to play with the others . . . that after three weeks of observation, it was Stewart who had made the call to send Dale home early—incidentally giving himself the U.S. record for time in space.

Fine. Whatever. Dale knew he had underperformed. Had circumstances been reversed, he would have dropped the hammer on Stewart, too.

But what was unforgivable was this: Zack Stewart had been too fucking cowardly to tell Dale face-to-face.

Besides, it was clear that Dale's problems extended beyond Zack Stewart. Chief astronaut Handler was notably cool toward him . . . and when, after eight months, Dale realized he had no new assignment, not as an instructor or even as a loanee to one of the new commercial companies, he made plans to get out of Houston.

He was drinking too much. From his childhood experiences with an alcoholic father, he knew that was a bad sign—

His postflight public relations tour gave him the opportunity . . . he had learned that ISRO, the Indian space agency, was looking for people who knew the *Soyuz* to help with their version of the venerable Russian craft.

He had gotten a résumé to them, been hired at twice the money he could have expected in a comparable job in the United States (assuming any space-related company would hire a NASA dropout), and the rest, as Dale liked to say, was history.

Now, well, shit had happened, and here he was, once again dealing with the same dynamics that had so frustrated him on earth. Not only Zack Stewart, but Shane Weldon, Gabriel Jones. Bad enough that Indian baggage like Vikram Nayar and Valentina Makarova had come along, but these guys from Houston! For Dale it was like being sent back to junior high school—

Things were going to be different now. He wasn't going to smile and play the game. . . . There was no game. There were no rules.

If he wanted something, he was going to get it.

With Valya's help.

Number one . . . punch that self-righteous fucker Zack Stewart in the face.

At the moment, however, his perpetual target was up, pushing Harley Drake and his chair toward him.

On the way, they were intercepted by Shane Weldon.

It was time for Dale Scott to declare himself.

"Hey, Shane," he said, interrupting an intense conversation. "Just wanted to say good luck on the election tomorrow." He offered his hand, too.

Weldon didn't hesitate. "You, too," he said, though it was clear that even saying that much was painful for him.

Then Dale turned to Zack. "Hey, Zack, we haven't seen each other in a while. Strange to be here like this, huh?"

"*Strange* is a pretty weak word for it."

"Sorry to hear about Megan and, well, all that." Whatever *that* was; he'd had a tough time getting information on the "resurrection" from Vikram or his little pet, Makali, the so-called exospecialist. But he had the general outline.

"Thanks."

"I've got to ask you one thing, though." He put his arm around Zack's shoulder, winking at Harley Drake, who looked as though he wanted to shoot him.

"Yeah?"

"Does *this* qualify as a spaceflight?"

Dead silence! Oh, it was wonderful! Neither Zack, Harley, nor Weldon had any idea what to say.

Finally Zack found his voice. "Why does it matter?"

"If it is, and you're the commander . . . could you work your magic and get me sent home early again?"

He waited for the trio to react to that. Weldon got red in the face. Harley actually rolled his chair six inches closer.

But Zack just stared.

"Hey, I'm just kidding," Dale said. "Just trying to . . . lighten the mood." He backed away. "See you at the polls!"

He turned, feeling really good about himself.

Until he realized that Valya and Camilla were gone.

Fuck. Fucking alien.

ARRIVAL DAY: VALYA

"Where are you taking me?" Valya asked Camilla, as the pair left the Temple and the clustered humans from Bangalore and Houston.

"I want to show you something."

"Should the others see it, too? Commander Stewart and Mr. Nayar?"

The girl smiled and shook her head. The gesture was rich with dismissal and contempt. "You're the only one who understands me here."

She glanced at the purse Valya had been clutching ever since their meeting. (Valya had the strap over her shoulder, and the purse itself tucked behind her right arm.) "Can I see what's in your purse?"

"Maybe when we get back," Valya said. "Sure."

Charmingly, Camilla took Valya's hand . . . and, for the first time in hours, seemed like a normal nine-year-old girl.

Valya Makarova had had many strange conversations in her life, seemingly with every trip out of Russia. Her gift for languages guaranteed that, of course; so did the fact that her jobs usually involved translating work, so she was often in situations where people didn't understand each other. Strangers on buses or in restaurants would realize that this otherwise grim-looking Russian woman could communicate with them, usually to their relief and pleasure.

For example, when working in Baghdad after the end of the American occupation, she had emerged from her hotel early one morning, hoping to get some exercise before the day's barrage of broiling heat, to find a skinny older man wearing jeans, a tank top, and a cap from some American sports team doing exercises with recitations that he claimed were the original human root language— her field of interest. They started in Arabic, and shifted to the mutual linguistic ground of American-style English, but were interrupted by the arrival of Iraqi commercial security, who put the run to this fascinating man before Valya could get a name or a cell-phone number—

None of these had prepared her for Camilla Munaretto.

To begin with, and allowing for the fact that Portuguese was not in her top five languages, Camilla was the most articulate child Valya had ever met. It wasn't just her vocabulary—which was better than Valya's—it was her apparent self-possession and confidence.

The girl was also quite pretty . . . dark-haired, yet blue-eyed, one of those luscious South American hybrids who had come to dominate the fashion industry in the past generation. Had she remained on Earth and grown to the appropriate height, Camilla would undoubtedly have followed in her mother's spike-heeled footsteps, onto some runway or into a catalog.

But even in Valya's former "normal existence," the fashion world was never high on her mental playlist. To think about such things here, in these particular circumstances, was quite silly to begin with. At present, Camilla wore a ludicrously large T-shirt proclaiming the virtues of a Ron Jon Surf Shop. Apparently, when first encountered, she had been nearly naked, saved from terminal immodesty only by some bizarre coating, flakes of which still covered her upper arms and thighs . . . at least those parts of her still visible around the edges of the billowing shirt.

She also had a nasty-looking scratch or bite on her upper left arm.

Their meeting had been arranged by Vikram Nayar, who had said, "She didn't arrive with either group. She was already here."

That had required some explanation, and with Zack Stewart assisting, Nayar had told Valya that Camilla Munaretto had been the niece of *Brahma* cosmonaut Lucas Munaretto.

"Had been?" None of that made sense to her.

Steward explained that Camilla had died of leukemia a year and a half before the *Brahma* and *Destiny* launches, and that she, like several other humans, had been revived here inside Keanu.

Valya knew something of this. She had heard that Zack Stewart's wife was one of these "Revenants," the term that seemed to be catching on with the refugees. She wasn't sure she believed any of it, of course.

"What do you want from me?"

"You're the only one who speaks her language."

"I'm barely fluent in Portuguese."

"No one else seems to know a word of it, so you are, by default, our expert." Apparently he felt he needed to make sure Valya understood. "She's a child in very strange circumstances; she needs to be able to talk to someone."

Valya had already felt uneasy around Camilla. Glimpsed earlier, the girl had been fidgety, moving quickly from group to group, like a beggar on speed. Then, given a candy bar by one of the Houston people, she had sat down in the shadows of the Temple to eat the treat.

Somehow, without Valya's seeing her, Camilla had crept forward, into the lit part of the Temple, where for some reason she had fixed on Valya quite some time before Nayar came to her with his "offer."

The girl's gaze was disturbing, and for an instant, Valya felt angry; she did not want to be tethered to this strange girl!

But she recognized the inevitability, if not the wisdom, of Nayar's plan. If Camilla had truly been "brought back," then she held vital information that would be lost without Valya's help.

She realized that she was happier knowing she had something to do. "What do you want me to ask her?" she said to Nayar.

"Whatever you want. I have no . . . guidance to offer, though obviously, anything you think important . . ." This was surprising; in the time she had worked with or around Vikram Nayar, he had *always* had a plan of some kind. Age and disruption were damaging him.

So she had introduced herself to Camilla and been rewarded with a genuine smile, though not one of surprise . . . it was closer to an acknowledgment, as if the girl were saying, *I've been waiting for you.*

Nevertheless, Valya stuck to the basics, asked if Camilla was hungry, how she felt, all good, all normal. Then, since she wanted to know . . . "How did you get here?"

The girl took a moment to organize her answer, or so it seemed. And then she delivered a narrative so precise that she might have been reading it. "I died in a hospice in São Paolo. I had leukemia from the time I was six. It made me very sick and very sad." And, yes, her eyes shone with tears at this point. . . . Valya felt her defenses weakening.

As if a switch had been thrown, Camilla was suddenly upright and happy again. "Then I woke here, in one of the boxes. It was difficult to get out." She made pawing gestures.

"You must have been . . . completely amazed, to be alive again." Valya tried to imagine it but could not get past the inevitable preceding step, which was dying of cancer.

"I died in my sleep," Camilla said matter-of-factly. "They gave me many drugs. It was just as if I woke from sleep . . ." And here she spread her hands, as if to say, *Look at me now.* "And I was well!"

Valya had to accept the story: The girl was here, after all. She had no clever way of confirming her story, only the information Nayar had passed along from what he knew about Lucas Munaretto, and about what unusual things had happened during the *Brahma* mission.

"Who brought you back? Who . . . made you well?"

"God did," she said.

At last, Valya thought, an answer that made sense . . . not to Valya's religious beliefs, which were non-existent, but for a young girl from Catholic Brazil.

"But he worked through the Builders," Camilla said.

"Who are the Builders? The builders of this *place*?"

For the first time, Valya saw confusion or doubt in the girl. "Yes . . ." she said, though she seemed quite uncertain. Valya had heard Zack Stewart mention *Architects* and assumed Camilla meant the same thing. But she couldn't be sure.

Valya looked around. Everyone was eating or sitting in an exhausted stupor . . . except for Zachary Stewart and his daughter and a few others, busily talking just far enough away that they could not be heard. Dale Scott was there, too.

They were watching her, of course, and especially watching Camilla.

"Have you told anyone about these Builders? Commander Stewart, perhaps?"

"Oh, he knows." She seemed quite certain, though Valya noted that she did not actually answer the question.

"Who are they? Will we meet them? Are they watching over us, helping us? What do they look like?" In spite of herself, Valya grew excited. This was a game she could enjoy . . .

But Camilla was suddenly done playing or talking. She shook her head, as if to clear it, then stood up . . . somewhat wobbly, as if her legs had gone to sleep. "Not here," she said.

And, without waiting for Valya, she headed for the Temple opening.

With a backward glance at Stewart and his party, who were now arguing with Dale, Valya painfully got to her feet, grabbed her bag, and gave chase as best she could.

Out in the twilight of the habitat, she saw Camilla fifty meters away, gesturing for her to come. She caught up with her and, after a brief exchange, wound up following her to the wall of the habitat opposite the Temple opening—literally behind the structure.

"Do you have a destination in mind?" Valya asked. "Or do you just want to take a walk?" She could easily understand the need . . . if, as claimed, the girl had been dead. Of course, Valya reminded herself, her body was new; it wasn't really as if Camilla had to shake off a year or two of cold sleep in a coffin. . . .

Physical issues aside, however, Camilla might well feel a spiritual need to walk, run, explore, to reconnect with her hereditary hunter-gatherer impulses. . . .

"I don't really know," Camilla told her. "But I have a . . . picture in my mind of a place against this wall." She stopped and glanced backward. "The Temple will be farther away." She turned down-habitat again, resuming her march.

Valya discovered that she was a little out of breath, and that her legs were weak . . . yet the exercise felt good. She was moving . . . granted, it reminded her of a joke Dale Scott was fond of repeating (as he was fond of repeating every witticism in his repertoire), about a country woman whose young son had spent his hard-earned chore money on a merry-go-round: "Well, you've spent your money and enjoyed your ride . . . but where have you *gone*?"

She was going nowhere but, for the moment, enjoying the ride.

"I'm sorry to keep asking this question, but I hope you understand," Valya said. "How are you feeling?"

Even in the dim light, Valya could detect a grown-up change of expression on Camilla's face. It was almost . . . re-flective. "Somewhere between troubled and giddy." Then she looked directly at her. "I hope *you* understand."

Valya then told Camilla, "You are very well spoken," and the girl smiled and said, "As are you." Not *You, too.*

She even followed up with a question of her own. "You can talk to everyone and you look like you be-long. How do you do that?"

So, even in their brief time together, the girl had spot-ted Valya's little working trick, the one that gave her so much success as a translator: Whenever she spoke another language, she acted it as well.

"When I was in secondary school, thirteen or four-teen years old, I noticed how, in moving from one lan-guage to another, speakers used different gestures, posture, and facial expressions. There was, in my school, a theater instructor named Grigory. He was very young and very handsome."

"Did you fall in love with him?" That was another question beyond Camilla's age.

"No," she said. "He was not likely to fall in love with me." Not because of age, but sexual preference . . . Valya did not want to discuss that with Camilla. Things were strange enough!

"But Grigory was so pleased that any student had even noticed, much less bothered to ask about it, that he gave me a master class in the value of these cues to the actor's art. He told me, 'Valyochka, voice isn't just words and volume, voice is where sounds originate in your mouth.'

"Of course, I had no idea what he was talking about. Then he said, 'Valyochka, you've watched many American and British films.' You don't know this, but almost every student in Russia studies English from the first year in school."

Camilla had only nodded, again, the gesture of a much older person.

"Part of that education was watching all these movies, and Grigory had done this, too. 'Valyochka,' he said, 'watch one of each again, and this time notice: British English originates in the front of the mouth, American English toward the back. If you speak American English, and wish to sound convincing, not only must you emulate the pitch and eliminate your accent and know the words by heart . . . you must locate the words in the right place in your mouth.' Then he smiled—I still remember this—and said, 'There's a reason they call a language a 'tongue.'"

Caught up in her own storytelling—her biggest weakness, aside from unsuitable men, was enjoying the sound of her own voice in any of her languages—Valya didn't realize that Camilla had stopped two meters back.

"Are we where you wanted to go?" she asked the girl.

Camilla said "Yes," but her body language and gestures lagged, a sign to Valya that the girl was unsure.

"And what are we to find here?" They were close to the wall of the habitat . . . which to Valya looked like the rocky face of a canyon rising to the sky. It was shadowed, of course, and relatively smooth . . . but even in the dim light she could make out different-colored striations.

There were bushes and trees growing here, too, making it difficult to see whether the place where wall met floor looked artificial, or had been cleverly engineered to look "natural."

Camilla was ignoring the wall and the trees, however. She was walking slowly parallel to the wall, eyes on the ground, like a child at the beach in search of shells. "Are you looking for something?" Valya said.

More uncertainty now. "I . . . think so." She stopped. "Here."

They were standing in an open patch of dirt indistinguishable from that around it, except for the fact that it seemed flat, with a suggesting of circularity. As if there were some kind of plate two meters across embedded in the ground.

"I see," Valya said, lying only slightly. "And what happens now?"

Camilla smiled. "Now I want to see inside your purse." She reached toward it.

Valya hesitated. For some reason, she didn't want to hand over her purse—which was odd, because back on Earth, she would have been happy to show a girl what she carried.

But, as every breath and sight reminded her . . . she

was not on Earth. "Why?" she said. "It's just ordinary stuff."

"I'm not entirely sure." But Camilla still held out her hand. "But I just know I need something other than the clothes we're wearing . . ."

She handed over the purse and watched as Camilla opened it and—with a fair amount of reverence, she had to admit—began taking out the items within. Phone. Package of Kleenex. Badges. A pack of chewing gum.

"Ah!" Camilla said, clutching a Chanel lipstick. She handed the other items and the bag back to Valya, then stepped into the center of the "plate" and placed the lipstick there.

"What's going to happen?" Valya said.

"Something," Camilla said.

Valya suddenly felt a vibration through her feet and sandals, an electric tingle that lasted less than a second. She smelled something unusual, even by Keanu standards: like plastic burning.

The dirt in the plate rippled once.

The light in the entire habitat flickered several times, bathing the scene in a strange strobelike effect.

Most human beings, in times of great stress or confusion, revert to their milk language.

Not Valya Makarova. When she saw that there were now *two* lipsticks instead of one, she found herself echoing her former lover, Dale Scott: "Oh, holy shit."

Camilla seemed equally surprised. Hesitantly, she reached out for the "new" lipstick. "It's warm," she said. She handed it to Valya.

"Shouldn't you keep the new one?"

"My mother told me I couldn't wear lipstick until I was twelve."

Valya wanted to laugh. This girl had died and been reborn on another planet! She had just taken part in some type of alien techno-magic! Yet she still remembered some argument with her mother! For an instant, Valya wished she could become mother to a daughter—just to know that one of her parental strictures would sustain itself across time and space, and through death!

"I'm sure that if your mother were here, she would allow you to have it. Besides"—Valya knew there was a risk to this, but felt it was time to confront the subject—"you've been dead for two years, right?"

"I'm not sure. Uncle Lucas said so."

"When did you die?"

Now the girl looked troubled and sad, and Valya felt she had made a mistake. "It was late in February. I had been in the hospital since before Christmas."

"The year was . . ."

"End of 2017. Beginning of 2018."

"And you were . . ."

"Nine."

"That was almost two years ago, Camilla. By my calculations, you are going on eleven. And you may wear lipstick. But let me test it first." Valya kept her tone light, but she was not sure that this Chanel knockoff would be lipstick.

She opened it and screwed it into position . . . noting that it seemed to have been used to the same degree as her original. It looked and smelled the same—odd to have a whiff of that waxy fragrance here.

She applied it, rolled her lips. "Perfect," she announced, and presented the lipstick to Camilla, who almost squealed with delight.

Valya knelt to examine the strange circle of dirt, which still showed frozen ripples, like Arctic snow. The original lipstick rested in a bowl-like depression perhaps three centimeters across. Wondering if what she had witnessed was less duplication than transference, she plucked it out, opened it, tested it.

No, it was still the same.

She considered the magic plate and the contents of her purse. "I wonder if it would duplicate my phone," she said.

She stopped.

Camilla was simply staring at her. The lipstick was in her hand, but the girl had made no move to apply it. "What do you think?" she said.

The girl said something in a language other than Portuguese. Valya recognized it: German. "About what?"

Camilla's eyes were bright, but vacant . . . much like those of eighty percent of the teenagers Valya had seen in the past generation, all linked to Slates and earbuds and even experimental direct-neural taps.

She was distracted and unable to respond.

By whom? she wondered. Or what?

"Let's go back to the others," she said.

Without a word, Camilla got to her feet and began walking, and never looked back or sideways.

Valya wanted to run.

ARRIVAL DAY: MAKALI

"Makali girl, when did you eat last?"

Vikram Nayar's voice jarred Makali like a slap. She was sitting against the wall of the Temple—or, as she persisted in thinking of it, part of an *alien structure* on an *alien world*!—writing in her notebook. Nayar was squatting, tailorlike, a few meters away. There was no one else around. The deadened air of the Keanu habitat made it seem as if she and Nayar were the only humans within kilometers.

"I don't know," she said. In the weeks she had worked with the *Brahma* mission director, she had grown to appreciate his fatherly side. She would have appreciated it slightly more if she'd believed his attentions to her were entirely fatherly. "Since the shooting."

Nayar grunted at the reminder. Although famously ill-tempered—Makali had not yet enjoyed the full force of the man's wrath, but she had seen it descend on any number of young and not-so-young men in the control center—he claimed to be bothered by violence. He claimed Gandhi as his model. Well, as Makali's father used to say, "We all need our ideals, no matter how short of them we fall."

"There isn't much food left."

She slid her Moleskine back into her purse and stood up. "Then why tell me to eat?"

"You need your strength. We all do."

"Humans can function on far less food than they know. I believe Gandhi proved that."

She knew she was provoking Nayar—knew also that a man his age might take that as flirtation, which meant that she ought rightly to share the blame for his attentions.

But she couldn't help it. Fighting back—all the while knowing that Nayar wasn't likely to explode at her as he would with a male subordinate—gave Makali a sense of power, which was a rare and precious thing for an Austro-Indian woman in India.

And all Nayar could do was grunt.

"How long have you been sitting there?"

"A minute, no more." His face told her he was under-estimating, that he had likely sat there for some time. "What are you writing so furiously?"

"Observations, of course." She had no need to lie about it. "I'm an exoterrestrial specialist in an exoterrestrial environment. Every breath is an observation."

"Or, rather, an interaction—and possible contamination." He smiled. He was reverting to fatherly, possibly even professorial mode.

"I've been forced to accept the contamination," she said. And she wasn't lying about that, either. For years exoterrestrial specialists had fretted about the possible damage alien cultures could inflict on each other, from cultural and religious right down to the biological. Astronauts who had accomplished the first few lunar landings fifty years back had been forced to endure two weeks of isolation upon returning to Earth, just in case they might be carrying virulent, deadly lunar organisms.

From the airless, sun-blasted, billion-years-dead Moon.

By those standards, the collision of humans with Keanu was so appallingly rich and uncontrolled that Makali was unable to study the matter. It was like obsessing about a potential scratch on your finger only to have your head chopped off. Air, water, the touch of Keanu soil—she had been exposed to all of it.

And now, as Nayar was reminding her, she needed to consume some of what grew here.

"I must confess, I was always bemused by the way you took notes." Makali preferred pens and pencils and expensive, pocket-sized Moleskine notebooks to even the most capable Slates and tablets. It wasn't a political decision, though she was proud of the green values of her method, but a practical one.

She had found that she remembered thoughts and observations if they were tactile . . . if she physically wrote words or drew images. Even the act of typing was insufficient to allow her to capture her discoveries—data flowed into her eyes and brain, and, apparently, right out of her fingers.

Of course, she owned so many Moleskines that she could not put a number on it. ("Sorry, Cedric!")

But thanks to her notebook and pencil, she was able to continue making her observations, about the weather, the light—and what was wrong with the light? Shouldn't there be a night and a day?—the smells, the soil, the dimensions of the habitat, the architecture . . .

The Temple structure fascinated her, of course. Aside

from the fact that Keanu itself was a structure, the oddly proportioned ziggurat was the first artifact she had ever been able to study. And she had been busy sketching the walls, speculating on what kind of material they were made of, when Nayar found her.

She was amazed to find that, in addition to studying this alien structure, she was also interacting with it . . . treating it as just another building to walk around. Makali wasn't alone in this; there were dozens of humans lingering around the base of the Temple, some sitting, others collapsed in sleep, a few arguing, one elderly Indian man staring into a far distance only he could see—

And several people devouring fruits and other vaguely edible-looking objects.

Nayar approached a young man who seemed to have taken charge of the distribution. "Xavier," he said. "Makali here hasn't eaten."

Xavier turned toward her . . . and favored her with a look she had not seen in many days and had never expected to see in this world: Makali was ethnic Hindu, but that was where her links to the subcontinent ended. She had been raised in Australia, had surfed and done martial arts, and was about as far from the bindi-wearing stereotype as a woman could get. She was wearing a loose shirt and khakis, but they still showed off a figure one of her girlfriends had described as "lean but oh so womanly."

Here, on an alien world, after two days of insane travel in an alien bubble craft, Xavier reacted to Makali as a pretty young woman. She didn't realize that she needed that affirmation, and perhaps she truly didn't back on

Earth, where she had tended to be too appreciative at times.

But she rather liked it now.

Not that it helped her get fed. "Sorry, dat's all there is." Makali tried to place the young man's accent; growing up in Australia, but having lived in the United States, England, and India, she had grown sensitive to the many voices of English. This was definitely Cajun, but with some other flavoring.

Nayar took her part. "Nothing! How could you let that happen? Aren't you keeping track? Are you certain everyone has eaten? Have you taken roll?"

One of Nayar's Indian engineers would have shrunk visibly from this assault, but the American teenager just looked more sullen and dug in.

"It's all right," she said to Nayar, reassuring him by putting a hand on his arm, a trick that never failed. "We got the food from those trees there," she said to Xavier.

He pointed down-habitat, toward the wall the Temple entrance faced. "I'll just pick something for myself."

"I can't allow that," Nayar said. "It could be incredibly dangerous."

"I rather doubt that," she said. "We've seen no signs of physical danger at all. This habitat was clearly designed for humans."

"Please don't put your theory to a field test."

"You're not going to wrestle me to the ground, are you?"

Even the mild suggestion of physical contact made Nayar uncomfortable. He merely shrugged, then gestured as if to say, *What's a fatherlike figure to do?* and stepped aside.

As Makali walked around the corner of the Temple, headed for the depths of the habitat, she saw, scrawled on the rough, textured side of the Temple, these words: *KAENU SUX.*

At first she was offended. *What kind of idiot thinks it's proper to scrawl graffiti anywhere—and on an alien artifact? And to misspell the name!*

But her second thought was more forgiving. It meant that the Keanu habitat was already feeling like home to some of them. Given that it was likely they would be spending a long time here—possibly the rest of their lives—that was vaguely comforting.

Her momentary satisfaction about Keanu and its human inhabitants quickly gave way to an emotion that was largely wonder (she was inside an alien spacecraft!) liberally spiked with fear (she had zero control over what was happening!).

Exhibit one: As she slipped away from the Temple, working her way through clumps and clusters of Bangalore and Houston people, some of them simply collapsed on the ground, she noted the bizarre way in which light kept changing.

The roof of the habitat—hell, it was so high you might as well call it the "sky"—contained several dozen long snaky shapes that seemed to provide illumination . . . but at a very low level, not much better than a summer twilight in Melbourne. (In fact, though it was difficult to tell, it appeared that fewer than half of the sky-snakes were actually lit.)

Suddenly, when Makali was halfway to the "wall" where the vege-fruit grew, the sky-snakes burst to life, a wave of bright light sweeping down the entire habitat, as if a swift-moving cloud had revealed the sun.

Fine, not so freaky; it was now dawn here in the habitat. Of all the humans who had been scooped up by the Objects, Makali considered herself—and should have been—the one best prepared to accept alien environments, life forms, means of communication. . . .

But then, within seconds, the sweep of light repeated itself, another bright wave washing over the entire habitat.

And another. And a fourth, the last two coming so quickly that they overlapped—the third wave was still lighting the "north" end of the habitat, where the humans had emerged from the tunnels, when the fourth wave blew through.

And then, as if nothing had happened, the sky-snakes resumed their earlier level of activity . . . and the light returned to twilight.

It wasn't hunger that made Makali want to hurry to the trees, get food, and return to the Temple.

It was a classic human emotion.

Fear of the unknown.

Makali Pillay's father had been the space buff in the family. Senior Pillay's favorite movie was *The Dish*, a charming account of the Australian astronomers who helped the crew of *Apollo 11* transmit video of the first steps on the lunar surface to a worldwide audience of millions.

When his daughter was born just after *The Dish* reached theaters, it was natural for him to give her an astronautical name . . . *Makali* meant "moon."

Makali had learned to share her father's interest in space, to some degree. Given the books and movies and pictures lining the walls of their apartment above the restaurant, she had little choice.

But she didn't necessarily share his interest in astronauts and space shuttles, nor ethnic pride in India's accomplishments, including becoming the fourth spacefaring nation on the planet.

Makali had become fascinated by the possibilities of First Contact and alien life forms. Her father had balked at this: "I like the idea, too, but it's still a science without a subject! You want to go to the U.S., fine! Go to the NASA Jet Propulsion Lab!"

Makali knew even then that although JPL had developed space probes for America and NASA for sixty years, it was not the home of exobiology.

Instead she had taken her double degree in biology and chemistry and gotten a fellowship at the NASA Astrobiology Institute in Houston.

It was there that she expanded her studies to include atmospheric physics and geology and even languages. She had spent six months at the South Pole searching for Martian meteorites and extremophiles.

It was there, also, that she escaped from her father's control, dating one unsuitable man (by her father's standards, that is) after another, and earning herself a slightly exaggerated reputation as a good-time girl.

Well, she had grown up in Melbourne, not Delhi. She

looked like a resident of the subcontinent, if you ignored the blue eyes and the broad-shouldered build, a gift from years of swimming and surfing.

She had not been able to decide which was worse: to have been condemned to the stereotypical studious submissive Indian woman role, or to be considered an Aussie tart. Obviously the party-girl image had made it difficult to gain responsibility and authority—even as it opened other doors and encouraged male supervisors to welcome her arrival.

But, while she had indeed run through a lot of boyfriends in a decade, she never overlapped them . . . no one-night stands, either, allowing for some liberal interpretation of the standards. She had spent the past five months in a committed relationship with Cedric Houghton, a thirty-five-year-old bachelor credit specialist in Pearland, Texas, who was probably frantic about what had happened to her. (Because of her assignment to Bangalore, they hadn't seen each other in a month . . . but they had video-chatted the night *Venture* and *Brahma* had landed on Keanu . . . which seemed, now, to have taken place a year in the past.)

Makali had been faithful to Cedric; even without the spur of a relationship, she would not have considered a relationship with any of her co-workers on the ISRO exo-intelligence panel.

Which was one of the reasons she had found Valya Makarova's wanton behavior appalling, especially with a loathsome male specimen like Dale Scott, who had propositioned her several times. Never crudely; oh, no, compared to the very direct Aussie boys Makali had known in Melbourne, for example, Scott was a master of sophistication . . . he didn't touch, he merely loomed. He didn't leer, he only shared confidences, winks, ostensibly harmless data.

He never took no for an answer because there was never a *question*.

All of this behavior was inescapably obvious to Valya, yet she had continued to swoon every time Scott entered a room, like a lovesick teenager in her first sexual relationship.

Which made Makali, briefly and unhappily, wonder if Dale Scott's bedroom skills were the reason for Valya's erotic stupor. . . .

Fortunately, the chaos of the discoveries from Keanu had driven all personal matters from Makali's mind. She had been scooped up from the wreckage of Bangalore Control Center, and after surviving the initial shock of what had happened, she had spent the trip from Earth to Keanu silently evaluating the data—Keanu's maneuvers at the time of the *Venture* and *Brahma* landings, the discovery of structures inside Vesuvius Vent, the habitat itself.

None of these had been a shock, frankly. Thanks to a bit of luck and data from underused and ill-funded Asian astronomers, ISRO and the Russians had detected unusual signals from Keanu long before its closest approach to Earth, hence the clandestine creation of an exo-intelligence panel staffed with the world's experts who were *not* American citizens. Makali and the other members of the team had suspected that the human landing on Keanu was going to lead to First Contact.

So far, so good. What they had not anticipated—and who could have?—was the discovery of resurrected or reincarnated or reconstructed human beings inside Keanu. Makali believed, and there had been hints in what Zack Stewart said, that these creatures had been deliberately "created" by Keanu's builders and operators in order to communicate with humans.

Perhaps that communication had been too easy—how else to explain the horrifying series of accidents that had led to, well, the bombardment of Earth by a pair of Keanu-launched Objects.

Makali's father was also fond of saying, "Don't look back." There was no point in trying to apportion blame; in some sense, Makali knew she should be grateful. When she took up exobiology, she had assumed her career would be spent constructing biospheres for newly discovered exoplanets and trying to determine which probe-gathered samples from Mars, asteroids, and the Earth's surface would give proof of alien life.

As her lost boyfriend Cedric would say, "You've got that covered."

("Thank you, darling!")

She reached the trees and, fully aware of the lack of food, immediately began searching for these vege-fruits.

The first problem was that others had been here first; the branches showed clear signs of having been stripped, eagerly, swiftly, and violently. She made a mental note to do some calculations relating the amount of available food to the daily needs of the population. She suspected the two lines would intersect rather soon, and they would run out . . . of course, why be pessimistic? Hadn't she just insisted to Nayar that the Keanu habitat was designed for humans? She had no data on how quickly the habitat would produce more food.

Right now, however, it was looking grim . . . she had worked her way along the habitat walls, through the "orchard," for several meters, perhaps ten, without seeing anything larger than an acorn.

And then she found something that disturbed her as much as the flickering sky-snakes had.

As far as she could see down-habitat, toward the far "southern" end, the trees were now covered with a black mold.

She touched it—what the hell, maybe it was Keanu packaging of some kind, like wax on an apple—and quickly regretted the gesture. Her fingers burned as if she'd dipped them in battery acid.

("Cedric, baby, this isn't good!")

Turn around, then. Go the other way.

She had not completed the maneuver when a shape appeared in front of her—

—and struck her!

For an instant, as terrified as she had ever been in her life, she shouted and lashed out . . . before realizing her assailant was a dog! It was a Lab that had been scooped up with the Texans . . . certainly the animal had not been aboard the Bangalore Object. Makali had seen it earlier in the day, running freely.

Now it kept leaping on her, licking her. She had never been a dog person—no pets of any kind. Her experience with dogs, in fact, was this: They always jumped on you.

Normally it made her want to shove the creatures

away, but circumstances had changed. In this environment, Earth beings needed to stick together. Wishing she knew the dog's name, Makali nevertheless made what she hoped were soothing sounds.

"You bad boy," she said.

The dog seemed to calm down. "You're probably hungry, too," she said.

Makali's human-canine communication skills were lacking—how arrogant she was, to think she could crack the codes of exobeings!—but she got the clear impression that the dog wanted to return to the Temple. He kept turning toward it, looking back, as if waiting.

Disturbed by the strange light and the Dead Zone, Makali decided it would be wise to pay attention to the dog.

As she came within sight of the Temple and the horde of refugees, she was suddenly sad. She missed Cedric, of course. But she also missed her father. She found herself blinking back tears.

It didn't help that she saw the same emotion on the faces of those she passed. Now in a state of collapse, fed but looking into the great unknown, each was probably thinking about a husband or wife, about missing parents or children, friends, co-workers, everyday Earth life now gone, likely never to be regained.

"Cedric," she said aloud, "help me get a grip." She had developed a bad habit of talking to him as if he were present . . . their whole relationship, in fact, was based on her telling him things. Making excuses, at first. The one part of Makali Pillay's existence that she had never been able to manage was money. Cedric Houghton had been the counselor she had been sent to when her credit card bills became a problem.

He had not cured her, of course. But he had stabilized her—and won her heart, at least for now.

Thinking about Cedric allowed her to put the sadness behind her, for this reason: On the day that the Object struck Bangalore Control Center, Makali Pillay still owed forty-three thousand dollars U.S. on five different credit cards.

And while she might never see Cedric or her father again, there was one bright side: She would never have to pay them off.

ARRIVAL DAY: ZACK

It was catching up with him. The strangeness, the loss, the endless strain.

Zack had collapsed inside the Temple, his back against one of its too-tall walls—in the same chamber where he and Megan had confronted the Architect or its avatar—and found himself unable to move.

Or even think.

Even now, two meters away, Vikram Nayar, Shane Weldon, and Harley Drake were carefully quizzing Makali Pillay about her journey into the Keanu twilight. He was hearing words like *blight* and *Dead Zone* and understanding none of it.

And, if possible, caring even less. He only had energy for Rachel . . . and she was presently out of sight. He knew, as a father, as a leader, that he should know where she was, who she was with.

Unlike, say, a typical Friday night in Houston.

That was how Zack knew he was at his redline, into a danger zone, beyond exhausted, beyond endurance.

He was paralyzed.

The only thing capable of drawing his notice was the dog wandering through the crowd, searching for food or water or a pat—or its master. Zack was not a dog person, but at the moment, he was happy the creature was around. It was a Revenant, too. And apparently immune to whatever caused human Revenants to wear out in a few days. Why? Because it didn't have to withstand the stress of communicating on behalf of the Architects?

"Hey, Zack, you listening?"

Harley Drake slowly wheeled his chair closer and leaned down. Zack couldn't help grunting in appreciation—once. Again, all he had energy for. "Yeah," he croaked.

"You need water."

"I need," he said, exhausted by the expenditure of energy required to utter three words more or less in a row, "everything."

Harley offered him a bottle of water. He had to hold it so Zack could drink from it. When Zack seemed full, he said, "Did you hear what Pillay was saying?"

"No."

Harley looked at him with resignation. "I don't want to have to go through it all again." But he did, or at least the highlights, talking about the blight, the Dead Zone, the flickering lights. "Is that right?" Harley said, when he was finished, speaking to the others, who stood off to one side like a jury.

"Yes," Nayar said.

The water had helped revive Zack. "It seems anomalous, maybe even troubling," he said. "But I don't have—"

"No one's expecting a solution or an insight," Weldon said. "But if this is anomalous and therefore troubling . . . well, I think it affects our next steps."

"Which are?"

"Sorry," Weldon said, "I don't have them. Or even one. Let me say, 'our next steps, whatever they might be.'"

Zack turned to the others. "If this habitat is changing or breaking down, we may have to move."

"Where to?" Weldon said.

"Another habitat."

"Is there another one?" Nayar asked. "Do you know this?"

"I don't. But Megan hinted that there was. And just do the math: Keanu's internal volume could hold a couple of dozen habitats this size . . ."

Pillay spoke up. "The last mass calculations we did would suggest that." To the others, she said, "Keanu is not solid."

"Good to know," Weldon said. "Our first order of business tomorrow, after electing Zack as mayor, might be to send out scouting parties."

"How do we get out of here?" That was Nayar. Zack had always suspected the man was an Eeyore; now it was confirmed.

"As I said, I was in another chamber . . . there was one passage. There might be others."

"And there are other access vents," Makali said.

All heads turned toward her. "Of course there are other vents," Weldon said, not bothering to disguise his impatience. "The surface is riddled with them."

"They were firing like RCS jets, too," Harley said.

"I'm not talking about those," Makali said. "We detected more vents like Vesuvius, where it appears you can actually reach Keanu's interior."

Finally Zack lost patience. "Everybody shut up! How many did you find, and where are they?"

"We never had a complete revolution of Keanu to observe," Makali said, happy to be an analyst rather than a combatant. "It was only once Keanu performed its venting-capture maneuver that we were able to detect differences in some of the vents.

"But we identified four where the spectra indicated outgassing of atmosphere rather than propulsive material. Vesuvius was one of these."

Shane Weldon wasn't ready to let the matter drop. "It would have been nice to know before Zack and his crew—and the *Brahma* crew—found out the hard way."

"I'm going to guess," Zack said, "that Makali's team didn't know until we were already on EVA."

"Even later," she said. She turned to Weldon and gestured to Nayar, including him. "Or we surely would have shared that information."

"Fine," Harley said, "we're all going to sing campfire songs now. What the hell does it mean?"

"One thing's obvious," Zack said. "Keanu is large enough to contain several habitats the size of this."

"We agreed on that some time ago," Weldon said.

"Okay, then, Shane, if our habitat could be reached through Vesuvius Vent, then it makes sense to assume that these other habitats might also be reached by these—what did you call them, Makali? Access vents."

"Of course," Nayar said. "And while all knowledge is helpful, what use is this?"

Now Zack knew what he wanted to say. He could feel his spirits lifting even before he said the words: "It means we might be able to reach these other habitats. We aren't trapped in this one. And Keanu has some amazing capabilities—we might find the control center for the whole operation."

He could see them all—each in his or her fashion—imagining the possibilities. Weldon was the first to reset to skepticism. "I don't see how we reach these other vents, even if they happen to be within walking distance. We don't have EVA suits, or maybe you forgot."

Weldon's tone infuriated him, but Zack remained calm. These people were just as tired and fried as he was. "I'm not saying we have the entire solution in our hands. I'm just saying . . . we have a literal *opening*."

Now Makali Pillay was nodding enthusiastically. "We should not only search for a way out and to the other habitats, we should go back to the vesicles."

"The what?" Weldon said.

"*Vesicles*," Makali said patiently. "It's a term from biology and means *a bubble*, which is sort of what brought us here—"

"The term isn't important, Makali," Nayar said, "but this is: Our . . . vesicle was literally dissolving as we disembarked. What do you suppose is left of it?"

"Ours, too," Weldon said.

"Probably not much," Makali said. "But we have all these people, and while keeping us fed and watered will occupy most of us . . . some should take the time and go back, find out what's there, what can be used . . . whether or not those landing chambers give access elsewhere." She smiled. "Sorry, I'm babbling. It's probably the hunger."

"Haven't you gotten anything to eat yet?" Zack said. He searched for Xavier, who was just a few meters away. "Hey," he said.

"Way ahead of you, boss," Xavier said. He held out a vege-fruit to Makali. "One of the leftovers, ma'am. Sorry we didn't have one earlier."

"Not a problem!" Makali said, biting into the item without delay and with considerable relish. With her mouth full, she said, "I just hope the blight doesn't destroy these . . . vege-things."

Weldon was like a gardener intent on killing a weed. "Even assuming we can get out of this . . . tin can," he said, "I don't think there's a high probability—by which I mean over one percent—that we'll be able to take control of this vehicle."

"We don't have to take *control*," Zack said, seeing another possibility that he had failed to present. And beginning to resent the fact that he was doing all the heavy conceptual lifting here. "We just have to be able to send a signal to Earth."

"You're thinking of, what, a giant signal fire? Maybe in the shape of an SOS?" Nayar said, joining the fun.

The group's manner had changed, from serious skepticism to outright mockery. It was a defense mechanism Zack recognized; he was prone to it himself. The only response was to play it straight and not get angry. It made you look like the dull kid on the playground, but sometimes you had to do it. "I don't think rescue is out of the question," Zack said.

"Let's run those numbers, then," Weldon said, moving from mockery to outright hostility. *He must be tired out of his mind,* Zack thought, trying to be charitable—and functional. "The world's entire near-term—by which I mean for the next couple of years—capability for sending manned vehicles to Keanu is three. Two *Destiny-Ventures,* one *Brahma.*" He turned to Nayar. "Unless you guys have a secret stash somewhere."

Nayar was shaking his head. "We would be lucky to launch *Brahma-2* in two years."

"Even if you launched all three vehicles uncrewed, that's twelve seats. Okay, you can squeeze one extra body . . . call it fifteen. We have a hundred and eighty-seven souls on board! What would you do? Have a fucking lottery?"

"Actually," Harley said, "it's a hundred and eighty-six." When no one responded, he added: "Minus Bynum."

That brought a savage smile to Weldon's face. "Well, that improves the picture. So we'd only have a hundred and seventy-one people condemned to death—"

"Shut up!" Makali Pillay placed herself in front of Weldon, who, probably to his great surprise, did not tower over her. Rather the opposite . . . she actually pushed the man back a step. "Since when does NASA run away from a challenge?"

"Since I've been around," Harley said, in a voice so low only Zack could hear. And he couldn't help laughing a little.

"Shane, you sound like my mother." Makali turned to Nayar; she wasn't going to spare him, either. "And you, too. Zack is talking about a chance, that's all. He can do the math; he knows we can't be rescued.

"But some of us could be! And the others . . . wouldn't it be great to be resupplied from Earth? Be back in touch? We might be exiles, but we wouldn't be alone! And how would this be any different from being colonists on the Moon or Mars? Fine, we didn't volunteer . . . but here we are! Let's make the best of the situation!"

The combination of youth, beauty, vehemence—and righteous fury—was successful. Weldon actually blushed. "Good point," he said. "Sorry, Zack, I—"

"No problem." It was probably valuable to have let Weldon have his say. He was the great soldier type: full of complaints and justifiable worries, but once allowed to vent . . . ready to take the hill. "So, do we have a plan for tomorrow?" Weldon said. "Election, then most of the company engaged in finding food, water, and shelter while some of us become scouts?"

The agreement was universal, but muted. Zack was amazed to see how quickly everyone's enthusiasm waned. His, too. Five minutes ago he had been ready to venture to the far ends of the Temple . . . now all he wanted to do was sit back down.

As he sank against the wall, Xavier sidled up to him, a half-smile on his face. "Say, boss, you know this vege-fruit everybody keeps talkin' about? Like it's alien food?"

"Yeah?"

"Any of them ever seen a pawpaw before?" Xavier giggled. "'Cause that's what they are." He waddled off, pleased with himself . . . and Zack couldn't blame him. All the supposed brainpower on display here in the Temple wasn't a match for a teenage fry cook from the bayou.

Zack resolved to keep Xavier in his sights. Who knew what other useful information the kid would turn up? Or what kind of unexpected trouble he might cause?

For the moment, he fell back on his training. This was like a long day on the International Space Station . . . just before bed, tomorrow's schedule would be uploaded. And in Zack's mental checklist, there was this: Return to the Beehive.

ARRIVAL DAY: PAV

After four hours of searching for, finding, then picking and hauling vege-fruits and herky jerky, followed by a frantic ten minutes of ravenous consumption, Pav Radhakrishnan decided he needed some Pav time.

So he hiked deeper into the habitat from the Temple—anything to get away from the insane mob—and found himself a rock to lean against.

Makali Pillay had told him that there were no monsters running around, no creepy alien snakes or shit like that, not that he was convinced anyone really knew the truth of the matter. Not even Makali, who was supposed to be the expert on Keanu, or so Pav's father had told him before the *Brahma* launch.

But Pav was willing to risk it, just to get away from Nayar's attentions. Fine, the man had been a close friend of his father's—his boss, in fact. It didn't mean he was responsible for Pav. It didn't mean Pav would treat him like his absent father.

Thinking of Taj made him wonder where he was. One of the Houston people had confirmed that the *Brahma* commander was aboard *Destiny* with two of his surviving crew members, that he could even be back on Earth by now. Fucking great—Taj had always mocked the United

States and its *Destiny* spacecraft because it had to splash down in the ocean. "Are we fish or mammals?" he would say.

"Bet he's happier now," Pav said out loud.

Then he began to wonder, for the hundredth time, if his father knew that he'd been taken. His mother knew, of course. (She had probably watched the whole thing on television from Russia. Good for her. Pav hoped she was crying her eyes out.)

But what would vyomanaut Taj Radhakrishnan think about the Object that had plastered the Bangalore Control Center and scooped up some of the survivors . . . including his son?

At some level, he would have to admit that it was kind of cool that his son—who had never given a shit about going into the space program—had now traveled just as far from Earth as he had.

Take that, Papa.

More likely, he was freaking out. He would probably find some consolation in the fact that Nayar and Makali and other associates were with Pav. One of the few life lessons Pav could remember his father telling him was, "Trouble goes better with company."

Well, Pav sure had company. He had been living at the control center since *Brahma* landed on Keanu, sleeping when he could on the couch in Nayar's palatial office suite. (The flight director was never there; for Pav it was like having a swanky hotel room.) He had spent most of his waking time in the control center itself . . . the thing reminded Pav of one of those Best Buy stores he'd seen in the United States, twice as big as it needed to be, crammed with screens and consoles—and not enough staff. He'd been able to lurk there for hours, largely unseen.

But then he'd begun to hear about problems with the mission. The other life lesson Taj had shared with him was, "Spaceflight is incredibly dangerous even in low Earth orbit. I'm going where no human has gone before. Don't be surprised if something goes wrong." So it wasn't technically a surprise, but learning that his father was out of contact with *Brahma* and Bangalore . . . hearing that one or more of the human explorers, from either *Brahma* or the American team, had been killed . . . then watching as the *Brahma* lander, the pride of ISRO and an entire nation, a twenty-meter-tall vehicle that cost a billion rupees for every meter of height, simply disappeared.

He would have gotten out of the center and gone home, but it was too far, and there was no one at home except his grandparents. (And what were *they* doing right now? Treating him as if he were dead?)

And Nayar wasn't letting him go. If, prior to the loss of *Brahma*, Pav had had to sneak into the control center, afterward he was not only welcome . . . he was required to be there.

So he had had an up-close-and-personal view of the approach of the first Object. He didn't think he'd ever forget the stunned reactions of the control team when they realized it was heading straight for them.

Only then had Pav directly disobeyed an order. He had tried to get out of the building and run, and while running, jump onto the back of a truck or a car that was making an escape.

He hadn't made it.

And here he was.

Sitting on the ground, which did, indeed, look like good old Earth dirt, he kicked off his sandals and rubbed his feet. He wondered how long they were all going to be on Keanu. Weeks? Months? Years?

The rest of their sorry lives?

How long would his sandals last? Would he wind up running around barefoot and naked?

Or would he die of starvation?

All he had been hearing from the other Bangalores— none of the *Brahma* control people, though—were rumors that NASA or ISRO would send a rescue ship. *How* they had any way of knowing that, Pav couldn't imagine.

It wasn't as though they were using their Slates. He had turned his on at various times and wasn't getting a link from anywhere or anything, not that he'd expected to. He'd disabled the Wi-Fi anyway, to save on battery life.

Pav knew the batteries on his Slate were running down, that there was no place he would be able to recharge them, and that once they were gone, they were likely gone forever. And along with it, his stories, his pictures, and especially his tunes.

He would have them in his head, that's all.

For now, though, he pulled the Slate out of its case and thumbed the on switch. He was tempted to let the speakers thump and wail, but that might let one of the others know where he was. He was just as tempted to access his private folder of female favorites. . . .

He didn't want to see or talk to anyone else right now. He wanted to slip in his earbuds, close his eyes, and pretend he was back in his bedroom in Delhi.

Or, at least, Vikram Nayar's big office.

Thinking about the office got him thinking about Nayar's attractive secretary, and, without the added spice of his collection of babes, next thing he knew his hand was sliding into his pants. Then he unzipped them. The potential shame of discovery was outweighed by the wicked certainty that he would score the first orgasm on Keanu.

Talk about your giant leap for mankind—

What was that?

Something had flown across his field of view!

Or had it? The light here was so low—like perpetual twilight—that he couldn't be sure.

Carefully returning his half-erect penis to his pants, he stood and scanned the scene . . . a slightly uneven landscape, part dirt, a few rocks, and some bushes. In the far distance was a hazy suggestion of a wall of some kind.

But close up? Nothing. No rustling leaves, no chittering birds, no buzzing insects.

Just the very clear *whump* of his heart in his chest . . . and the insane rhythms of Summer Jihad in his buds.

Nothing else.

He sat down again. No possible way he was going to resume the quest for the Keanu jack. All he could do was relax, and think about . . . how the fuck this had happened.

It was his father's job, of course. Pav could barely remember the time before Taj joined the space program.

He had been a fairly young Indian Air Force pilot, where your long-term goal was to be able to drop a nuke on Karachi or Islamabad, when the Indian Space Research Organization made a deal with the Russians to fly a vyo-manaut on a *Soyuz*, one step toward the building and launch of an indigenous craft of its own.

Taj and Wing Commander Asahi had been selected . . . and the whole Radhakrishnan family had relocated to Star City outside Moscow.

Pav had been eight at the time, and what he remem-bered most about the new home was that it was cold and dark, and nobody spoke Hindi.

ISRO sent a small support team to Star City; they were the only people the family could talk to, and not one of them was under the age of twenty-seven. They were forced to depend on each other—perhaps too much, because Pav's mother, Amita, had fallen in love with . . . Vikram Nayar. When that got discovered, Taj had thrown her out—and Nayar had, too.

Amita had taken up with a Russian guy at Star City. And Pav's life, not especially good at that time, had got-ten much, much worse.

Pav had had to learn Russian in a hurry. His first words were *chorny mat*—"black ass," the charming term his Russian classmates had for a person of color.

Eventually things had gotten better (Russians would still roll over for anyone who could play classical piano, which was Pav's big skill), though never great, or even good. In fact, at the moment, Pav still thought the insane floating smelly ride in the Object and the crazy weird day on Keanu weren't as bad as those first months in Russia.

Another one! Something had definitely hit the fucking ground about ten meters in front of him.

Pav slowly got to his feet, slipping on the sandals. He was going to have to check this out—

Carefully, he crossed the distance to the landing spot. . . .

Two objects lay in the dirt. Pav picked them up . . . a lipstick and a coin, an American quarter—

"Boo!"

He had been ready for it, but he still started. "Goddammit," he said. Really, it was all he could think to say.

"Sorry. I couldn't resist. You're Pav, right?" It was Rachel, Zack Stewart's daughter. They had met at least twice back on Earth, but years ago, when she was, like, eleven. She'd grown up and filled out. But so had Pav; he stood almost six feet now.

"How long have you been watching me?"

"Not long." Rachel's voice was neutral, and in this fucked-up half-light it was impossible for Pav to tell whether she was giving him an I-saw-you-playing-with-yourself smirk.

"Do you want your things back?" He held out the lipstick and the quarter.

"Not unless you can show me where I can use them."

"Well, I think the quarter's no good. But you might need that lipstick—"

"When, for prom?"

But she took it and jammed it in the pocket of her jeans.

"What are you doing out here?" he asked her.

"Same as you," she said, in a voice that was so

noncommittal that he began to relax; he hadn't been caught.

"Just had to get away?"

"Duh." She saw the Slate in his hands. "God, you have music?"

"For a while."

"Can I listen? Who is it?"

"Summer Jihad."

"I know them!"

"Really." He didn't believe her for a second, but he handed over the unit, anyway.

"Shit, yeah! 'Blow Me, Blow You,' 'Down, Up, Down,' I've got them all on my Slate, too."

"Where's yours?" he said, having to shout a little, because Rachel had the earbuds locked in and was actually dancing around, already immersed in music.

"Buried it!" she said loudly. "In my mom's grave!"

Pav knew all about Megan Stewart's death, of course; he and his father had been present at the Kennedy Space Center when Zack got the news of the accident . . . had stayed in the United States to attend the funeral.

And in Bangalore Control, he had also heard the strange rumors that Megan Stewart had somehow been brought back to life here, on Keanu.

"Which one?" he said, daring to joke about what was likely a very sensitive subject.

And he hit home. Rachel removed the earbuds. "There only is one," she said, suddenly very serious.

"Well, what happened, then? They were saying all kinds of strange shit. . . ."

"Such as . . ."

"That whoever is running this place had made some kind of copy of her—"

Rachel was fiercely shaking her head. "No! No, it wasn't a copy . . . it was my mother! She came back to life. I talked to her. I mean, she couldn't fool me." She was waiting for him to agree with her. "Wouldn't you know your mother anywhere?"

"Not sure," he said, "but my mother and I—"

"Fine. Not that I care, but just trust me: She was back."

"And . . . ?"

"She died again."

She started to put the earbuds back on, but Pav stopped her. "Then where is she?"

"We don't know. I mean, my father said she . . . she . . ." Rachel's eyes filled with tears. "We don't know, okay? Why don't you go back to beating off!" And she wrenched his earbuds away and put them on again.

Which is why Pav heard the rumble, a groaning vibration that seemed to come from beneath them. It lasted maybe two seconds . . . but it freaked him out so completely that he forgot his embarrassment.

"What the hell was that?"

Rachel blinked and pulled off the buds. "What?"

"Didn't you *hear* that?"

"Hear what?"

"Wait . . ." He put an arm out to steady Rachel, and himself. "I thought it was starting again."

"What are you talking about?"

"Some kind of quake."

"I didn't feel anything."

"Well, no, not dancing around like that—"

"Fine, then." She shoved the Slate into his stomach.

"Look," he said, "I'm sorry. Keep it for a while. I just . . . felt something. It's like this whole place shivered."

"You're freaking me out." She did look terrified. "What do you think is going on? Keanu's a spaceship . . . do they even have things like quakes?"

"It's really a small planet," he said, having heard Makali Pillay state this fact half a dozen times. "It not only has quakes, it probably has worse quakes than Earth."

"Is that supposed to make me feel better?"

"Yeah. We understand earthquakes. An object this size would have a lot of them, just because it's in a tug-of-war between two really bigger bodies. Earth and the Moon," he added, unnecessarily, of course. (Her father was an astronaut, too!)

Rachel stared at him. "What are you, some kind of astro geo guy?"

He was embarrassed again. He wasn't all that sure of his facts, for one thing. And he never talked science, ever. He was into music; *that* was what he talked about, *especially* with girls.

Maybe he was just really changing the subject. "You know what it's like when your family is in the space business. You can't help hearing things like that."

Rachel said, "We should probably go back. My dad used to freak out when I was late coming home, and that was in Houston." She smiled. "Things are a little different here. . . ."

"I hear you."

By silent agreement, they turned and began walking toward the Temple and the others.

"Hey, what if that wasn't a quake, though?" Rachel said. "What would all that shivering mean?"

"It would probably be very bad. As in, the place is falling apart . . . or about to change, and if it changes, it's not likely to be good for humans."

"You're not very cheerful, Pav."

"Not lately."

ARRIVAL DAY: HARLEY

The last thing Weldon said to Harley Drake, while helping Harley out of his wheelchair and onto a mat of some kind of leaves that Sasha had arranged, was, "Stick with me tomorrow."

"I ain't going anywhere, Shane."

"You know what I mean. We've got a lot of folks who've gotten through the first day like stunned cattle. They're going to be more agitated tomorrow, once it sinks in that we're stuck here."

"Didn't you listen to Zack? We aren't necessarily *stuck* here, my friend."

"Stewart is a goddamn optimist," Weldon said, using a tone more appropriate to describing him as a registered sex offender. "These access vents could be twenty clicks away, across a frozen vacuum we can't possibly cross."

"Or they could be ten clicks away, or right next door, if we just find the right passage."

"And even if we get to the next habitat, then what? We've only seen one, and aside from food, water, and one useless building, it doesn't have much. Why would you assume you're going to find Keanu mission control?"

"Does it hurt to give people hope?"

"Not until they realize it's bullshit, and then it hurts a whole lot."

"So they'll be hurting later rather than sooner."

He was flat on his back now, and Jesus, did it feel good.

"Are you fucking arguing with me, Harls?" Weldon and Harley had always had a commander-pilot relationship, with Weldon in the commander's seat. Which was funny, because Harley's chops and flying experience were substantially more varied and flashy . . . but Weldon had commanded Marine units, then moved into NASA management. Harley had commanded an airplane and did not enjoy telling other people what to do.

"Just helping you shape your argument, my friend." He was troubled by Weldon's reversals on the subject. Usually, once consensus was reached, he was Mr. Consistent. "Besides, didn't you sign on to Zack's bit about sending a signal?"

Weldon chose not to answer, finding another distraction.

Which was fine with Harley. They were all too worn out and stressed to have rational discussions. What they needed was sleep.

Assuming that was possible on the slatelike floor, even with the "cushion" Sasha had so thoughtfully provided. "You're too good to me," he had told her. Harley was, in fact, astonished to realize that he and the woman from Yale had been inseparable since the Keanu crisis went critical . . . four days ago?

"Oh, don't worry: I know," she said, rubbing a smudge of dirt off her face.

"What I can't figure out is why." He knew this was a stupid question. *If she starts asking herself that, she'll be gone!*

"You mean, why is this goddess of a woman spending all her time with . . . ?" She made a comic gesture toward Harley, including his useless legs.

"I know I've got tons of charm, but—"

"Well, sure. And fame. Let's not forget the fame."

"Yeah, me and your local member of the state assembly. Can you name him?"

"Her. Actually, I can." She blinked, and he couldn't tell whether she was joking. "But I take your point." She thought for a moment. "Are you at least rich?"

"I make a living." He had a pension and a little money put away in an IRA. No significant property, no anticipated inheritance.

And no sense of just how and why a casual conversation had turned into a game of Where Is This Relationship Going?

"Don't worry, I have money." She smiled.

"The question remains."

"Well . . . maybe I was just between boyfriends."

"I can live with that."

"And you are kind of cute and funny." She actually reached down to muss his hair. "Aren't you just totally fucking tired, though?"

"I'll shut up." Just in time, too.

The moment Sasha was on the mat next to him, however, she said, "What do you mean, other vents and habitats?"

So he told her. And was gratified by her interest. In

spite of his public position supporting Zack, fatigue, or innate pessimism, had convinced him that Weldon was essentially correct: Zack was giving them false hope. They were trapped here inside Keanu and would die sooner rather than later . . . new victims of the space age, like the *Challenger* and *Columbia* crews . . . just more numerous. Even getting back in touch with mission control—hell, anyone on Earth—meant little.

Barring some miracle, Keanu was where they would spend the rest of their lives. The challenge was to make that time less than "nasty, brutish, and short."

Food, water, consumables—that was one major and likely ongoing challenge. And, in spite of what Zack Stewart had pitched, lack of rescue, lack of hope.

No one was talking about danger! About the fact that one of the first astronauts to enter Keanu had actually been killed . . . and that two of the others hadn't survived the mission, either.

They'd been brought here against their will. Told nothing. Helped in no way that he could see, other than the simple fact that the environment wasn't immediately fatal.

"Hey!" Sasha said. "Look who's here!"

Camilla had approached them. The Brazilian girl looked unfazed by the suicide or accident or whatever she thought had happened.

"Hi!" Harley said, in his best tourist-friendly voice. He knew Camilla didn't speak English.

Then the girl rattled off a phrase in a language that Harley recognized. "Is that German?"

"Yep," Sasha said, and spoke quickly to Camilla. "I

did two years of grad work in Geneva. I'm pretty fluent."

"Lucky for her."

Sasha didn't miss the sarcasm. "Come on, she's nine years old and the only person who speaks Portuguese is that weird Russian woman. Would you like that?"

"No," Harley said, feeling selfish. He also felt that feeling selfish was a survival mechanism. "But I like so little these days."

"Ha," Sasha said. "Come on, let's go back to bed."

Harley accepted the new reality: He and Sasha were Camilla's adoptive parents, much as the two of them had served in that role for Rachel Stewart back in mission control . . . four days ago.

Four days, or an entire lifetime.

As they settled down in the cool, theoretically safer interior of the Temple, Harley noticed that Camilla was scratching at a place on the back of her left arm. Even a quick glance confirmed that it was lumpy and inflamed. "What happened there?" he said to Sasha, who had seen it, too.

"Bug bite, I guess."

It wasn't until they were all resting on their sides and backs, fighting off sleep, that Harley asked himself:

What bug?

Part Three

To the people on Keanu:

My name is Taj Radhakrishnan. I was the commander of the *Brahma* mission to the Near-Earth Object Keanu. My vehicle was destroyed two days after landing, two days after my crew and I joined Commander Stewart's team in the first explorations of Keanu's interior.

The exploration was . . . we were unprepared for what we found. I don't believe anyone could have prepared us—

Only four of us made it home safely. Three others died. Zack Stewart bravely . . . stayed behind.

Bangalore and Houston have tracked the Objects back to Keanu. We assume that these things were a kind of transport system—why they took you, we don't know.

But we hope you are alive. We are doing everything we can to contact you and see what we might do.

For my son, Pav, if you are listening . . . be brave.

BROADCAST FROM MOSCOW MISSION CONTROL TO KEANU
BY TAJ RADHAKRISHNAN, SEPTEMBER 3, 2019

There are 186 or 185 or maybe 180 of us, it turns out, depending on who's gone bugfuck and killed somebody that I don't know about.

We've got some food, a bit we brought along, other stuff we've found. Some water, same deal. And the clothes we were wearing.

THAT'S IT! No alien masters, no mission, no instructions . . . just a big habitat like a mall, only instead of a Gap or Martin Spencer or GUM . . . there's one building we call the Temple.

We've had an election, and an American astronaut named Harley Drake won, though I don't think he considers it winning. He's a good guy; my dad mentioned him a few times. Got crippled in the same car accident that killed Megan Stewart, Zack's wife and Rachel's mom, which is how, I guess, he wound up babysitting Rachel and getting caught up with the Object.

As for the whole Megan Stewart thing . . . the fact that she was alive here when Zack and my dad got here, don't ask me. No one seems to be quite sure how the fuck that could happen, or even if it did. I'm willing to believe it, because it's no weirder than anything else I've seen.

I just wish someone would tell us WHY we're here and WHAT THE FUCK WE'RE SUPPOSED TO DO.

And WHEN WE GET TO GO HOME.

This officially sucks.

I'm scared. I hate typing those words, but it's true.

I've never been more scared in my life.

THE PRISONER

The only way the Prisoner was able to maintain any mental stability was through routine. It would wake, it would eliminate, it would exercise, it would eat. It would then perform an examination of its prison, carefully pacing the x and y axes.

An objective observer would have called it foolish, because obviously the measurements didn't change.

Except once, exactly seven sleeps back. During that waking period, the Prisoner had discovered that its chamber had grown wider and shorter, as if reshaped. In search of confirmation, it had measured the area seven times, and—allowing for slight variations due to the imprecise nature of its instruments—confirmed that the prison had indeed been reshaped.

It was the same sleep period in which the Prisoner had felt numerous anomalous vibrations in the wall and floor. Obviously there was a connection, but what?

On the next sleep, it performed the measurements again, and found to its disappointment that the chamber had returned to its previous dimensions.

There were no strange vibrations during that sleep period, either.

In one sense, the Prisoner was happy; it had concocted a dire scenario in which every successive waking period would show that the chamber was growing fatter and shorter by the same amount each day . . . until it found itself pinned like vegetative matter.

It had been quite easy to speculate, during the darker moments of that calculation, that this was how its Keepers would punish it. . . . Exile having been judged insufficient, they would simply, slowly, crush the Prisoner.

The threat vanished with the return to normal measurements, and left the Prisoner feeling even more despairing.

Because it could live for years, decades, in this chamber.

The second stop on the Prisoner's waking routine—and the last before swim and sleep—was the special place on the outer edge of the chamber . . . it was where the builders had embedded tiny assemblers to apply heat, light, and information to the raw materials of the habitat in order to synthesize food, skin, or other materials.

It was also where it expended its own waste.

The Prisoner had located certain tools. They had been woven into the fabric of its prison by Powers-Beyond-the-Keepers. The Keepers themselves would be greatly angered to know that their Prisoner was using them.

One tool allowed the Prisoner to leave the prison, for brief periods.

There was no access to the larger Keeper environment, of course, but there was a means of going another direction.

Out, to the bleak surface of the vessel.

Of course, this required protection and support, but the Powers-Beyond-the-Keepers had prepared for this, equipping each environment with adaptives, self-shaping garments that would provide protection for one cycle.

Donning one of the adaptives was a rigorous challenge, though not much more rigorous than challenges the Prisoner had faced and overcome while growing up in its birth habitat. Indeed, diving into the adaptive fluid had much in common with a rite that all had to endure before being allowed to divide: the triple, involving exposure to surface and air as well as sea. It was not meant to be fatal to participants, though it often was.

Donning an adaptive suit was not meant to be fatal, either.

Since this was the Prisoner's fourth time donning the adaptive garment, the feelings of suffocation and loss of sight and hearing were almost familiar.

Once enclosed in the adaptive garment, out on the surface, the Prisoner had one cycle to find a weapon, a tool, anything to improve its existence.

ZACK

"I think this is going to be a giant waste of time."

It had been two days since the vesicles had arrived on Keanu, one day after Megan's burial, and Zack Stewart faced a wall, where Makali Pillay's pronouncement was as obvious as it was discouraging.

"Hold on, for Christ's sake," he said, his voice ragged and harsh. "We just got here. We already know that these walls come and go."

"I'd be happy to see you make it go," Makali said. He had to fight the urge to turn on her and scream. Some microscopic vestige of his training and sense of command allowed him to absorb her sarcasm, charging it off to (a) the exhaustion and (b) the foreign accent.

Besides, Makali hadn't already devoted an hour of her life to searching for a "missing" passage, as Zack had yesterday. He turned to his team, which, in addition to Makali, included Wade Williams, Dale Scott, and Valya Makarova. "Why don't we all spread out and see what we can find."

He immediately began probing the surface of the habitat with his fingers, which were scraped and filthy. He would have happily delayed a trip back to Earth for a ten-minute dip in Lake Ganges.

His last fatherly function had been to persuade Rachel to take her bath this morning. Harley Drake had set up a rotation for bathing—women one day, men the next. Logical, doable, for the moment. But Rachel's participation? Not easy. "Daddy, it's so gross!"

"It's what we have."

"But we're drinking from it! We're drinking from the same water all these . . . people are using!"

"Upstream."

"What *stream*, Daddy? This is a . . . scummy pond." He couldn't argue on facts; his only appeal was, "You're setting a bad example."

That was the magic phrase, giving him victory, but at a cost. Rachel had begun stripping off her clothes, forcing him to turn away. His only real choice at that moment was to depart, heading back to where the new mayor was trying to lead.

There he had run into Makali, Williams, Valya, and Dale Scott, several of the people he least wanted to see. Williams was busy sharing his extensive knowledge of life with Harley Drake, who wore an expression that proclaimed his disgust and indifference.

Makali Pillay was busy expressing herself in similar terms to Vikram Nayar, at least if body language was an indicator. She was half a head taller than the Bangalore flight leader . . . and far more animated.

"Hey, Zack!" Harley headed toward him, clearly anxious to get away from Williams. "When do you head off to see the Wizard?"

"Now. What about you?"

"First priority, checking on Gabe. He's not looking

too good." Zack could see the man leaning tiredly on the wall of the Temple, nodding as half a dozen people tried to tell him things at the same time.

"And the rest of us are?"

"There's dirty and hungry and tired, and there's sick. Morning, Wade!"

Zack realized that Wade Williams, the sci-fi writer who had somehow managed to be included in Harley's alien Home Team, had joined them.

On first meeting the man, Zack had looked at Williams's outfit, a safari jacket and rumpled khakis, topped with a floppy jungle hat, and judged it pretentious and ridiculous. Now he was less sure. Of course, living in a filthy space suit undergarment for a week had lowered his standards for male attire. He would gladly have swapped his long johns for anything from a Victorian frock to a spandex superhero costume. "I've been trying to persuade your friend here to let me accompany you on your exploration this morning."

That had alarmed Zack. What he'd had in mind was a quick loop past the tunnels where the Houston and Bangalore groups had emerged from the vesicle "dock." Makali was a good companion for the mission; anyone else would just be baggage.

"And I," Harley said, smirking in triumph, "think that would be an excellent idea."

"It's a long hike," Zack said, searching for a counterargument.

"Until going to Houston last week—or was it a hundred years ago?—I was regularly walking one point five miles every day. Or over three kilometers, for you Metric

Nazis." Even with his dirty khakis, ridiculous safari jacket, and smudged spectacles, Williams seemed determined. "I fancy I can keep up with you, Commander."

"Call me Zack—"

"Besides, saving your experience of the past week, I'm still more familiar with exotic propulsion systems and concepts for alien spacecraft than anyone here. Before I started telling stories for my beer money, I worked at Hughes."

Zack had no idea what that meant, but it was clear he was not going to win an argument. When in doubt, embrace the inevitable—

"Fine." To Harley, he said, "Anything else before I go?"

"Just for grins, and since Weldon and Jones seemed unclear on the motivation, what are you hoping to accomplish here?"

"First, I get to see where you guys came from," Zack said. "Your magic bubble spaceships."

"You're going to be disappointed; they sort of dissolved. We're talking gone with the wind."

"There must be *something* left." Zack couldn't believe that a vehicle capable of ferrying several dozen people across four hundred thousand kilometers could just vanish.

"Zack, it was nothing but a pile of powder."

"That just makes no sense to me. Why build something so . . . so capable, then throw it away!"

Sasha Blaine had been lurking nearby. "Nothing in this place seems to be permanent. I mean, just look at this stuff." She scooped up a handful of Keanu dirt and let it drizzle through her fingers. "I get the idea that if you just zap it with the right amount of energy, you can turn this into anything you want."

Well, one shitload of energy . . . "It isn't just, you know, add power."

"I know that," Sasha said, changing the subject while reminding Zack of every supremely bright, hyperfocused, slightly awkward grad student he'd ever known. "The goo still has to be programmed, doesn't it? And I have no idea how."

"From what you told us, Commander," Williams said, "the Architects seem to be pretty good at managing information."

Zack stared at him. Surely this pompous ass wasn't going to use Megan's resurrection as a debating point. He decided to end this now. "Well, even if all we find is white powder, we'll have something to start with."

Harley sensed the looming problem. "Hey, Zack, look at it this way: Human beings have been throwing televisions and computers away for years, rather than repair them or recycle them. Why should your friends the Architects be any greener?"

"Fine," Zack said. He had a team of three now. He glanced at Scott and Valentina, who were waiting patiently.

"Why do I need them?"

"You don't. I just don't want Scott hanging around here all morning, spreading his brand of cheer. And his girlfriend is attached at the hip." Then he said, for all to hear: "Since Valya Makarova is our exolinguist, it seems that she would be most valuable in your mission.

Suppose you gain access to a passage. Suppose you find a message or one of those Keanu Markers. She's right there; she can translate for everyone."

Valya immediately protested. "Really, Mr. Drake, how can you promise something like that—?"

"I'm kidding, don't worry. No one's expecting you to be a human Baretta Stone."

"I think you mean Rosetta Stone," Dale Scott said.

"Either one."

As they moved off, Zack kept his eyes on Harley. "And what about Dale?"

Harley pulled two Tik-Talks out of the bag on the side of his chair, handing one to Dale. "As you may recall, Zack, Dale here was quite the communicator during his astronaut days. He's your radio guy."

"Jesus, we're just taking a hike."

"It's a couple of clicks. You don't have to go real-time. In fact, given that the batteries can't be recharged, you should call only if you need help."

"I think I told some of you—or some of you heard me— that Megan and I made it to another habitat, a much larger one that looked like it contained a whole city of some kind."

"How far away was it?" Scott said, still sounding reasonable. "From this habitat, I mean."

"Had to be on the order of a couple of kilometers." He pointed directly down the length of the habitat. "But it was on the other end there, and as of yesterday, it was blocked just as completely as this one is."

"So, what, we just turn around and go back to the group?"

"We can't simply do nothing," Zack said. "We have no idea how long we can survive here. I want to know if we've got resources, and possibly a way out. I just have this feeling that there's still a way to get everyone back home."

"Why?" Valya said.

"Because someone *brought* us here. Someone built all this, adapted it for humans. Believe me, I saw it taking shape right in front of me. If there's any order to the universe, this has to be some kind of test—we just have to figure out the rules." His vehemence shocked him as much as it did his companions.

But Makali was saying, "Mr. Williams, what are you doing?"

"Feel that?" Williams said.

Zack realized he had grown aware of a pulsing hum. Troubling . . . Got it. "I remember now: I felt that same vibration in the Beehive."

"The what?" Dale was looking at Valentina. Even Makali seemed confused.

"The place where Keanu seems to generate new life," he said. He quickly explained about the cells and the second skins that covered the Revenants when they emerged.

Makali and Williams looked at each other. Scott and Valya, too. "What is it?" Zack said.

"To hell with the tunnel and the vesicles," Williams said.

"Yes," Makali said. "How far to this Beehive?"

RACHEL

"I suppose you were watching."

Rachel Stewart found Pav Radhakrishnan fifty meters from Lake Ganges. He was hidden in the rocks, Slate in his lap, with his back to the water and the female bathers, but still: He was a boy, he could see naked women by turning his head. He would peek, count on it.

"What?" He pulled the buds out of his ears, startled by Rachel's sudden vault into his field of view.

"All of us. The gir-ls," she said, stretching the word to two syllables. "Without our clothes."

He made a good show of acting surprised when he turned and saw that, yes, Lake Ganges and its current occupants were extremely visible. "Hey, you're right. I could have seen all of you . . . the underage and the really old. In all your hotness, too."

Rachel sat down next to him. She was hungry again. Breakfast had consisted of more crunchy vege-fruit, and not nearly enough. She had the feeling that wasn't going to change any time soon. "What's on your Slate?"

"The usual. Music, some school stuff—"

"Porn."

Pav looked at her. For a moment, Rachel thought he was going to go all red-faced and defensive . . . but no.

He blushed, yeah, but he also grinned. "Got my needs," he said.

She took advantage of his momentary relaxation to snatch the Slate away. "Hey!"

She ran.

Her hair was still wet. In spite of total immersion in water, she felt greasy and dirty. Her flip-flops were not the ideal footwear for a race.

But bolting away from Pav and heading for the farthest wall of the habitat . . . well, it was the most fun she'd had in days. Her father always told her she was healthier and happier when she worked out—or got any type of physical activity at all. Maybe he was right.

She left Pav far behind as she raced through a stand of reeds so tall they were over her head, but spaced in rows. Which was kind of odd, though not insanely odd by Keanu standards.

Off to her left there was a dead patch. She avoided that, partly because she didn't want to be seen in the open, partly because it looked . . . brown and white and spoiled somehow, like mold.

Then it was into a newish forest, short green bushes and trees.

The only sound she heard was her own breathing . . . and then, far off, barking.

That stupid dog again. All during her "bath," Cowboy had insisted on splashing into the lake and either sniffing her or the nearest woman. A couple of the bathers, especially those from Houston, seemed okay with the idea, but Rachel had been furious.

Eventually someone had lured the animal away. But now he was on the prowl again. . . .

As Rachel emerged from the new forest, she felt her side beginning to ache. So she stopped. The far wall, the one that was opposite the Temple, still lay at least a kilometer or more away. Between the new forest and the wall was a series of gentle hills made of rounded rocks.

Rachel plopped down behind the nearest one and opened Pav's Slate.

For a moment, she felt bad about that. Not for the invasion of privacy—anyone near Rachel's age assumed that every computer or Tik-Talk or Slate was hackable, that any images, music, or data stored there was certain to be seen by someone else, eventually.

What bothered her was wasting energy. She promised to only peek for a minute . . . and started clicking on the desktop.

Which was an immediate disappointment. She realized it was all schoolwork or music—an amazing amount of music, and many of the names unknown to Rachel—and, yes, the predictable private folder under a stupid cover name. "'Physics stuff,' Pav? Really?"

"Actually, my porn is in the file labeled 'Porn,'" Pav said.

It was her turn to be startled. "How long have you been there?"

"Five seconds." He was still panting, in fact. "See anything you like?"

"Well, no, not in your 'Hot Euro Bodies.' None of them are real, by the way."

"Okay, but not relevant."

The dog barked again. "Is he coming after us?" Pav asked.

"He's a Lab or a retriever," Rachel said. She recognized only half a dozen dog breeds, but Labs and retrievers were among them. "They're herders. Maybe he thinks we're cows."

Pav sat down next to her. "Let me," he said. Rachel allowed him to take the Slate back. "Were you there for the launch?"

"What launch? Oh, my dad's. Yeah." Two years ago, the last time Rachel had gone to Florida and the Cape for Zack Stewart's first attempt at a *Destiny* mission, her mother had been killed. This time, Zack had encouraged her, and had arranged for Amy Meyer and her family to go along. So, dutifully, she had stood at the press dome three miles from Pad 39A as Zack's *Saturn* had lifted off. The launch excitement lasted ten minutes; the rest of the day had meant driving, parking, walking, unparking, and driving back to the motel in horrible heat and humidity. None of this had done anything to improve Rachel's attitude toward Florida and rocket launches.

"I couldn't go to my dad's."

"Why not?"

"It was in French Guiana. The European Space Agency owns it and they really aren't set up for many visitors. And the Coalition was worried that if something went wrong, they'd have to deal with a few thousand witnesses."

"Well, nothing went wrong—"

"*Then*, you mean."

"Yeah." Pav showed her the *Brahma* launch . . . the

massive *Ariane 6* rocket rising on a fountain of steam, then arcing over the Atlantic.

"Wait!" Rachel said. "What was that?"

"What?"

She took the Slate and clicked on the pad, freezing the footage and opening another window, where Pav had called up another view of the *Brahma* event from MSNBC. She froze that image . . . which showed her mother Megan's publicity portrait.

"Oh," Pav said, seeing the picture. "I guess they were doing some kind of recap. . . ."

Rachel resized the image so it filled the screen. There was Megan Doyle Stewart, probably from four years ago, when she finally broke down and got new images made. Brunette, brown-eyed, unable to appear serious even when it would be a good idea—

It was the same woman she had seen most recently on images downlinked to Houston from Keanu. The same woman whose horribly mutilated body she had just helped bury.

She couldn't see it. Her eyes were filled with tears.

"Hey," Pav said, "let's just . . . save on the batteries." He gently took the Slate back and closed the windows—

—just as Cowboy trotted past.

The dog veered away from his path, which seemed to be taking him toward the near wall, just long enough to pant and sniff them. Then he continued on his canine journey.

"Where do you suppose he's going?" Pav said.

"We should probably get him . . ."

"Are we responsible now?"

"I think we're responsible for everyone and everything now." She got up. "Besides, if we don't chase the dog, we'll have to go back to the Temple, and they'll put us to work at something crappy."

"You make an excellent point."

Cowboy was easy to follow . . . his tracks were visible on the smooth dirt surface. And whenever they lost sight of him in the rocks, they would hear him yap. "Do you suppose he's chasing something?" Pav said.

"I hope not," Rachel said.

Pav laughed. "Another excellent point."

"Eventually he's going to run out of room, though." They were close to the wall now. It rose above her, like one of those giant office towers in downtown Houston, only rocky and sandy rather than shiny glass. Stopping, she let her head tilt back and saw that the wall began curving toward the ceiling, which made her feel light and dizzy—

Not far away, Cowboy started barking furiously.

Pav slipped one of his tattooed forearms around her. To her surprise, she rather liked it.

"It's creepy to know that we're living in a giant tube."

"Hey, if you think about it, we were living on the surface of a big ball of rock. How was that better? Come on."

Cowboy's barking had grown irregular but was enough to let them know where he was . . . to their left, down-habitat, and right against the wall.

Here stood a collection of rocks and weirdly shaped structures that reminded Rachel of cave stalagmites. Their surface was studded with tiny crystals of some kind, like mica or fool's gold. And they all seemed fresh, somehow. Moist.

The dog had gone silent.

"Where did he go?" Rachel said. Then she called, "Cowboy!"

"Who knows? He came out of nowhere, right? Maybe he went back."

"No, he was chasing something. And if he went back, we would have seen him."

Pav was in the lead, and suddenly he stopped. "What's the matter now?" Rachel said.

"What if he's found something we don't want to find?"

"Like what? An alien?"

"High on my list."

"I hope so. I have a lot of questions for the first alien I meet." And she slipped past him.

Around the last cluster of rocks, almost hidden in shadows, they found Cowboy on his hind legs, pawing at the wall.

And the wall was pulsing and flowing.

"Holy shit."

There was a slit of some kind, as if the wall were either creating an opening or closing one. Cowboy kept leaping into the slit. With every movement, the pulsing stopped for a few seconds. "Whatever's going on," Rachel said, "it looks as though he's interrupting it."

She stepped forward, but slowly and carefully. As she got closer to the dog, she began to smell something—an odor that blended swamp with diesel exhaust. It wasn't unpleasant, but she wouldn't want a bottle of it, either.

"Here, Cowboy . . . come here . . ."

The dog stopped moving long enough to glance back at Rachel and Pav. Then he turned away and dove right through the opening.

"Well, shit," Rachel said.

"What do we do now?"

Rachel wasn't sure. "Look," she said, "my father is all freaked out because there doesn't seem to be a way out of the habitat. . . ." She was already edging toward the opening.

"Are you out of your mind?"

"Probably, but . . . it's solidified." The opening had developed edges that gave off wisps of steam, like a lava flow that hits cold seawater.

"Which is good for us how?"

She was within a meter.

"What do you see inside?"

"Not much," she said. It appeared that the ground surface continued into the opening. "It's dark."

"Oh." Suddenly Pav was past her, raising the Slate and clicking on its flashlight.

The light didn't do much, but it showed a foggy tunnel that descended gently for a few meters, then seemed to turn to their left. "Cowboy!" Rachel called.

"I don't see or hear him." He turned to face her. "What do you want to do?"

"The dog is important, I think. And so is this tunnel thingie. Let's just . . ."

"Okay."

He took her hand, which Rachel found she liked, and both stepped and stepped again. Half a head taller, Pav had to stoop to get through. "How far do you want to go?" he asked.

"Two meters."

"Why two meters."

"I don't know. 'Cause I can jump two meters, okay?" She was finding Pav a tad pedantic. "Cowboy!" she yelled.

"Now, that was weird," Pav said. "There was no echo."

True; something had struck Rachel as wrong, but she had not realized there was no echo. "What do you suppose that means?"

"Either this passage is kind of small, or the walls are coated with some material that absorbs sound."

She kept going forward, half-step by half-step.

Pav was playing the Slate light up, down, and sideways. Up showed a low ceiling with the same texture—smooth dirt and rock—as the floor. The walls were different, however. They looked . . . moist, like the opening, now a full two meters behind them.

Just then the dog barked. "He's not far," Pav said, "not if we can hear him."

"What do you think?" Rachel said. "Good for another two meters?"

"Sure," he said, slipping the Slate back to his belt and taking her hand again.

They stepped forward confidently—

—and fell into darkness.

XAVIER

"You don't look so good, mister."

Xavier Toutant found Gabriel Jones flat on his back behind a rock, out of sight of the Temple or, indeed, anyone.

Xavier had just returned from one of several trips to the rubbish heap, a newly designated area near the down-habitat latrine that now served as the resting place for any garbage.

Not that there was much. Manufactured items brought from Earth were the closest thing the combined HBs had to money; no one would be throwing even a milk carton away. Hell, cut off the top of a milk carton and you've got a pot or a cup!

But there were rinds and leaves and stray bits of vegetation that needed to be collected and removed from the eating area up against the Temple's south wall, and without hearing any discussion, or seeing anyone doing the work, Xavier had started the cleanup. It wasn't that he was especially tidy by nature; his room back in La Porte never passed one of Momma's infrequent inspections. But he was clean.

And he knew from experience that you didn't want trash around when you were dealing with food. Bad enough that there were no tables, no pots and pans, no fire, no utensils. This was seriously stone age, except that, from what Xavier knew, even stone-age people had fire.

Mr. Jones opened his eyes. "Hey, brother," he said. His voice was weak.

"This ain't the best place to be resting."

Xavier offered his hand and helped Jones up. "I didn't plan to rest," Jones said. He looked ashamed.

"Well, we're all so tired and strung out that I'm surprised we aren't trippin' over bodies."

Jones smiled now and seemed to be stronger. "You got that right. Xavier, right?"

"Right, Dr. Jones." He and Jones had been introduced at least twice before, but Xavier was used to the fact that it seemed to take a while before he got really noticed.

"Gabriel." The two of them resumed Xavier's journey back toward the Temple. "You've been doing a hell of a lot of work around here," Jones said. "Don't think no one's noticed."

Xavier thought that was nice, if funny, given that Jones barely remembered his name. "Things gotta be done."

"That's right." He nodded toward the Temple, which rose in front of them, fifty meters away. "Like figuring out how to work this thing."

"Is that what you're doing?" Xavier wondered what Jones and the other NASA guys, including the new mayor, were actually up to. It had seemed that they spent most of their time shaking their heads and complaining to each other.

Jones must have sensed his contempt. Now apparently fully recovered, he smiled, took Xavier by the shoulder, and said, "Come see."

Like most of the Houston-Bangalores, Xavier had been inside the Temple, but only as far as its massive ground floor. The scale of things—everything seemed to be twice as high as needed, including the ceiling—unnerved him. But it also had benefits; the high ceiling and open side let in enough light to let the ground floor serve as a shelter.

Not that the HBs needed it, yet. There had been no rain. There was light, but no harsh sunlight. No wind. The temperature had not changed in any way that Xavier could determine. It was all very . . . well, Momma would have called it the Garden of Eden.

Xavier knew better, of course.

He followed Jones to where most of the members of the new HB Council were clustered. Weldon was one. So was Vikram Nayar. The pretty tall girl, Sasha. "There you are," Weldon said to Jones. He glanced at Xavier, as if to say, *What the hell are you doing here?* But only for a moment.

"What are we up to?" Jones said.

"Based on what we see and think we understand from looking at the exterior, we've got three stories of structure," Sasha said. "And those stories are double height."

"So . . . close to thirty meters high?" Jones said.

"Right." Sasha was moving around the floor, pointing up, then to the corners. "That's in one dimension. This chamber here is twenty meters by fifteen. But the outer perimeter is twenty by twenty."

"So we've got a hidden chamber on this ground floor?" Jones looked at Xavier, as if to say, *Someone's got to state the obvious*.

"And two double-sized floors of possible chambers above us."

Nayar said, "But how did they access them? There are no stairs, no elevators."

"These Architects build ramps," Weldon said. "At least, they did in the vents outside."

"Zack said the Architect guy was big, on the order of twice human height," Sasha said. "I don't know, maybe they just . . . climbed up?" She smiled awkwardly, knowing it wasn't the best suggestion.

Harley said, "Maybe this is easier for me because I'm closer, but look at the floor."

To Xavier it appeared as if a third of the floor had been scraped. "Well," Jones said, "were they moving something? A piece of equipment, maybe?"

"They could have been peeling off a layer," Nayar said.

"Something moved across this floor," Harley said.

Xavier squatted down and touched the scraped area. He could feel tiny grooves. He looked at the near wall. "I think it was the wall," he said. He walked over to it . . . something about the combination of the position and the grooves on the floor convinced Xavier that that was what had happened. "They moved it," he said.

"Maybe," Jones said. "Why?"

"To give us room?" Harley said.

As the great minds debated this, Xavier followed the wall to where it joined the adjacent one. This wall was also featureless . . . except for one object up high, as much as four meters. It was a round plate probably a third of a meter across, slightly darker than the dun-colored wall.

"What do you suppose that is?" Xavier said.

Jones was with him now. Xavier was aware of the man's heavy breathing; shit, he was one sick dude. "Some kind of sensor, maybe?"

Xavier looked around. Between Jones, on the verge of another collapse, and Harley in his wheelchair, it was hardly an able-bodied group. But between Weldon, Nayar, and Sasha Blaine—

"I need you guys to boost me up there," Xavier said.

Fortunately, there was limited discussion. Jones did point out, "We're dealing with a lot less gravity, folks." He showed his spirit by steadying Xavier as he raised his foot to step into Sasha Blaine's clenched hands. Sasha and Jones boosted him onto Weldon's shoulders.

Xavier told Weldon to take him right up to the adjoining wall. Steadying himself with his hands, he carefully pulled himself up. Finally he was standing . . . still a good half-meter short of the plate.

"Do you see anything?" Jones asked.

"Get ready," Xavier told Weldon. "I'm gonna—" *Jump* was the word he didn't say. He popped up and slapped the plate with his hand.

Weldon went tottering backward, and Xavier scraped against the wall as he hit the floor. But Jones had been right about the low gravity. He had almost felt as though he were flying . . . and the fall took twice as long, giving him sufficient time to tuck and roll.

Nevertheless, the floor was hard. As the others complained about the silliness of his actions, Xavier lay on his back, looking up at the plate—

Which had changed color, from a dull purple to a brighter shade. "Anyone feel that?" Sasha Blaine said, alarmed.

Xavier had; a pulse had just rippled across the floor.

"Everybody out!" Jones was saying, because the ripple was clearly a signal that something was about to happen to the Temple.

First the wall began to move back to its prior position . . .

And the ceiling began to drop. "Move, move!" Weldon shouted. "It's going to squash us!"

Xavier stood his ground for several moments, fascinated by the relative smoothness of the operation. There was no horrific grinding, no screech of stone or metal or whatever it was being wrenched from place to place. Just a slow, relentless glide. He could see a fluid of some kind forming at the top, bottom, and side edges of every moving slab, as if the elements were self-lubricating.

The fluid had a funny but familiar smell, too, almost like the pawpaws—

But then Sasha Blaine tugged his shirt and pulled him away.

He joined the others just outside the big opening. A larger crowd had formed, too, mostly Bangalores. Like those who had fled the Temple, all of them stared in openmouthed amazement as they watched the interior of the Temple rearrange itself. "Should we move farther back?" Nayar said.

"Excellent idea," Weldon said, pointing to either side of them.

The exterior walls were moving now, too, shrinking the opening to a third its original width and two thirds its original height.

As a final touch, once the new exterior seemed to be settled, a doorlike covering swung into place, too. Unlike the other surfaces of the Temple—exteriors layered and textured, interiors flat and smooth—the door bore markings and irregular bumps. "Bas relief," Sasha said to Harley.

Who said, loud enough for Xavier and the others to hear, "But carved by a crazy person."

"Carved by an alien," Jones said.

"What's the difference?"

"How long do we wait before we go in?" Sasha Blaine had somehow managed to pick up the baby and was sitting next to Harley, rocking. It had been fifteen minutes, by Xavier's best guess, since the shiftings and movements inside the Temple had stopped.

"Jones, Nayar, and Weldon are walking the perimeter," Harley told her. "Let's wait until they get back. Besides," he said, indicating the new door, "we don't have a key."

Hearing this, Xavier rose from the ground and marched directly toward the door. Harley called, "Hey, friend, what's the rush?" But Xavier was simply tired of waiting.

He was also quite curious.

He stopped in front of the door, which was still wider and taller than any door ought to be. The various protuberances made it look odd, too.

And there was no obvious handle.

Well, what the hell. He simply pushed on the right side, hoping the Temple had thought to create alien door hinges on the left.

Nothing. He only established that the door was solidly in place.

So he pushed on the left side, reasoning that alien beings might not share his particular preferences regarding right and left. Even some humans didn't.

Nothing again.

"Xavier, what the hell are you doing over there?" Gabriel Jones and Shane Weldon had returned from their scout around the Temple.

Xavier was tired of the timidity.

"Trying to get the door open!"

More out of frustration than logic, he simply leaned forward and pressed in the middle.

The door divided itself in two from top to bottom, swinging open to reveal a ground floor that was smaller, but now internally lit.

"Xavier," Jones said, still a good distance behind him, "before you enter . . . be sure there isn't something nasty waiting for you."

"Yes, Momma," he said, but under his breath. Did the

man think he was an idiot? Xavier stood in the opening and looked at the interior . . . which was now shorter, smaller, more normal looking.

There were lighted tubes all around the room, where the walls met the ceiling. They looked a little funny: too bright. When Xavier took a step inside, he noticed that the dust and who-knew-what-kind-of-fragments on his shirt gave off a glow, which reminded him of the black lights used in bars. His teeth were probably blinding.

And along the right side, rising to an obvious opening in the ceiling, was a long, gently sloped ramp.

"It's okay," he said.

As Sasha carried the baby in, right behind Harley in his wheelchair, she said, "So the aliens use French doors. Didn't see that coming."

"Yeah," Harley said, "maybe *Architects* is the wrong name for them. Maybe we should call them the Interior Designers."

Once the whole council, and a dozen HB bystanders, had reentered the Temple, human bravery had reestablished itself. Weldon and Nayar were the first to charge the ramp, disappearing through the opening for several moments.

Weldon returned with the breathless news, "There's a second floor up here."

Then Nayar returned with more interesting word. "There are some structures or facilities or machines on the second floor, and many more on the one above it."

Sasha said, "It's as if the Temple was in caretaker status."

And Harley said, "You mean, waiting for us?"

"This *habitat* was. It's got the right air, gravity close enough, temperatures—"

"Look at the light, both interior and exterior. And while the proportions of the building are still a little off, it's pretty close to human standard, don't you think?"

Other HBs slid past them, going up the ramp and likely higher.

Sasha and Harley noticed that Xavier wasn't moving. "Don't you want to see what's up there?" Sasha asked.

"Time enough when the crowd dies down," he said.

Xavier emerged from the Temple to find that the crowd had grown even larger. It was as if every one of the HBs wanted to climb to the top of the Temple now.

To Xavier, it just meant that it took him longer to edge his way through the throng, bumping up against a number of women with hair still damp from a dunking in Lake Ganges.

What the hell, he still had one more trash trip to make . . . just in time to get ready for the afternoon feed, whatever it was.

He gathered a final armful of greens and set off toward Lake Ganges and the dump, following his newly established path through the nearest trees.

He had gone only a few dozen meters when he heard laughter, and someone singing a song. Emerging into a clearing, he found Camilla dancing around, eyes closed, blissfully unaware of his presence.

She was the singer, something in Portuguese, he assumed. It sounded like a nursery rhyme, something about a "*rato*." Rat?

"Hey, hi," he said, not having much experience chatting with nine-year-olds even in normal circumstances. And this one, he knew, had been brought back to life by the alien Architects.

She ignored him. It was as if she couldn't even hear him.

Fine. He just kept going. Mindful of Camilla's strange nature, Xavier did glance over his shoulder a couple of times. The first time showed Camilla still in mid-dance.

The second time she was gone.

Xavier dropped the final load of trash and was on his way back when he heard a scream. For a moment, he thought it might be Camilla, but it came from the direction of Lake Ganges.

It was only a few dozen meters. He sprinted through the rocks and field and emerged at the pond to find one of the Bangalores, a lady who was completely naked, pulling another woman, this one clothed but limp, out of the water.

He helped her get the limp woman completely out of the pond. She was young, another Bangalore, and not moving. Water flowed out of her nostrils.

The naked woman kept telling him something. He had no idea what she was saying, though he could make a good guess.

Xavier had no medical training except for what he'd seen on television. That was enough to give him the basic moves of CPR—pinching the nostrils, opening and clearing her mouth, breathing in.

He didn't have time to think, which was good, because she tasted like cold and mud and something worse. He repeated the breathing several times, then did chest compressions.

At that moment the naked woman edged him aside and took over. It was quickly apparent that she was better at this than he was.

But neither seemed to be successful. After what seemed like half an hour—likely ten minutes—of pounding, breathing, compressing, both of them sat back, exhausted.

The limp woman was dead.

The naked woman had tears in her eyes. She spread her hands in a universal gesture of futility.

Only then did she stand up and start searching for her clothing.

Xavier realized that he needed help—if only to be able to communicate with the naked woman. He stood. "Wait here!" he said, adding a gesture he hoped would help her understand.

Then he ran for the Temple.

"Look at this," Gabriel Jones said. He and Shane Weldon knelt over the body. Vikram Nayar was talking to the formerly naked woman.

Xavier could only stand there wishing he were somewhere else. He was still panting from the run to and from the Temple. "Xavier, come here," Jones said.

Now he really got nervous. Had he somehow hurt the limp woman? He was even more unhappy when, with Weldon moving to keep anyone else from seeing, Jones turned the dead woman's head and pushed back her lank hair. "Look at this," he said, so quietly that Xavier barely heard him.

There was a bloody, bruised lump on the side of the woman's head, just above and behind her left ear. "Did you see that?"

"No," Xavier said, feeling sick. "She was already in the water when I got here." He nodded toward the formerly naked woman. "She had already pulled her out. We tried CPR. . . ."

Jones and Weldon glanced at each other. Some kind of silent message passed between them. "It would have been easy to miss," Jones said—

"Oh my God!" Sasha Blaine said. Xavier had not seen her arrival. Now she was right behind him, baby in her arms. "Oh my God, oh my God!" She was flat-out hysterical, something that surprised Xavier.

Weldon, too. He grabbed Sasha and turned her away from the body. "Settle down, Sasha. You must have seen a dead body before."

"Goddammit, Shane, that's not the problem. It's just—" Xavier realized that Sasha wasn't freaked out by death . . . she was angry. "It's the *mother*, Shane." She indicated the baby in her arms. "The baby's mother!"

Gabriel Jones literally sat back on the dirt. "Holy fucking shit."

Weldon wasn't convinced. "Are you sure?"

"I actually spent time with her," Sasha said. "Her name was Chitran. She was twenty-three. Her husband worked at BCC, okay?"

"Settle down," Jones said. He was on his feet now, but still in quiet mode. "Did she have any obvious enemies? Was she fighting with anyone that you saw?"

"No. Why?"

Jones showed Sasha the bruise. "I think she got clobbered, then pushed into the water to drown."

Sasha shook her head, careful to keep the sleeping baby calm. She whispered, "If you'd told me she walked into the water and drowned herself, I'd believe that, sure. She was in shock from the get-go. Barely able to speak."

Jones and Weldon looked at each other again. Then Jones took Xavier aside. "So now we've got a murderer in our group. Don't tell anyone about this," he said. "Not a soul, you understand?"

Part Four

Zack!

It's Tea.

Hi or hello . . . I never know how things like this are supposed to start. It won't surprise you to hear that NASA public affairs has been no help at all.

I've been back in Houston for four days and in the middle of some pretty . . . serious debriefs.

I hope things are going well for you, you and Megan. The two of you. I hope the people who were taken are with you, too, including Rachel.

I miss you, baby. In spite of everything—your smile, your voice. And want you to know we're trying to work something out here, some kind of rescue.

Come back. Come back safe and sound. All is forgiven, you know.

BROADCAST FROM HOUSTON MISSION CONTROL TO KEANU
BY TEA NOWINSKI, SEPTEMBER 3, 2019

Have I made it clear that I hate this place? HATE, HATE, HATE.
Want to go home.   KEANU-PEDIA BY PAV, ENTRY #3

THE PRISONER

The first rush of freedom was always sweet, reminding the Prisoner of its youth . . . the long swims juniors were permitted, before the time of dividing. Playful. Endless.

Cold.

The other residents shared stories—seven-times-removed memories—of such swims on the home world before they traveled to the warship. The distances frightened the Prisoner . . . in fact, they were not believable, no more so than any of the old ones' seven-times-removed nonsense.

The Prisoner was happy to relate a freedom swim with its own direct experience, before division, five cycles gone.

It was enough.

On each of the three prior free swims to the warship's exterior, the Prisoner had visited the shell. There had been little to find; the shell had been resting in the cold emptiness for seven times seven times seven cycles, and everything useful had already been harvested. (By other prisoners, the Prisoner wondered?)

Nevertheless, the shell had provided a destination, a place to rest and contemplate. To plot. To dream.

However, this fourth surface swim was different. The Prisoner had sensed vibrations in its chamber: several large events in a cluster, followed shortly by two smaller ones . . .

then one large event that actually produced heat, and seemed to illuminate the thinner walls of the cell.

Given those startling signs, the Prisoner felt that an examination of the shell was required.

Ascending through the vent and into the open, the Prisoner noted little obvious damage. There was more open soil than seen on prior swims, but that might have been due to the warship's rotation and exposure to external heat and light.

The Prisoner wondered whether that large event had been caused by extremely close passage to a star. It seemed unlikely, given the short duration of the event.

There was more debris, too, as if a giant wave had washed over the surface of the warship. From the distribution, the Prisoner judged that the source of the event wave was beyond the shell.

The garment was good for an entire cycle. The Prisoner would swim for less than half a cycle before returning. Surely that would produce results.

This surface swim required only a seventh of a cycle before the Prisoner found evidence of a catastrophic event: an area of the surface that was freshly molten. The debris patterns extended outward from a point here, not far from the edge of another vent—one the Prisoner had suspected, but never swum far enough to locate.

There was wreckage, too. Fragments of one shell, the Prisoner suspected, and the toppled remnant of a second.

Had there been a battle here? Two shells blasting away at each other with star weapons? Surely not; using one star weapon at this range would mean the destruction of both . . . which must have been what happened.

The Prisoner's people had used star weapons, though not for seven cycles. (At least, not the small group of people resident here within the warship. The Prisoner had no knowledge of events on the home world.)

The Prisoner knew that star weapons left behind residual effects, poison in the water, soil, and air that would result in death within seven cycles.

Nevertheless, seeing that the toppled shell was sufficiently intact, the Prisoner elected to risk further exposure.

The shell was fragile compared to the ancient one that had brought the Prisoner's ancestors from the home world. Perhaps the star weapon had damaged it.

Yet it retained a common rounded, pointed shape—surely required when blasting out of the sea—and a massive propulsion section.

The Prisoner's first challenge was entering the shell. There was an obvious portal that, with a brief period of scratching and tugging, opened to reveal the chamber within.

But it was so small! The Prisoner could fit through the opening, but feared damaging the garment it wore.

And yet even a quick glance inside the ruined shell revealed it to be filled with treasure! Again, it was the next risk the Prisoner would have to assume.

Carefully, the Prisoner extended one, two, three fins through the opening. The first attempt to push through almost met with disaster—stuck!

The Prisoner gently rocked back and forth, each movement resulting in inward progress . . . and possibly damage to the garment. (The Prisoner knew that the garment had the ability to repair itself but did not prefer that mode. There would be heat and discomfort.)

In!

The habitation chamber was lit only by the starlight that entered through the opening. The Prisoner had to move forward carefully, almost blindly.

The first impression—intolerably small! The creatures who made this shell and swam it across the Great Emptiness must have been tiny! From the Prisoner's youthful lessons about the home world, it knew that most small creatures lacked the capability for great intelligence.

Yet here was evidence. Even if other, larger creatures had constructed this shell—small beings had operated it.

And, so the evidence suggested, destroyed it.

And themselves.

Since there were no bodies, there must have been survivors—or one survivor, to remove the others. Conversely, perhaps the survivor(s) also became prisoners like the Prisoner.

That seemed unlikely, given the vaporized state of the opposing shell. No, the crew of this shell must have won the battle. Then departed.

What would they leave behind that would have value? Metal. The Prisoner longed to rip away several pieces of hanging equipment. It had no tools to work metal, but brute strength often gave results—

The Prisoner discovered that the walls of the shell were lined with many smaller chambers that opened easily, after sufficient pressure and violence.

The contents were baffling. Fabrics. Shiny objects whose functions were mysterious. Containers with colored substances suspended in fluid or paste.

The Prisoner's elation at discovering the shell, its satisfaction at gaining entry, began to fade. Perhaps the only item worth salvaging was metal.

A tentative tug at one hanging structure proved the flimsiness of the shell's construction. It came away almost instantly—

Revealing another being!

The creature lashed out, driving the Prisoner back against the material it had torn away—

Screaming in pain and fear.

DALE

Dale Scott was reluctant to enter the Beehive. For one thing, the simple idea was not especially inviting. From Zack's description on the trek from the former-vesicle tunnel, it sounded like an unholy mixture of animal womb and factory. Why would he want to stick his precious neck into that?

For another—

"There are a shitload of animal tracks here, have you noticed?" Dale said. "And they look *fresh*."

He was with Valya, several steps behind Zack and Makali. Wade Williams was behind and off to one side. Dale didn't know whether the man was just wandering or doddering. He had kept up, though, so it didn't matter.

"They do indeed," Makali Pillay said. "And they're not just impressions in soil. They're moist, as if they were made by creatures that just crawled out of the primordial ooze."

"Revenants, fresh from the incubator," Zack said. "They've been resurrected, just like their human counterparts."

"Mmm-hmm. And big ones, too. Like that cow you saw."

"Wherever it went. Not just walking creatures, either," Zack said. "I was pretty sure I saw some birds."

What was beginning to matter to Dale was the nature of this particular mission. He had automatic, permanent issues with Zack Stewart. Now he was growing quite unhappy with the Indo-Aussie woman, Makali, who had apparently decided she was Miss World NEO Explorer. Her incessant, chirpy observations about the rocks and soil and sky and temperature were no doubt accurate and helpful . . . if you gave a shit.

Which Dale most definitely did not. Not that he had a great alternative plan; getting away from the Temple, where the two available activities were (a) collecting food and (b) cleaning up—well, this little walkabout was a fine way to kill a morning.

But he was getting hungry and saw little prospect of a meal any time soon. He felt sure that the Beehive wasn't going to turn out to be the Keanu version of McDonald's.

A thought struck him. "Hey," he said, "do you suppose we could eat that cow?"

"It would be smarter to use it for milk," Wade Williams said. "We do have a baby, don't we?"

"Fine," Dale said. "Do you suppose we could eat *a* cow or the second one we find? Assuming we find *any* cow, of course." He turned to Makali. "Apologies if that offends your religious sensibilities."

"I'm not Hindu," she said. "But thanks for asking."

"Why couldn't we?" Valya said.

"Are you worried that a Revenant animal might be poisonous?"

Dale said, "I'm more worried that it's just useless. Not nutritious."

"You mean, literal empty calories," Williams said.

"No," Zack said. "I believe that the whole Keanu system proves that matter and energy are never lost. They are just arranged in different states. If we cook and eat cow meat we find here, I'm willing to bet it's just like doing it on Earth."

"Well," Williams said, "it seems to have worked with the plants we've consumed."

"So far," Dale said. "Our bellies are full . . . but are we getting the vitamins and minerals we need?"

The others glanced at each other. Zack shrugged. "There's not much we can do about it. And there's the Beehive." He and Makali trotted ahead, leaving Dale with Valya and Williams.

The sci-fi writer turned to Dale. "You are just a ray of sunshine, aren't you?"

The entrance to the Beehive was a classic cave mouth. The opening was roughly three meters high and half a dozen wide, though irregular. The ground was churned up, muddy. "It looks like a herd went through here," Williams said.

"Or came out of there," Dale said. "And did some fighting on the way." The edges were streaked with some kind of yellowish goo, and in one case a reddish substance that Dale took to be blood.

Makali picked at the wall. "You're right," she said to Dale, holding out her finger. "Animal fur."

"Great."

"Well, folks," Zack said, "our choices are stand here . . . or go inside."

He voted with his feet and disappeared into the mouth, followed closely by Makali and Williams. Even Valya seemed eager to enter the chamber.

Dale had no choice but to follow.

It opened up once you got past the entrance—indeed, the Beehive was as big as a small warehouse inside—though the ground still squished, and there was a horrific smell of blood, shit, and urine.

Nevertheless, Dale was impressed by the rows of chambers rising around him . . . all shapes and sizes, from shoebox to piano crate. All but a few gave off enough yellow light to provide illumination. Most were still sealed, their sides encased in what appeared to be thick plastic. Some were newly opened, though, with moist, squishy fragments of the sealant spilling onto the dirt floor. "I don't remember it being this big," Zack said.

"All the walls seem to keep changing," Williams said. "Why should your Beehive be any different?"

"And *this* section here is all new," Zack said, pointing to the larger units.

"New in the past four days?" Makali said. Zack nodded. "Well, I guess we know this is an active site."

"The question," Wade Williams said, "is why? Is Keanu just creating some kind of Noah's Ark? Replicating two of every kind of animal?"

"They started with Pogo Downey," Zack said quietly. He moved off several steps. Downey had been a member of Zack's *Destiny* team and was an old colleague of Dale Scott's. He hadn't realized that Pogo had died and been turned into a Revenant.

"Does that mean we'll see that Bynum character again?" Williams asked.

Dale had to remind himself: the man Zhao had gunned down.

"Don't think such things," Valya hissed.

At one end of the Beehive, a passage led elsewhere.

"Where does this lead?" Makali said, clearly eager to explore further.

"That was how we entered the Beehive and the habitat from Vesuvius Vent," Zack said. "Allowing for the fact that it all might have changed, there's a decent-sized tunnel that runs probably twenty-five meters to a kind of airlock. We called it the Membrane."

"I have to see this," Makali said. Without waiting, she vanished down the other passage. Zack said, "Maybe some of us should wait here."

"Great," Dale said, "I vote for anyone but me." It wasn't a sense of adventure that drove him; it was the desire to walk on dry ground.

He caught up with Makali quickly. And Zack was right behind him.

The tunnel was just like the Beehive proper, only smaller. There were yellow chambers here, mostly small ones, though not all. And no inactive or recently opened ones.

Zack said, "These weren't here before."

After two mild turns, they reached the end of the passage. There were chambers here, too, at least a dozen of them, all human-sized, all open. What drew Dale's attention, though, was a shimmering curtain that seemed composed of plastic bubbles.

"This is the Membrane," Zack said.

"What's beyond it?" Makali said.

"Vacuum. A big passageway, the base of Vesuvius Vent. A ramp and the surface."

"And the wreckage of *Venture* and *Brahma*," Dale said. Zack didn't react.

Makali approached the Membrane, reaching out for it. "Is this all right?"

"I don't think you can hurt it by touching it. Or vice versa," Zack said.

"Too bad we don't have EVA suits."

"We've got *pieces* of one," Dale said. "But, seriously, what good would it do?"

"Well," Makali said, "just for science, I'd like to get another look at that Marker Zack and Pogo found on their way in. We got imagery, but we didn't get close to solving it. And I think it held a lot of important information."

Dale tuned out of the conversation. His eye had been drawn to a chamber a few meters back . . . the largest in this part of the tunnel.

As he watched with paralyzed fascination, the yellow side bulged and split, unleashing a torrent of fluid that spilled onto the ground—and revealing a large snake-shaped creature that seemed to be wrapped in oilskin. "Zack!" Dale shouted.

The creature immediately began thrashing around like a cat in a bag. Now Dale saw that it had appendages—four short ones. It was vocalizing, too, though the cries were muffled.

Zack arrived, with Makali a step behind. "Give it room!" he shouted.

Dale retreated back toward the Beehive proper. Williams and Valya had come to investigate. "Stay behind me," he ordered.

The creature scraped its hands or feet on the wall of the chamber, and savagely rubbed its head, too, peeling the covering from its mouth and eyes. Dale wondered what damage and pain the process caused—

But such concerns vanished when he recognized the creature. "Is that a fucking crocodile?"

The general size, shape, and snout suggested so. The animal flopped on the ground, writhing again, working to continue peeling away the covering.

It gave Zack a chance to slip past, joining Dale, Williams, and Valya. "Makali," he said. "Come on!"

Makali was slow to react. "Don't study the fucking thing," Dale said. "Get over here!"

Before she could reach them, however, the creature roared and snapped to attention.

It looked at Zack, dismissed him, then, long tail swishing, turned toward Makali. "Give it some room!" Zack shouted.

Easier said than done, Dale thought. Especially since the croc started slithering toward Makali.

The Aussie woman retreated, but Dale knew she didn't have a lot of room . . . and she had no way out. "Please do something!" Valya said, grabbing Dale's arm.

In fact, they had nothing, could do nothing, except

Valya and Williams reached them. All four crowded against the farthest reach of the passage as the croc suddenly thrashed its way out of the open pod, tail whipping so close to Dale's face that he felt the breeze.

The croc uttered a series of snorts and snaps and then, to Dale's amazement, turned away from them and skittered up the tunnel, heading away from the Membrane and toward the Beehive proper, and likely the habitat beyond.

Zack was already diving into the damaged chamber, calling, "Makali!"

But only for a few seconds. Covered with slime, he backed out of the chamber, gagging and gasping for breath. Valya and Dale used their shirts to wipe his face.

"Is she in there?" Williams said.

"Didn't see her. It opens up, but it's dark and filled with . . ." He didn't need to finish the statement: filled with fluid.

"What happened to her?" Valya edged toward the chamber and gingerly stuck her head in. Like Zack, she couldn't tolerate more than a few seconds.

"Makali!" Zack shouted. The effort was too much for him; he began coughing, spitting up fluid.

Williams turned to Dale. "Think your phone works here?"

"Worth a try," he said, still unconvinced that calling the Temple had any value beyond spreading bad news.

He had it in his hands when Williams said suddenly, "Oh dear merciful God!"

He pointed at the Membrane behind them. It was rippling like a sea in a storm. As one, the four of them backed away from it.

stay several meters behind the croc—w

making terrifying guttural noises—as it st   aga

Zack was looking at the various pods a   de

"Goddammit, about half of these look read   so

"We can't leave," Dale said, wishing with a

that they could.   to

"Why is Keanu doing this?" Valya said.   te

"Who knows?" Dale said. Valya's tendency   t

and moan was the major reason he had stoppe

her, a close second only to his desire to sle

younger women.

Zack was grim. "Dale, I want you to call Harley

Let him know, uh, he's got a lot of company he

his way."

Dale had just reached for the Tik-Talk when he

the others heard a horrific thrashing from down the p

sage. "Oh, God!" Valya said.

"Shit." Dale could see Zack steeling himself. Then h

plunged forward, on the trail of the croc and Makali

Dale followed. It was dangerous and stupid, but better

than hanging back and doing nothing.

When they reached the end of the line, the passage

just this side of the Membrane, they saw the rear half of

the croc, still in its flaking second skin, sticking out of a

large Revenant pod.

Fresh fluid covered the ground . . . and in the middle

lay a large wrapped-up creature that could have been a

cow or a big dog. It wasn't moving, though. "Where is

Makali?" Zack said.

"I'm guessing inside that chamber," Dale said. "She

probably ripped it open, pulled out what was inside—"

"Something's coming through . . ." Valya said.

The Membrane parted, and a human-sized creature wrapped head to toe in a yellowish covering emerged.

It seemed to have trouble walking and seemed fatter than a human, with thick masses around its waist.

But then it raised its right hand.

And Dale heard a muffled but all-too-human voice, complete with Aussie accent, saying, "It's me! Makali!"

Zack immediately tried to free Makali from the second skin, but she pushed him away. "Don't!"

"When I found Megan she had to get out of that—"

"It's different," Makali said. She turned and pointed to the Membrane. "I was out there, in vacuum! It's some kind of protective suit. I can breathe. I can see." Each statement was accompanied by broad gestures. "I'm pretty comfortable."

"How the hell did you get into it?" Williams said.

Makali pointed at the reincarnation pod the croc had torn open. "I crawled in there and kicked through to the next one. Fell into it, actually." Dale heard a terrible coughing sound, then realized it was Makali laughing. "I thought I was drowning!"

"What did you see on the other side?" Dale asked.

"Not much; I didn't get far: a big, symmetrical cavern." She nodded at Zack. "Rover tracks."

"How long do you propose to stay in that outfit?" Zack said.

"As long as it will support me," Makali said. "I'd like to go back through the Membrane."

"Not by yourself, you aren't. Sorry. We can try this some other time—"

"Can you feel that?" Wade Williams was holding his hand at the opening of the shattered pod. "Airflow."

"Going in or going out?" Dale said, not liking the first thought that came to his mind.

"Out."

Zack stepped up. So did Dale. Everyone felt the same thing . . . air being sucked from the tunnel, the Beehive, and possibly the habitat, into the open space of the tunnel beyond.

"We need to seal this," Zack said.

"Fuck that," Dale said. He had no interest in any of this, or in remaining here in a very dangerous place. But Valya shrieked again, and Dale knew that this was not her standard startled shriek.

This was terror.

Two freshly revenanted cows were thundering toward them down the narrow passage, driven toward them by, from the sounds of it, the croc.

The creatures were all stuck at the moment, thrashing, fighting, eating and being eaten.

And in the process destroying the passage. Dale could feel his ears pop, a very bad sign in a chamber separated from vacuum only by what appeared to be a meter of vegetative material mixed with rock.

"What do we do?" Valya said. The shriek had gone out of her; she was plaintive, almost helpless.

"Everyone pick a pod," Zack said. He turned to the nearest one and began clawing at it.

"What are you suggesting?" Williams said.

"Do what I did!" Makali shouted. She was already helping Valya, though her efforts were hampered by the thick skinsuit "gloves" she wore.

And it was getting hard to hear. Dale's ears ached.

He needed no further encouragement. Shoving the Tik-Talk into his waistband, he commenced his own clawing at the nearest pod large enough to hold a human-sized item.

"We're going to die in these things!" Williams said, unnecessarily.

"Possibly," Zack snapped. "But you're going to die for sure out here."

The last sounds Dale heard, other than the horrific squeals and crunches of two animals in mortal combat, was a series of rips and gushes as four reincarnation pods spilled open, followed by the thud of whatever lay inside hitting the ground.

"Good luck, everybody!" he shouted, and dived into the dark, moist suffocating space.

ZHAO

After four days of life in the Keanu habitat, Zhao realized that he had finally found the one environment he hated more than India.

It was a shame that he had had to travel four hundred thousand kilometers to experience it. The light was wrong; the companions were not of his choosing; the food was limited to non-existent. There was nothing to read, nothing to watch, nothing to study. He could perform calisthenics if he wished, but he enjoyed more structured physical activities like golf and tennis. There were few potential sexual partners and zero potential sexual venues and opportunities.

He had no tasks, no useful work.

And he was the only criminal around.

He had not been mistreated; far from it. He had been treated exactly like everyone else . . . which, of course, was a form of mistreatment.

He had taken his turn with the gathering of food, though always in isolation. Even if he hadn't carried a virtual mark of Cain, as the only Asian in the population, he stood out. The Houston group shunned him; the Bangalores simply pretended he didn't exist.

The only benefit was that this position allowed him the opportunity to observe.

Observation one: The activation of the Temple under Nayar, Jones, Weldon, and Drake was proceeding in almost comic fashion.

Zhao had managed to join the throng that surged into the Temple once its walls and floors had rearranged themselves to more human proportions. Unlike most of the others, he had stuck around. His initial impression—marvelous! If he hadn't already been impressed with the Architects' mastery of molecular manufacturing, he would have thought their mechanical engineering to be the most fascinating thing he had ever seen . . . allowing for some obvious anomalies that hinted at a system on the verge of a breakdown. (But he should withhold judgment on that issue; what, really, did he know of these Architects and their motives?)

No, for the better part of an hour, he simply lurked in the corner of the main floor of the Temple, amused by the sudden, inexplicable changes in lighting and bursts of loud noise. It all reminded him of a long drunken evening with a potential source in a Hong Kong nightclub.

There were even blasts of suddenly cold, then hot air. At one point Zhao could have sworn that he smelled bacon frying.

Each environmental shift was accompanied by not-so-distant torrents of profanity in American English and Hindi from the floor above.

Zhao was trying to concoct a reason for going upstairs when Harley Drake wheeled in from the outside. (He had been one of the original "explorers" of the upper floors but had been called away an hour ago on some strangely urgent matter. Gabriel Jones had gone with him.)

Now he was here, alone; his companion, the large American scientist Sasha Blaine, was not with him. Drake pushed himself to the ramp . . . attempted to climb the slope by sheer muscle, and failed. He tried again with the chair's motor, and that, too, was inadequate.

Then he looked at Zhao. "Could you push me up there?"

"No problem." No problem at all!

The upstairs was a disappointment—not for lack of wonders. It was filled with strange shapes and structures, including an object that had to be a table (rectangular, perhaps a meter wide by two long, and three centimeters thick), made of the same substance that made up everything "artificial" in the habitat, from Temple walls to . . . well, what looked like appliances or electronic gear on this floor.

There were even three stools . . . crude and basic, more like dumbbells laid on their sides. But the right height.

"Amazing, isn't it?" Harley said.

"Someone is looking out for us, it seems."

Nayar and Weldon, accompanied by a woman from the Houston group, were busy touching various surfaces on a control panel. Nayar was using a pen and the margins of a magazine to record positions and results: which lights went on or off or changed color, which temperature changes were triggered. "Goddammit," Weldon said, "I wish we had a few pieces of clean paper so we could write this stuff down."

"Is there any logic to it?" Drake asked. "I did some cockpit design for *Destiny*; we kept falling back on grouping systems."

"Sadly, no," said Nayar. "Of course, we've just begun our survey. For every panel or button we've found to be active in some way, there are two that are inert."

"So far, you mean," Drake said.

"Noted," Weldon said. "Besides, we've got three upper floors to go through." He indicated the "counters" and "consoles." "They're all packed with stuff like this."

"Do you suppose any of it links to guidance, navigation, or propulsion systems?" Zhao said. He hadn't exactly intended to speak up, finding fly-on-the-wall mode to be useful. But he had not given up on the idea of returning to Earth. He completely approved of Zack Stewart's mission to examine the vesicles and learn whether they were useful, and he was all in favor of finding some way to control Keanu itself.

Besides . . . he had worked with Nayar and the ISRO team. It would not surprise them to hear from him.

Weldon was another matter, however. He looked at Zhao with irritation. Nevertheless, all he said was, "We haven't forgotten—"

A pair of Indian engineers, one slim and Zhao's age, the other fat and older, came down from the floor above. As if presenting a gift to a feudal lord, one of the men carried an object that looked like a super-sized candy bar . . . only blue.

He gently set it on the table. "We believe this is nutritious," he said. Jaidev, Zhao remembered; that was his name. He was deadly serious, but not a bad engineer.

Drake, whose nose was close to the table already, leaned over and sniffed at it. "Doesn't smell bad."

The second engineer—Daksha—was openly enthusiastic. "In texture and aroma it reminded me of military food. Meals Ready to Eat."

"Where did you get it?" Nayar said.

Jaidev turned to his compatriot. "Directly above. We were testing buttons and revealed a cabinet with a faucet."

"Did it work?"

Jaidev frowned. "While we were trying, one of the machines activated, and this popped out."

Weldon was clearly skeptical. "Blue food?"

"Whatever," Drake said. "There it is. What do we do with it?"

"Someone probably has to taste it," Zhao said. And before anyone could protest, he picked up the bar and bit into it.

The engineer had been right; the texture was much like that of an energy bar. The taste was undefined; nutty. As he chewed, Zhao said, "This *is* one of the things prisoners are for, isn't it?"

"Nobody likes an asshole," Drake said. "Even a brave one."

"Think of all the time I've saved you, searching for a volunteer."

Nayar was all business. He *would* have suggested Zhao as the test subject. "Well?"

Zhao was considering that exact question. His stomach was quite empty; what little food he'd had for the past four days had been unfamiliar, close to inedible. So initial conditions were challenging.

Yet, for the first minute or two . . . the blue bar rested happily inside him.

Then—

"Excuse me—"

He ran as fast as he could down the ramp and out the front of the Temple, where he vomited in front of Gabriel Jones and Sasha Blaine.

Weldon had followed him, less out of concern, Zhao felt, than out of curiosity.

Fortunately, it was only a single episode. Unlike the many times he had suffered food poisoning—another affliction he associated with warm climates—Zhao felt fine again, and quickly.

Weldon was busy explaining the experiment to Jones and to Sasha Blaine, who was cradling the sleeping baby in her arms.

Which led Zhao to his second great observation of the day: Something bad had happened in the general direction of Lake Ganges. A drowning? Zhao couldn't be sure, but it was clear from the tones and body language that someone had died.

Two deaths now. If this trend continued, in three months they would all be dead. Of course, that was pessimistic; things rarely progressed on such straight lines.

Still, it wasn't promising—

Jones was louder now. "Have we heard from Zack?"

Weldon said, "Harley got a squawk from Dale about half an hour ago, something about watching out for more animals from the Beehive."

"It just gets better and better," Jones said.

Harley Drake and Vikram Nayar had emerged from the Temple, Nayar pushing. The blue food bar lay in Drake's lap.

"You've recovered," Drake said.

"What are you going to do with that?" Zhao said.

"Throw it in the garbage, I guess."

"Let me try it again."

"Are you just a glutton for punishment?"

The same thought occurred to Zhao. "I've eaten nothing but crap for four days. I'd have probably thrown up anything new."

Drake was reluctant, but Weldon saw the wisdom of another taste test. "If he's right, we gain a lot," he said. He didn't add, nor did he need to, that if Zhao was wrong, he wouldn't miss him. He smiled. "Bon appétit." And handed him the bar.

Zhao took another bite roughly the same size as before. He used every trick of feedback and disassociation he knew—and his training in Guoanbu had equipped him with many such techniques—to suppress the urge to vomit.

He found, however, that he didn't need them. As he had suspected on his first test, his discomfort was temporary. Jaidev and his friend had been correct; this object was edible.

"So far, so good," he announced. "Whether it provides real nutrition or energy—"

"Yeah, yeah," Weldon said. "We won't know for a while yet." He turned back to the other members of the council. "Meanwhile, we've got work to do." And he led Jones and Nayar back toward the Temple.

Harley Drake remained behind, however. He handed Zhao the rest of the bar. "If you can stand it, you might as well finish it. Even if you ate a Power Bar, you wouldn't get much benefit from a single bite."

Zhao accepted it. Then Sasha said, "Harley, have you seen Rachel lately? Or Pav?"

"Not for a couple of hours." He looked alarmed and guilty. "Have you?"

"Last I saw, she was at the lake. But she isn't there now, and no one seems to know where she went."

"Shit," Drake said.

To Zhao, he seemed genuinely distressed. "I'll go take a look," he said. The offer was partly an attempt to get away from the Temple, but real nevertheless; he was stuck with these people. Their plights and problems were his.

"Are you just in a mood to volunteer?"

"Everyone has a job but me." Zhao tapped his stomach. "While we're waiting to see if I die or not, let me find Rachel." He smiled. "Tracking people is one of my skills."

Drake didn't hesitate. "Go. And when you find her, feel free to subject her to intense criticism."

Sasha slapped him on the shoulder, but Zhao sensed that Drake wasn't kidding.

The last person he saw, glancing back at the Temple, was the little Brazilian girl, Camilla, watching him go.

PAV

The landing had been surprisingly gentle. For that matter, the fall had been surprisingly slow . . . a moment of sick panic—*I'm falling!*—followed by the drop into darkness, with enough time to wonder what lay below. And what had happened to the walls.

When he was nine years old, Pav had fallen off a slide and broken his right wrist. This felt the same, but took ten times longer.

At least nothing appeared to be broken.

He was on his side at what could easily be described as the bottom of a well. It was dark enough. The only light came from the slitlike opening, which appeared to be ten meters up.

"Rachel?"

"Right here," she said, very close by. "I thought you were going to land on me."

"Are you okay?"

"Yeah, I guess."

He felt a hand on his hip that slid onto his butt. "Careful," he said. "This isn't the time or place."

"God, be serious."

Well, he usually was. But for the past few days, he had felt the urge to at least pretend to be like a movie hero . . .

quipping to hide his terror. If he hadn't already found Rachel immature and irritating, her lack of understanding would have done the trick.

He rolled onto hands and knees. The ground here was harder and more rocklike than that of the habitat. As he got up, he bumped into Rachel, doing the same. "Thank God for low gravity," she said.

"How much room do we have here?" He stretched out his arms.

"A lot," Rachel said. He could hear her walking around.

"Don't go too far."

"Where's your Slate? Let's get some light and see if there's a way to climb out of here or call for help."

Pav realized that he had been holding the unit when he fell. "Shit." He got to his knees and began feeling around for it. So did Rachel.

"It can't be far. . . ." In fact, it was only a meter away. "Well, got part of it," he said. "The back broke off and the battery must have fallen out."

Then Rachel pressed both items into his hand. Pav went to work reassembling the Slate. "By the way," he said, "I'm pretty sure there's a way out of here."

"Really? Do we just sprout wings and fly?"

"Not up," he said. "Sideways."

"Don't get your hopes up—"

"Rachel," he said, "Where did the dog go?" And he clicked the last pieces of the Slate into place.

"Fine," she said, unwilling to admit error. "Give us some light."

There wasn't much, but there was enough to show

that they were in a good-sized tunnel. "He could have gone one of two different directions."

"What do you want to do? Split up and find him?"

"Are you insane? We are not splitting up!" she said. "Call my father."

He showed her the Slate display. "No link."

Rachel walked away from him. "Cowboy!" she shouted. "That missing echo is so weird," she said. "Let's find the way out of here."

"You don't want to sit tight and wait?"

"Who's going to be looking for us?"

"I don't know. But if we wait, we could hear somebody calling from up there."

"Really? I just shouted for the dog and I felt like I had a pillow over my head. I don't think sound carries in here."

"Well, we can't climb back up, and we've got two choices. Which one?" He aimed the light at the ground. "It's not like we can follow the dog, 'cause there ain't no tracks."

Rachel turned around and around until she faced Pav and the opening behind him. "Okay, this is the direction of the Temple. When we . . . buried my mom, we went . . . that way." She raised her right hand. "That was down-habitat, my dad said. And where he had seen a passage and another big habitat."

"Down-habitat it is," he said. "Uh, we should probably turn off the light, if we can. Save the batteries."

Rachel slumped. "Yeah, good idea."

He killed the light. "Our eyes will adjust."

"You hope."

VALYA

For Valya Makarova, diving into the reincarnation pod and surrendering to it was ten times worse than being sucked into the Bangalore Object.

She had had no time to think or comprehend what was happening. Aided by Zack Stewart, she had clutched her purse and plunged into the hideous yellow light of the pod.

She had easily pushed through its interior wall and fallen into a much larger chamber beyond that. Or so it seemed; it was entirely dark. She was suspended like an insect in a medium but could not touch sides, floor, or ceiling.

As she thrashed about, she bumped into something, or someone.

Within moments she felt a thick coating covering her ragged clothes and the purse against her middle. It reminded her of a mud bath at a spa, a luxury she had experienced exactly once in her life, but all-encompassing.

And invasive, too. The wrap invaded her armpits and her vagina and anus as well as eyes, nose, and mouth. For several agonizing seconds she was convinced she was drowning. But the fabric quickly liquefied, and if it got into her lungs it either dissolved or got absorbed.

Either way, she was still breathing and, though her vision was clouded, still able to see—

—and beginning to see light, and other shapes that were human.

She found that if she moved her arms and legs, she could swim, after a fashion, though it was also likely that the fluid around her was dissolving or changing.

She took her first big breath and found it welcome and easy, even though she was now securely enclosed in a full-body cocoon.

The fluid that had filled the chamber around her began to transform, turning first to Membrane-style bubbles, then to powder, which quickly began to wisp away, blown across her legs by either convection or the air leak.

She was sitting on the floor with three other encased humans. "Dale!" she screamed, as loud as she could. (Which turned out to be loud only in her ears. It was like trying to shout underwater.)

He must have heard *something*, however, since the figure nearest turned toward her, nodding vigorously and making flapping gestures with his skin-coated hands. He clambered to his feet . . . a bit unsteadily . . . then reached for her.

Meanwhile, a third figure—Zack?—was helping the fourth, likely Williams.

"Valya, can you hear me?" Dale said.

She could, to her surprise, though it wasn't exactly hearing with ears. The "sound" seemed to originate in the bones behind her ears, likely some kind of inductance. "Yes."

"How do you feel?"

"Like a sausage."

The wind was whipping the powder around. The four rips in the inner wall seemed to have grown. "I hope there's some mechanism that seals it off," Valya said.

Then, from an entirely unexpected direction (Dale was to her right, with Zack and Williams beyond him), a hand landed on Valya's shoulder.

Makali. In her suit, she had poked through the chamber's outer wall. "We've got to get away from here," she said.

It was like escaping from a collapsing circus tent. The outer wall of the annex turned out to be more like fabric than a harder, plasticlike substance. Makali's in-and-outs had created an opening that was tearing apart under the assault of the now-massive air leakage.

One by one, they exited into a dark, rocky chamber that reminded Valya of a modern-day mine shaft: wide, twice as tall as a human, clearly carved out of rock.

There was a bright patch a hundred or more meters farther down the shaft. The eyes of Valya's skinsuit adjusted for the transition from dark to bright and back without the telltale green tinge of night-vision goggles, which surprised Valya more than she'd expected. Well, the Architects were thousands of years more advanced technically—as if the reborn animals and skinsuits weren't sufficient examples. But those were, frankly, magical.

Having a great low-light vision system . . . that was something she could more readily appreciate.

The others were performing the same skinsuit familiarization. "I guess that's Keanu day," Makali said. "The sun is shining down to the base of Vesuvius Vent."

Zack stood silently, regarding the scene. Valya realized that this was the route he had taken a week in the past. Finally he spoke. "How are you all doing?"

There was a flurry of grumbled assents. "Everyone breathing without difficulty?"

"I lost my glasses," Williams said.

"How well can you see?" Valya really wanted to know, because she was finding that the skinsuit enhanced her abilities.

"Much better, actually. Whatever this suit is, it has a vision correction."

Zack said, "At the moment, I'm really curious about where oxygen and water come from, and where does the heat go?" Zack was pointing at the bulges around the hips of Makali's suit. "These seem to contain life support equipment."

"Like what grew inside the vesicles," Makali said.

Williams pointed to Valya. "Looks as though she's got an extra bulge."

"My bag," Valya said. She was happy she hadn't lost it but realized it was now useless.

"Him, too," Williams said, indicating a smaller bulge near Dale's hip.

Dale patted at it. "Feels like the T-square," he said.

"So whatever we were wearing just got enclosed?" Valya said.

Zack shrugged, to the extent he could. "Seems so."

"Where do we get food and water?" Makali said.

"Maybe they don't have that capability," Dale said.

"Maybe these were just for emergencies. You aren't supposed to be in them long enough to get hungry or thirsty."

"Hell," Wade Williams said, "even if they are emergency suits, good for X duration—we don't know what X is for Architects. Could be twenty years. Could be twenty minutes."

"All I know," Zack said, "is that they fit us. So I have to assume the support systems match."

Dale had more questions. "Which gets to a good point: How the hell did this happen? How did we wind up in human-sized space suits?"

Makali pointed back to the shattered chamber. "It's like it was part of that Membrane thing. You dived into the 'suiting room' and it wrapped you up." She wriggled a bit, which Valya interpreted as laughter. "I'm not suggesting that we used the preferred method of entry."

"I don't get how or why you could dump four different human beings in a vat and come out with four suits that fit them," Dale said. "And, by the way, assuming we eventually get back to a pressurized environment . . . how do we get out of these things?"

"I'm still trying to figure out the system that could detect, identify, and retrieve a dead human soul from space," Zack said. "These suits are a lot like the second skin that Revenants are reborn in." To Valya, Zack seemed to be talking to himself. "The whole suiting business . . . that seems to be about a ten on which the soul retrieval is a thousand."

He looked down the tunnel toward the light again.

But Dale grabbed him by the shoulder and turned him back toward the chamber. "Goddammit, Zack! Why don't we crawl back in there! A hole big enough to let that much air *out* will let us back *in*!"

Zack and Makali took steps toward the chamber, where flaps of material still fluttered weakly. "What do you think?" he said to Makali.

"It's not like this leak would empty the whole habitat," Makali said. "The annex was sealed off from the Beehive proper." She reached for one of the flaps. Before her skin-gloved fingers made contact, however, the entire chamber simply collapsed. "Get back!" Zack shouted.

It was a strange sight, almost in slow motion, the "tent" vanishing under a cascade of rocks and soil. There was no cloud of dust; in the vacuum and low gravity, particles simply fell to the surface.

There was a long moment. Finally Dale said, "I withdraw my suggestion."

Williams spoke for the first time in a while. "Well, now what do we do?"

"We go out," Zack said. "Uh, gravity might be less than you're used to . . . try to slide rather than step."

Before they could emerge into the harsh sunlight of Vesuvius Vent, they reached an intersection where four different tunnels branched off.

"Where do these go?" Williams said.

"We never had time to investigate," Zack said. "We were too focused on this."

He pointed to the Marker, a stone plate mounted at least two meters off the ground. Makali was already camped beneath it.

Valya had seen one brief image of the Marker, the first definitive sign that the *Destiny-Venture* and *Brahma* explorers were dealing with an advanced civilization. Keanu's maneuver from flyby to Earth orbit had been one clue, followed by the existence of the ramp in Vesuvius Vent . . . but both events had other explanations. Not this 3-D-like image of a helical galaxy that shifted to a DNA helix, and who knew what else, depending on the observer's viewpoint.

"God," Makali was saying, "I wish I could get higher and see what it looks like from above."

"From Architect height?" Zack said.

"Yeah." She was clearly getting frustrated. "I'd love to see what that guy would be seeing."

"You think it was different?" Dale said. "The basic image is the galaxy, our galaxy, we assumed."

"And there's not much point in showing another one," Williams said.

"It's not the galaxy image. There was also the DNA one, and a third that we decided was a schematic of Keanu itself."

That news energized Zack Stewart. "We never saw anything like that, and I was here when we found it!"

"Bangalore got a ghost image from Lucas's helmet cam hours after you passed by," Makali said. "I don't think he even saw that angle—"

"What do you remember? It might be important."

"Not much. A big sphere with a dozen squat tubes inside it, all connected by spidery lines." She gestured in frustration. "But I can't seem to find the right viewing angle."

"Nothing we can do, then," Dale said.

"There's something else," Makali said. "When we processed the galaxy image, we saw several illuminated or indicated points." She turned to Williams. "Remember that?"

"Hell, no, we never got that far with it."

"Oh. Well, there were at least six of these points, and they were all clustered. They were in our local stellar neighborhood, if you will." She pointed at the Marker. "Now there's only one bright spot."

"So it's changed in the past week," Zack said.

"Oh, yes."

"Was it damaged, do you think?" Zack said. "By the detonation?"

"Not damaged," Makali said. "Affected, maybe."

"What is this 'detonation'?" Valya said.

"He means that the *Destiny* crew carried a small nuclear device to guard against alien organisms or actual creatures being brought back to Earth," Makali said. "It was set off by Yvonne Hall."

"I had no idea!" Valya knew there had been an explosion aboard the *Venture* lander, an event so devastating it had crippled the nearby *Brahma* spacecraft, too. But that was all. "Dale, did you know?"

"No. But I'm not surprised." To Zack he said, "Let me guess: You didn't know the thing was on board."

"That would be correct," Zack said.

Valya felt sicker than she had during her worst moments inside the Object. It only confirmed the brutal things her Russian and later Indian friends and neighbors had said about the United States and its disregard for international norms.

No, she told herself. *Don't surrender to that emotion. Be a professional.* "What about these bright spots?" Valya said.

Makali said, "We concluded that they told us where Keanu came from. Waypoints, stops along its galactic voyage. They seemed to match up with exosolar systems. . . ."

"And what about now?" Zack said.

"Now I think it's telling us where Keanu's *going.*"

"Which is where? Back where it came from? Or the next stop on the journey?"

"Speaking of going," Dale said, "what's the plan?"

Zack indicated the different tunnels around them. "We should explore these shafts and see where they lead—"

"If anywhere," Williams said.

"Well," Makali said, "there are five of us and four branches."

"I'm sorry," Valya said, and she felt no shame in admitting it, "but I have no interest in exploring a tunnel by myself."

"Fine," Zack said. "You and Dale take that one." He pointed to the tunnel on the far right, and quickly assigned the others, too. "We don't have clocks," he said. "And we have no idea how long these suits are good for. Take fifteen minutes or your best guess, see what you can see, and report back."

Dale immediately headed for the right branch. "Wait!" Valya heard herself saying. Although physically she felt fine—better than she had in years—she hated not having anything to contribute, to being reduced to following Dale Scott around.

But she persisted, following him into the dark tunnel. Within ten minutes they had negotiated one major twist and found themselves staring at a brilliant spot of light. Dale loped forward into the clearing, where, arms outstretched, he bent backward to look up. "Looks like a shaft that goes to the surface," he said.

"Are there any other openings?"

He turned around twice. "None that I can see."

When they gathered again, the verdict was two shafts of some sort—"Possibly exhaust ports for propulsion," Williams suggested—one flat-out dead-end (Makali: "There was a blank wall"), and one collapsed tunnel.

"Okay, that clarifies things," Zack said. "The Marker suggests that Keanu is moving. Given the tools we've got, which would be none, the best way for us to know for sure is to get to the surface and look." He pointed to the opening.

Valya knew Dale well enough to realize that he was spoiling for a fight. He did not want to go beyond this point.

But suddenly Makali took off.

"Now what the fuck?" Dale said.

"I don't know about you," Zack said, "but I'm inclined to follow her."

HARLEY

"How's it going, Mr. Mayor?"

Her arms free of sleeping or writhing baby for the first time today, Sasha Blaine plopped down next to Harley Drake.

"Could be better."

Sasha brushed her red hair back from her face. In spite of all the stress, lack of sleep, and shortage of soap and water, she looked remarkably healthy and happy.

Another reminder that she was too young for poor old Harley Drake. "It's not as though I needed a lesson in the futility of politics. Two days as HB mayor . . . hell, everyone is coming to me for decisions they could easily make themselves."

"Maybe. But it's a good sign. They trust you. They're thinking of themselves as part of a community and not just freelancers."

"It's terrifying, Sasha. I don't have the answers! I'm finding out how the Temple works right along with Nayar and a dozen other guys. In fact, given that they're real engineers, unlike me, they walk in there knowing a hell of a lot more about moving walls and strange appliances and what any of it does."

"You got the whole water business sorted out."

"Nayar, not me. And it didn't take a lot of political genius to say, 'girls today, men tomorrow.' The food thing . . . everybody's off hunting and gathering. We just organized them into groups. So at least we've got food coming in. And this Xavier Toutant guy came up with garbage disposal on his own. Not my idea. I mean, that's all I've got on my side of the ledger. Shall we look at what's going wrong?" He began to tick them off with his fingers. "Zack Stewart has gone off to investigate the Objects, or vesicles—and, by the way, where the hell did that word come from?"

"One of the ISRO engineers."

"It's driving me crazy. Fucking engineers, always inventing names for things that already have perfectly good names. Where was I? Right, Zack goes for vesicles, somehow winds up at the Beehive—where, based on one message from Dale Scott, things aren't going too well. Thanks for that, Dale. Very useful . . . Rachel Stewart is missing."

"She's a teenage girl," Sasha said.

"I know, but I'm still responsible. I'm the reason she's here." He could feel his face flushing, but he simply couldn't stop himself. "I'm the reason Megan Stewart *died* and *everyone* is here!"

He took a breath. "What else? Gabriel Jones is seriously ill and I haven't had thirty fucking seconds of privacy to be able to nail him down on what the problem is. And the icing on the coffee cake . . . someone murdered the little mother, not only depriving the baby of its primary care, but forcing you to take the job—"

"You know I don't mind," she said. She was rocking back and forth, clearly upset.

"And last, but not remotely least . . . her death has created a goddamn mystery for us to worry about. So, really, in addition to being small-town mayor and de facto long-duration space mission commander, I'm supposed to be a criminal investigator, a judge, a logistics manager, a technical program director, and a social worker. It's a lot for a guy who's really just an airplane jockey—"

He stopped. He was worn out by his own vehemence. And he was finally hearing what he was saying.

"Finish it, Harley. You really live to fly airplanes and, what, nail cocktail waitresses?"

That was pretty close; Sasha knew him quite well for an acquaintance of only a week. "It's a lot for a guy who's in a wheelchair."

He knew it was lame, but he also knew he'd overdone the complaining. The wheelchair card was the closest thing to a trump he had in his conversational deck. "Let me start over. What's up?"

Sasha laughed out loud. "God, Harley, I came to tell you to hang in there, that you're doing great and everyone thinks so."

That wasn't the response he'd expected, and it made him angry again. "Sorry for being such a disappointment."

"Lighten up, Harley. Remember, we're as good as dead; everybody knows and doesn't need a reminder! Stick to the basics. 'How are you doing?' 'Fine!' 'Fine!' I mean, you could just ask me about the baby."

"Okay, how's the baby? What's his name?"

"Her."

"Her name."

"Chitran never said. She never said a word that I heard. I'm calling her Chandra. It means 'moon.'"

"Is it okay to say I think it's a nice name?"

"Not yet."

And she got to her feet. She was a tall woman and would have looked down on Harley in his best days. From the chair? She looked like an angry Amazon. "Oh, and by the way—I'm just fucking fine, too!"

She walked off, leaving Harley Drake more alone than ever.

RACHEL

"I think this is far enough."

Pav had simply stopped walking. They had been at it for twenty minutes or so, using the Slate intermittently to light their way.

Rachel said, "But we haven't found anything."

"Exactly. We haven't heard or seen the dog. Nothing's changing here. No turns, nothing to see. This tunnel could be fifty kilometers long."

"Unlikely."

"Fine, then." He seemed really irritated. "We're running down my battery."

"Too bad! Afraid you won't be able to access your porn collection?"

There was a pause. With the light off, Rachel couldn't see Pav's expression or posture. His voice, however, showed that he was hurt. "Why the hell would you say something like that?"

She felt mean. "Sorry. I'm just . . . frustrated. Where is the stupid dog? How do we get out of here?"

"Don't know and don't know. Which is why I want to go back to the opening. I keep thinking someone will come looking for us."

Rachel realized that she was ready to give up. "Well, now that you mention it . . . I'm kind of thirsty."

"Thirsty and starving." She sensed that he was waiting for her to make a move. "How far have we gone, do you think?"

Rachel looked back. "Well, I can still see a spot of light."

"Come on, let's go back."

"Okay."

She started off in the opposite direction. "It's also that I really hate tunnels and darkness," he said.

"God, me, too. I'd rather be anywhere else, frankly."

The fact that he would admit that when he clearly thought it a sign of weakness . . . maybe Pav wasn't so immature after all.

Halfway there, Pav came to a sudden halt again. "Okay," Rachel said, "will you stop doing that?"

"Ssshhh!" He put out an arm to steady her, as if lack of motion would improve the acoustics. "I heard something."

"No you didn't—" Then Rachel heard a distant bark from somewhere ahead of them. "Cowboy!" she shouted, and started running.

"Hey, careful!" Pav said.

The tunnel was a smooth rocky cylinder with one flat side, the floor. No piles of rock or uneven patches. Even so, it was hard to keep track of your feet when you couldn't see them, so she slowed down.

They heard another bark when they were within a hundred meters of the opening. "I wish he would find *us*," Pav said. "Isn't that what dogs are supposed to do?"

"Maybe he's found something more interesting."

As they reached their landing spot, they saw Cowboy . . . and the more interesting object: an Asian man in a white shirt still brushing dirt off his slacks.

"It's Zhao," Pav said, stopping short.

"I don't—"

"The guy who shot that other guy?"

Rachel was suddenly more afraid than she'd been when falling down the shaft. "What do we do?"

It was too late to run. Zhao had seen them. He waved and said, "Well, mission half-accomplished. I'm Zhao."

Rachel realized there was no point in running away. "I'm Rachel; this is Pav. What was your mission?"

"Find you two and bring you back." He looked up at the opening, then back at them. "Didn't you hear me calling?"

"No," Rachel said. At the same time, Pav said, "We were down the tunnel."

"Chasing the dog," Rachel finished.

"So where is he?"

"He was just here a moment ago," Rachel said. "Barking at you."

"Never saw him, never heard him."

"Well, the acoustics—" Pav said, stopping when Zhao dropped to his knees and began brushing the ground.

"Looking for something?"

He stood up with a water bottle. "This." He offered it.

Rachel drank, reminding herself to take only a couple of sips. There were three of them on a bottle, and who knew how long it would have to last. "Thank you."

Pav wiped his mouth, then said, "Uh, how did you get down here?"

Zhao shook his head. "I seem to have fallen."

"Us, too," Rachel said.

"Chasing the dog?" Zhao stepped back to look up the shaft. "I was actually quite careful. I'm not sure I wasn't pushed."

Rachel looked at Pav. Even in the low light, she could see his eyes widen, as if to say, *Weirdo!* "Well," he said, "I don't think the dog is the only animal on the loose up there. . . ."

"I would have smelled or heard a dog," Zhao said. "This was a person."

He stepped from side to side, trying to get a better look up where they'd come from. "Hey, up there!" Without much success, he tried to pull himself up on the rocky wall. "We're down here!"

"What are you doing?" Rachel said.

"He's still up there," Zhao said.

She and Pav both looked toward the top of the shaft. Zhao was right; somebody's head popped into view, then out again.

"What the hell?" Pav was getting angry. "Help us out!" he shouted. "Throw a rope or something!"

Nothing. "Can you hear us?" Pav shouted.

Still no response, but the figure appeared for another instant.

"Who is that?" Pav said.

"I think it's Camilla," Rachel said.

"The Portuguese girl?" Zhao said. "If she was the one

who pushed me, I'm going to fire my martial arts trainer."

"Camilla!" Rachel called. "Get my father!"

"Can she hear us?" Pav said.

"She's ten meters away!" Zhao said.

Then the opening—not large to begin with—got smaller.

"What the hell?" Pav said. "Is she putting stuff in the opening?"

"Hey, Camilla!" Rachel shouted. Zhao, too. And Pav.

Their pleas had no effect. The opening above them suddenly closed, leaving them in darkness.

Rachel wasn't sure, but it seemed that the strange little Portuguese girl had walled them in.

MAKALI

Feeling as if she could run forever, Makali Pillay led the charge up the ramp out of Vesuvius Vent. In a ragged line, with Zack closing in on her, Williams—surprisingly—in third, followed by Dale and Valya, they emerged into the harsh bright sunlight of a Keanu day and quickly headed upward to the surface.

She had only studied the imagery of the original exploration by the *Brahma* and *Destiny* crews . . . the snowy, shadowed crater with the obviously artificial ramp spiraling up one side. But she remembered the ramp as relatively clean, bare rock. Now it was covered with debris . . . easily avoided or jumped over, but obviously new.

And great swatches of snow were gone, especially in the higher reaches. "It looks so different!" she said.

"Setting off a nuke will do that," Zack said.

Makali and now Zack were taking giant leaps as they gained altitude. "Careful," Zack said. "It's easy to over-shoot in microgravity."

Makali acknowledged the warning without really altering her actions. She judged the vent to be at least thirty meters deep, a hole big enough to swallow a ten-story building. She also realized that as they got farther from the junction and the tunnels, gravity seemed to diminish sharply. She lost traction once or twice but was saved from a spill by Zack. "What did I tell you?" he said.

In the exuberance of exploration, and low gravity, Makali found it hard to slow down. Even Williams was springing up the ramp not far behind.

"Let's be smart about this," Zack said, trying to get Williams's attention. "There's no guardrail!"

Makali thought his worries were unfounded. To her it was obvious that a fall from the ramp would be slow and painless . . . assuming you even hit the base of the vent at all. She knew that most asteroids and other astronomical bodies were so small, so lacking in mass, so bereft of gravity that a human runner could literally leap into space.

Thinking about that made her worry more about becoming a human satellite of Keanu than about a serious fall.

Reaching the top, she and Zack stopped as quickly as the slick surface and low gravity would allow.

Williams was not so ept. He lost his footing and landed on his backside, sliding up to and into Zack and Makali. Makali was afraid they would topple like bowling pins, but Williams only bounced and spun.

By the time she and Zack had helped the writer to his feet, Dale and Valya had reached the top of the ramp, too.

"Hey, Makali," Dale said, as soon as he was within touching distance. "Now that we're here, mind telling us why you took off?"

God, he was an irritating human being. Had she been his commander on a long-duration mission, she wouldn't have just sent him home early . . . she would have ejected him from the airlock. "Because we were about to turn back and go into the tunnels," she said. "This would be my only chance to walk onto the surface of Keanu."

"Well, is it worth it?"

"Look for yourself." Her first impression was that she had entered a world possessing only two colors: black and white. Even the advanced adaptive optics of her skinsuit struggled as she looked from surface to sky.

Makali had seen as much imagery of Keanu's surface as anyone. It looked like any other large, icy comet or asteroid . . . rocks interspersed with ancient ice and snow, visually a lot like Iceland in the winter.

No longer. While the distant hills looked much the same, here most of the snow was gone . . . and in its place lay a shiny, smooth surface. "What the hell is this?" Zack said.

"I take it it looked different a week ago."

"Correct." He walked onto the shiny material, toeing it. "These are actually big plates," he said.

As her eyes adjusted, Makali had seen edges, too. "Do you suppose this is the real outer skin of the Architect's starship?" Williams said.

"It's not uniform," Dale Scott said. He had walked off a dozen meters. "The plates end here."

Makali surveyed the area at the top of the vent. "Yeah, it looks as though there's plating all around the rim."

"It's as if Vesuvius were built, not found," Valya Makarova said.

"Well, they used it and the other vents like giant rockets," Dale said.

Wade Williams wasn't wandering around the shiny white plates. He pointed to the sky. "Raise your eyes, friends."

Makali did, not seeing anything but black for several seconds. Oh, there it was! Planet Earth, a bright crescent in the sky across the vent, forty degrees above the horizon.

"It looks smaller than I expected," Makali said.

"It's a lot smaller than it was last week," Zack said.

"So we *are* moving," Williams said. "I suppose it would be prudent to figure out *where*."

"And how to turn around before it's too late," Zack said. "Come on."

"We landed two hundred meters from here," Zack said. "*Brahma* wasn't much farther." He was already moving; Makali sensed that he was tired of explaining his actions to Dale Scott.

She wondered, briefly, what Dale Scott would look like sailing over the rim of Vesuvius to the hard ground thirty meters below.

The *Venture* landing site was a sheet of greenish ice, likely discolored by the heat of the nuclear blast. In the center, ten centimeters of a lonely gold landing leg stuck out. Its top was melted. "That was *Venture*," Zack said.

"Dear God," Williams said. "That whole spacecraft— a two-billion-dollar item—vaporized."

"Along with two of my crew," Zack said.

"And one of *Brahma*'s team," Valya added.

Unbidden, she put her arm around the former *Venture* commander—clumsily, but heartfelt. Makali could hear labored breathing; she realized that Zack Stewart was struggling with his emotions.

Well, he was entitled. Makali felt as though she'd been

through enough fright and wonder in the past four days to last several lifetimes . . . and Zack Stewart had been living at the same intensity for three times as long. She was amazed that he was upright.

Dale was looking around. "So where was *Brahma*, anyway?" His question broke the mood, but he had the grace to speak softly.

Makali launched herself. She knew the landing site—at least, as it had been the day both spacecraft touched down. She remembered Bangalore Control Center's worries about orbital maneuvers and who landed first. What a waste of time and energy that had been.

The distance from the melted *Venture* landing leg to the *Brahma* site was no more than five hundred meters. Both spacecraft, NASA's *Venture* and the Coalition's *Brahma*, had been targeted for Vesuvius Vent, so their proximity was no accident. Still, it must have been thrilling to be on *Venture* watching *Brahma* touch down so close . . . or to have been on *Brahma*'s flight deck seeing *Venture* already waiting on the icy ground.

But where was *Brahma*? She was still on the green ice, though it was no longer uniform; there were patches of regular ice now, and even some rocky areas. Had she gone the wrong direction?

"Zack, over here!" It was Williams. "I found *Brahma*."

He was pointing to a large silver can lying on its side. It looked as though some giant foot had tried to crush one side of it, but it was still amazingly intact.

Yes, *Brahma*, pride of the Coalition . . . the first

mission beyond low Earth orbit ever flown by astronauts who weren't Americans . . . and here it was, space junk, blown on its side and destroyed by a fantastically misguided decision.

Makali skipped closer and was startled at how large the vehicle was. "It's tall, even on its side," she said.

"Twenty meters high, five across at its widest," Dale Scott said. Of course, Makali thought; he had worked closely with the *Brahma* teams. "It looks as though the crew cabin is sort of intact."

While the lower or left half of the spacecraft showed severe damage, crushing, and melting, the conical nose looked scorched, but whole. "Makes sense," Williams said. "The return capsule's designed to withstand the heat of reentry. Heat from a pocket nuke wouldn't be an order of magnitude worse in this environment."

"How comforting," Valya said, not hiding her sarcasm.

"I want to go inside," Scott said. "If the interior is intact, I guarantee you there's food and water, enough for a crew of four for a week. Some tools, who knows what else we'd find that might be useful."

Makali hadn't been thinking of useful supplies, either, but of sheer curiosity. "There are two hatches, right, Dale?"

Scott was loping around the nose of the craft. "Correct. The EVA hatch on the lower deck, and the side hatch on the return vehicle."

"Stupid question, but are they locked?"

"Not the EVA hatch. But there might have been a guard on the return vehicle, something you'd enable only on reentry. You know, to keep someone from blowing the thing in flight."

Makali was searching for the EVA hatch, a squarish piece of metal a meter and a half on each side. "I can't remember," she said. "The *Brahma* crew was not aboard when the bomb went off, so that hatch would be open?"

"Correct," Scott said.

"Got it," Zack said. He was on the opposite side of the wrecked spacecraft. Makali circled around the left, skirting the twisted legs and shattered propulsion module. Valya followed her.

Williams was with Zack. They were pointing to a slab of crumpled metal on the underside of *Brahma*. "There's the EVA hatch," Zack said, "open—

"—and completely inaccessible," Williams finished.

Makali had to agree; *Brahma* had fallen on the side where the hatch lay open, crushing it and burying it. "It might be possible to push it back," Williams said.

"Maybe," Zack said. "But that material looks jagged and we're wearing . . . skin."

"Hey, good news and bad news, friends," Dale Scott said. He was at the *Brahma*'s front end. "I found the return vehicle hatch."

The rounded nose of *Brahma*, and the silvery skin, looked singed on one side, the one facing *Venture* and the blast. Other than that, and the fact that the vehicle was on its side, it looked intact, much as Makali remembered it from pictures.

Of course, none of those pictures showed it with its circular hatch open, flopped to one side like a small access platform. "Didn't you say it was locked?"

"Only a possibility," Scott said.

"Locked or unlocked, why is it open now?" Williams said.

"From the blast?" Zack said. "Or from being tipped over?"

"Not the hatch I knew," Scott said.

The five of them were circling the nose and the hatch, as if wary of going closer. *The hell with this,* Makali thought. She skipped right up to the hatch, which was almost at eye level. Her skinsuit wouldn't allow her to pull herself up to it, but low gravity meant that she could hop fairly high, high enough for a peek inside.

"The cockpit looks intact," she said. "And some of the displays are still lit."

"How is that possible?" Valya said.

"*Brahma*'s batteries were good for another week," Scott said. "If the cockpit is still intact, it means that the force of the blast probably wasn't severe enough to sever the connections."

"Are we going to talk about this all day?" Makali said. "Or is someone going to give me a boost so I can get inside?"

Even though she had more than a layperson's familiarity with the *Brahma* cockpit, Makali's entry was quite disorienting. Had *Brahma* been in its nominal, upright position, the hatch opened to the right, allowing ingress and egress to the middle two of four couches. But those two couches folded under the other two for orbital or landing operations.

When Makali stepped through the hatch, she found herself looking up at the commander's couch and its folded companion, and trying to stand on the other pair. The control panel was to her right. The "floor" of the spacecraft, and the access hatch to the lower, airlock deck, were above and to her left. The immediate left was taken up with the bulkhead covering *Brahma*'s ascent motor. Which was, she suddenly realized, filled with toxic fuels. She hoped there were no leaks.

The cockpit seemed dark, deserted, and cramped. Of course, the lower deck doubled as a habitation area, a fat doughnut surrounding the ascent stage. This was where the four *Brahma* travelers rode through launch, maneuvers, and touchdown on Earth.

Had they finally gotten home? The three surviving *Brahma* astronauts had joined *Venture* crew member Tea Nowinski aboard the *Destiny* orbiter, which, if Makali remembered correctly, had been crash-landed onto the surface here . . . and safely launched toward Earth.

She knew the crew members, some better than others. The Indian commander, Taj. How horrifying to have him survive the mishaps on Keanu, to return home and find that his son had been snatched away. Lucas Munaretto, so handsome and charming—and so unsuited to the rigors of spaceflight.

Makali barely knew Natalia Yorkina. But she had been good friends with Dennis Chertok, the oldest and most experienced member of the *Brahma* team—and its only fatality. Poor Dennis! So focused, so driven, so knowledgeable. He had spent almost two years in space on half a dozen different missions going back almost thirty years, every one of them marked by some equipment failure that he had been able to solve.

She wished he were here now.

"Looking for anything in particular?" Dale Scott was two steps behind her.

"Well, your food and water would be a good start."

"Most of that would be below." He edged into the cockpit with her, wrenching himself around to reach the access hatch. "It's open, but—"

Makali could see past him. "Damaged."

"Yeah. I don't know if I can even fit in there."

"Forget it," she said. "It would be great to have extra goodies, but they'd be gone in an hour."

They both straightened up. Then, gingerly placing their feet on the sides of the couches, they moved away from the hatch and toward the control panel. "So, who *did* open that hatch?" Makali said.

"No fucking idea."

"There must be something we can take, something that will be useful."

"It's a spacecraft, lady. Especially this module. It's all instruments, controls, computers, comm, none of which is useful in our present situation." He pointed to a panel mounted above them. "Since it's technically a wreck, I suppose we could take the cockpit recorder. . . ."

"There's a *black box*?"

"Yeah. I mean, it's not as though anyone expected *Brahma* to crash, or if it crashed, to be found. It was just a data storage device, all the uplinks, maneuvers, imagery."

"I want it."

Scott looked at her as if she were raving. "Why?"

"When we get back to the habitat, it will give me something to do." That wasn't the answer, of course. The black box held data, and data was her life. Especially data on exo-environments, possibly on the postblast environment. She had been nursing dark thoughts about the radiation levels here—

Scott braced himself in order to reach above his head and detach the recorder unit. "Whoa," he said.

"What?"

He gestured at several cabinets directly in front of him. Because of her need to brace in mid-cockpit, Makali had not been able to see them before this.

Two cabinets had been ripped open, their covers literally torn from the hinges. One contained clothing that, she could now see, was dumped below her in the dark bottom of the cockpit. The other cabinet had been cleaned out.

"What do you suppose happened?" Makali said. "Is that damage from the crash?"

"Could be, but look lower."

Below the vandalized cabinets was another damaged area . . . a third door that looked as though it had been punched in. It was jagged and some pieces were missing . . . and there was a film of frozen red or orange fluid on it.

"I think," Dale said, "that someone opened the hatch and did some damage in here."

"And to himself," Makali said, deciding without any justification that the red fluid was blood.

Scott handed her the recorder unit. It was just too big

to fit comfortably in Makali's hand. Scott could see that as well. He must have learned something from his abortive ISS mission, because without being asked, he tore some netting from a corner of the cockpit. "You'll need this," he said, adding a tool kit and several pieces of cable and clips from another cabinet. "I don't know how helpful it will be—

Just then Zack's rounded, skinsuited head rose above the open hatch. "Come out here. We found something."

"So did we." He told Zack about the cabinets and the possible blood.

"Yeah. I think you need to exit, now."

Head bowed, Wade Williams was carefully searching an area directly in front of the *Brahma* nose, moving deliberately. He reminded Makali of a beachcomber using a metal detector to search for coins.

"So, what do you have?" Scott said.

"Tracks," Williams said. Zack had told the others about the possible "incursion" into the *Brahma* cockpit. Zack's description made Makali think of a black bear attack on a campsite.

In the glare, with the diminished acuity of the skinsuit "eyes," the tracks weren't easy to see, but they were unmistakably present: a series of long scrapes on the thin layer of ice and snow. Each one was half a meter long. "Bipedal, I judge," Williams said. As a sci-fi writer, he was in heaven. "And a big fella."

He was following them away from *Brahma*, to where the ice and snow-covered regolith gave way, again, to the white plates. "They're hard to see on the white stuff," he said, "but still present."

Scott was still examining the most visible tracks. "I'm not sure it's just one creature," he said. "There's a scattering of other markings, too."

"Two sets?" Valya said. She sounded alarmed.

Zack walked over for a second look. "Well, we know that at least two nonhuman life forms exist on Keanu—the Architects and the Sentries. Who's to say there couldn't be others?"

"Who's to say this is two different creatures?" Williams said. "Maybe it's just your Architect."

"I hope so," Zack said. "I've got unfinished business with that guy."

"So let's find him," Makali said. "*Follow* him."

She pointed straight ahead.

"Where?" Valya said.

"Mt. St. Helens," she told her. "The next vent."

"How far is it?" Williams said.

"Check me on this, Zack, but ten, maybe fifteen kilometers."

Zack had frozen into apparent immobility. He knew what Makali was proposing. "At least."

"A bit of a hike," Williams said. "Of course, we still don't have any way back into our habitat, and don't know how long these suits are good for—"

"This is officially fucking crazy!" Scott said. Perhaps he was being protective of Valya, or maybe he was just using common sense. "I agree that going back through the Beehive seems not too promising, but I have a hard time believing that the next best option is to hike overland to some other vent. Suppose it gives us access to another habitat—suppose that habitat is filled with the creatures that ransacked *Brahma*! How is that good?"

"There are no good options," Zack said. "So we make the best of what we've got."

"Which is?"

He pointed at the plates on the surface leading in the general direction of Mt. St. Helens Vent. "Follow the blinding white road."

GABRIEL

"It's kidney failure," he said.

It was the first time he had uttered those words to anyone. Not to his chief of staff at JSC, not to his girlfriend or his mother.

Certainly not his daughter.

No one.

The diagnosis was recent, of course. The definitive word had been delivered to him at Baylor only, what, less than a month ago?

"How advanced?" Harley Drake said. The HB mayor had found him slumped against a rock a kilometer from the Temple, in the direction of the opposite wall, beyond Lake Ganges.

How had he gotten there? Jones wasn't sure.

"Far enough. Stage four, they call it. I've got elevated creatine levels, family history of diabetes and high blood pressure.

"You were on dialysis?"

"Just started! My third session was scheduled for the day we got scooped." He smiled. "I guess I don't need to tell you about shitty luck."

"No, got that covered, thanks. What would make you feel better?"

"Got any calcitriol?" That was one of the medications he'd been given, a hormone. He was so new to suffering from chronic kidney disease that he had yet to really read up on his condition and treatment. No time.

"I'll check on the top shelf, but meanwhile try this." Jones had noticed a beer bottle in Harley's lap but had been too tired and distracted to ask why.

"A Miller Genuine Draft is supposed to help me how?"

"Oh for fuck's sake, Gabe. It's not beer. One of Nayar's guys has learned to play the Temple food controls like a virtuoso. He's pumped out an amazing variety of foodstuffs, so far. It's a little like playing Battleship— he's just adjusting one parameter one way, a couple of others a different direction. And out comes nasty food, and finally this. Go ahead, take a drink. I did."

Jones sipped from the bottle. "Tastes like cold coffee!"

"We think it *is* cold coffee."

His head hurt, and not just from his physical condition. "This is all too magical for me. How is that *possible*?"

"We're doing nothing but speculating, but I keep going back to what Zack knows, what we've established so far. The Architects were able to pull a human consciousness out of space and attach it to a rebuilt body that seems to have been identical to the original. That shows not only that they are aware of and able to detect and manipulate a whole class of information we know nothing about, but they can search it, re-form it into something useful."

"Turn that information into a program, you mean—"

"Then use their molecular machines or gray goo or whatever it is to duplicate the original item.

"My point is, if their machines can do people—"

"—Dead people."

"Yeah, even better. If the Architects have machines that can find and capture whatever it is that makes up a human soul and regenerate that person, they can certainly scan a dozen or ten dozen human beings and generate the right atmosphere or a properly sized table." He pointed to the beer bottle. "A cup of Starbucks ought to be pretty basic. Come to think of it, I'm going to get Jaidev and his guys working on cups, plates, and flatware. That beer bottle is one of the better containers we have."

Gabe had grown quite interested in Camilla's activities, but he'd needed Sasha Blaine to translate and couldn't find her, either.

Then, feeling tired, he had just sat down to rest. . . .

It was a good thing he hadn't been elected mayor. For the first two days, from the scoop to maybe two hours past the landing—to the point where the Chinese man had killed Bynum—he had fancied himself a modern-day Moses.

Yeah, he was Moses, all right. Not the Moses who brought the Israelites to the Promised Land but died without reaching it himself.

He was the Moses who was lucky to get the Israelites across the Red Sea, where they then faced forty years of wandering and uncertainty.

He felt weak again.

"Hey, Gabe," Harley said. "Drink up. We don't think

it'll hurt you. Jaidev's been guzzling the stuff for the past two hours and he seems to be happier than any of us."

"It seems like a waste of resources." But he drank. It was cold and thick and tasted coffeelike, not that he was a judge. Nevertheless, out of thirst or desperation, he drained the bottle. As Harley was saying, "We have a lot of resources. We've just started learning how to make use of them."

"Fine, I'll concede that you can feed and maybe clothe people; that that's what the Architects had in mind when they brought us here. But I don't see medicines; I don't see a hospital. Hell, Harley, we don't even have a doctor in the house!" He belched loudly, and so strongly that he thought the Temple coffee was coming back up.

But no, he was safe. All he did was spark amused laughter from Harley Drake. "Come on, Gabe, allow yourself to hope! If, in the space of a day, we can get the Temple to turn out food, water, furniture, and what appears to be cappuccino . . . who's to say that in a week's time we can't be replicating a dialysis machine?"

"I find that preposterous."

"Okay, a month. Two months."

"I won't last that long."

"Stranger things have happened, my friend. Or haven't you noticed?"

Gabriel stood. He was feeling better. Maybe that damned drink from the Temple was worthwhile—

No, idiot. All it was was fluid that filled the hollow in your stomach for a few moments. It's fooling your body into thinking it's worthwhile.

You were a dead man the moment the Object scooped you up.

"Any word on Rachel? Or Zack?"

"Nada. I sent Zhao after Rachel."

"Was that wise?"

"It's not as though he's going to run off," Harley said. "And Rachel's a smart kid. She'll turn up."

For the past minute, Gabriel had thought he was hearing singing but blamed it on his illness, as if tinnitus were something else he would have to endure as he fell apart.

Now it was unmistakable. Somebody was singing—

Camilla walked around the rock, a smile on her face, unself-consciously presenting what sounded like a nursery rhyme, but in Portuguese.

The only odd thing—

"What happened to your arm, sweetheart?" God, he had fallen back into the parental voice. His staff used to tease him, saying that he used it with department heads who were being especially stubborn.

She didn't resist as Gabriel took her left arm and gently turned it, noting that the girl seemed hot, almost feverish.

Harley rolled closer. "Yikes," he said, softly, not wanting to alarm the girl.

She had a palm-sized carbuncle on her upper arm that had split and now oozed a glistening liquid. Not blood, not pus.

But clearly nothing good.

"Let's take her to Sasha."

"Wait—" Gabriel realized that the girl was holding something in her hand. "What have you got there?" He squeezed her hand and gently tried to turn it. Camilla didn't resist; she opened her hand, revealing a bug of some kind.

It was squarish, almost freakishly so . . . and brightly colored: yellow, blue, red, none of them natural to his eye. "What *is* this little thing?" he said.

"Don't ask me," Harley said. "I'm good as far as mosquitoes, bees, and spiders, and that's it."

"Well, I know a bit about the insect world, and I can't place this."

"How are you on insects found in India?"

Harley had a point. "About as good as you on insects in general. Someone at the Temple will recognize it."

"Unless it's native to Keanu."

"We haven't seen anything like that yet."

Gabriel smiled at Camilla and let her close her hand on the bug again. Continuing her song, she bowed her head, then resumed her journey. "Looks like a Woggle-Bug," Harley said. "It's actually kind of cute."

"Okay, what's a Woggle-Bug?"

"From Frank Baum, the guy who wrote the Oz books."

"Ah, fictional."

"Yeah, sorry. I know more fictional bugs than I do real-life insects."

He maneuvered his wheelchair around to follow Camilla. Gabriel got in position to push.

He *was* feeling better. He wondered how long it would last.

Part Five

Hello, my darling niece!

Camilla, this is your uncle, Lucas. I am safe at home with your loving mother, my sister, all your family . . . all of them so interested in the magic that brought you back to me, to all of us, however distantly and briefly.

We are following your journey into deeper space with hope and love and prayers for your safety.

We think of you every day, every moment . . . praising God for allowing you a second chance at life, and trying to understand his purpose in giving you that chance on Keanu.

BROADCAST FROM KOROLEV MISSION CONTROL TO KEANU
BY LUCAS MUNARETTO, SEPTEMBER 4, 2019

My favorite video game was *Satan War*, where you got to shoot your way out of the deepest part of hell while crossing rivers of fire and oceans of shit and fields of spikes.

All the while being chased by demons and hoping you could get to heaven.

So far my life in Keanu has been a lot like *Satan War*, only WITHOUT THE POWER UPGRADES AND WEAPONS AND THE GOAL OF HEAVEN. KEANU-PEDIA BY PAV, ENTRY #4

THE PRISONER

Struck by the long-finned creature, the Prisoner did not lose consciousness, but it was stunned, almost paralyzed.

The strange creature continued to approach, perhaps to conduct an examination. Which worked to the Prisoner's advantage; it would conduct its own examination of its assailant.

The Prisoner realized its assailant was smaller and, most unusually, not wearing any kind of garment to protect it against open space. When the assailant spread itself, it revealed many fins—arms, nonaquatic beings called them.

For a moment, the Prisoner thought it one of the broken vessel's crew.

But now the Prisoner recognized this creature. It didn't belong here any more than the Prisoner did. The Prisoner knew, of course, that its people were not the only residents of the warship. There were others, some of them quite dangerous. The Prisoner had never met any of these others, of course, dangerous or not. But it had been warned since youth about one in particular:

This type, a Tall Fins.

The Prisoner was never quite sure what was so fearsome about the Tall Fins. They were relatively small, for one thing.

They did not appear to possess the traits of an intelligent race—no clothing, no tools, no transport vessels.

No communications. There was no chance the two could strike a truce. So went the stories. Yet apparently wherever the Tall Fins went, other creatures died.

However, this was not the Tall Fins's environment. It was forced to scramble along the sharply angled walls of the interior, which took time and allowed the Prisoner to recover and pry a metal rod from the vessel's interior—

A quick swipe of the rod sent the Tall Fins flying into a wall.

The Tall Fins seemed momentarily stunned. Brandishing the metal rod, the Prisoner maneuvered blindly toward the vessel's hatchway, knowing an exit was going to be difficult because of the small dimensions of the opening.

The Prisoner considered the next move. The Tall Fins did not appear to be strong enough to engage in a duel of metal rods. But what other weapons did it have? Poisons? The warship's builders had stocked the resident environment with a menace long extinct on the home world: a round floating creature that defended itself with a shower of needles—

Shifting within its protective suit of skin, the Prisoner brandished the rod. The Tall Fins reacted, retreating. In the combat games of youth, the Prisoner had learned to feint with the major arm, then shift the weapon to a lesser arm for the killing blow.

But the wound in its back! Much worse than the Prisoner had believed. It felt pinned, almost helpless. The only option was to wait for the Tall Fins to come close enough to strike—

To the Prisoner's surprise, however, the Tall Fins skittered away, toward the opening, then out. For a moment, the Prisoner feared that the creature meant to seal the opening, locking it in.

But fractions of a cycle passed . . . and the opening remained clear.

The Prisoner knew that the garment would eventually seal itself around the wound, but the shard . . . the Prisoner bent forward—some pain, though bearable.

But no freedom. Every place it went, it seemed, the Prisoner was fated to be constrained.

The only option was to rock from side to side, resulting in substantially more pain, and the fear that the garment's seal would tear.

With a crack the Prisoner could feel in its dorsal side, the shard separated.

Freedom! The garment remained sealed . . . but the shard remained.

The pain was comparable to dividing . . . only it promised to last far, far longer.

And might kill the Prisoner before it could return to the relative safety of its cell.

In agony, the Prisoner began the slow, unpleasant process of squeezing through the opening.

A long, painful walk lay ahead.

ZHAO

"This is really starting to freak me out," Rachel announced.

She and Pav and Zhao had walked, by Zhao's estimate, half a kilometer down the lightless shaft. Discovering that the Indian boy carried a Slate, Zhao invented a game: Every two hundred paces, which had to be counted by Rachel, then Pav in turn, the trio would stop and flash the Slate's light.

They had accomplished five such illuminations, none of which revealed anything different, just a smooth, rocky floor and walls that curved enough to confirm that they were in a cylinder.

Zhao was growing a bit unsettled himself, given the bizarre circumstances . . . being essentially walled into the tunnel by a nine-year-old girl . . . theoretically chasing a dog—a *reborn* dog, let's not forget—with limited resources, to wit: a Slate, a bottle of water, and a candy bar he had bartered from Xavier Toutant.

All in the company of the only two teenagers in the population, both of them children of the *Destiny* or *Brahma* astronauts.

Looking at it from Pav's point of view, or Rachel's, the

situation was even more unsettling, given that they knew him as either a spy or a killer.

Rachel said, "Shouldn't we be finding a cross-tunnel or some other way out by now?"

"In a human-built mine on Earth, yes," Zhao said. "But I don't think we can *expect* anything here."

"Well," Pav said, "Keanu is what, a hundred kilometers across? If we're walking in a straight line, eventually we'll get to the other side."

Zhao forced a smile, even though he knew the teens couldn't see it. *Stay in character,* he thought. *Follow your training.* He didn't feel the need to point out that while this shaft seemed straight, it likely wasn't . . . that it would not be a vector through the sphere that was Keanu, but could just as easily be an arc, curving and curving. . . .

Well, that was a pointless mental exercise. Even if Pav were correct that following this shaft might lead to the other side of Keanu . . . they couldn't walk a hundred kilometers without food and water.

They couldn't walk twenty.

"My hunch," he said, offering fake optimism, the kind you gave a prisoner undergoing interrogation, "is that we will find a branch or a turn or an exit once we've reached the end of our habitat."

"Shouldn't we be pretty close to that by now?" Pav said. He was a young man—inked, wired, impatient. Zhao knew quite a few like Pav, not just from his time in India, but in posts in China, too. He found them all difficult to control past a few hours.

Not that he was expecting to have to control Pav past

a few hours. "Let's keep going," he said. "Pav, your turn to count."

Both teens started walking again.

Rachel was a greater challenge than Pav. Zhao knew what buttons to push to keep a bright, immature teen male in line. He knew of no equivalent training buttons that would produce predictable results with a bright, immature teen female, especially an entitled American.

Especially an entitled American teen female whose father was in her life and affecting her behavior.

Or an entitled American teen female whose dead mother had been recently in her life.

They had reached 140 in Pav's count when all three of them stopped.

"Do you feel that?" Rachel said.

"It was like I was being pulled toward the wall!" Pav said.

He was quite agitated, and Zhao couldn't blame him; he had felt something, too . . . a tingling that started with the soles of his sneaker-clad feet and shot up one side of his body. "Light, please," he said.

The Slate flashed and held, and Zhao was surprised to see that the shaft was no longer cylindrical, but squared off; that the surface looked shiny, white, and polished, like the tiles in a new subway station; and that there was a branch leading to their right . . . what Zhao took to be the direction away from the human habitat. The main shaft continued.

"When did everything go so weird?" Rachel said. Her voice held her usual teen sneer, but Zhao could hear the hint of panic.

He touched her shoulder firmly. "Kill the light," he told Pav. "I didn't notice a specific change—"

"—Unless it was that zap we got," Pav said, finishing Zhao's statement, which Zhao found annoying.

"Now I know what's freaking me out," Rachel said. She had moved close enough to Zhao that he could feel her trembling. "This isn't a tunnel, it's a pipe."

"What's the difference?" Pav said.

Zhao was struck by Rachel's insight. How had he missed it? "People and machines use tunnels for access. Pipes are for the transfer of fluids—" He didn't have many phobias, but drowning in an enclosed space in the dark would top the short list.

"The walls were dry," Pav said, clearly trying to make a case they all wanted made.

"For now," Rachel said, almost hissing.

"The question," Zhao said, "is whether this new branch is less like a pipe than what we just walked through."

"I vote we take it," Rachel said, already edging toward it.

"So we've given up on the dog?" Pav said.

"We haven't heard or seen him in the past hour," Zhao said. "I think—"

Just then he and the other two felt the strange tug and tingle again.

Only this time they were slammed against the wall and instantly dragged toward the new branch shaft like metal filings to a magnet. They were left hanging halfway up the wall . . . then released, sliding to the floor.

It wasn't painful, though their clothing likely prevented scrapes, but it was frightening.

Fortunately, it lasted only a few seconds. Pav was the

first to regain his feet, and he helped Rachel, then Zhao. "That," the young man said, "was officially weird."

Rachel turned to Zhao. "So what was that?"

Zhao realized that he could see Rachel and Pav. The new shaft was bathed in a blue, actinic light, but distorting. "Look!" Pav said.

As Zhao and Rachel watched, with considerable horror, the shape of the shaft ahead of them deformed, a wave passing away from them like a silent tsunami.

"To answer your earlier question," Zhao said, "or your next, I have no idea."

"Whatever it was, the first time it felt like it was headed up the shaft, the way we came," Rachel said. "This time it came back—"

"—And made a turn and went down this tunnel," Pav said.

"It looked like—God, this is going to sound stupid," Rachel said.

Zhao was curious. "What did it look like, Rachel?"

"Like a little ball—as small as a marble—was being sucked through the wall of the shaft."

"I didn't see that," Pav said.

"Well, I did."

Rachel laughed. "This is funny?" Pav said.

"No, just . . . I played with marbles when I was little. You had steelies and agates. My favorite was a cat's-eye because it had all these different colors—"

Zhao wasn't ready to concede the idea that a small particle somehow distorted gravity—but on further reflection, why not? Based on its mass and density, Keanu's gravity should be a fraction of what it appeared to be (about half Earth normal, one of the Bangalores had calculated). "Something is adding or changing gravity," he said. "It could be we just saw it. Your cat's-eye."

"We sure *felt* it," Pav said.

"Poor Cowboy," Rachel said. "Even if he didn't get squashed, he probably got thrown around. . . ."

Rachel trailed off. Zhao felt a moment of disorientation, as if he had suddenly been picked up, spun, and dropped, all in less than a second.

Something was happening again, and not just the flyby of some gravity marble—

He felt heat on the back of his neck.

"Now what?" Pav was saying.

Zhao turned . . . a wall of yellow goo was rushing at them, a gelatinous mass the size of a subway train, and leaving just as little room for escape.

DALE

If he hadn't been wrapped in the cocoonlike skinsuit, forced to work with Zack Stewart and crazy Makali, tagging along with his ex and with an ancient sci-fi writer, with no real knowledge of his destination or how long he would have life support—

Dale Scott would have enjoyed the trek to Mt. St. Helens, which was the next vent—one of the Keanu features given terrestrial names by clever, unimaginative Earth-based astronomers.

The path was blessedly smooth, better than any road or sidewalk Dale had seen, even allowing for the fact that his most recent exposure to roadways was in Russia and India, where the standards fell considerably short of, say, Beverly Hills.

He decided that the closest thing to this white Keanu surface material was a basketball court, specifically the parquet of the old Boston Garden. (His father had taken him there when he was eight. He'd never forgotten the smooth, solid-but-yielding beauty of that floor.)

The sky was the black of space, though lots of it. Dale had seen that sky, of course, but only through small windows. He had never walked out in it, in the open. By raising his head, he could see stars, a very strange sight over a sunlit landscape. Thank God the crescent Earth lay behind them; he would have found it distracting and, given his chances of ever walking on it again, sad.

Physically, he was still feeling fine. In another time or place, he would have been eager to dissect the skinsuit to see what techno-magic allowed it to provide a breathable atmosphere (he assumed that the same sort of nanobuilt gear that developed in the vesicle was wrapped around his waist right now) while keeping him from being thirsty, hungry, or tired.

He and the others had reported feeling a series of pin-pricks up their spines and in their stomachs; Dale was pretty sure the suit was giving him water and calories that way, and possibly even the Keanu equivalent of an energy drink.

As for other life support matters, he hadn't tried to urinate yet, but then, he hadn't felt the urge, either. Given the challenges of elimination in even the most advanced human space suits, which Dale knew better than almost anyone (EVA suits had been his first tech assignment as an astronaut), this was the true innovation, worth millions or tens of millions on Earth.

But he wasn't going back to Earth.

At least, not yet. Not that he could see. Given that, he was doing okay.

He just wished he could touch his medallion, the lucky item he wore around his neck.

Because this wasn't an ordinary medallion. No, sir, no St. Christopher medal for him. This was a genuine 1974 Incredible Hulk medallion he had bought with his allow-ance when he was eleven.

He had displayed it in his room for the next three

years, next to his comic books and action figures. He was ashamed to admit that he liked the Hulk, the green-skinned alter ego of mild-mannered professor Bruce Banner when circumstances demanded . . . rage and muscle, not brains and timidity, not because of the Marvel comic books, but because of the CBS TV series.

Whatever. Nobody but Seth Bryant ever asked him, and Seth was a comic book snob and geek. Dale Scott was, to the rest of the world, a jock.

Who relied on the Hulk to keep him safe.

That was necessary around the Scott household, because John Jeremy Scott was a blackout alcoholic—a fact Dale realized when he was eleven. Until that time, he had just thought J. J. Scott, a police officer in Anaheim, was tough because he had to be. He would yell and stomp around the house and break things—not always, not even very often, but enough—and, when Dale was younger, slap him when he got out of line.

From the time he got the Hulk, however, Dale never got slapped. Not once, up to the day his father finally moved out.

And Dale discovered that his Hulk was gone! Stolen from its place of honor on his shelf.

He didn't have to wonder who (his father) or why (because J. J. Scott was always doing nasty things and once had teased Dale about spending his time watching the Hulk on TV).

But Dale had his revenge. After J.J. moved out and then moved in with some other woman, he settled in Fullerton, not far from Anaheim. He shared custody of Dale and Dale's sister, Chelsea, though he wasn't very rigorous about keeping to the schedule—a relief to both children.

The one time Dale found himself in J.J.'s apartment, he had sneaked into the master bedroom . . . and found the Hulk medallion sitting in the top drawer of a clothes chest.

Dale had pocketed the medallion and escaped clean with it, though he lived in trembling fear that J.J. would discover the theft—or, rather, the recovery—and turn on him in one of his terrible rages.

Dale feared that right up to the night, two years later, that J.J. Scott died in an off-duty auto accident . . . drunk.

He had had it put on a chain, so he wouldn't lose it, and the Hulkster had accompanied him to Cal Poly Pomona, then to the Navy and flight training and grad school, to Iraq twice, and test pilot school and NASA, and even aboard the International Space Station.

And now here . . . wherever this was. Some godforsaken hollowed-out planetoid pushing itself out of the solar system back home. He wondered how far they'd traveled in these few days. Keanu would still be visible from Earth with the naked eye, even if its trajectory was due solar south. Someone in New Zealand or Chile, or Byrd Station, South Pole, would have a good view.

Keanu could probably keep accelerating for a long time—hell, centuries, maybe, meaning it could reach some fraction of the speed of light. But so far . . . hell, they weren't even as far from Earth as the planet Mars!

Zack and Makali were in front, like lead mutts on a dog sled. Williams was in the rear, probably because of age and an inability to keep from stopping every few dozen steps just to take in the view. Well, what the hell; he had been imagining shit like this for fifty years. Dale guessed that it was okay for him to take it in.

Especially knowing that he wasn't going to live any longer than Dale.

He looped close to Valya and asked her, in his below-average Russian, how she was doing. He had detected growing tension back at the *Brahma* site, along with real reluctance to press forward.

"How do you think?" she growled. Okay, obviously still some tension.

"I wish I could cheer you up," he said.

"What would you do?" she said. "Sing me a song? Tell me a joke?"

"It worked before."

"You had many charming techniques that worked before. We are in different circumstances."

"Copy that."

He let her mush on ahead of him and fell back with Williams. "Is it everything you dreamed it would be?" he asked.

"Less and more," Williams said. "Even though I wrote it a few times, I surely never thought I'd be doing a traverse across an alien starship."

"Funny how dreams come true."

"Or nightmares."

"That would be the 'less' business."

"I keep telling myself that I also imagined and published miraculous escapes for my heroes. So if I have the true predictive vision . . ."

"Here's hoping."

Dale noticed that for all his bravado, Williams was

actually limping a bit. Before he could ask, however, he heard a shout from Makali.

"Oh my God, look at that!"

Though still better than a NASA EVA garment, the skinsuit's biggest drawback was limited field of view. The cowl-like hood was fairly rigid; in order to look up or sideways, you had to turn your body. You had almost no peripheral vision.

And the view forward wasn't glasslike, either. You were looking through a filmy fabric about a centimeter in front of each eyeball.

Which was why Dale pressed forward, asking, "Can you see Mt. St. Helens already?" Zack had said "ten to fifteen kilometers," which Dale took to mean "fifteen or more." They could not have gone halfway yet.

"It's not the vent," Makali said, completely unnecessarily by that time, since Zack and Valya and Williams and Dale could all see what she'd found.

It appeared to be another spacecraft.

At least six stories tall—taller than *Brahma* before the accident—it was a rounded cylinder like a big fat bullet, or something out of an old Jules Verne novel. There were bumps and protruding blisters on the skin, which appeared to be metallic.

"Look at the pitting on this thing," Zack said. "It must be really, really old."

"How do you know it wasn't designed that way?" Makali said. *Of course,* Dale thought, *be argumentative.*

"Just a hunch," Zack said. "And no landing legs. And

I believe it *was* designed that way." The vehicle rested perfectly upright but lacked legs or any obvious landing aids. It rested on material that reminded Dale of a collapsed balloon.

"It must have crunched down on that skirt," Makali said. She was close enough to toe the material, which was bleached an ugly white. "Hard."

"Petrified," Williams said. "More fuel for the argument that this is really, really old."

"Whom did it belong to?" Valya asked. "Who landed it here?"

"Nobody from Earth," Dale said. "And with that kind of landing, I get the impression this was a one-way trip."

"Both *Brahma* and *Venture* had ascent motors inside them," Makali said.

Dale couldn't decide which annoyed him more, the fact that exospecialist Makali Pillay would presume to argue matters of spacecraft engineering with him, or just that she kept talking, period. "And both were modular," he said, knowing he should not engage the woman. "With obvious separation lines. I'm looking at this baby, and it all seems to be one big piece."

"—With an open hatch on this side," Wade Williams said.

The hatch was a thick plug that opened downward rather than to the side, creating a platform for occupants going EVA.

And at least ten meters off the ground, preventing any

of them from seeing inside the opening . . . or from reaching it.

"This gives me some idea of who it belongs to," Zack said. "Look at the proportions of the Temple . . . the Architect was twice as tall as a human being."

Dale could hear Wade Williams sputtering. "Surely the Architects are more advanced than this thing. They launched the vesicles, for God's sake. This vehicle looks as though it could have been built by China, now!"

"Well," Makali said, "whoever built it, a ladder would have been nice."

"Shame on the Architects for not realizing you'd be coming along and wanting to go aboard," Dale said. He had decided he might as well declare war on Pillay in the hopes of getting her to shut up. Otherwise, he would be provoked to violence.

Zack ignored the exchange. "They probably had a rope ladder of some kind—"

"—A thousand years ago," Williams finished. "Even something metal would have gone brittle in that time, baked and frozen a few million times. It must have eventually blown away like dust."

"This is all quite fascinating, I'm sure," Valya said. "But since we can't go aboard, we should press on to this vent, since I believe it represents our only hope for survival. Or am I overstating matters?" For a non-native English speaker, Valya had perfect pitch when it came to sarcasm. Dale had always enjoyed it, at least on the few occasions when it was directed at someone other than him.

"Oh, I think we can go aboard," Zack said.

"Zack, how?" Makali said. She was almost sputtering.

"Because in this gravity, we can throw him ten meters," Dale said. They were all experiencing low gravity. But apparently not all of them were thinking of its potential advantages. Not even the famous exospecialist. "Or, really, you could throw me ten meters. You're mission commander, Zack. I'm expendable."

Zack considered this for a moment. "I guess, if you count Keanu as one, I've already been first to enter an alien spacecraft. It's someone else's turn."

"Not the exospecialist?" Makali said.

"After me," Dale said. He gestured to Zack. "May I?"

In Keanu surface gravity, it was a simple matter for Dale to step into Zack's hands, which were clenched waist-high, steadying himself with a hand on Zack's head. "Okay, I'm just going to propel you."

"That should do it. Look out below if I miss."

"You might not hit the ground for a minute. I'll have time to duck."

"Or catch you," Williams said.

"Remember," Makali said, "you still have to get *down*."

"*Then* you can catch me," Dale told her.

It took only one toss. Dale's flight up the side of the alien ship reminded him most of a roller coaster ascent; it seemed to have the same speed.

Which gave him plenty of time to reach for the hatch while not smacking his head on it. "It's bigger than it looks from down there," he said, holding on. He glanced down at Zack and the others once, then resolved not to do that again.

The trickiest maneuver was getting on top of the

hatch. Fortunately, the plug itself had layers and notches in it, sufficient to allow him to take a grip. Once secured, he swung his feet to the side of the vehicle, then Spider-Man-walked his way up.

He actually had to climb over the rim of the hatch. How tall were these guys?

There was an airlock of sorts—or, rather, a large chamber with a hatch on its inner bulkhead. The chamber was as featureless as a sewer pipe, and, stained and corroded, not much better looking. He wondered how much of that was due to age, and how much was in the original design.

Beyond the inner hatch was simply darkness . . . a metallic deck and a high ceiling. With no light but what came through the hatch, which was itself in shadow, there was nothing to see: no equipment, no tools, not even an access ladder or hatch to an upper deck.

The interior confirmed Dale's impression of the exterior; it was like an Egyptian tomb in there.

He turned and almost jumped out of his skinsuit.

Makali Pillay was standing just inside the outer hatchway. "Makali, what are you doing up here?"

"You said, 'after me.'"

"I meant on the order of days or weeks." He stepped aside. "Well, take a look. You're not going to find anything."

She said nothing, merely slipping past him into the big, empty deck.

Which left Dale with that rarest of things in any space excursion . . . time to enjoy the view. *Especially since this might be my last beautiful vista.*

It wasn't much . . . a white surface that could just as easily have served as the parking lot for an interplanetary sports arena. Around its edges lay dirty snow and ice, and rock, all of which looked exactly like equivalent surfaces on every comet or asteroid humans had ever photographed.

There were low hills, more rock than snow, on the horizon—which was freakishly close. As he scanned from one heading to another, Dale noted the change from rock to snow and ice, and—

"Hey," he said to the others. "I can see Mt. St. Helens!"

"Great!" Zack said. "How far?"

"Wow, hard to tell—maybe five clicks, might be less."

If he took the bearing directly out the hatch as zero degrees, the next vent lay at forty. He pointed in that direction, and was rewarded by the sight of Zack Stewart repositioning Valya and Williams in that direction. (He must have found that the shiny white surface repelled marks.)

See, Stewart? Dale thought. *I could have been useful on a long-duration space flight. I could have finished my tour on ISS. You stupid son of a bitch.*

Makali emerged. "What took you so long?

She pointed upward. "I got up to the next floor."

"Deck. And I didn't see any access."

"It was sort of a tube against the wall."

"Bulkhead."

"You can stop that any time," she said. "Especially since you didn't find any whatever-you-call-it."

"Whatever. What was on the upper floor?

"I'm sure it was the . . . the flight deck, okay? But it was just scraped and messed up, mostly open pipes, as if it had been stripped." She thought for a moment. "It looked a little like the inside of *Brahma*."

"Hey, you two!" Zack was calling from the base of the spacecraft. "Let's go!"

The jumps down—Makali first, followed by Dale—were easy, with one exception: They both landed on two feet like parachutists, then bounced at least two meters in the air like trampoliners, before coming to rest again . . . this time like tumblers.

"Suits okay?" Zack said, sounding worried.

"So far," Dale said. Zack was already turning away, with Makali following him, rushing out ahead of Valya and Williams, leading the march toward Mt. St. Helens Vent.

Dale found himself bringing up the rear with Williams, who was moving slowly. "How are you doing, friend?"

"Not good. I've had a kind of stitch in my side the last mile or so." God bless him, he was a metric refusenik. "I'm finding it rather difficult to breathe. And my vision . . . it's like there's a blue-colored overlay on everything now."

Now that Williams had mentioned it, Dale realized he was seeing the same thing. "How blue, exactly? I'm getting a kind of sky-blue tinge—"

"Dodger blue."

They were talking quietly, walking within a meter of

each other. Dale had no idea who had heard what. "Hey, everyone! Have you noticed any changes to your suit, and vision?"

Zack stopped to let everyone catch up. "Now that you mention it," he said, "I'm seeing some blue sky in my vision. I thought it was the skinsuit reacting to all the brightness."

"Mine is darker," Valya announced.

"How are you feeling?" Dale asked her.

"Steps are beginning to be hard work."

"Are you still feeling the pinpricks?"

She seemed surprised by the question. "No."

Dale got a sick feeling in his stomach. "Zack," he said, "I think the suits are trying to tell us they're running down."

It was impossible to read expressions, difficult even to read body language. Dale had to give it to Zack; he revealed nothing of what had to be real concern. "That's a good thought, and a good reminder that we should pick up the pace," he said. "Everyone! Off we go again!"

Instead of leading, however, he stayed back like a Marine drill instructor, as Makali, Valya, and Williams passed by.

Zack grabbed Dale and moved with him, pointing directly at Williams's back without saying anything. The message was obvious: *Help him.*

"Any thoughts on what we do when we get to the next vent? The process of getting into these things was . . . unique. Do they have a machine that cuts us out of them?"

Makali said, "Remember the vesicles? They just dissolved."

Williams stopped. "I'm sorry, folks. Dodger blue has given way to indigo . . ."

He swayed visibly, then pitched forward onto his face.

Zack and Dale reached him at the same time, rolling him onto his back. "Is he breathing?" Zack asked.

"Hard to tell—" In fact, it was impossible to tell. Wait! He managed to see Williams's face through the skinsuit mesh. His eyes were open. "Hey, Wade, stick with us, friend! We're within sight of the vent," Dale lied. "We'll carry you."

With Zack's help, they got Williams upright, then onto Dale's shoulders in an awkward fireman's carry. "Can you manage this?"

"Zack, he weighs about five kilograms." While he had to remind himself not to turn too sharply, it wasn't difficult carrying Wade Williams.

It was just frightening. With every step Dale took, he wondered if the next one would see Williams's suit dissolving into dust . . . and Williams suffering an agonizing death-by-vacuum in his arms.

There was also the matter of his own skinsuit status. "I'm darker than blue sky right now," he said.

"Substantially darker here," Valya said. Christ, someone was going to have to carry her next.

He really wished they hadn't stopped at the alien lander.

HARLEY

"All right then, how long has it been?"

"I make it eight hours," Weldon said. "Not a word from Zack since what, according to my watch, was about nine a.m."

"And nothing from Rachel, either."

"Or Zhao?"

"No."

Harley was in front of the Temple, under the gauzy, eternally twilit sky, out of his wheelchair and sitting on a bench, which was a fresh furnishing, thanks to the Jaidev team of Temple Operators and Reconstructors, his newly favorite human beings. He had drunk some Temple coffee and eaten some Temple energy bars. He couldn't honestly say that this made him feel great, or even good.

He just felt a lot better than he had this morning. Tired, yes, but workout tired, not depressed tired.

That was the physical side. Mentally? Quite the opposite.

He had a college buddy named Kirk Dearborn who had become a television director. Fifteen years ago, Harley had visited Kirk in Los Angeles on the set of some crime procedural drama. He had done the whole day in the life, showing up with Kirk and the crew and staying until wrap. (Kirk had insisted, because he hoped to do a project set at the Johnson Space Center and was setting Harley up for a reciprocal day.)

The one memory Harley took away from that day—beyond the efficiency of the crew, the constant availability of food, and the notable physical attractions, even when wearing lab coats, of the female cast members—was the constant barrage of questions aimed at Kirk. Lighting. Lenses. Lines. Times. Clothing. Makeup. At one point, he asked his friend, "Are all these things up to you?"

"Hell, no! I'm just a hired hand. Every real decision is made by the show runner." He had smiled. "But I'm the director on the set, so everyone asks me over and over, just to be sure."

That was what Harley Drake felt like after his first two thirds of a day as mayor. As if dozens of people were constantly approaching him for decisions that either they could have made themselves or were not makeable by Harley Drake. He rubbed his eyes.

"And what about our investigation?"

Weldon shrugged. "Oh, I don't think there's any doubt; someone broke that gal's neck."

"Who?"

"Jones is working that. First cut is, it could have been something basic and stupid—an argument over water or food."

"And what's the second cut?"

Weldon hesitated.

"Shane?"

"My sense, it's some hostile force inherent in the environment, likely some entity we don't understand."

"Hostile? You mean like, alien murderer? Are we ready to go there, Shane?"

"Remember what Zack said about this Sentry. This habitat only *looks* empty. Things could be hiding anywhere, or moving in and out of here at will."

Harley held up his hand, as if by gesture he could change Weldon's whole worldview. "We're just refugees, Shane! We're not at war."

"Our planet was attacked, we were kidnapped and dumped. . . . With all due respect, Mr. Mayor, that feels like war to me."

"'Poland first?'" Harley couldn't help remembering an old comedy routine.

"More like Pearl Harbor." Shane Weldon, however, had not risen in the cutthroat world of NASA and the Johnson Space Center by being openly confrontational. His tone immediately changed. "Remember, of course, that my default setting is paranoid."

"So noted."

"I came out here to see how you were holding up."

"Fine," he lied. "What about you? What about . . . everyone else?"

"I'm great, Harls," Weldon said. "There's nothing better than *not* having responsibility."

"How did you manage to get out of the mayor's job again?"

"Fast feet, I guess." He put his hand on Harley's shoulder. "Look, I have some idea what you're going through. But my impression? Most folks are happier now than since they got scooped up. This has been a good day for the Houston-Bangalores."

Harley had to laugh. "Every time I hear that, I think you're talking about a minor league baseball team."

"Another few days like we had with the Temple today, we'll be ready for the bigs."

"You think so?"

"Stability looms. Water's a question, of course. But, given that we've been able to pull drinkable liquid out of the Temple system already, I can't believe potable water is a problem." Weldon smiled. "Before long, we'll be able to start manipulating this environment."

"We'll probably have to create our own EPA to keep us from polluting the place."

"Not if I can help it," he said.

Harley knew that Weldon was a passionate hater of most government regulations. "Where did Sasha get to?"

"She's off with the baby."

"Of course. Hi, Xavier." The young garbage collector had approached and was waiting patiently. Back to Weldon: "How is the new food turning out?

Weldon smiled. "More of it all the time, and more variety—"

"—and better." To Xavier, Harley said, "Don't take this the wrong way, kid, but I'm pretty sure I'm never going to eat a fucking pawpaw again."

"They aren't number one on my hit parade, Mr. Drake. I just want the Indians to make some utensils."

Harley turned to Weldon. "There's an order from the mayor for life: utensils, plates, cups."

"And food to fill them. Got it."

"Did you need something from me?" Harley asked Xavier.

"I was supposed to tell you this: It's not from India."

"What isn't?"

"Your Woggle-Bug."

"Really?"

"One of Mr. Nayar's guys says so. He has a degree in etymology."

"Entomology, you mean." Harley turned to Weldon, then back to Xavier. "How can he be sure? I mean, even if I knew a lot about bugs, I don't think I could say for certain that a specific one *couldn't* be found in North America." Harley thought back to what Zack had said about this Revenant process. "Maybe it's a prehistoric bug, from some floating racial memory."

"I was there, too," Weldon said. "Nayar says it is not a terrestrial insect. It has none of the required features."

"Why didn't you just say that?" Harley frowned. Another mystery. "Well, thanks—"

"They want you to come see it," Xavier said.

Harley sighed. "Shane, can you help me into my chair?"

In a corner of the ground floor of the Temple, Nayar and Jaidev's team had created a habitat within a habitat for the Woggle-Bug: a flat, hemispherical glass jar resting on the floor.

"What was this supposed to be?" Harley said. "This little glass cage?"

"A serving dish, we think," Jaidev said. "It's not really glass, any more than anything else we've replicated is plastic or ceramic or metal. But we have found a sort of menu in the commands. . . ."

"When you get back to it, we need more things like this. Real dishes."

"We want to replicate a table next," the Indian mission director said. "I don't like this on the floor."

"I don't think furniture for the Woggle-Bug terrarium is a priority," Harley said. "I'm surprised you bothered with this . . . upside-down dish. Won't it suffocate?"

"We were prepared to drill some tiny holes," Nayar said. "But we did a little test; being without oxygen doesn't seem to bother it."

"What bothers me, a little, is that you tried," Harley said. "It's a bug, so what? Don't we have bigger problems? Don't we need other goods?"

"I think," Weldon said, seeing that Nayar was stiffening at the idea of having to defend his decision, "that the position here is, we really don't know what this critter is. Let's keep it isolated and under control."

Harley was happy to express his objections through Weldon. It was becoming a familiar method. "In theory, fine. But I'm not convinced it's alien, or dangerous, or either way, that sticking it under glass is going to make any difference. We don't know what any of this stuff really is! It's not as though we were handed the directions when we showed up!" He turned to Nayar. "Vikram, your guys have done a fantastic job unlocking the secrets of the Temple. I think it would be better for all of us if that's what they kept doing. We'll get our exospecialist looking at Woggle-Bug here."

"And where *is* our exospecialist?" Nayar said in his most quiet voice.

"Expected back any minute."

Nayar pointed at the bug. "Mr. Drake, have you *looked* at this creature?"

Mr. Drake? "I saw it in Camilla's hand—" Harley said, then stopped. Well, no, he hadn't examined it. The Woggle-Bug, to him, had looked like a cartoon version of an insect, all bright colors and edges. "Okay, I'm looking now."

Nayar knelt down so his finger touched the glass. "The more closely you observe it, the more strange it seems. It doesn't seem organic, not as I recognize such things. It's almost . . . fractal." He straightened up. "And it's bigger."

"Bigger than what?"

"Bigger than it was when we first put it in the jar," Jaidev said.

"How can you tell? Did you replicate a ruler, too?" Harley was getting frustrated.

Jaidev pulled a pen out of his shirt pocket and was about to give Harley a demonstration, but Nayar stopped him.

"Three of us examined it and three of us came to the same conclusion."

"Okay, fine," Harley said. "It's weird and it's growing. Where's the entomologist? Let's ask him."

"I'm the entomologist," Nayar said. "It was my undergraduate field of study before I joined ISRO."

Harley was not a card player, but he knew when he held a weak hand and should consider folding. "My apologies. What do you suggest we do, once we have the bug properly isolated and under observation?"

"By default, we're starving it," Nayar said. "We don't know what it uses for nourishment, anyway."

"What if the critter takes being starved as a hostile act?"

"Yeah, like me with the Objects," Weldon said. One of the Indian engineers laughed, but only for the time it took Nayar to shoot him a cold look.

"Tomorrow we try adding different substances to its environment. Water, for example, to see whether it reacts."

"That would be fine," Harley said. He couldn't imagine what good or bad it would do. But he needed Nayar and his team happy, and if playing Mr. Wizard with an alien bug would help—

"Thank you," Nayar said. He signaled to Jaidev and the others, and they all headed for the ramp and the upstairs.

Watching them go, Harley noticed Camilla sitting quietly in a corner, apparently having watched the whole exchange.

He rolled toward her. Even though she seemed alert, she looked pale, even sickly, to Harley. There were actual shadows under her eyes. Knowing she couldn't understand him, he smiled and pointed to her arm. "Better? *Bueno?*"

She seemed to understand, nodding politely. Sasha must have scrounged a Band-Aid from the RV or another source. It covered the wound.

Then he pointed at the bug and the dish. "You can go over there, if you want."

Hesitantly, she went over to it. With a glance back at Harley, as if for permission, she sat, smoothly assuming a posture that in Harley's world could be attained only by a yoga instructor, or a rubber-jointed child.

"Shane," he said to Weldon, "can you get Sasha for me?"

"Have you forgiven me yet?"

Harley almost jumped. He had been so intent on the girl that he hadn't noticed Sasha sneaking up behind him.

"Shouldn't I be asking for forgiveness?" he said.

She sat down next to him and took his hand. "No. My father always told me, if you're ever in a personal argument and it turns out that you are objectively right, apologize at once." She smiled.

"I accept?"

"Correct response."

"How's the baby? Chandra." He was pleased that he remembered the name.

"Sleeping. One of Chitran's friends is talking to the engineers about getting some baby food out of the dispenser upstairs." She lowered her voice. "One of the Texans is on the trail of a cow, whether to milk it or—" She shook her head. "What do you need?"

He told her about the Woggle-Bug and Nayar's plan. "Since this appears to be an alien life-form, I wanted to know more about where it came from. Could you ask Camilla when or where she got bitten? And how she's feeling?"

Sasha smiled, then sat down next to Camilla, who had been examining the bug and its habitat with a fervor Harley associated with children and beloved TV cartoons.

The girl seemed pleased to see Sasha, hugging her and jabbering in German.

"She says she's tired and hungry. And she got bitten at the plate."

"The what?" It turned out, *plate* was what Camilla called the node where she had duplicated Valya Makarova's lipstick. Which raised other questions in Harley's mind. "Yeah, how did she know about this plate? Did she just find it by accident? Are there others?"

More German. Camilla seemed to be answering freely and with enthusiasm. "She just knew to go there. And there are others."

"How many?"

"She doesn't know. She just . . . knows when she's near one, and she's passed at least"—she checked with Camilla again—"three others."

Four duplicating nodes. "What I want to know," Sasha said to Harley, "is how the plates are different from the dispenser in the Temple."

Harley's head began to hurt whenever he considered these matters. "I think Camilla's magic plates are for straight duplication, places where the habitat concentrates enough raw material, programming, and power to copy something."

"I wonder if it could copy food? Or a cat?" she said.

"Don't know." *And don't care much for the implications.*

"The Temple's dispenser is far more sophisticated. It's got more power, more raw materials"—so Jaidev theorized; no one had yet found a pipeline for goo—"more processing, more whatever. You can make something from nothing. I'm guessing, at the plate, you can only copy what you bring."

Sasha patted Camilla on the shoulder and stood up.

"God, can you imagine what it would be like if we had something like this back home?"

"Yeah," Harley said, "like American manufacturing after container ships opened up China, times a thousand. Total fucking disaster. Assuming a big ship from Earth ever shows up, I'd advise the commander to quarantine this habitat and make sure none of that magic stuff got out for about five hundred years."

"I don't understand that! You could end poverty and hunger!"

"Oh, come on, Sasha. We could have ended poverty and hunger any time since World War Two. The technology has existed. It's the will. All this think-it-make-it would do is destroy manufacturing. The only jobs would be for people who haul the raw materials around and tend the power plant. You really want to impress me? Show me the big nuke or anti-matter core that keeps the lights going in this place. That's technology Earth could use."

She pointed a finger right in his face. "You know what's really stupid?"

He braced. "Tell me."

"Arguing about this."

He laughed. She smiled and wagged her finger in a substantially friendlier manner. "But you are a dark man, Harley."

"You knew that when you hooked up with me."

"Actually, I didn't know anything about you before I showed up in Houston."

"We're even, then. Wait—" Harley realized that Camilla was singing that little song Xavier had mentioned, the one with "*rato*." "She keeps doing that. Any idea—?"

Sasha was shaking her head. "It's not German. It sounds like 'rat' and 'wall'; those are the only two words I sort of understand."

"She said she was hungry. We should get her some food."

She went away with them to the upper floor.

Harley occupied himself with leadership tasks for a while, among them setting up a "food rotation" with Weldon and Nayar.

Every now and then he would stop and think, *Come on, Zack! You know the drill! Don't leave a buddy hanging! Check in! Come back!*

When he rolled past the Woggle-Bug terrarium on his way out, he noticed that where there had been one . . . there were now two.

Odd. "Sasha! Shane! Anyone!"

ZACK

Dale said, "Zack, I think Wade's stopped breathing!"

Hearing that message, three words compressed to one came unbidden to Zack Stewart: "Shitandgoddammit!"

They were within sight of Mt. St. Helens Vent, which meant they were no more than half a kilometer from a Membrane, and possible rescue. Or escape. Or improvement in their really difficult situation.

Given that, Zack didn't want to stop. He truly didn't want to have that reason to stop. "How do you know?" he said.

"He stopped talking ten minutes ago."

Zack hadn't noticed, largely because the skinsuit-skinsuit communications were spotty and he'd already grown used to relative silence from the rear of their little column. "Wade!" he said. "Wake up, please! Talk to us!"

No response.

He could hear a faint echo as Dale tried the same tack, with no better results. "I've got to tell you, he feels like dead weight."

"Zack, for God's sake, stop so we can check him!" That was Valya, her voice blaring inside Zack's skinsuit cap. He hadn't realized she was only a meter behind him.

Fine, he stopped. So did Makali, who was actually ahead of him.

They ran to meet Dale, then helped lower Wade Williams.

He's right, Zack thought. *Dead weight.* To Makali, he said, "Can you see his eyes? Anything?"

"I'm trying. These fucking bug eyes . . ." Wade had given the skinsuit goggles the name, appropriately enough, from classic sci-fi.

"Do something!" Valya said.

Dale was growing more agitated. "It's not like we can do CPR, honey!"

"Oh, shit," Makali said, suddenly rocking back from Williams.

She had a piece of his skinsuit in her hand, from his head. "It just . . . peeled off!"

As Zack and the others watched, unable to take any kind of action, Wade Williams's skinsuit began to crack and vaporize, as if melting from within. "Oh my God," Makali said. "It's just like the vesicle!"

Then Williams's entire body shuddered and clenched, as if dumped in icy water. In a way, it was like that, as his skin came into contact with the extreme temperatures of Keanu's nearly non-existent atmosphere—an effective vacuum—both unbelievably hot and chillingly cold.

"Help him!" Valya screamed.

All Zack could think to do was place his hands on Williams's chest. He felt as though he were trying to keep the poor man from exploding. Williams's blood was trying to bubble; skin, muscle, and bone were holding it in.

But not prettily. There was a second clench, then another rippling spasm.

A last breath escaped from his lips, turning to vapor, then icy crystals. Williams's body immediately hardened, as if surrendering to the environment.

Zack uttered a silent prayer from his youth. *Let the angels watch over him.*

Assuming angels could turn their eyes to this part of God's universe.

"Tell me he was dead before . . . that," Valya said.

"I believe he was," Zack said. "Terminally unconscious." He believed it, too.

"Well, that's that," Scott said.

Allowing for the limitations of the skinsuit, Valya hit Dale as hard as she could. "How can you be so callous? The man just died!"

"Shut your face! I carried him! And now we've got to get moving!"

"Knock it off, everyone," Zack said.

Makali helped to defuse the situation. "Dale, what was the last thing he said?"

"What's the—?" Scott caught himself. He realized that not only was Valya shocked by what she'd just witnessed, she was terrified that she was next. "Ah, I think it was, once I had him on my shoulder, he said, 'The view from here is tremendous.'"

"Good. Something to remember and tell his family," Makali said.

Assuming we're ever in contact with Earth again, Zack thought. *Assuming we live past the next hour.*

A lot of assumptions.

"I want to leave," Valya announced. "My indicators are almost as blue as Wade's!"

"Good idea," Dale told her, suddenly Mr. Supportive. "Are we going?"

"One thing," Zack said. Since Williams's body weighed almost nothing, Zack elected to carry it. This wasn't just courtesy or a desire not to leave a comrade on the battlefield—

The others hadn't realized it yet, but Zack would never forget: People who died on Keanu didn't necessarily stay dead.

They didn't need to have died here, and apparently their bodies could be torn asunder, too.

What would happen to Wade Williams if his body were returned to the Beehive?

God help him, Zack took Wade Williams's body with them as a science experiment.

"Zack," Makali said, "Why did Williams's suit fail so quickly?"

He would have loved to know that answer, though it was still fairly far down the list of Keanu questions he wanted answered.

"I can think of two possibilities," he said, shifting the body as he turned to check on Valya, who was being hustled along by Dale. "One is that he was a lot older than the rest of us, and the suit burned up more of whatever that suit burned keeping him alive.

"The other is . . ." And here he hesitated, because it was a theory that had been taking shape ever since he and

Megan had met the Architect. "The other is, Keanu is really old, on the order of a thousand years, maybe ten thousand years."

"Yeah, I saw that alien ship. It looked as though it had been sitting there a long goddamn time. . . ."

"I think that a lot of this place's advanced, miracle technology is malfunctioning or breaking down or worn out."

"So his suit just . . . failed."

"One possibility." He looked for Valya. She and Dale were ahead of Zack and Makali now. *Yeah, I'd be hurrying, too.* "Valya, how are you doing?"

He couldn't hear her reply, but Dale Scott flashed a clumsy thumbs-up.

Even though the white tiles remained regular and flat, it seemed to Zack that they were walking uphill. "There's the rim!" Makali said.

She ran forward, passing Valya and Dale.

"There's no way down!" Makali announced that grim news as Zack, now feeling out of breath and worrying about his own blue indicator, reached the rim. He set Williams's body down.

Mt. St. Helens Vent, on first, fragmentary glance, was larger than Vesuvius, and less symmetrical. Given the rockfalls and other features, it also looked older.

"What do you mean, no ramp?" Dale said. He and Valya had just caught them.

"What she means," Zack said, "is that we can't see a ramp yet." He turned directly to Makali. "Right?"

But she didn't answer . . . instead she began loping around the rim of the vent.

"Zack," Dale said, "we need to get Valya out of that suit ASAP."

"We all do." He watched Makali growing more and more distant. She must have expected an obvious, easily accessible structure like the ramp at Vesuvius. (He recalled his own shock at seeing it . . . the ramp was the first undeniably artificial alien structure humans had ever seen, and Zack was one of the first to do so. How quickly that seminal, world-changing moment had gotten lost in the avalanche of later discoveries.) Given the distressed nature of the Mt. St. Helens walls, Zack wasn't ready to announce that there was no ramp.

He had to remember, too, that for all her physical fitness and hearty Aussie cheer, Makali was still an academic with limited operational experience, much like Zack when he first joined the astronaut office. She wasn't used to dealing with this kind of stress.

"Zack, are you leaving us?" Valya's voice sounded in Zack's ears.

"No!" he said. "Just looking for a route to the bottom!" In spite of his professional optimism, he was forced to admit that Makali had some support for her verdict; there was no obvious ramp wrapping around the inside of the vent cone, not on this side. The crater wall itself had crumbled in places, spilling tons of rock to the flat bottom.

Zack was suddenly worried that even if they found a way down, the tunnel into the expected habitat would be blocked.

Wouldn't that just be the shit?

"Over here!"

Had he heard that? Makali calling to him?

"Zack! Dale, Valya, over here!"

Zack quickly retraced his steps, catching up with Dale and Valya, who had not managed to get far. "I see the ramp now!" Makali said.

Zack could see her now . . . a third of the way around the rim of the vent, half a kilometer distant, literally jumping up and down like a child saying, *Pick me!*

Dale and Valya ran right past Williams's body, and Zack considered leaving it where it was, to hell with honors to comrade or science experiment.

But one lesson he had learned in his NASA career was this: When you make a good plan, stick to it. *Better* is often the enemy of *good enough*.

He made sure to pick up Williams's body.

"It doesn't go all the way to the top," Makali was saying. "That's why we couldn't see it."

Makali was being generous when she described the ramp the way she did; the top ten meters of the ramp had collapsed some time in the past.

"Is there no other way down this? A second ramp?" Scott said.

"I didn't see anything," Zack said. Makali said the same thing at the same time.

"How do we get down?" Valya said. She sounded tired; her suit was likely close to failing.

"Jump," Zack told her.

"I can't!"

"We don't have time to fuck around. Dale, grab her and start running."

Dale Scott might have been a greedy, petty prick . . . but he knew that time was short and physics was their friend.

He literally picked up a struggling Valya, circled back to give himself a running start . . . then sailed off the rim, down a distance equivalent to the height of a two-story building . . . and slid, ass first, down the ramp.

Makali turned to Zack. "Can you handle this with the body?"

"Dale just did."

No more arguments. She took her flying leap, landing more or less on her feet and skipping to a controlled stop.

Looking at the gap, at the sheer rock face below the ramp itself, at the appalling distance straight down . . . he hesitated.

Idiot. As if you're going to live another hour in this suit—

He was airborne before he knew it, but his takeoff foot slipped and he realized he had made a bad launch.

He hit low, just below his knees, and flopped forward on his face, skidding into the vent wall, meanwhile losing the body in his arms.

He might have had low gravity working for him, but he had ancient stone working against him. He felt as though he'd been tackled in a football game—could even taste blood in his mouth from where he'd bitten his lip.

The impact stunned him. For the first time in his life, he lost consciousness—likely only for a few seconds. But it was terrifying.

Then he was being helped up. Makali. She was speaking to him, but he couldn't seem to hear her. Nevertheless, he let her drag him farther down the ramp, toward the blessed darkness below.

His indicator was indigo now.

Blind, deaf, exhausted, he simply trudged down the ramp. With each step, he felt the growing sense that exploring space with him was a bad deal.

Look at the record. Dale Scott kicked off the International Space Station, the first and so far only person to suffer that fate.

Then there was his *Destiny-7* crew. Yvonne dead. Pogo dead, brought back to life, then dead again. (Did that count as one loss, or two? He knew what Dale Scott would say.)

There was one dead in the *Brahma* crew, too: Dennis Chertok could be added to his butcher's bill.

And Megan, of course.

And now Wade Williams. Possibly Valya.

"Don't mumble," Makali said. "We're almost at the bottom."

"Williams," he said.

"Worry about him later, Zack. Come on!"

And just like that, they were at the bottom, on level ground, at least, picking a path through rubble. "Someone went this way recently," Makali said. To Zack it sounded as though she were panting now, too.

He didn't have the strength to dispute or query, but Makali continued. "I saw two long, scraping tracks," she said. "Frozen stuff, bright yellow like the goo that made the skinsuits."

As they reached the broad, now-familiar access tunnel and left Keanu daylight behind, Zack found his voice. And apparently, his mind. "Maybe it's from Dale and Valya." He hoped they were ahead of them.

"It looked like the tracks we saw leading away from *Brahma*."

Deeper and deeper. Their suits had no lights, but the optics shifted into some kind of night vision. He could see Scott ahead of him, Valya in his arms.

They had stopped at the shimmering curtain that was another Membrane. Seeing it, Zack laughed out loud.

"It's funny?" Makali said.

"I'm just relieved it's here . . . I made a big assumption that this vent would have the same features Vesuvius did."

He hurried forward, taking Valya by the arm. "How are you?"

She was swaying. "Look," Scott said, pointing to her skinsuited legs.

A crack was forming even as Zack watched. "Let's go. Everyone, through the Membrane!"

It was just as he remembered it . . . walking into a chamber filled with bubbles of varying sizes, from pea to marble, that clung to the skinsuits. "Just keep walking," he said, not sure whether Valya could hear.

But she was still upright, still moving. Deeper and deeper they went. Surely they were no longer in vacuum—

Through a final cascade, like a rinse at a carwash, and they were out . . . standing in another Beehive annex.

Makali and Dale Scott pushed through moments later.

"Holy shit," Makali said.

Zack shared the sentiment; this Beehive was obviously a cousin of the one in the human habitat, but far older. It looked used, almost abused. Most of the reincarnation cells were broken, their fluids dried or dissipated. "They're bigger here," Makali said.

Yes, while they came in different sizes, most cells here were far larger than those Makali had seen, even those sized for cattle or crocs.

"Oh my God!" Zack turned away from his examination of the Beehive just in time to see Valya's skinsuit enter its terminal phase, cracking into pieces and flaking off to dissolve in a cloud of dust. Pieces of it clung to her, but clearly not in any logical pattern—one on her right arm, one around her breasts.

Wide-eyed with understandable fear—"Do it," Zack said; "we're all going to have to!"—she took the first breath.

And immediately began gasping and wheezing.

Makali looked at Zack. Even swathed in the skinsuit and hidden by the goggles, her expression was obvious: *Oh no!*

But Valya waved off assistance and began breathing more comfortably. "It's okay," she said. "Feels like oxygen. It's just . . . the smell! And it's cold!"

Zack could feel his suit going terminal. There was a moment when he thought, *I can't breathe*, but it passed. Overall, it was like having a wetsuit drop away.

He immediately understood why Valya's first breath was so difficult. There was air, yes, but probably less than humans wanted—it was like being at a mountain observatory above three thousand meters. Cold, too.

And the smell! Like the worst rotting fish he'd ever encountered. He almost gagged.

Scott's and Makali's suits began to dissolve now, too. They were all committed to entering this new habitat—

"Zack," Valya said. He was facing her, his back to the rest of the Beehive. She pointed past him.

A creature blocked the passage—a tall, multi-armed being Zack recognized as a Sentry, the same kind of alien that had killed Pogo Downey.

And Megan Stewart.

RACHEL

She couldn't breathe. She couldn't see. She couldn't move.

And something nasty was happening to her face.

Suddenly she inhaled, choked, coughed, spit, and, terrified, began to thrash.

Okay, you can breathe! She was hot, still couldn't see, but air was coming in, going out.

A gooey film covered her eyes. The same goo pinned her like an insect in a science experiment.

For a moment. With a bit of effort, she was able to tug her right arm free of the goo and wipe her eyes. The only difficulty was that someone or something kept bumping her and, strangely, wiping her face.

"Stop that!" she screamed, though she heard nothing and started coughing again. Finally she got both hands free and cleared her eyes.

She was still in the passage, more or less sitting up, though cocooned in a settling, hardening, drying sea of goo . . . and Cowboy was flailing around in it, too.

He barked. At least, his gooey muzzle opened twice. No, she couldn't hear. Goo in her ears, too.

Her first move was to grab the dog. He seemed terrified. No wonder; he'd been in the dark for hours, and now he'd been swept up in some kind of tsunami. "It's okay, boy, everything's okay," she said, knowing the words made no sense, but hoping the sound of a human voice would calm the animal.

And when he grew calm, so would she.

A human touch seemed to work. The dog began licking her face again. Normally this would have been annoying, but this was not a normal situation.

She did more work on her ears, wiping away some of the goo, improving her hearing considerably. "Pav!" she called. "Zhao! Where are you guys?"

With the tunnel so filled with plasm and the sound so deadened, she didn't expect a response.

They might be dead, she realized. Before long, she might be dead, too.

Then Cowboy barked—she could hear him now—and struggled out of her arms. He began digging at a mound of goo to her left . . . which quickly revealed itself to be Pav, who was shouting in Hindi.

Zhao was to Pav's left. They were both alive, trying to extricate themselves.

Rachel dug in and helped. Allowing for a considerable amount of struggle as well as grunting and groaning, it went quickly. Rachel realized that the goo was not only hardening, it was drying out, turning to powder.

Pav was able to stand up and hug her. "Thank you," he said, his voice muffled and old-sounding.

Cowboy bumped up against Pav. Though there was almost no light, they could see that the dog's coat was crusted with goo. Flakes fell off every time he moved.

And even with all this activity around him, Zhao just

sat there, head down. "Come on, get up," Rachel told him.

"We have nowhere to go," Zhao said.

"Oh, for God's sake," Rachel said. She and Pav tugged Zhao upright. "Are you just going to sit there and wait to die?"

"At the moment, that seems to be the practical choice."

Rachel understood his feeling. In that first instant after regaining consciousness, feeling herself trapped, blind, deaf, she had considered simply . . . letting it all go.

Some force inside her had taken charge and made her fight. And now she was glad she had. Yes, the situation was grim. But everything about her situation on Keanu was that way.

She would be letting her father down if she simply died. Maybe it was that simple.

"We're walking," she said. "That way."

That way was simply farther down the passage in the direction they had just been carried by the wave of goo. It didn't seem smart to go back the way they had come.

She just hoped they would find an escape before their little supply of water ran out, along with their energy.

The good thing—the only good thing—about the goo was that in an hour's time, it dried up and flaked off, leaving little residue.

The bad thing—being buried continued to have a bad effect on Zhao, who seemed numb. Rachel and Pav had had to wipe the stuff off him; he wasn't much help. Even after he could breathe and stand up, he was pretty much a zombie.

After an initial burst of enthusiasm about being alive, Pav wasn't much better. "Do we just keep walking until we drop?"

"If the only other choice is sit here until we die, yes." She realized she had to do better than that, even for herself. She patted Cowboy, who was happily walking with them and not getting one step ahead. "The dog seems fine. Maybe he found water or a way out."

"If he did," Zhao said, emerging from sullen silence, "why is he still trapped with us?"

For a moment, Rachel wondered if she and Pav and Cowboy wouldn't have been better off if Zhao had never emerged from the goo. Even back in the habitat, her initial impression of the man hadn't been positive. He was a spy and a foreigner.

Until Rachel ran into the beings that built Keanu and killed her mother, Zhao was the closest thing to an alien she had ever met.

"When I figure out how to ask him," she said, "I'll let you know."

An hour after their bath in plasm goo, Rachel and Pav looked and felt the same as they had before.

The passage looked the same. There had been no further appearances of the gravity marble. The dog had been content to trot with them, bumping into their legs for reassurance. Things weren't exactly good . . . but they could have been worse.

And Pav had resumed talking. "Hey, Rachel, how far do you think we've walked?"

Rachel knew a human could cover half a dozen kilometers in an hour, with a steady walk. But their progress had not been steady. On the other hand, they had easily walked for three hours. "I don't know. Ten kilometers?"

"How long was the habitat?"

"Less than that, from where we started." There was no point ignoring the obvious problem. "But we haven't been going in a straight line."

"Yeah," Pav said. "We could be going around the end of the habitat."

"Right!"

Zhao spoke up now, too. "Or completely away from it into the interior of the NEO."

Rachel had an idea, something her mother had taught her. "Would that be so bad?"

Zhao turned to face her. His expression showed disbelief bordering on anger, which was an improvement over his zombie-like silence. "If we want to return to human beings with human food, yes."

"How do we know there isn't water and food elsewhere in the NEO?"

"We don't!" he said. "We don't know anything!"

"Oh, we know a little, don't we?" she said, making sure to keep walking, dragging Zhao and Pav and Cowboy with her. "I mean, look," she said, waving at the passage around them. "We know that somewhere, there was a race of beings that just wanted to let the universe know they existed. So . . . they took one of their moons—"

"Whoa," Pav said. "We don't know this was one of

their moons." With the authority only a sixteen-year-old boy could assume, he said, "Planets like Earth can only have one."

"Turns out Earth used to have a good-sized second moon," Zhao said.

"That's just a theory," Pav said. Rachel smiled to herself, not that anyone could see her expression in the near-darkness. *Pav's getting into the game.*

Zhao said, "A theory with more foundation than your assumption that the Architects originated on a planet like Earth."

"Fine," Pav said. "But am I wrong if I say that, somewhere in the galaxy, there's a race that has the power to leave its home planet, fly across space, reach this planetoid, and put some kind of engine on it to move it into orbit around its home planet? Or that they spent a century or five centuries hollowing it out, creating habitats, rewiring it, replumbing it?"

Pav smiled, clearly enjoying his fantasy. "Or that they put some kind of shithot miracle motor inside it, antimatter, maybe? And then they put some of their people aboard and sent it into space?"

"It's obvious that *something* like that must have happened," Zhao said. "But why would anyone do such a thing?" Listening to his growing agitation, Rachel feared she was going to be personally challenged to justify the Architects and all their actions. "Exploration?"

"How about invasion?" Pav said.

"I don't know," Rachel said. "Although I can't imagine what you would find on another planet that would be worth a trip of a thousand or ten thousand years. What?

Water? Slaves?" She had heard some of this from her father. He would often sit with her and watch old sci-fi movies like *Independence Day* or *War of the Worlds* . . . but he would never sit quietly.

"How about our music?" Pav said.

"What, they came here for Beethoven?"

"A thousand years ago they wouldn't have heard of Beethoven."

"You were the one who suggested music," Rachel said. "Besides, they could get our music by listening. They wouldn't have to *come* here."

"He just means art," Zhao said. "Which is as valid an argument as any, given the utter lack of information." He not only seemed engaged in the conversation, he was actually striding out with purpose. "Exploration, maybe. Invasion, no. But there is another motivation: the search for new products and ideas."

Pav laughed out loud. "That's China for you. 'Give us your ideas and we'll build them more cheaply than you. And sell them back to you.'"

Zhao's head turned to Pav with such energy that Rachel expected a punch to follow. But the Chinese engineer and spy merely smiled. "That has been China's philosophy for thirty years," he said. "We learned it from the Japanese and the Americans and the English before them."

"Speaking of business," Rachel said, "I wonder how expensive something like Keanu is. I mean, could the Architects afford to build one, or a hundred?"

"And how does it support itself?" Zhao said, clearly

warming to the subject. "Are these habitats filled with objects or machines or materials that can be traded?"

"I don't think so," Pav said. "If they came here to trade spices and furs, why did they scoop us up? As I recall, they weren't even stopping until we landed here."

"Maybe the landing showed them that we might have something worth trading," Rachel said. She was having a tough time concentrating on these subjects—normally they would have bored her. And she thought she might be seeing a turn in the tunnel ahead.

The others said nothing, however, and the dog stayed where he was, pacing them.

"But then why did they acquire two hundred human beings?" Zhao said.

"Maybe they trade *people*, not stuff," Pav said, shooting a *gotcha* smile behind Zhao's back at Rachel.

"Nonsense," Zhao said. "If anything, they would be trading information, which really wouldn't require a vessel this size or a mission lasting thousands of years. There would be . . . no point."

"Speaking of lack of points," Rachel said, "do you really think Keanu was a giant starship filled with aliens or machines?" She knew it was all speculation, but she had a strategy. Megan Doyle Stewart had once told Rachel, "Some people don't want to talk, or think they don't, especially after a trauma like a train crash or a tsunami. Get them to argue. Get them talking about money or religion or politics, and they'll open right up."

And it had worked! Rachel had been burdened with two men who were like statues, and in order to get their spirits back from wherever they were hiding, Rachel had provoked them into an argument! Pav had picked up on it!

Maybe he wasn't so dim. "What else would it be?" he said.

"Well," she said, grateful again for the hours of space-related chat that her parents had bored her with, "if you don't have some magic stardrive, you know that anything you launch is going to take thousands of years to reach its destination. Machines simply don't last, right?" She directed the last question at Zhao.

"It's difficult to think of materials lasting a millennium," he said, "much less anything that uses heat or energy or moving parts."

"So, what I think they did," Rachel said, and she really was enjoying this, "is they had this goo, this nano-stuff, that didn't have moving parts and wasn't some kind of brittle material. It was just the stuff you could make anything out of, assuming you had enough energy. They probably didn't have to bring a thousand workers to Keanu . . . they didn't have to build anything. They'd already built it on their home planet." To Zhao, she said, "Whatever it looked like. They sent the goo and the instructions here. It built itself. And it keeps building itself."

Zhao laughed. "But the instructions! The programming! The macro controls . . . I can't imagine the complexity, the processing power. It's as if . . . you might need a good chunk of the time and energy of an entire star!"

"Maybe that's what they had," Rachel said. "They

were doing whatever they were doing a thousand or ten thousand years ago."

"I can't see it," Zhao said.

"I see it," Pav said.

"Oh, really—" Zhao's tone was sarcastic, but he never finished the sentence.

"Not your argument," Pav said. "That."

He pointed ahead of them, where there was more light—and sufficient light to see shapes and structures.

Cowboy barked and took off.

Rachel began jogging toward the light.

"Looks fresh," Pav said.

Rachel and Pav arrived within a couple of minutes to find not only an intersection where another passage crossed theirs . . . but that one of the branches opened into a small Beehive.

And, as Pav had noted fairly recently, the walls were dripping and the cells pulsed with light.

"Maybe that was what all that goo was doing," Rachel said. "Flowing down here to, I don't know, rearrange things."

Zhao had finally caught up with them. Panting, he said, "Why were you running?" Then, seeing what was around them, he stopped. "Oh."

"This is what they call a Beehive," Rachel said. "And that is one of the pods that just hatched . . . something."

Pav grabbed her arm. "Some*one*," he said, pointing down one of the passages.

Looking a bit like a revived mummy from an old monster movie, a human figure was shambling away from them.

Rachel gasped. It had happened before; why couldn't it happen again?

"Mom!" she called.

"Hey," Pav said, grabbing her. "Wait."

He pointed down the passage to their left, the one that terminated in the Beehive.

The entire cylinder was rippling.

"That's not good," Rachel said.

The ripples were moving toward them, and they looked bigger and stronger than anything she'd seen. A big, nasty cat's-eye was headed directly toward them.

VALYA

This had, without doubt, been the worst day of Valentina Makarova's life. It wasn't as long as the agonizing day when her father had been struck while walking drunk on a Moscow highway and been taken to a hospital to die. It wasn't as physically taxing as the time she had contracted pneumonia and was out of her mind with fever and fear.

It wasn't as disorienting as last week's transit from Earth to Keanu in the vesicle.

But this day combined the worst of all three.

And it did not appear to be over yet.

In fact, confronting a large, terrifying alien just as she and Dale, Zack, and Makali had reached some kind of shelter meant there was only bad yet to come.

Valya knew she had not been an example of plucky pioneer spirit or gritty determination on the trek from Vesuvius Vent to this one. She had, in fact, spent most of the hike on the edge of hysteria—

To her amazement, Zack was right in front of the alien. Of course, there was almost nowhere else to go. Valya, Dale, and Makali were crowded behind him.

The Sentry was half again as tall as a human being, roughly symmetrical; it had a head, a torso, two arms, and two legs. But it also had two other pairs of arms protruding from its midsection. All arms ended in similar flaplike hands—each with half a dozen long fingers, at least two of them opposable.

The left lower arm was brandishing what looked like a piece of aluminum tubing.

The creature was blue-green in color—that was either its skin or clothing or possibly armor. The skin looked shiny and hard to Valya.

The face was shadowed, hard to see. Complicating everything, the creature seemed to be swathed in the same flaking skinsuit material as the four humans.

"You know this thing?" Makali said.

"Its type. I've seen two," Zack said. "Killed one."

The Sentry, if that was what it was, remained motionless . . . like a jungle cat waiting to pounce, Valya thought. As Zack slowly moved side to side, apparently looking for a chance to dash around the Sentry, the alien reacted, rotating its big, thick body. On the second move, Valya saw something shiny and anomalous, a silvery piece of metal embedded in the Sentry's back, and what looked like blood discoloring it.

Not that she had any right to think this, given her limited experience, but it seemed that the alien had trouble moving to its right.

"Zack," she said.

"Something to offer, Valya?"

"I think he's hurt!"

As if to prove her wrong, the Sentry took a swipe at Zack's head, prompting a scream from Makali and, from Dale, "Valya, just shut up!"

But Zack easily ducked the blow, and Valya grew more convinced that the alien was wounded.

"He's not going to be able to hit you, Zack."

"I hope you're right!" he said.

"Zack, what are you trying to do?" Makali said.

"Get past him—" He tried it again; the Sentry took a second swipe at him, but this one was so slow and clumsy that Zack was able to grab the tube.

And yank it out of the Sentry's grasp!

"Way to go!" Dale yelled. "See how he likes it!"

Fortunately, instead of clobbering the creature—which, given its size, would still be a bit of a trick—Zack merely brandished it . . . and was rewarded with the sight of the alien backing away and sinking down.

"*What* is going on?" Makali said.

"I told you," Valya said. "It's injured. Look at the back."

The Sentry had lowered itself, folding its legs, until it was only as tall as they were. It leaned its good side against the wall of the Beehive . . . and now they could all see the obvious injury.

"Zack," Makali said, "we can get past him."

But Zack was regarding the creature, which was now gesturing with five of its six arms. (The one closest to the wound was hanging limp.) "I think it's trying to talk to us."

"I don't hear anything," Dale said.

"Sign language," Valya said.

Dale turned to her and smiled nastily. "Oh, good, right in your wheelhouse. Translate, will you?"

"Fuck you," she said. But Dale's mean-spirited suggestion wasn't too far wrong; Valya knew two different sign language systems. If anyone could figure out what the Sentry was trying to say, she would be the one.

Of course, it might take years. And given its physical condition, she wasn't sure the Sentry would last another hour.

But Zack was already taking the lead. He slowly laid the tube on the ground—out of the Sentry's reach, Valya hoped. Then he pointed to himself and his fellows, saying, in turn, "Human, human, human, human." Then pointed to the Sentry, and opened his hands in what, for human beings, would have been an obvious *Who are you?* gesture.

The Sentry flapped its hands in what seemed to be a reply. If, looking from left to right, you numbered the alien's upper hands as one and two, its middle pair as three four, and the lower, almost vestigial pair, as five six, the response went: *two, one, four.*

Or so Valya chose to see it. It would be difficult enough to decode these gestures in normal circumstances; the creature was wounded and likely not using hand number three. How would that change the message?

Zack was holding palms up, gently waving them, saying, *We mean no harm.*

The Sentry had no reply.

Zack carefully pointed to the wound. Then he tapped himself on the chest. "Ow!" He made a creditable howling-in-pain sound.

"Christ," Dale said softly, but loud enough for Valya to hear.

All she could do was shoot him a dire look. Was he stupid or just evil? Any extraneous sound or movement was going to confuse the Sentry!

The Sentry used all three major arms to touch its chest. Then it pointed to the wound as best it could, all three hands.

And made a sound of its own! It was *loud*, like having a whale singing a meter away!

"Holy shit," Makali said. This time Valya did not feel the need to offer censure; she was thinking the same thing.

Holding up his right hand, as if to say, *Let me try this*, Zack slowly reached toward the Sentry . . . toward the wound.

The Sentry's head turned slowly, cautiously—or so it seemed to Valya. But it did not raise a hand to block Zack's move.

Zack actually touched the metal shard with a fingertip.

The Sentry remained frozen, though clearly wary.

Zack closed index finger and thumb on the shard and tried to wiggle it.

The Sentry made a sound, but not the roar; this was closer to a growl.

But, Valya noted with fascination . . . no hand gestures at all!

Zack slowly moved his hand away. He thought for a moment, then brought his hands together, almost in prayer. "Stuck tight," he said. The Sentry merely looked at him.

Now Zack turned to Makali. "How are your surgical skills?"

"Non-existent," she said. "And I hope that doesn't mean—"

"We're going to take that thing out. A little goodwill gesture."

"Like Androcles and the lion?" Valya said, as amused as she was horrified by the idea.

"Didn't the lion wind up eating Androcles?" Dale said.

Everyone ignored him. "It looks to me as though our friend was wearing one of the skinsuits, which really gives me some crazy ideas, given the blood you saw, and the fact that this piece of tube looks terrestrial. But to the point: I think the skinsuit sealed around the wound and is keeping that shard in place."

"Why would it be better to have it out?" Makali clearly didn't want to become the designated space surgeon, and Valya couldn't blame her.

"If you had a bullet or an arrow stuck in you, you'd want it out."

"I'm human."

"The Sentry is a living being. I think the rule still applies: Foreign objects should come out."

"Yeah," Dale said, "we don't want this guy to develop an infection. Although it might make it easier to get around him."

"We can get around him now," Zack said. "Consider that the habitat beyond is his. And that there might be a dozen just like him waiting for us."

"One thing: You're calling this guy 'him.' Can we just say 'it' for now?"

Zack ignored, that, too, turning back to Makali. "If you want me to do it, fine. But I'm a little shaky—"

"Okay, I'll do it." Makali smiled. "I'm the exospecialist, right? My bailiwick. What do I do, just . . . pull the thing out?"

Zack pointed to the ratty Hermès bag mushed against Valya's stomach. "Anything useful in there?" he said. Valya shook her head.

Then Zack indicated the mesh bag around Makali's neck. "Okay, then, what's in that?"

"Probably screwdrivers and pliers."

Zack smiled. "I think a pliers would be just the instrument."

"I hope there's a staple gun in here, too," Makali said, slowly removing the kit and kneeling to open it.

"Why?"

She smiled, getting into the spirit of the insane adventure. "To stitch *it* up."

Zack turned back to the Sentry, who seemed, to Valya, to be fading. Loss of blood? Or some similarly vital fluid? If so, given the paucity of fluid on the ground, it was likely internal bleeding.

Which argued in favor of Zack's surgery.

"Needle-nose pliers," Makali said.

"Let me have it," Zack said. He plucked it from the kit and slowly brought it into the Sentry's view. He opened it once, twice. Then he slowly, carefully moved the pliers over to the shard, then back.

The Sentry gestured—one flip of the number two hand. *It's a lefty*, Valya thought. And said, "It was a simple gesture. It's either yes—"

"Or no," Dale said.

"Let's assume yes," Zack said. He was slowly handing the pliers back to Makali. Then, after again establishing eye contact with the Sentry, he moved Makali into position with the pliers.

"Okay, doc," he told her. "Do your thing. Just move slowly."

Valya could see that Makali's hands were trembling. But her body language was completely resolute, like a high diver on a platform.

She took two slow, almost bridelike steps, which put her within reach of the Sentry and its shard. Then, like a mime, she slowly unfolded her hand and the pliers, and locked the nose onto the shard.

At that moment, Zack turned to the Sentry, clutching his left hand with his right, as if the left were injured, and making a growling sound.

Then he opened the hands and smiled, as if to say, *It'll all be over in a second.*

And he told Makali, "Proceed. And everybody be prepared to jump back."

Makali made a first, tentative tug, with no results, not even a grunt from the Sentry.

"He's the size of an NFL lineman," Zack said. "You're going to have to pull harder than that."

"I have no leverage," Makali said. "It's too high—"

"Just do it."

Another tug. Nothing.

"Goddammit," Makali said. But she kept her right hand on the pliers, using her left to wipe sweat from her eyes.

The Sentry made a gesture and a sound. This was unlike its early communications: the gesture used the lower working hand, and the sound was more high-pitched.

"It's telling you to go ahead," Valya said, unable to stop herself. *How can you be sure of that?*

"What if he bleeds out?"

"That's a risk *it* will have to take," Dale said.

As Valya watched, Makali put more and steadier pressure on the pliers, moving it ever so slightly from side to side.

And the shard began to move.

Valya could see the Sentry shudder, likely with pain.

In a few seconds, the bloody shard was out, dropping to the floor.

Makali was rooted where she stood, in shock at what she had wrought. Zack gently edged her aside and examined the wound. "Some bleeding," he said. "Doesn't look infected, though I'm not sure I would know it."

The Sentry seemed to have its own idea about how to treat the injury. It used both upper hands to hammer at the covering of the nearest intact cell. Breaking through, it withdrew a handful of yellow substance that it swiftly transferred to the wound, which was now within reach.

Then it turned away and began shambling deeper into the Beehive.

"What, not even a thank you, masked man?" Dale said.

"It made some gestures," Valya said, not entirely

untruthfully; the creature had flapped its good lower left hand several times in what seemed to be movement unrelated to scooping and placing the goo. She chose to interpret that as *Thank you*, or even *You can go now*. She said, "It may not have a cultural history of gratitude. Even some human cultures are like that."

"What next?" Makali said. She was busy trying to clean the bloodied pliers on her pants leg, then replacing the tool in the kit—all with trembling hands.

"I don't know about you guys," Zack said, "but I'm getting hungry."

"And thirsty," Dale said.

"I think we follow our friend and see if he has a cultural history of hospitality."

XAVIER

Xavier Toutant doubted he would ever be as comfortable in the Keanu habitat as he had been in Houston—even though he hated Houston. Life here was too raw, too unfamiliar, and too complicated. He missed Momma and his friends, he missed television, he missed having fun.

He was having no fun here. None.

But the one thing in Keanu's favor . . . there was no real night. No spooky wolf hours. Xavier had never liked the dark. Nothing good had ever happened to him much after the sun went down.

The lights in the Keanu sky never dimmed. It never got much brighter than twilight, but it never got much darker.

He loved that. It made him daring. He set off for the Beehive, on his own, without having to ask permission—without expecting to see anyone dogging his path. Should he be stopped, he had prepared an answer to the question, "Where do you think you're going?" And it was, "To see if we're going to have chickens or ducks." He wasn't doing any cooking, because there wasn't any cooking to do yet, but Mr. Drake and Mr. Weldon knew that he had been a cook and wanted to cook again.

He even had a motive that he would keep to himself, which was this: He had gotten by for a couple of days trading those candy bars. But he was down to his last two, and when they were gone, he would need new currency.

He couldn't get close to the machines on the second floor of the Temple, but he could explore the Beehive. Surely there would be something of use here.

Not that he expected to be stopped and questioned.

Whether it was having more and fresher food in their bellies, or cumulative exhaustion, the HBs turned in early and en masse that night. The only exceptions were Vikram Nayar's Temple team; veterans of projects in the IT world, they seemed eager to work all night unlocking secrets of the Temple.

Xavier wished them all the luck in the world. He was grateful that they'd figured out how to get some food out of the place, and even a few utensils.

They'd made a lot of progress in one day. Who knew what would be spilling out of the Temple over the next week or two months?

They might even build a house or twenty!

They could even build a whole town . . . complete with a farm, of sorts. Maybe a barn, too.

Because Xavier was seeing and hearing about animals emerging from the Beehive.

Xavier had seen the dog, of course. And then a cow, which some of the Houston people had claimed and were trying to feed.

And toward the end of this day, as operations and experiments in the Temple continued, he had seen birds flying against the strange ceiling of the habitat. He hadn't been close, and the lighting was strange, but they looked like sea birds. Gulls.

That was all he needed. There was some weird shit going on in this Beehive place, and he wanted to see it for himself.

It wasn't really very far, no worse than walking to Le Roi's from home the time his truck broke down. And substantially less dangerous: no drunken cowboys gunning past him in their vehicles.

All he had to do was walk.

The whole trip took less than twenty minutes. Actually, he had a clue that he was approaching the Beehive before he could see it . . . there were muddy tracks everywhere, most of them leading out and spreading.

Xavier was no outdoorsman. He had never been hunting or camping or fishing in his life. So he wasn't sure exactly what kinds of tracks he was seeing, but even to his untrained eye there appeared to be at least half a dozen animals . . . and a couple of them with big hooves or paws or whatever the hell you called them.

And they diverged, too, some of them going up-habitat, back toward the vesicle port . . . some of them down-habitat.

Some unwary HB was in for a hell of a surprise, because whatever these animals were, they were sure to be hungry.

That thought made him nervous, because he realized the animals might be eating each other. Xavier was used to dealing with chickens and lobsters, so the thought of sundered animal flesh wasn't itself a problem. But he didn't look forward to the sight of a cow's head ripped from its body, or a pile of entrails. No, thank you.

With tracks came animal shit. Lots of it, and fairly fresh, from the looks of it.

Suddenly the idea of exploring the Beehive was much less attractive.

The trail of tracks and shit led him right to the main opening, which looked like a cave from some old movie, one where you can easily see that the "rocks" are papier-mâché or rubber.

Xavier stopped before entering, because he could hear noise from inside the Beehive, some kind of terrible screeching and scratching, and his mind went right to his nightmare of an animal devouring another animal.

But the noise lasted only a few seconds. He waited, listening.

Nothing.

He looked around. No one watching, of course. And no four-legged thing approaching.

Xavier entered the Beehive.

He was instantly sorry that he had. While it was immediately impressive for its size and the collection of odd-shaped cells, some of them recently opened, others clearly in the cook phase, it smelled like locker room and garbage pile and flower shop and maybe something else, all at the same time.

It wasn't all stinky . . . but it was thick. It made him sniff and made his throat itch, which was very unpleasant.

The ground was all slimy, too, not just muddy, but with some kind of yellow goo that was either drying or nowhere near dry.

He decided to ask Nayar and Jaidev to have the Temple give them shoes. *Size ten, anything you've got.*

After a couple of minutes, however, and a few dozen meters deeper into the Beehive (which turned out to have branches leading in three different directions, making him wonder how big it really was), Xavier was feeling more comfortable and confident.

He hadn't heard any further screeching, so that was good.

He hadn't found anything worth bartering yet . . . *but let's see now.*

He turned up the nearest branch and found that the cells here were all large, and new-looking, and busy. *Don't hang around here,* he told himself.

So he doubled back to the main chamber and struck off farther down what appeared to be the old, primary passage.

He hadn't taken ten steps when he realized he ought to stop.

He heard screeching from somewhere in front of him. And close!

The passage was twisty-turny and the light was low—really nothing more than the eerie glow from the cell fronts—so it was difficult to see much.

But Xavier saw a terrifying and familiar shape coming around the corner.

A goddamn monkey!

It wasn't a big monkey—not gorilla-sized, for sure. But it was waving its arms and looking unhappy.

So, as Momma would have said, Xavier ran like Satan himself was in pursuit. Back to the main chamber, then outside . . . he made sure to put about fifty meters between himself and the Beehive before he slowed, stopped, and, panting, dared to look back.

He stopped next to a large rock that sat on a low hill. There were trees and bushes to his left . . . if he had to, he could slip in there and likely lose his pursuer.

The monkey had gone silent and hadn't emerged. Maybe it found a banana or a pawpaw to gnaw on.

Xavier was happy to leave the creature to its business. It made him feel stupider than usual, however, having come all this way with such high hopes, only to end the adventure running in terror.

The one thing he had liked about Keanu seemed about to vanish, to go wherever other great notions went, when they turned out to be crap.

Well, if he hurried back, he'd still get most of a night's sleep.

Even before he started back, he thought of something cool. He knew about this monkey. Drake and Nayar and Weldon and Jones would want to know, too. They would want to take care of it; otherwise, it would be scaring off anyone who tried to enter the Beehive.

And who would be the guide? Who would be the hero? Why, Xavier Toutant—he would lead the first monkey hunt on this new world.

He had gone no more than a dozen steps when he heard another sound.

This wasn't an animal grunt . . . it was a moan.

Xavier tried to remember what kinds of animals could

make sounds like humans. Panthers? Something like that.

Since he didn't know, why worry about it?

But he wanted to check it out. Sounded pitiful . . . maybe some kind of cat that got mauled by some bigger, meaner animal.

The sound was coming from the trees. Xavier carefully approached, pushing an overhanging branch aside. He smelled tree of some kind.

And that weird Beehive smell.

Another moan, much closer.

Human! He was sure of it.

He pressed on and stumbled across a body lying near a tree.

It was a woman not much older than Xavier . . . but she was covered in some kind of brownish material, clinging to her like caramel on an apple.

She had scratches on her face where she must have clawed the material away.

She looked at Xavier and, sobbing, said something.

In two days of working and living with people from Bangalore, Xavier had learned a few Hindi words and phrases.

One of them was this: "Help me!"

PAV

Pav's father, Taj, had a saying. "As the rabbit said while screwing the porcupine, 'I've enjoyed about as much of this as I can stand.'"

Pav's mother hated hearing such talk. . . . In retrospect, Pav realized, his mother, Amita, had grown more openly proper and Victorian as her illicit relationship with Vikram Nayar progressed.

Wing Commander Radhakrishnan wasn't usually so racy, either, but he had a naughty side that emerged under the pressure of socializing at Star City, where vodka, as one of Pav's friends there joked, "wasn't only a breakfast beverage."

Running ahead of Rachel Stewart and Zhao toward a mummy . . . trying to reach it before the cat's-eye rolling toward them . . . Slate bouncing against his back (after being soaked in plasm, it was probably broken) . . . Pav had totally enjoyed as much of this as he could stand.

That was, if he had time to think.

The dog got there first, barking ferociously and jumping in front of the mummy like some sheepherding animal.

From the way the mummy threw up its hands, trying to protect its face, it was frightened by the dog.

Which made Pav even more terrified, because he could

see the cat's-eye rolling closer and closer, the strange blue light pulsing. It was like a slow subway rolling toward him . . . but there was no doubt that it was going to arrive—

Wait!

There was another tunnel to their left! He'd just passed it as he closed to within two meters of the mummy. "Rachel," Pav shouted. "That way!"

"What about it?" Rachel shouted.

"You and Zhao—go there!"

Pav reached the mummy, performing a good American football—what Wing Commander Radhakrishnan called "carry ball"—tackle, knocking it down.

Then picking it up. Pav was fairly tall, but no taller than the mummy.

Nevertheless, he had gravity and what was surely his final surge of adrenaline on his side.

It was a fireman's carry, something he'd never actually attempted, but, *whoof*, up on the shoulders, turn around, scream "Come on!" to the dog.

Start running toward a stupefied Rachel and Zhao. "Into the fucking tunnel!" he screamed.

They weren't far away and he actually reached the tunnel just at the same time, bumping into Zhao and losing the mummy.

But only for a moment. He grabbed the mummy's arm, and to his surprise, the mummy grabbed back. "Go, go, go!" he shouted. He could hear the cat's-eye's approach as the main tunnel groaned like metal under strain.

Then he could *feel* it on his whole right side, as if he were being tugged that way.

Ten meters now, maybe twenty from the main tunnel—

And getting dark.

The cat's-eye passed behind them with a crunching *whoosh* that made the light pulse.

Pav lost his footing, not because he stumbled, but because he was flying.

All of them were flying and falling down, down, down a dark tunnel.

Pav had time to count to a hundred, which meant that they fell or floated for probably three whole minutes, because he was too freaked out to think for part of the time.

He was afraid they were going to hit hard, like they'd been dropped off the top of a building.

But he could see no bottom . . . Pav could barely make out the sides.

Then they bumped the wall, lightly, but firmly, and began to tumble slowly, which, in normal circumstances, might have been fun . . . but surely wasn't, here.

During one of the gentle rotations, Pav saw a circle of light ahead of them . . . or below them.

And it grew. "Hang on!" Rachel said.

"To what?" he said.

Two seconds later, they all fell into a giant cavern that, to Pav's disoriented vision, looked like their own human habitat. But wasn't.

More specifically, he and the others had emerged from the floor of a similar habitat and were looking and falling *up* at a set of squiggly glowworm lights. Pav turned his head and saw that the floor, still separating as the five of them rose into the air, was completely built up! Filled with structures making it look like a Lego city. There were odd open areas, like pools or lakes. Far in the distance, a jet of bluish material shot toward the roof, then died.

Meanwhile, like rockets launched from a city park, Pav, Rachel, Zhao, Cowboy, and the mummy were now arcing high—

—and helpless to do anything but fall.

Some force was altering their trajectory, however . . . "Do you feel that?" Zhao shouted. He was below Pav, splayed like a skydiver.

"It's like a wind!" Rachel yelled. She was above him, gently tumbling, as he was.

The mummy? Not in Pav's field of vision. Nor was Cowboy.

"Air current!" Pav said. How was it supposed to go, maneuvering in microgravity? His father had shown him video from his space station mission . . . *Tuck your legs, arms, and you'll spin faster. Spread them, and you'll slow.*

He extended his arms and legs, which felt very strange indeed. But he was essentially weightless . . . like hundreds of space travelers. Like he'd been for two days in the Bangalore vesicle.

You'd think he'd be used to it! *Tell that to your stomach!* He couldn't escape the horrifying feeling of falling, falling . . .

And that he was going to die.

Along with several massive globular clusters of plasm, the quintet seemed to be aimed at one of the open spaces . . . what might have been a city park in a terrestrial city, but oblong in shape, and huge.

At this height—even as it rapidly decreased—Pav couldn't tell what the park surface was. Not green grass, certainly . . . it was yellowish in color.

He hoped it wasn't brick or stone—

"Take my hand!"

Distracted by the spinning, growing landscape, Pav hadn't seen Zhao flying up to him . . . with Rachel, Cowboy, and the mummy (who now looked more like a black female in a disappearing covering) all strung out behind him, Rachel holding Zhao's left foot and clutching Cowboy's paw, and the mummy, like flying children from Peter Pan.

Pav grasped Zhao's hand, felt himself tugged and turned.

Now! With his other hand, he clutched the Slate to his chest and braced for the fatal smash—

He landed on his right side, and found that instead of being flattened and killed . . . he splashed, then bounced!

As he did, however, he slammed into Zhao, catching a shoe against the back of his head—and that hurt.

Then he skidded and settled, just in time to see Rachel and the mummy making their own inelegant landings.

He was lying on his back on what felt like sabudana pudding, thick and yielding. And, fortunately, either not too deep . . . or just thicker with depth. He was able to sit up.

Aside from what would surely be a lump on the back of his head, he was unhurt.

The others were arrayed around him, each one rising or sitting. "Is everybody okay?"

"Fine," Rachel said. "God, that was freaky."

"Where's the dog?"

"I lost my grip the last few meters," Rachel said, looking around. "Cowboy!" she called.

Zhao was slow to respond. "I may have turned my ankle." He was trying to stand.

The mummy was seated facing them, giving Pav his first real look at this stranger, the human female wearing a layer of brownish material that had been torn off in various places, notably her face, which showed her dark skin.

"*Namaste,*" Pav said, adding, in his native language, "Do you speak Hindi?" Then he said, "What about English?"

"She speaks English," Rachel said. She had gotten to her feet and now stood at Pav's side.

"How do you know something like that?" Zhao said.

"She knows me," the mummy said, turning to Pav. "*Namaste* to you, though."

Pav flinched. He knew that voice, too. And, as she continued to peel off the second skin, the face.

It was Yvonne Hall, flight engineer for Zack Stewart's *Destiny-7* crew . . . the first human to step onto Keanu's surface.

And who had died here more than a week ago, vaporized in a nuclear blast.

The introductions were quick and, to Pav, strangely low-key. "Yvonne, Zhao. Zhao, Yvonne." "Nice to see you again," and so on. Pav thought they should be shouting, that each of the humans should be jumping up and down.

Maybe they were too tired or weak. Or maybe they had just seen too many crazy things. Their supply of wonder and amazement had been used up.

Certainly Yvonne seemed used up. She stared at the plasm pooled around her feet, raising her head to speak, then slumping, like a puppet on strings.

"You're sure it's her," Zhao said.

"It's her," Rachel said. "She used to come to our house for Fourth of July."

"Yeah," the woman said, her voice raw and raspy, "it's me. But I wouldn't blame anyone for doubting it." She blinked, as if getting used to seeing after being in darkness. "I feel . . ." She was unable to complete the sentence; she began to shiver, as if her whole body were regaining functioning. Well, Pav thought, if this was really *Destiny* astronaut Yvonne Hall, and she had been brought back to life, that was what was going on.

Zhao knelt beside her, taking her by the hand. "What do you remember? What happened?"

Yvonne focused on him and finally forced a smile. "First, you guys tell me what the hell you're doing here. I'd have to have been dead for fifty years before I'd believe that NASA could send you three to Keanu. And looking at these two"—meaning Pav and Rachel—"I know it hasn't been fifty years."

"More like a week," Pav said.

"Okay, tell me how. But first, can we get out of this shit?"

The trip to "shore" was like a slog through coastal mud—amazingly tiring, even for a distance of less than a hundred meters.

Without discussing it, the group had simply headed en masse for the nearest "dry" place, which was an open space between two tall, featureless buildings. Rachel was the first to emerge. "Careful," she said. "There's some kind of step here."

Pav saw that there was a solid border around the giant pool of plasm. He had to pull himself up, another procedure that was far more taxing than he expected. "Is gravity higher here?" he said aloud.

"I think it's just that stuff," Rachel said. "It grabs you."

"This plasm . . . it looks like the same sabudana that got pumped through the tunnels," Pav said.

He saw that Yvonne was struggling to extricate herself, so he stepped back in to help her. Then he helped Zhao, who was trying to hop on one good ankle. Eventually they were all together, bent over and panting, in what looked, Pav thought, like an alley in a terrestrial city—minus the graffiti, dirt, and noise.

"What did you call this?" Rachel said.

"Sabudana," he said. "Like tapioca."

"Okay." She sniffed. "Sure doesn't smell like pudding."

"I don't believe it's supposed to be edible," Zhao said.

"Too bad," Pav said. "I could eat a liter or two."

Suddenly Yvonne stepped away from them, vomiting against the nearest wall.

Rachel was already with Yvonne, holding her from behind as she retched. "I'm all right," she kept saying, clearly lying.

She was sobbing now, too. And who could blame her? Pav knew few of the details, just that the American *Venture* lander had carried a small suitcase nuclear weapon . . . and that to protect the vehicle from some menace—Pav didn't know exactly what—Yvonne Hall had detonated it, destroying *Venture* and *Brahma*, which had landed nearby, and vaporizing herself.

Pav couldn't imagine being in a situation where he would pull that trigger, knowing he would be killing himself dead dead dead.

Even if, as it turned out, it was not so permanently dead.

Then, to wake up . . . where? In some kind of alien cocoon?

Pav wanted to vomit in sheer sympathy.

"Here," Zhao said, offering Yvonne the water bottle—which still had a couple of centimeters of water in it! He'd been holding out on them. Fucking figured.

Rachel was rubbing Yvonne's back, looking and acting very grown-up. It was fascinating how different this teenage girl turned out to be. She wasn't completely a brat, anyway.

"This is so . . . strange," Yvonne said. "One second, I was . . . fighting off Downey. Then . . . I'm in some vat of some kind, trying to breathe—"

"We know," Rachel told her.

"How can you know?" Zhao said. "None of us can know what this is like!"

"I talked to my mother after she came back," Rachel said, suddenly sounding like someone twice her age. "I haven't had the experience, okay, but I've been thinking about this for days now."

"It's not just . . . coming back," Yvonne said. She was steadier on her feet now. "It feels as though I just saw that timer count down to zero about fifteen minutes ago. I was there, then I was nowhere." She forced a smile. Then she pointed to Pav. "Then you tackled me. Why'd you do that?"

"To save you," Rachel said, "from a cat's-eye."

"Which is what?" Before Pav could venture an explanation, which was sure to be argued by Zhao, Yvonne waved her hand. "Never mind about that. I think I could ask a million questions and still not run out." She raised her eyes to the unfamiliar structures around them. "What happened to me, where we are. And what the hell *you* people are doing here."

Rachel's account of the twin vesicle/Objects, their launch at Bangalore and Houston, and their "collection" of almost two hundred humans, took several minutes. It would have been completed more quickly, but Yvonne kept interrupting. She was especially troubled by the connection between her detonation of the nuke aboard *Destiny* and the launch of the Objects. "So you're saying *I* caused it? Nobody has any idea what was going on there . . . what my orders were! I mean, look at this place! Are they saying I was wrong?"

"Nobody is making any judgments," Zhao said. Fair enough; in Pav's view, based on subsequent events, the Coalition and NASA would have been better off staying away from Keanu—or, if they had to land, bombarding the place. "Everyone understands that you were only following instructions."

"Shit, yeah! They should ask the White House or headquarters. They could ask my *father* about my instructions."

Mention of Gabriel Jones caused Rachel and Pav to look at each other. Zhao knew of the relationship between the JSC director and Yvonne, too. He gestured to Rachel. "Go ahead, tell her."

"Tell me what?" Yvonne said.

"Your father was one of the Houston people who got scooped," she said.

"He's *here*? My father is here?"

Pav thought Yvonne was about to collapse. He and Zhao took her arms, but she steadied. "Okay, okay." She was shaking her head, as if recovering from a punch. "The others in the crew? Tea, Zack. The *Brahma* guys . . ."

"Tea, Taj, Lucas, and Natalia went home on *Destiny*," Pav said.

"On *Destiny*?" Pav had to explain the bizarre "snowplow" landing the orbiting *Destiny* had made on Keanu's surface.

"Where's Zack Stewart?"

"With us," Rachel said. "Well, with the others back in the habitat."

"Good. He's a good guy." Yvonne still looked uncertain. "You know, as we talk, I've got another input. It's sort of a voice, but not a voice."

"In your head?" Pav said.

She nodded. "It's like having . . . sound and some kind of video streaming right past your ears and eyes."

"What about?" Zhao asked.

Yvonne closed her eyes and put her hands over her ears.

"Yvonne," Rachel said, only to have Yvonne flap her hands and shush her.

"Let me think! Jesus!" She walked away.

Rachel turned to Pav. "Did you ever see Cowboy?"

He wanted to laugh; with all this, the girl thought about the dog. "No." Just the one sea of plasm was large enough that it was possible the dog had splashed down some distance away, unseen but still safe. It could have hit another lake.

But the animal could just as easily have slammed into one of these buildings. "We can start looking whenever we—"

Yvonne suddenly returned, all business. "Okay," she said. "I think I'm getting used to what's going on. Somebody or something is telling me or making me feel things. And they can make it kind of urgent. Right now they or it are telling me there's something we all need to see." She looked up, then scanned the tops of the buildings. "It's that way," she said, nodding forward.

Zhao was shaking his head. "We have no time for sightseeing. We need to find a way back to our habitat."

Yvonne turned to look at him. She was taller than Zhao and loomed over the Chinese spy by half a head.

Her expression was odd, too. "We said, you need to see this."

We? Pav looked at Rachel, then Zhao. Suddenly none of them felt inclined to argue.

JAIDEV

From the time Jaidev was seventeen until he was fired by Vikram Nayar, his life had consisted of work or furtive sex. Money, status, none of those had mattered. It was all about doing the work and finding a partner for the night. Or the hour. Or the next hour. So far, life here in the Keanu habitat had been much the same.

Minus the sex.

In the few moments in which he was not consumed with the giant toy store that was the Temple and all its wonders, Jaidev tried to prepare himself for a celibate life among the Houston-Bangalores.

Now, basic demographics suggested that a group of 180 or so humans, all but a few of them adults, would have at least three dozen gays, if you believed the information so widely believed in the community. Other studies might drop that number to ten or so.

That was hardly a dating pool, at least by Jaidev's standards. Especially when you had to allow for the fact that some or half of those in the community might be women.

Of course, Jaidev was well aware that he might not be facing old age—or a life span that stretched more than a few days or weeks.

Thank God he had the work. Having Nayar and the other leaders kissing his ass, having Daksha to boss around—priceless additions.

And not only were they making real progress in learning how to operate the Temple's marvelous 3-D printing system, they were branching out into other areas. "These bugs," as Daksha called them.

"What about them?" Jaidev said, snapping. He was midway through a tricky assembly sequence, hoping to replicate the functions if not the design of a Slate or cellphone battery, something that would have almost as much value as food or water, and much like trying to rearrange a Rubik's Cube blindfolded. In short, he was unhappy about the interruption.

"They're intelligent, I think," he said.

"They're not much bigger than mold!"

"Intelligence is not related to physical size."

"Let me know when you find an intelligent molecule." He turned away. It was fun having a serf; less fun having to pretend to care what he had to say.

"Assemble a few molecules in the right sequence, and you have an entity capable of processing information and duplicating itself. Aren't those the definitions of life?"

"Life, not intelligence. Can't you be precise?"

"Whatever," Daksha said, throwing up his hands. "They're trying to communicate with us."

"Fine," Jaidev said. "I'll allow the speculation; how do you know?"

And, to his surprise, Daksha related a whole series of not entirely unintelligent tests he had conducted on the Woggle-Bugs, from changing their environment (covering the habitat, for example) to bombarding them with sound at a variety of frequencies, and basic imagery.

"I got responses for almost half the methods."

"Which actually undercuts your argument," Jaidev said. "Couldn't they just be responding autonomously? Like machines."

"Look," he said, clearly beginning to lose patience, "they actually rearranged themselves when I started putting pieces of paper up against the habitat walls. They put themselves in little fucking shapes! They were in the process of reproducing . . . I bet if you repeated the experiment, they'd line up like soldiers on parade!"

This was more interesting, possibly useful, and, theoretically, dangerous. "Good job," Jaidev said, unable to stifle the compliment.

Which somehow caused Daksha to give him a hug. And for one horrible pair of seconds, Jaidev wondered if Daksha's pre-Object hostility, not to mention the eager punch to his face, was the result of some complicated, sublimated, unhappy homoerotic attraction. Daksha to Jaidev.

He hoped not. Jaidev's range of sexual partners was, as one of them had once sneered, broad, but shallow; he was attracted to a certain physical type, and Daksha was pretty thoroughly not that.

The hug ended when Vikram Nayar passed through the work area, making his usual queen-of-England-style pause to ask after the latest developments ("How are we doing now, hmmm?"), which allowed Jaidev to say, "The Woggle-Bugs are communicating."

"Who says?"

And here Jaidev made himself happy. "I do," he said, and gave a quick recap of the information Daksha had just shared with him.

Nayar got as excited as Jaidev had ever seen him, telling Jaidev and Daksha to follow him downstairs—and not waiting for them.

"So now we're even?" Daksha said. "You steal my idea, payment for punching you?"

"Not even close," Jaidev said. "But it's a start."

GABRIEL

Noisy in the Temple . . . why? Gabriel Jones wanted everyone to shut up; *can't you see a man's trying to sleep here?*

He said something, grunted, maybe. Rolled over and felt better now. Really needed his rest, needed to be strong for tomorrow, for all the days to come.

Wondered how long he had been lying here . . . What time was it?

Not too long, he was sure. He'd been busy talking with Harley and Nayar and Weldon and the two Hindi guys and the Blaine woman . . . something about Wiggle-Bugs or Woggle-Things, whatever. There was one, now two, maybe four or sixteen or, hell, five hundred, some big number.

Trying to say something, supposedly. God damn, he wished they would move the Woggling Thing somewhere else . . . felt as though it were close enough to touch!

Those things *saying* something . . . what? How? They were bugs! Tiny little things you could squish if you wanted.

Maybe they rearranged themselves to spell out words! That was it! The Woggle-Bugs had spelled out *Help!* or

Let us out! That was why everybody seemed to be in such an uproar.

That idea was so funny, he laughed out loud, though that hurt and made him cough.

"Gabriel, how are you doing, man?"

Who kept bothering him!?! *Oh, Harley. Good man. Suffered a lot. Got to be patient with Harley Drake.* "Resting."

"Sit up so you can get something to eat and drink."

"Not hungry."

"I don't care. Doctor's orders." All Gabriel saw was a wheel from Harley's chair half a meter in front of his nose. Careful! Close enough to run over him! "Come on, help him sit up."

Hands on him . . . he didn't like that, struggled. "Hey!" he said.

Weldon and Sasha Blaine. Sasha put a cup to his lips, made him drink. Water. Gulped some, started choking. He tried to push her away, damn woman, bothering him like this.

Then she put a spoon to his mouth, something on that . . . tasty, like cold stew. Treating him like a baby, though. Wanted to tell them it wasn't nice, he was a grown man with two doctorates and director of the Johnson Space Center! They all worked for him—!

"What can we do for him?" Weldon said.

"He's sick, not deaf," Harley said.

"Hiding a man's physical condition is too old-school for these circumstances," Weldon said. He turned to Gabriel. "You're a grown-up, Gabe. You're in bad shape, renal failure or close enough it doesn't make any difference. Nayar and his team have just started to get the hang of programming items from the Temple. You're drinking some water and eating some of the food. But it's going to take time. You can't just lie down and die; we won't let you."

He took the stew from Sasha, sat Indian style in front of Gabriel, and began feeding him rather more forcefully. Gabriel wanted to fight, but no strength! And . . . well, the food tasted good, best he'd had in the longest time! Maybe that was all he needed—a decent meal! None of this alien fruit stuff or leftover junk from a cooler!

"Mr. Drake!"

More noise suddenly, all around. Harley wrenched his chair away. Gabriel was too tired and too busy eating to pay much attention. Delegate! He'd learned that lesson. Can't do everyone's job. He was the director of the Johnson Space Center . . . he had a lot on his plate. *Bring me the big decisions—!*

Then Shane Weldon stopped feeding him and said, "Holy shit . . ." He stood up.

Slumped over, unable to raise his head, it was tough to see, much less understand what was going on. But Gabriel knew the voice of that Katrina kid, Xavier. He was all excited and upset about something.

And there was a woman crying. Gabriel heard the name *Chitran*. Indian name. Bangalores, yes, one of them. So what was the big deal?

Then Sasha Blaine was saying, quite loudly, "She was *dead*, Harley! Just yesterday!"

"Well, she's back. We knew that was possible, didn't we?"

"You're pretty fucking casual about this—"

Weldon was still standing where he blocked Gabriel's view. "She was killed, Harls. Murdered."

"Okay, then, back from the dead, the perfect person to ask . . . who did it?"

Now it was Vikram Nayar's voice, saying, "She said it was the girl. She said it was Camilla."

Sasha said, "Oh, for God's sake, she's a nine-year-old girl. She's probably still addled from whatever has happened to her—"

"Vikram," Harley said, "get her to calm down."

"She wants her *child*," Nayar said. "And she wants us to punish Camilla."

"Where is the baby?" Harley said. "Sasha—?"

"Sleeping with the Bangalores. I was just going to check on her—"

"Better get the baby."

"Better find Camilla, too," Weldon said.

"She shouldn't be far," Nayar said. "She's been living right here with these bugs all afternoon." Weldon handed the food to Nayar and started for the opening.

"Wait a second," Sasha said. "What are you going to do?"

"Bring her in for questioning, I guess." Weldon turned to the others. "Right?" Then he was gone.

Sasha seemed upset. "Harley, is this spinning out of control?"

Harley laughed so loud it startled Gabriel. "When was it ever in control?"

Gabriel must have moaned, because suddenly Sasha knelt next to him. "What do we do about Gabriel?"

"Might as well let him rest."

Gabriel rolled over and sighed. The woman was still crying about her baby. What was the passage from the Bible? "Rachel weeping for her children"? Gabriel felt that . . . weeping for Yvonne, for the stupid decisions he had made that cost her her life . . . had cost him his life.

More sleep.

MAKALI

"What are we expecting from this?" Dale Scott asked.

Makali and Zack and Dale and Valya had followed the Sentry farther into a Beehive chamber that was a good cousin to the one adjoining the human habitat.

Makali realized that she no longer found Scott's comments irritating, likely because of fatigue, familiarity, and the realization that he was merely vocalizing her own thoughts. "I don't know about the rest of you, but I could use water, then food."

Makali had wondered about that, too. The skinsuit had tended to that vital need but was no longer available. It wasn't as though they could melt ice and snow from the Keanu exterior. . . .

What was Zack's plan? Did he have one? It seemed that ever since turning away from the sealed vesicle passage, they had been reacting or running, grasping the only option available: flee the croc, dive into the goo, head for the surface.

Head for Mt. St. Helens.

"How about safe passage into the Sentry habitat?" Zack said.

"You make that sound almost reasonable," Dale said. "But it just makes me ask, and then what?"

Zack was slow in answering. Makali was quite sure that their commander had not reached an accommodation with Dale Scott and probably wished he had been left dead on the surface like Wade Williams. Finally he said, "If there are other Sentries, maybe they'll know how to get us back to our habitat."

"Or how to control the NEO," Valya said. She had cheered up considerably since shedding the skinsuit and finding a purpose in establishing communication with the Sentry.

After several turns they saw branching passages that seemed decayed and otherwise disused, except for a central one.

As the Sentry slipped out of sight, Dale hurried to keep up.

Makali and the others heard what sounded like a yelp and a splash.

They came around the corner to a central chamber, clearly a collection of Beehive cells . . . and a floor that was half-ground and half-pool.

Dale Scott was rising from the pool, which seemed to be about a meter deep.

The Sentry was looking at him with what Makali hoped was curiosity.

"Well," Dale said ruefully, "I found some water."

It was obvious that the Sentry lived here; around the pool were pieces of what had to be furniture, including a table and a stool, both of them too large to be of use to humans.

The facings of the cells had been stripped—there were objects or substances stored in several. One of the larger cells was clearly a sleep or rest chamber for the Sentry.

In one corner were piles of organic material . . . some looked like tubers, others like flattened fish or animals.

"Home sweet home," Dale said. All the humans could do was stand and watch as the Sentry went about its business, pulling objects out of one chamber, transferring them to another. It found one device, roughly the size of a Slate, and held it up to its chest. Apparently satisfied with the data revealed—if that was what happened—the Sentry replaced the unit.

Then it turned to the pile of food and supplies in the corner. Kneeling, it carefully picked through the material, finding what it wanted—first, a flask that contained some kind of liquid, which it drank. ("I hope that's water it might share," Valya said.) Then, a silvery morsel that looked to Makali like a flattened eel; it used one of its good middle arms to smash the thing against the chamber wall.

"Savage," said Dale, who had, with Zack's help, emerged from his soaking and was standing there dripping. Fortunately the temperature was tolerable, even on the warm side. Dale would be uncomfortable until he dried off, but he wouldn't be in danger of catching pneumonia, at least. As for other alien bugs, Makali couldn't say.

Zack suddenly stepped between them and the Sentry. "Careful, everyone—"

Makali could still see the giant being . . . it was removing another item from deep inside a chamber. Clearly the item had not been used in a while; the Sentry literally rubbed it against its chest and examined it.

Then it inserted it into the vest it wore. A middle hand touched various spots on the vest. Then the Sentry addressed them: "DSH," it said. It was one syllable that seemed to contain two sounds, *deh* and *sh*.

The Sentry pointed to itself.

"I think that's communication," Makali said.

The Sentry pointed directly at Zack, who said, "Zack." Then Dale, who said his name, then Valya, who did likewise.

Finally it pointed to Makali. She couldn't speak. She knew what to say; she approved of the way the others had offered their names.

She just wanted to be sure. *Don't anthropomorphize!*

"DSH," the Sentry said, pointing to itself again.

"Help him out," Dale said. "Its name is Dash; he wants yours."

"Makali," she said, drawing out the name. She hoped that was the right thing to do.

"The voice is coming from that unit on its chest," Valya said. "I assume it's a translator."

Still focused on Makali, the Sentry—Dash—began speaking again, but it all sounded like grunts and whistles, with the exception of a sound that could have been the word *help*.

Oh. "It needs vocabulary," Valya said. "I think the device records sounds and structure. I need to keep it speaking, then exchange sounds and words. We'll build from there." For the first time since Makali had met her, Valya seemed happy.

Over the next couple of hours, Valya Makarova worked her magic with Dash, carefully taking him through the Roman alphabet, then numbers, weights, measures, body parts, colors, directions, units of time—every word she could think of that would be useful in creating a vocabulary for Dash's translator.

It didn't take long for Dash, or its machine, to begin uttering brief phrases, offering its own story, bits of which registered with Makali, as she sat with her back against the nearest intact Beehive cell, either dozing from exhaustion or attempting to unlock *Brahma*'s black box recorder.

She wanted to give Valya and Dash closer attention but found it frustrating, like listening to a mother explaining something to a not-very-bright child.

Nevertheless, several facts registered.

Much like the fabled broken clock, Dale had been right at least once today. "It's not a 'he' or a 'she,'" Valya proclaimed. "It's gender neutral. Sentries reproduce by fission."

Dash was not in the cell by choice. It had lost some sort of power or political struggle and been unfairly locked away in the Beehive . . . the equivalent of solitary confinement. "I think it wants us to help with some sort of scheme," Valya said.

"The hell with that," Zack told her. "Ask it why its people don't need the Beehive's function." Like Makali, he had tried to stay out of the mutual education process in order to allay confusion. But now he had found a reason to join the exchange.

"They come," Dash said, in the first coherent answer Makali heard. "When they want, they come. I move." And Dash pointed farther down the Beehive.

Dash also kept saying, "Don't trust!" without being clear about the untrustworthy party, though Makali felt the Sentry was talking about other Sentries.

Or did it mean Zack, Makali, Dale, and Valya?

Eventually, if Makali closed her eyes, she was able to imagine that Valya was conversing with an immigrant who had a machine-based speaking voice.

One bit of intriguing information: Dash's major enemy was its fission partner! "Disease hurt me," Dash said.

"'Disease' as in 'illness'?" Zack said.

"No, 'Disease' is another name," Valya said. "Think of it as 'DSZ.'" With a bit more back-and-forth, it turned out that their fission parent's name was actually more like XYZABCDIYTMIDS. New connates adopted the last two designators, and added a third.

"So they've got, like, literal blood brothers," Dale said.

"Or connates," Zack said. "If you wanted to use the correct biological term."

"Yeah," Dale said. "I need the correct terrestrial biological term for a fucking alien."

He spoke loudly enough to draw Valya's stern look. She spread her hands as if to say, *You're making my work difficult!*

"Maybe Dash can add profanity to its human vocabulary," Makali said.

All the while it was patiently answering and asking,

Dash continued to perform its own inexplicable rituals. At one point it dipped its flask into the pool and filled it. It drank, then offered the flask to the humans, directly addressing Valya. "Drink," it said.

Valya did not look well to begin with, but she grew even paler at the thought of putting her mouth on the alien container. In fact, Makali realized, none of the humans looked healthy. She was suffering from the queen of all headaches, likely from hunger. . . .

Makali set aside her tool kit and the black box. She stepped up, took the flask, and drank.

It was water, though it had a briny taste. For a moment, she feared she had drunk seawater . . . and in another moment, she concluded it didn't make much difference; this was the only water available. If it was bad, they were dead.

Then Dash offered up a squirmy mass of flattened eel.

Makali had been raised in a restaurant. She had sampled a broad range of unlikely foods in her life on Earth, from haggis to eyeball of yak. How much worse could this be when it came to taste or texture? "I'll try it," she said.

"It could kill you," Dale said.

"Worse yet," Makali told him, "it could fill my belly but give me zero nutrition." She wasn't going to explain restriction enzymes and other digestive challenges; besides, Zack knew what she meant. "But I think we have to try. We're going to need food. Besides, I am the exospecialist."

Zack smiled. "You've talked yourself into it. What are you waiting for?"

396 DAVID S. GOYER & MICHAEL CASSUTT

She took the proffered food in her hand and transferred it to her mouth, forcing herself to chew (it was
drier and tougher than she'd expected) and swallow.

She regretted it instantly. The Sentry food slid down
her gullet like a horse pill without seeming to land in her
stomach. It made her feel queasy.

"Texture, not so bad," she said, hoping that by
speaking she would be able to forgo vomiting. "Like
one of those crunchy rolls you get at a high-end sushi
place."

"How about taste?" Zack said.

"Kind of overwhelmed by smell, unfortunately." The
Beehive smelled like a rain forest in the high heat of summer: moist, mixed, rotten.

Gulp, better now. The morsel had somehow worked its
way to its intended destination. She forced a smile. Turning to Dash, she said, "It's okay." Then had to ask Valya
if the Sentry understood *okay*.

Dash saved her the trouble. "Okay," it said. Then it
indicated that the other three should eat, too.

"Tell Dash we want to wait," Zack said, glancing at
Makali. "Just because it went down, don't assume it will
stay down."

"I'm not."

But now Dale Scott surprised her, stepping forward and saying, "Commander Stewart, with all due
respect . . . we are beyond faint from hunger. I need
something in my system, even if it's rejected later." He
turned to Valya and Dash, spreading his hands. "Is there
more?"

Once the four humans had drunk and eaten, Zack had begun to quiz Dash. "Why were your people so hostile when we arrived?" He recounted the death of Pogo Downey.

"I know nothing of hostile acts. When the People"— Makali wasn't surprised that when Dash's translator related the Sentry's term for its race, it used that particular word—"were judged to be unsuitable candidates for the vessel's needs, we were given a new task. Serving as guards."

Zack said, "Who did the judging?"

"The Builders," the Sentry said, through the translator.

"Which could easily mean 'Architects,'" Dale said.

"I thought it said 'vessel,'" Makali said. It was a struggle to keep the terms straight, especially since Keanu seemed to carry different classes of beings.

With further encouragement, Dash gave a halting, almost incoherent account of how the Sentries had landed on the NEO "seven times seven times seven" cycles ago, and found themselves enlisted in a war.

"Against the Architects?" Zack said.

"With."

"Then, against whom? Who was the enemy?"

Here Dash got very agitated, so much so that Zack jumped back. The only sounds emerging from its translator were squeaks and squawks. "Valya," Zack said. "Help."

"I don't know any more than you do."

Makali stepped forward. "This enemy," she said to Dash, "where is it? What planet?"

"Enemy controls many planets, many warships, many, many," Dash said, and then abruptly rose to its full height. "You help me, yes? Yes," it said, answering for them.

Then, in a process Makali wished she could have seen in slow motion, the Sentry seemed to collapse on itself, compressing its limbs and torso into a giant ball, which rolled into the pool.

And sank so that its top barely touched the surface.

Zack stared, openmouthed and wide-eyed. "Was it something I said?"

"If it's like us," Makali said, "I think the Sentry is just exhausted. Are any of you feeling headaches?"

"Is that the feeling where there's a hatchet pounding on the center of your skull?" Dale said. "That headache? Hell, yes."

They all were suffering, news that caused Makali to revise her diagnosis. "Zack, we're all hungry, which might explain the symptoms, but—"

"It might also be low O_2," he said. He was shaking his head, as if chiding himself. "I should have remembered. The Sentries I saw in our habitat . . . it wasn't so much that we defeated them. They weren't equipped for our environment. I think they died because there was too much oxygen."

"Well, shit," Dale said. "If their habitat's ideal O_2 level is low, that's not good for us."

"Right. We've got to get out of here," Zack said.

The situation wasn't critical, merely urgent. The lack of oxygen—rendering them weaker, like climbers on Mt. Everest—would require them to rest more frequently, though true rest would be difficult to find.

Especially with Dale Scott still running his mouth. "Does this make sense to you?" Dale said. "To any of us?"

Zack was clearly tired now, almost dopey, but still about to lose patience. "What's your problem?"

"First Dash says its big enemy is its connate"—he made a big show of using the term—"but now it's this other enemy the Architects are at war with." He laughed. "This reminds me of Earth! Interstellar civilization my ass. They're like . . . fucking Somalia."

"Why would you expect it to be any better than Earth?" Makali said.

"Didn't they have to learn to get along in order to travel between the stars?"

"That's always been an entirely human assumption," Makali said. "Based on hope and zero information. Maybe they needed fear or war to make them travel between the stars."

Zack laughed. "Worked for getting us to the Moon. No *Sputnik*, no fear of Soviet domination, no *Apollo*."

"You mean, none of us would be here," Dale said.

"Right."

"If I ever get a time machine, I'm going to look up the guy who launched *Sputnik* and strangle him—"

"All right, everybody," Makali said. "We have larger problems, such as this: Are we going to help Dash or not?"

"I don't know why we should," Dale said.

Zack looked at Dale. "This surprises me as much as it does you, but me, neither."

It actually surprised Makali more than Dale. "I thought you were a huge proponent of brotherhood of intelligence and all that."

Zack looked at the ground, but shook his head. "In theory, sure. But I'm not sure I trust these beings. And every moment we spend here, with Dash, is a diversion from the mission."

"And what is that mission?" Makali said.

"Finding a way off the NEO."

"Do you really think that's possible? Not as a vague way of motivating us, but as a concrete goal. Because I don't see how—"

"I'm convinced that if Keanu had the means to grab a couple of hundred humans and bring them here, it has the means to send them back. Yes. Though, realistically, the first goal should be getting control of the whole operation. Dash ought to be able to help with that. . . ."

"But Dash is a prisoner. And his people aren't flying this thing *now*. Why would we expect that to change because of us?"

"Hey, we're the *human* race," Dale said, sarcastically. "We rule, don't we? We kick alien butt. We're the meanest, smartest—"

Valya slapped Dale on the arm to shut him up. "Enough!" She turned to Zack and Makali, saying, quietly, "I think we should join forces with Dash."

"In spite of my objections?" Zack said.

"Because our other options are poor," she said, "and because I believe Dash can help us return to Earth."

"He doesn't have a vesicle," Makali said.

"But he does," Valya said, looking surprised.

"What do you mean?" Zack said. He jerked a thumb in the direction of the pool. "The Sentry prisoner has a *vesicle*?"

"Not exactly," she said. "But when he learned how we'd arrived here, he told me all about them: the way they're 'grown,' the fact that there are usually three of them in storage . . . he said something about the Builders doing everything in threes, but I'm not sure that wasn't a joke—"

Zack was on his feet. Makali said, "What are you planning to do? Dive in there and wake it?"

Zack hesitated, then grinned. "That would be pretty pointless, wouldn't it?"

Dale spoke up again. "Yeah, some people really hate being awakened."

Zack slumped with the rest of them. "So we wait," he said, then smiled grimly. "Conserve oxygen, okay?"

ZHAO

"You're quiet," Rachel Stewart said.

Pav, Rachel, and Zhao had been following the wandering, uncertain lead of the being that called itself Yvonne Hall through a maze of structures. They were too blank, too solid, too lacking in architectural style to be called buildings. They were just big blocks towering over them.

"Is anyone talking?"

"No, but you're the closest thing to a functioning adult we have . . . I was hoping."

It had taken him several hours to learn to properly hear this girl's voice. She continued to say things that were frivolous and inappropriate . . . until you realized that her tone was actually quite serious, and that she might even be voicing what everyone was thinking—and afraid to say aloud. He couldn't decide whether it was immaturity or a supreme wisdom beyond her years.

Or, possibly, the voice of her father. Zhao's research had suggested that Rachel was, in manner at least, clearly Zack Stewart's child.

"Try her again." He nodded at Yvonne's back.

"No, thanks," Rachel said. "I figure she'll tell us what we need to know, when we need to know it."

The resurrected woman—"Revenant," as Rachel and Pav called her—had simply given them orders and marched off. She was a bit unsteady on her feet, and every few dozen meters she was forced to stop, retching or just trying to steady herself.

The young man, Pav, had tried to help. "Do you want to rest?" he'd asked her, only to be waved away. "We've given you the only water we've got—"

"You have to follow me," Yvonne had said, her voice as raw as that of a lifelong smoker.

"Where?" Pav had demanded.

"Where they tell me!" she said, an answer that was incomplete, thus unhelpful, and a little disturbing, especially when she said, "It's like I've got a GPS in my head. Someone is telling me where to go, and it kind of hurts when we stop or go off course."

That had been fifteen minutes ago. Zhao hoped that wherever they were headed, they were closer. He was about to collapse from lack of water, lack of food, and exhaustion.

As he trudged next to Rachel, he saw Pav stopping ahead of them. He turned carefully to his left, bent as if trying to see or hear.

Then quickly back to Rachel and Zhao. "Did you hear that?"

Zhao had heard nothing.

Then it didn't matter, because the missing dog emerged from an "alley" and launched itself at Pav. "Cowboy!" Rachel shouted, running to join the scrum.

Yvonne Hall stopped and turned back. For a moment, Zhao feared some kind of biblical rebuke. But she blinked, shook her head, and, sounding for the first time like a normal human being, said, "Is that a *dog*?"

The dog seemed to think Yvonne was perfectly normal, because it trotted over to her. She bent for the ritual licking and patting as Rachel explained, "He's a Revenant, like you."

Which left Yvonne almost smiling. "Whatever you say."

Zhao was emboldened, gesturing to the habitat around them. "Do you know what this place is?"

Yvonne raised her head from the canine interaction and looked at him for a long moment, the way one responded to a query about directions from a stranger on a street.

"They tell me it's for 'processing,'" she said.

"I wish you'd tell us who 'they' are," Pav said.

"Whenever I . . . put that question in my own head, what comes up is 'Builders.'"

"Architects?" Rachel said.

"Yeah."

"My dad said that's what happened when my mom came back. She was kind of channeling the Architects."

"Let me tell you," Yvonne said, "it isn't easy. It's like having . . . five earbuds and a bunch of direct neural inputs all going at the same time. It's making me sick, for one thing, and I'm not really getting what I want to know, not in any coherent fashion."

She blinked again, but this time there were tears. "I was really dead."

Rachel looked to Zhao, as if to say, *What do I tell her?*

"Yes," Zhao said, firmly. His position was always *Work from the facts*. "Do you remember anything of dying?"

"White light. Burning. Falling. Drowning. Falling some more. If I believed in hell, I'd think that's where I was. There's something I have to show you. It's important. That's all I know, that and the feeling that once we're there, some of the noise in my head will stop."

And they resumed their journey.

Zhao had not been a popular child, not with his brother or playmates. One of the reasons was the fact that he *was* a brother: every other boy in the neighborhood (and there were only a few girls) was a single child, an honored son . . . and saw Zhao as an unfair ally in sports and war games.

The other reason? Zhao never believed any of the stories the other boys told, not about Chang Liu's father being a taikonaut or Du Jincheng's DVD of *Halo III* and especially not Mrs. Yang showing her breasts to Mang Senlin—even once, much less twice.

His constant refrain? "Show me."

This personality trait—which he defined as healthy skepticism—had served him in his intelligence work.

He wasn't sure it was serving him on Keanu. Start with the vastly improbable scooping of Bangalore humans by a giant alien space bubble, to use terms that would have come out of Chang Liu's mouth in 1998.

Then the arrival on the NEO, the discovery of the highly unusual events of the *Destiny* and *Brahma* missions (Zhao had known that there had been a Close Encounter, but few of the details), and the astonishing business of Megan Stewart's resurrection two years after her death, followed by, apparently, astronaut Pogo Downey's return from a more recent fatal accident.

What had driven Downey, anyway? Some twist in his personality? Zhao's research pegged the astronaut as extremely religious, suggesting that his death and resurrection might have unhinged him. Or was it a more rational desire to protect Earth from infection by the dangerous entities aboard Keanu—?

Zhao could sympathize with both motives. He was still emotionally numb from the wonders and terrors of his experiences since leaving the habitat, which, looking back, now seemed like a haven of sanity and logic. Being trapped in mysterious tunnels! Swimming in a stream of plasmlike goo!

Then falling to what surely should have been his death, only to survive . . . and find himself in the company of resurrected astronaut Yvonne Hall!

The only truly logical conclusion was that he had actually been killed when a kinetic-energy weapon struck Bangalore. Perhaps, as Yvonne suggested, this was some kind of hell. Certainly he had been shown a great many things . . . he just didn't know what they all meant—

They were skirting another lake, this one filled with churning bluish fluid, when the dog suddenly began barking, and not the friendly sounds even Zhao recognized.

Warning sounds, complete with growls.

With a clap of thunder so loud the sound flattened them, the lake exploded. Thrown flat on his back, Zhao could only watch in amazement as a gusher of blue fluid shot toward the roof of the habitat . . . to disappear into a rooftop portal.

It was over within seconds, the only evidence of the massive eruption being the empty lake . . . and a misty rain.

"God, that tastes awful!" Rachel said, wiping her mouth.

"Don't drink it!" Pav said, but it was difficult, since they had been coated with the fluid.

"Will it hurt us?" Zhao asked Yvonne. "And what was it?"

"Good questions," she said. "I'm putting them both in the queue. Meanwhile, we're here."

Zhao immediately classed the structure—four stories tall, and twice as wide, looking much like the Temple in the human habitat—as a public building of some kind. It just had a more majestic aspect, like British colonial centers in India.

Except that whereas those would face a broad avenue or a public square, or even this bizarre exploding lake, this rested at an odd angle to those next to it. At least two "alleys" simply dead-ended here, as if this building had been dropped into the neighborhood long after the others.

Yvonne stopped in the front, with Pav, Rachel, Zhao, and Cowboy looking the place over . . . and waiting. "Okay," Rachel said. "We're here. Now what?"

"We go in."

The building not only wasn't barred or locked . . . it wasn't even closed in; an entire side was open to the elements, such as they were. Or visiting strangers, in their case.

Entering its shadowy interior, Zhao was struck by the sheer size, the darkness, and what appeared to be illustrations along the walls.

"It's like a museum or something," Rachel said. Actually, to Zhao it was a planetarium; the exhibits were star fields. As they approached the first one, a solar system emerged from the stars . . . one more step and a giant green planet grew prominent.

There was no actual lighting, but the exhibits—there was no better word—provided their own light. "I count a dozen of them," Yvonne said.

"*You* counted, or the voices in your head?" Zhao said.

"The voices are quiet right now, thank God."

"Whoa!" Pav said. "Check this out!"

He had gone closer to the first planet exhibit. "What happened?" Rachel said.

He simply took her by the hand and pulled her with him. "Oh!" she said.

The planets disappeared, replaced by a landscape—and several alien beings. They were two-legged, but with three appendages. Their world, judging by the illustration, was heavily industrialized and densely populated.

"Okay," Rachel said, "we're being shown different worlds, and the beings who live there, right?"

"I have no better suggestion," Zhao said. He had shifted to the next one, which showed a ringed world and several moons. The landscape on display was mountainous, covered with patchy ice, and drenched in a dark rain. The inhabitants were squat, flat creatures . . . alien centipedes.

A third world, a banded gas giant like Jupiter, showed no surface landscape at all, but rather a sea of clouds and floating islands of vegetation . . . and beings that reminded Zhao of jellyfish.

The fourth . . . brilliantly scarlet desert, and an alien whose head looked like the bleached skull of a long-dead steer, wearing a monk's habit.

Rachel was already two exhibits ahead of him, in front of the first Earth-like world Zhao had yet seen . . . though this one looked to be ninety percent ocean. "This creature looks like the Sentry my father talked about."

Before Zhao could go closer, Pav said, "You know what these guys have in common?" Without waiting for an answer, he said, "Clothing." It was true; even the alien jellyfish wore delicate armor of some kind.

"What did you expect?" Rachel said. "They'd be naked?"

"In all the sci-fi I used to watch, aliens usually were naked."

"Maybe they've all eaten from the Tree of Knowledge of Life and Death," Yvonne said. Zhao knew what she meant, but Rachel and Pav looked at her as if she were gibbering. "The Garden of Eden," she explained. "Adam and Eve were running around, happily naked, until Eve took a bite of the apple and got Adam to do it, too. Next thing you know . . . loincloths. Don't know why I remembered that. I haven't looked at a Bible since I was twelve."

"Maybe the voices in your head are Christians," Zhao

said. "Speaking of the voices, we're hungry and thirsty and I think we need to know what's going on."

"In a minute," Yvonne said. "It's not as though they just shut up . . . it's just that the volume dropped. It's like I have ringing in my ears, only all through my head."

"Well, what would we be learning?" Rachel said.

"You're eager for more unfounded speculation?" Zhao said, remembering the talk in the tunnel.

"Sure!"

"I assume," Zhao said, "that these are races the Architects know." He waved farther down the row of exhibits. "It may be that we're looking at the Architects themselves."

"I don't think so," Rachel said. "My dad told me a little about the ones he'd met, and these don't look right."

"Here's a question," Pav said, gesturing to Yvonne. "Why did your voices guide us here? So we know all these aliens if we run into them? It's not like we can talk to them—"

"It's more than that," Yvonne said abruptly. "There is something these races all have in common—"

"Hey, what about this one?" Rachel said.

Zhao realized that Rachel had separated herself from the group. She was standing in front of a being far off to the side.

All of the half-dozen aliens Zhao had seen could be classified as strange, but this one was strange in a unique way. It looked a bit like a human-sized anteater, all legs and snout and spindly arms . . . but either wearing a garment composed of fractal elements, or—

That was the unusual thing: This alien was naked!

Zhao also realized that, approaching it, he saw no related planetary display.

His training in espionage had sensitized him to dangerous situations. Right now, all his internal alarms were sounding—

Rachel reached for the creature. "When does the image change . . . ? Oh!" The image didn't change; Rachel actually touched the face of what now appeared to be some kind of lifelike statue.

"Get away from there," Yvonne said.

"Why?" Rachel said, turning back to her. "It's not like it's going to—"

It moved!

"Rachel!" Pav shouted. He shot toward her, swiftly moving her out of the anteater's immediate reach.

The alien unfolded itself, head swiveling right and left, as if recording the positions of each human. To Zhao, it seemed to be measuring their distance and threat potential.

He wished for his Glock. He wished he carried something more weaponlike than an empty water bottle.

With the others, he backed away carefully. He allowed for the possibility that the alien was not hostile . . . but would take no chances. "Yvonne, what is this thing?"

"I'm getting the name 'Long Legs,' that's all."

"What does it do?" Rachel said.

"Nothing good," Yvonne said.

"What the hell does that mean?" Pav snapped.

"All these other exhibits, the voices in my head just sort of drone on. This one . . . it's like an alarm went off."

As if to demonstrate its hostile nature, the Long Legs extended its arms, showing multifingered appendages, like fingers with nasty claws. With more speed than Zhao would have believed, it sidled toward the opening. As it did, the Long Legs sliced through the exhibit next to it, destroying it, and not seeming to care.

Now it blocked the exit. Then it began to close on them.

Cowboy rushed forward at this point, barking savagely. The Long Legs stopped, as if to recalibrate.

"Any ideas, anyone?" Zhao said.

"Upstairs!" Yvonne said. "Uh, this way!"

She waved them toward the darkest corner of the museum. Zhao realized there was a ramp back there. "Everyone, go!"

He pushed Rachel. Pav shouted, "Cowboy, come on!" The dog held its ground right to the moment when the Long Legs swiped at it, the tip of its claw grazing his fur. Cowboy yelped and retreated.

Zhao let Rachel, Pav, and Yvonne head up the ramp first. It wasn't chivalry, but practicality: Yvonne was the only one of the four with any idea what lay upstairs.

And Zhao wanted another look at this Long Legs. Was it trying to grab them? Touch them? Kill them?

He almost regretted it. The alien charged directly toward him, one arm extending so far its claws missed him by only half a meter.

He made it up the ramp with a speed that was surely his personal best.

The second story was dark, no windows, filled with objects that might be machines or furniture, he couldn't tell. "Keep going!" he shouted. He could hear the Long Legs chittering up the ramp a few steps behind him.

"Next ramp's on the far side," Yvonne said, leading the way.

Another story. Lighter here, as if the walls were translucent. Another collection of boxlike objects, like personal possessions placed in storage.

But the Long Legs was still in pursuit.

To the top.

They emerged on the roof of the museum, but a roof unlike any Zhao had ever seen. It wasn't flat, for one thing, but rather bowed, as if the space underneath were a flattened dome. Nor were there any pipes, vents, or power lines—no obvious infrastructure.

"It's still coming!" Rachel said. She was hugging the dog, who looked as tired and frightened as the girl.

Pav had worked his way to the edge. "Can we jump?"

"Where to?" Zhao said. "Every other structure is higher! Or too far away!"

"How about down?" Rachel said. "Gravity is lower here, right?"

"Not enough, honey," Yvonne said. "We'd be lucky to just break our legs."

"That doesn't leave us any options," Pav said.

The Long Legs emerged. It was probably his imagination, but to Zhao the creature looked bigger. *It's your senses telling you you're going to be sliced and diced by something big and nasty.*

Then it hit him. "Everyone, back up to the edge!" he said.

"What good will that do?" Yvonne said.

Zhao didn't answer. He watched the Long Legs approach, searching for a weakness. "It's got some of that plasm on it," he said.

"Yeah, that's helpful," Pav said.

It wasn't—yet. Maybe never.

"Spread out!" Zhao said, "as close to the edge as you can, as far apart as possible. Rachel, you and the dog, next to me!"

He was pleased that the others followed his suggestion. In moments they were arrayed across one side of the roof . . . the Long Legs would be able to reach only one at a time.

Zhao was first. He had positioned himself closest. "Come on, you ugly piece of shit . . ." The Long Legs was within three meters.

Then he said, "Rachel, the dog!"

Rachel let Cowboy loose. It charged the Long Legs from behind.

The alien swiveled its head and whipped both arms around to deal with the attack—

—giving Zhao the opening he needed to hit it from one side.

Knocking it off the roof.

"Way to go!" Yvonne shouted.

They looked down. The Long Legs lay in three distinct pieces. "Wow," Pav said. "I bet he felt that."

What Zhao felt was triumph. Ever since volunteering to go in search of Rachel, he had felt lost, out of place, and useless.

No longer.

As they watched, however, tiny bits of the three

segments of the shattered Long Legs *began to crawl toward each other.* It was like watching a time-lapse movie of a building being built.

"What the fuck?" Pav said.

"It's reassembling itself," Zhao said, amazed.

"Well," Rachel said, "let's not stick around to watch."

They headed for the ramp going down.

ZACK

So Dash needed their help.

That was Zack's takeaway from several hours of terrible sleep and intermittent conversation between Zack, Valya, and Dash, with a bit of help from Makali.

Quizzing Dash was the only useful activity available to them, especially as they were hampered by lack of oxygen. They had tried the Tik-Talk several times and failed to get any kind of response from the human habitat, which was no surprise. "They're essentially walkie-talkie tech," Scott said. "We're way out of range, and even if we had another Tik-Talk close enough for a signal, the rocks here would probably kill it."

"So it's a paperweight," Zack said.

"Until we get closer, yeah." It was easy for Zack to get curt with Dale Scott, but in this case, his anger was triggered by worry about Rachel. Bad enough to have lost one parent for the second time . . . What must she be feeling, having her father lost somewhere on Keanu, out of touch?

Then there was Harley, not only worried about what had happened to Zack and what that might mean for the Houston-Bangalore group's survival . . . but just having to answer all the questions about where Zack went.

And now their new alien friend was in trouble. He had a plan, however, which reduced itself, in Zack's mind, to several one-word steps.

"Escape" was part one. Specifically, get out of this prison cell in the Sentry Beehive annex.

"Transit" was next. Get *through* the Sentry habitat.

The third was "Locate," as in find the NEO's control center or *a* control center. That was followed by "Reboot."

"Why do we need to reboot anything?" Zack had asked.

For the next fifteen minutes, Dash recounted the failures of the Keanu system over the past many cycles. "I think he means a century," Valya had said. She had been working to convert Sentry definitions of time and measure to figures humans could use.

Zack put the question directly to Dash. "How can you tell?"

"Terminal habitat loss," it said, which sounded terrifying in its blandness. "Random generations," whatever that meant, though Zack suspected it had to do with resurrections and Revenants. "Equipment failures."

That was clear enough.

It had been difficult for Zack to conceive of the technology on display in Keanu—propulsion, the creation of environments, access to an entirely unknown form of universal information, the ability to manipulate that information.

The idea that it wasn't working properly . . . yikes.

It added more urgency to a situation that was already quite urgent.

So, "Reboot."

Then, the final step, which was even more disturbing. "War."

"You mean, armed conflict?" Zack said, not really sure the term had been correct.

"The warship is infected," Dash had said, clearly struggling with the right terms. "It must be disinfected in order to function properly."

"Sounds more like fumigation than a war," Zack had said to Valya. "What or who is the enemy?"

"Pillagers," Dash said.

"Or Reivers," Zack blurted. During their time together on Keanu, Megan—channeling the Architect—had mentioned "Reivers," just the sort of vaguely Irish word she would have used for entities that could be pillagers or destroyers or wreckers.

Valya looked at him. "You know this term?"

He explained, then said, "Ask Dash who the Pillagers or Reivers are."

"The Builders' enemy," was all Dash would say.

"Okay, I think that's the best we can hope for," Zack told Valya. "Is it my imagination, or is everything really slow with Dash?"

"I would imagine that translation at this level—even for human languages it requires tremendous bandwidth—creates a lag."

"Sure," Zack said, "if we were using our level of technology." He nodded at Dash. "These people are centuries or millennia beyond us. And it's not just speech. It's *everything*. Movements, too."

Makali had been busy fiddling with the black box from *Brahma*. Now she said, "It's the problem of scale, one of the things we investigate in exobiology. Muscle response times and even the transmission of thought in beings of different sizes."

"As in, 'a brontosaurus would be slow to react'?" Zack remembered a statement like that from a comic book he had read when he was thirteen.

"Something like that."

He thought it was exactly like that, especially based on his experiences with the even larger Architect . . . which had been, no fooling, really slow of foot.

"If you're going to talk *about* Dash rather than *with* him," Valya said, suddenly assuming the role of hall monitor, "shouldn't we let him go about his business?"

"Sorry," Zack said. He addressed the Sentry. "How does your connate DSZ relate to the Reivers?"

"Ally," Dash said. It rose at that point, as if fatigued by the interrogation—or just dismissing further questions.

"'Ally' of which party? The Reivers or us?"

But Dash returned to its pool without answering.

"I think you offended him," Valya said.

Zack wasn't going to debate that with Valya. He turned to Makali instead. "Not a whole lot on which to base a plan of action."

"Actually," Makali said, "it's more than we've had since we got scooped."

"Point taken." He asked Valya, "When does it want to start with the war?"

"One-seventh."

Which Zack took to mean . . . "soon," or whenever Dash emerged from the pool. He was growing impatient.

He needed his team to be moving, somewhere, any-where.

Valya dozed off while Dash remained submerged. Zack lay down and got what he thought of as waking rest. His headache was still present, but he'd been deal-ing with physical discomfort for so long that it hardly mattered.

Dale Scott had proven he could sleep anywhere, any time; he actually snored.

Makali gave up on sleep and, unbidden, did a bit of exploring. When she returned, Dash was out of the pool, dripping wet and performing some obscure alien rituals involving the closing and opening of its outer shell, the apparent inventory of tools and other objects in its prison cell, and what seemed to be grudging responses to repeated questions from Valya. "I don't think he wants to talk," she said.

"It's got to talk, or we're not going to help. Tell it that." He emphasized *it* over Valya's growing use of *he*. Dash was not a human *he*, and Zack wanted the team to remember that.

Makali told Zack, "I can't find a way out."

"For Dash, maybe." Zack had been considering this. "Remember your scale issue?" To Dash, he said, "Food and other supplies come in here, correct?"

"Yes."

"Show me where."

The giant Sentry didn't have to go far; its prison cell abutted the last chamber separating the Beehive from the habitat beyond. In that chamber was a slit about a meter tall and at least that wide . . . two meters off the ground.

"Here's the Mouse Door," Makali said. It was clearly an opening of some kind. "It's got stuff in it," she said, tentatively probing with a screwdriver from her tool kit. To Zack, the stuff was a cross between the bubblelike material of the Membrane and the yellowish goo that filled the Beehive cells. Makali had sunk her arm into the opening up to her shoulder. "I think you can push through."

"Any thoughts on what it might be?" he said.

"So far, all I've got is filling. Maybe it serves some disinfectant or sanitizing role for material coming in—or going out. Maybe it would cling to Dash or harden if it tried to escape. I'm just speculating, of course."

Dale Scott was awake now, standing with Valya just behind Zack and Makali. "We're half the Sentry's size! One of us ought to be able to squeeze through there!"

Zack realized that, all things considered, he was the smallest human. Scott was bigger and heavier; Valya, bless her, shorter, but rounder.

Makali spotted him ten kilos, but barefoot, she was at least two centimeters taller.

He regarded the Mouse Door, then his clothing; he was still wearing his EVA suit undergarment, essentially a thicker pair of classic long johns, only with the added discomfort of a network of plastic tubing. He had been able to get out of it, wash himself, and at least rinse the outfit yesterday at Lake Ganges before having to re-don it. In spite of that, if he had the opportunity to shed it now . . . it might walk away.

And, trouble was, not be available.

Zack had trained for many uncomfortable situations in his astronaut career. EVA. Launch in a cramped *Soyuz*; landing in a cramped, spinning, vomit-inducing *Soyuz*. Microgravity toilets and showers. Winter and ocean survival training. Cold, water, vertigo—all good.

He could not face this war naked.

"Let's try it," he said. He knelt in front of the opening and put out his hands. As Makali had suggested, the bubbly material gave way. Zack couldn't pull it out, but he could compress it.

"I think we're going to have to shove you," Scott said.

"Don't look so happy about it," Valya said.

"One question," Makali said. "Assuming you get through . . . what about the rest of us? What about Dash?"

Zack thought for a moment. "Give me the screwdriver. If I make it through, I'll start trying to widen the opening."

Makali handed him the tool and leaned closer. "For Dash, that's going to be a lot of widening."

"I'm hoping this material fractures easily." He grinned. "Hell, maybe I'll find a big button out there that says *PRESS TO OPEN BEEHIVE*."

Holding his breath, he inserted himself into the bubble-packed opening. He could feel Scott's hands on his feet, raising him and transforming him into a battering ram. As if through cotton, he thought he heard Scott saying, "Here goes!"

He was propelled deeper into the opening . . . and

then, just as quickly, he slid right through it, like a watermelon seed spit from a child's mouth.

And tumbled face-first down a sloping rock wall onto a sandy beach.

Aside from a few scrapes to his palms—the rock wall had jagged edges—and a sense that he had been slugged in the midsection by some invisible assailant, Zack was unhurt. He got to his feet and regarded the scene.

The Sentry habitat had the same glowworm illuminators in its ceiling and seemed to have roughly the same shape as the human habitat. But beyond that, everything was different.

There was *fog* here . . . roiling, purplish, London-in-Sherlock-Holmes-era soup. It made it impossible to see very far, for one thing. Not that there was much else to see; the Sentry habitat was essentially a large lake. Aside from what appeared to be small islands in the distance—islands with trees and structures—the entire floor was liquid.

And no watercraft that Zack could see.

He knelt to scoop some, getting a minimal taste. Yes, water . . . the same brackish taste and texture as that in Dash's pool.

Straightening up and looking back, he saw that there were structures embedded in the wall to the left and right of the Mouse Door. One was a platform that led to giant steps that marched right back down to the beach where Zack was standing.

424 DAVID S. GOYER & MICHAEL CASSUTT

Okay, getting back up would be easier.

The other structure, to the right of the Mouse Door, looked to be funicular—for delivery of materials? Removal of same?

There was also a ramshackle building near the base of the steps. A shed twice as tall as Zack, and clearly not in use for quite some time: flat-roofed (absent weather, why would you need a peaked roof?) and entirely open on the side toward the beach (for launching a watercraft?), it was assembled from oblong plates, some of them missing. To Zack, the shed looked like a worn-out gingerbread house.

Realizing that Makali and the others were probably curious as to his fate and whereabouts, he searched the place quickly, finding it filled with . . . junk. Discarded containers, bags of who knew what, odd bits of cabling, several exterior boards or plates, several long pieces of oxidized pipe.

All of it, to Zack's mind, at least half again as big as it ought to be.

The pipe looked promising. He was able to heft it, though its diameter was too large to be comfortable in his hands, and the length was awkward. He felt like an out-of-shape pole-vaulter as he lugged it up the stairs toward the Mouse Hole.

"Anybody hear me?" he shouted, only then wondering just how smart that was: (a) It wasn't likely that Makali, Dale, and Valya could hear him, and (b) if Dash was a prisoner . . . wouldn't there be guards or surveillance?

Well, no one answered . . . and the Sentry habitat equivalent of a prison siren didn't blare.

Zack positioned himself in front of the Mouse Hole, debating the wisdom of shoving the pipe through the bubble goo. *If you do it slowly enough, they'll know it's you.*

But then what? Would they know to start banging it on the edges of the Mouse Hole to widen it?

Would that even work? Zack scratched at one of the edges with his fingernail. It did crumble. This might work—

Suddenly the stuffing in the Mouse Hole bulged, and Makali's head emerged. Like Zack, she was slipping and sliding, but she had Zack to catch her, though her inertia caused them both to fall flat on the platform. "There you are," she said. "We were getting worried."

"Sorry."

She stood up, then went through the same reorientation Zack had, with the advantage of remaining on the platform, half a dozen meters above the beach. "Okay," she said, "this is going to be a challenge."

"What, getting everyone else out? I didn't think you'd fit—"

"Nah, we can probably use your"—she nodded at the pipe—"big tool to open things up." She waved at the habitat-sized lake.

"I'm just wondering how we get across that," she said. "Swim?"

Extracting Dale, Valya, and Dash took hours and made Zack feel faint. It was true that the pipe was a useful tool for banging away at the Mouse Hole walls, especially when Zack squeezed back into Dash's prison and worked from the other side. (This also had the advantage of allowing him to brief the others on this phase of "Escape.")

It was still a tight fit for Dash, even with Zack remaining behind to push him. But eventually the Sentry was out, free for the first time in however many cycles.

The big alien immediately fell on its face on the nearest flat surface. "Well, it's been a while since it could stretch out," Dale said.

"I think he's praying," Valya said.

The posture did remind Zack of human religious ceremonies he'd seen. But his view was soon blocked; as arranged, Makali was poking the pipe back through the stuffing . . . Zack grabbed it and let himself be pulled through, marveling that with all the traffic through the Mouse Hole, and the serious beating it had taken, its weird colloidal stuffing was still present at all.

He emerged to find that Dash had now motored down the stairs to the beach and, as Makali, Dale, and Valya watched with varying levels of interest, was busy rolling around like a polar bear on a hot day at the zoo. "I think Dash is happy," Valya said.

With their pathetic equipment—essentially Makali's mesh bag and a pair of containers they had liberated from Dash's prison—they descended to the beach and the shed.

"Okay, well done," Dale Scott said. "I mean that sincerely."

"Now what?" Valya said, likely beating Dale to the question. "Where do we go from here?"

During the hours it had taken for the tedious banging and scraping to widen the Mouse Hole, Zack had been "working the problem," to use mission control terminology. (How he wished he had access to that back room and its great minds! Or even Harley, Weldon, Nayar, and Sasha!) He had the germ of an idea. But given his fatigue, and recent track record, he was reluctant to pitch it.

Besides, it was crazy. "Let's ask Dash," he said. After all, this was its own habitat. Maybe the water got sucked out every "cycle." Maybe there were shallow places where you could walk—

Valya picked a moment when the Sentry surfaced, and put the question to it.

The immediate result was not promising. "We swim," Dash said. It pointed down the rightward bank of the habitat.

"No way, Jose," Dale said, not waiting for Zack or Makali to protest. "I did that fucking Russian sea training and almost drowned. I don't do well with this much water."

Makali was ready to argue on Dash's behalf. "We can do this . . . it's floating, not swimming—"

"Oh, bullshit, honey," Dale snapped. Zack would have preferred more tact, but had to agree; this was a several-kilometer swim, and they weren't in shape to do it.

Valya and Dash were having an exchange; the upshot was that the Sentry was amazed and horrified to learn that humans weren't especially aquatic. For a moment, Zack thought the big alien would simply dive into the water and leave them.

"I think he's pleading with me," Valya said. "It's as if he wants us to transform somehow. . . ."

Zack realized that it was time for the crazy pitch. "There's one possible alternative."

The three humans fell silent while Dash kept complaining, which, for the Sentry, consisted of repeating the words *lie* and *stupid* and *dryers*, which sounded derogatory, even in the neutral voice of the translation unit.

Eventually Dash expended its energy, and looked to Zack.

"Ah, one of my favorite books is *Huckleberry Finn*," Zack said.

Makali got it first, clapping her hands. "A raft!"

"With what?" Valya said.

Zack pointed back at the shed. "With that."

Zack turned to Dash again. The Sentry had been watching the human antics with its usual stolidity. "If we get across the habitat, is there a way out?"

"Yes, yes, yes," Dash said, with what Zack took to be impatience. "Escape. Transit. Reboot." As if to say, *Are you idiots? What have I been telling you!*

Dale was the first to respond. "Fuck it, let's build a raft."

HARLEY

"Just tell us what happened."

Nayar, Weldon, Harley, and Sasha had taken Chitran first to find her baby. Then, with great difficulty, they had gotten her to accompany them to Lake Ganges.

They'd had to bring three of the Bangalore women along, for support and for translation. Nayar could have handled it and would provide a second voice . . . but Chitran was literally clinging to the women.

They'd also had to promise her that they were actively looking for Camilla and would arrest her the moment they found her.

"Assuming her story makes sense," Weldon said to Harley, as they stood alone on the shore. Nayar and Sasha were helping Chitran retrace her steps from yesterday morning. "I still don't see how a nine-year-old girl overcomes and kills a grown woman."

"Stranger things have happened," Harley said.

"Really?" Weldon said. "I'm trying to think of any event since *Venture* touched down that hasn't been bugfuck weird. I'd be hard-pressed to pick a number one."

"Oh, no challenge," Harley said. "Dead people coming back to life, that's easily number one through five—"

"—Out of five hundred strange things. I hear you."

Weldon was silent for a moment. "I keep feeling as though we just learned something really significant, like discovering fire. And haven't had time to think about it."

"We're not in a place where we can afford the luxury," Harley said. He, too, had been mentally buffeted by meeting aliens, being hauled from the Earth to a NEO, then trying to survive.

But finding proof that there was life beyond death—however temporary. That there was something more to a human being than blood, bone, and brain . . . some spirit or soul or bioelectric field that could be recorded, stored, uploaded . . . yeah, that was fairly important.

Weldon said, "I suppose we can always fall back on the excuse that NASA didn't hire philosophers."

"Or theologians."

"NASA didn't hire many police investigators, either," Weldon said, nodding toward the "crime scene," where Nayar and Sasha were trying, with some difficulty, to get Chitran to restage her death.

"I still can't get my head around the mechanics of this resurrection," Harley said. "The principle, yeah. But how do you find a soul in the big empty universe—a specific one. And why? Why Megan Stewart? Why Camilla?" He pointed to Chitran. "And why *her*?"

"Stewart said something about them being communicators. Messengers."

"Same thing as angels, if you know your Bible."

"And, since I don't, I'll take your word for it."

Sasha disengaged from the crime scene investigation and walked toward them, shaking her head. "Not going as planned?" Weldon said.

"She says the Architects are talking to her."

"So I heard," Harley said. "But what are they *telling* her?"

"Apparently . . . find Camilla."

Weldon groaned. "Yeah, yeah. And why would they do that? Wasn't she one of the Revenants?"

"I hope you don't expect me to have those answers," Sasha said.

Harley added, "Me, neither."

"I just want to be sure we get them."

Now Nayar approached. He looked as unhappy as Sasha.

"She says she was kneeling by the water, washing a shirt, when she got pushed down from behind. The assailant was on top of her, her hands around her throat. She fought, realized that the hands were small—"

"And so didn't get away because . . . ?" Weldon said.

"She got hit with a rock."

"Thrown or held in the same small hand?" Harley said.

"Yes. She was stunned, fell into the water, and died there."

"Still from the broken neck?" Harley said.

"She's not really sure," Sasha said. "And I wish you guys would cut her a little slack. She was *killed*. God only knows what it's like to go through that Revenant process. I mean, she's still not quite right."

"The language barrier isn't helping," Nayar said.

"She doesn't speak Hindi?"

"Yes, but it's not her first language. She grew up with Urdu, and none of us are good at it."

"I thought the two languages were kissin' cousins," Harley said. At least, that was what he'd heard in the past few days.

"At a higher social level," Nayar said. "In the technical world, or the political." He frowned. "Chitran was a maid."

"There are almost certainly native speakers in the rest of the Bangalore population," Sasha said.

"Then we should get one of them to speak with her, stat," Weldon said.

"We won't learn much more," Nayar said. "But conversation might be . . . more productive." He was looking past Harley.

"Vikram, are you satisfied with her, uh, testimony?"

"Yes. Implausible as it might sound . . . I believe her."

"A nine-year-old girl, yay high," Weldon said, holding his hand out not much above his waist, "takes out a grown woman."

"Come on, Shane!" Sasha said. "Chitran barely comes up to my shoulder. She's weak, she's distracted—"

"And children can be savage," Nayar said.

"Especially children who are Revenants?" Harley said. He hadn't permitted himself to class the reborn humans as Something Other Than . . . but the sample was small: a bit of anecdotal evidence about Megan Stewart and even less about Pogo Downey; Chitran, who wasn't proving to be especially useful yet . . . and Camilla, largely untested or examined. "Where did she get to?"

No one had seen her for hours. "We're looking," Weldon said.

"Sure you don't want some burly men to help with the fugitive?" Sasha said, not hiding the sarcasm.

"Anyone who wants to help is welcome," Weldon said, his tone even.

"Before you go," Nayar said, "one thing, and I don't know if it's significant." He seemed reluctant to say it aloud. Finally: "It goes to this language issue. Chitran is not saying, 'Camilla killed me.' It turns out that what she's saying is 'Camilla killed *us.*'"

"Does it make a difference?" Weldon said.

"Well, yes," Sasha said. "Remember what's in Chitran's head right now . . . images and terms from the Architect. That could be a warning . . . that Camilla's actions were aimed at everyone."

"And possibly not just humans," Nayar said. "Perhaps every living thing on Keanu."

He knew he was growing petulant—understandable, given the fatigue and the stress. *A good leader doesn't allow that,* he told himself.

And answered himself: *Who said you were a good leader?*

Well, at the moment, through no fault of his own, Harley Drake was the best leader the HBs had. And he needed to act the part even though he didn't feel the part. It had worked for presidents and prime ministers . . . why not him?

He said as much to Nayar, when the Bangalore leader caught up to him. "Sorry I was so short."

"I hadn't noticed," Nayar said. "I am more concerned about the Temple." *Oh, what now?* Harley thought. "Did you happen to look at the Woggle-Bug terrarium before you left for the lake?"

"I might have, but something is telling me I didn't really."

"You know that our single bug turned into two, and later four and eight."

"Ah, no, I got as far as two." Harley looked at Nayar, trying to determine just how worried he was. It was so difficult for him to read the Indian engineer's expressions and manner. *Christ, no wonder we keep having problems with an alien environment and its inhabitants—we can barely understand people from a different continent!*

"Oh, it's much worse now. Given a geometric progression every hour, it might be several hundred or a thousand . . . not that they are truly individuals."

"How the hell are they doing it? What are they using for food or fuel or extra mass?"

"It appears they are eating the terrarium itself, or possibly the flooring underneath it."

"Okay, I need to take a look at this, then."

They were still two hundred meters from the Temple. As Harley had expected, and hoped, the population was quieting down for the "evening." Rhythm and regular schedules—astronauts required those for productive work in space. Hell, for productive work at home! If only the damn habitat would accommodate them . . . this permanent twilight was tiring everyone out.

Not that that was the only reason. "Vikram, earlier

you were talking about the Woggle-Bugs communicating. I never heard how."

"Jaidev discovered that the first pair, even the first four, seemed to be arranging themselves in obvious patterns. Things that had a mathematical element. It was as if the creature or creatures were searching for some shape we would recognize, then respond to."

"Well, obviously you've recognized something. Did you make any kind of response?"

"I was not part of the team."

They reached the Temple. The first thing Harley saw was that the ground floor was almost deserted. Several Houston types were clustered in the far corner, talking or sharing meager food.

Then Harley saw Gabriel Jones, curled up asleep on the floor . . . he hoped.

Only then did he see the terrarium—"Oh, shit."

It had been tipped over. The composite shell was still intact, but the thing was now wide open. And a smear of Woggle-Bugs stretched from the former spot on the floor—which had been eaten away as if by termites—right out the front, where it spread and appeared to seep into the ground.

And no one seemed to be paying attention! "Vikram!"

"I know, I know." The Bangalore leader was looking over Harley's shoulder. Now he began shouting orders in Hindi. "Get Jaidev down here now!"

"What will Jaidev do?" Harley said. "For that matter, what do *we* do?"

"We treat this as a chemical spill," Nayar said.

"In spite of the apparent intelligence of these creatures . . ."

"Yes! I'm afraid if unchecked, they'll overrun the habitat in a week!"

Harley agreed completely. He just wanted to know that Nayar was on board for an extermination.

Jaidev and his fellow magicians arrived from the upper levels, skidding to a halt like cartoon characters when they saw the upended terrarium. Harley noted that Xavier Toutant was with them. "How did this happen?" Jaidev said. "I was down here half an hour ago and it was fine!"

"How many bugs were there then?" Harley asked.

"Too many. I had the feeling they were going to overrun their habitat in a few days. But not this!"

Xavier said, "You don't suppose they did this themselves?"

"No," Nayar said, and Jaidev nodded in agreement. "Not unless someone suspended the laws of physics for these bugs. They have insufficient mass to gain leverage." He turned to Harley.

"Someone tipped this over."

"Who would be fucking stupid enough to do that?" Xavier said.

Harley didn't have to think long. "Camilla," he said. "This is probably what Chitran's message was when she said that this girl was killing *all of us*." He was growing numb from the repeated blows to his perceptions and well-being. Spilled Woggle-Bugs = my death? Impossible.

Yet . . . possibly not. "Okay," he said, "even if it's too late, we need to clean this up. Good-bye, bugs. Do we have anything?"

"Too bad we don't have the RV," Jaidev said. "We could drain gasoline from its tanks, douse the creatures, and burn them."

"Do we know for sure that we don't?" Weldon had the inventory of gear from both groups. Harley looked at Nayar. "We should find out what we have in the way of weapons."

"We can probably synthesize something, too," Nayar said. "Poisons, other chemicals."

Jaidev rubbed his face. He had not slept for two days, Harley realized. Now he was being asked not only to keep performing his Keanu Temple magic, but to do so for the group's survival. "We'll get to work."

"Thank you," Harley said. "Meanwhile, Shane Weldon is out there somewhere, looking for Camilla. Xavier, can you find him for me?"

Xavier nodded and took off without a word.

"Okay, everyone," Harley said. "You have your orders."

Within moments he was alone, watching the spreading stain of the Woggle-Bug infection.

Before long, Sasha joined him in his vigil. "What in God's name—?" He explained what had happened. "Should you be sitting this close? What if they're infectious?"

"Then they got me an hour ago. Can't infect me twice, can they?"

"How should I know?" she said. She sat down next to him.

"Well," Harley said, "if they can infect me, they can infect you. Shouldn't you be getting some food or sleep?"

"Doesn't seem right, with you sitting up like this."

"You aren't going to try to talk me into going to bed?"

"I've learned one thing, Harley, and that's not to try to talk you into things."

"You really do know me, darling," he said. His tone was sarcastic, but he realized he had let down his guard.

And so did Sasha Blaine. She touched his shoulder. "Our timing really sort of sucks, doesn't it? It would have been fun to, you know, meet normally."

"Yeah. But on the bright side, we've packed a whole lifetime of adventure into a week and a couple of days."

"There's that," she said. "You know, in spite of that cynical, bitter exterior, you are pretty much a glass-is-half-full guy."

He laughed. "Not exactly. Do you want to know what kind of things go through my head at a time like this?"

"Do I?"

He pointed to the growing smear of multiplying Woggle-Bugs. "If we manage to kill every one of those things," he said, unable to keep from smiling, "do they all come back as Revenants? I'm hoping that there's some sort of personality threshold the Woggle-Bugs don't reach. Maybe they're all one big entity . . . when a few of them die, it's like, I don't know, skin cells that flake off a human." *Keep trying,* he thought. *Eventually you'll convince yourself—*

Xavier Toutant appeared in the entrance. Seeing Harley with Sasha, he marched directly toward them. "Xavier, you look like a man with a message," Harley said. In fact, he looked worn out and troubled.

"Mr. Weldon's on his way back. Said to alert you."

Oh, shit, he's got Camilla. Harley immediately pictured the unpleasant scene in which he ruthlessly interrogated a nine-year-old girl.

But when Weldon arrived, he didn't have Camilla. He was escorting a naked adult male who was moaning, weeping, and wheezing, an unholy trinity of unattractive activities.

It was Brent Bynum.

DALE

Building a raft—that worked fine. They wound up using one entire side of the shed, which was large enough to easily hold the four humans. Removed from the structure, the material proved to be light, like balsa. "I think it'll float," Zack said, in that bright, chirpy way that made Dale Scott want to drown him.

"Fine," Dale said, wondering why it was his job to keep the group focused on operational details. Probably because he had been an engineer and a fighter pilot—an operational type—while Zack and Makali and even Valya were academics. "How do we get this thing moving across the water?"

"Paddles?" Makali said. She had already been at work, stripping several long, narrow pieces of material from the shed. She began searching for some kind of thin, flat flap that could be attached to the base of the paddle.

They settled on one of the leftover tiles for the shed, attaching it with cable. Which worked for one sweep before separating.

"That ain't good."

Even Makali, usually so sure of herself, looked worried. "Zack, what are we going to do?"

Zack turned to the Sentry. "Do you see what we're planning?"

"Yes," the alien said through its translator. "You wish to construct a platform to allow you to float."

"Correct. But we lack propulsion for the, uh, platform."

"Obviously."

"Can *you* provide it?"

"I don't fucking believe this—" Dale said, but Valya shushed him again.

"Easily," Dash said. "I've been ready to do so for an entire cycle."

Which was how the four humans wound up floating on a thin slab of Sentry shedding across the vast, unpleasant sea of the habitat . . . propelled by Dash.

Now Dale Scott dozed and remembered his Navy days, not that you ever felt much in the way of gentle ocean swells on the carrier *Ronald Reagan*. (If you could feel a ship that size rolling on the water, it was time to be worried.) But Dale had spent some time in smaller boats. The motion was soothing; it made him reflective. He touched his Hulk medallion, finding reassurance in its presence.

He thought about these Sentry creatures and how they had wound up with a colony on Keanu. They'd developed spaceflight; the abandoned vehicle on the surface proved that. Quite an achievement for folks who seemed to spend most of their time in the water.

(And swam so strongly and gently. Dash had submerged himself behind the raft and proceeded to nudge it forward with each long, regular stroke. Dale had amused himself by counting to ten between nudges.)

Had they ever found spaceflight to be more practical and useful than humans had? Hard to tell; all Dale Scott knew was that NASA's *Destiny* and *Venture* program was hanging by a thread the day Keanu was discovered in the sky. The space agency had managed to pull off a pair of lunar landings, creating a brief buzz of public interest that lasted about a month, and soon subsided into boredom if not outright hostility over the expense (large) compared to the return (zero).

Zack's mission, redirected to Keanu instead of the Moon, would have likely been the last. There was hardware in the pipeline for two more, but the budget cutters were sharpening their little blades. The Coalition program, *Brahma*, might have been able to mount a second landing mission in five or six years, depending on a variety of factors.

No human had yet to devise a good rationale for these programs behind prestige, "science," and the nebulous idea that watching an astronaut bouncing across the lunar surface was somehow going to encourage kids to sign up for calculus . . . so they could build another limited vehicle to allow another group of astronauts to bounce, and so on. Dale had found that argument the weakest of the three.

Had the Keanu mission changed all that? Humans now knew they weren't alone in the universe . . . better yet, from a motivational standpoint, humans also knew that the other beings in the universe could show up on their front door and behave quite badly.

Yeah, it was going to be raining money on the big aerospace companies . . . and Dale Scott wasn't going to be able to run around with his own bucket.

If he didn't already despise Zack Stewart for destroying his astronaut career, the fact that his actions had cost him the chance to make a fortune would have put him at the top of Dale's shit list.

He regarded the ragged, stubbly man in the soiled long johns, curled up in the center of the raft, his back to Valya—who had her own place on Dale's shit list.

Makali had stayed awake, content to fiddle with the black box she had liberated from *Brahma*. She had asked Dale a technical question once—"Do I need an external device to play this back?"—and he had told her no, that the unit was designed all-in-one, a recorder with sound, video, data, and playback.

He had then offered a helpful comment about which screws to loosen first, only to be ignored. So he had redirected his gaze . . . noting that, thanks to Dash's unwavering nudges, they seemed to have made good progress, crossing more than half of the distance from Beehive Beach—itself located about a third of the distance from the "north" end of the Sentry habitat—to the "south," where, Dash assured them, there was an exit.

Dale hoped so. The roiling mist allowed only brief glimpses of this far shore. It could be hiding other Sentries.

By now the raft had floated past half a dozen "islands," though some of these pieces of land were actually peninsulas connected to a hard, dry surface that actually rimmed the habitat. ("We could have *walked* to the south end," Dale heard himself saying to Stewart. And being ignored again. Well, to be fair, they hadn't realized the habitat had a land border . . . and the raft was likely a quicker method.)

On those islands . . . some vegetation, of course, none of it familiar. And ancient-looking structures, most of them rounded rather than rectangular. Many of them had docks that extended over the water.

One interesting absence . . . no boats. Of course, if you were big and lived in the water . . . why would you need a boat? Dale wondered just how long the Sentries had been captive here on Keanu. Hundreds of years, maybe. Could humans survive that? Would they have to?

Just then a creature of some kind breached far behind them . . . it was purplish, smooth, so large it was impossible to see more than a flank covered with tinier wriggling creatures, like krill.

The startling sight made Makali flinch so abruptly she caused the raft to rock. "Careful!" he told her. He looked back at the creature, but it had sunk out of sight.

Their actions caused a piece of the raft to detach, which was bad enough, but the stray third of a plank also attracted a small flying fish that shot out of the water, then disappeared before Dale could fully register its looks.

Except for teeth. The flying fish clearly possessed piranha-like teeth.

Makali hadn't seen it and was already back in geek mode, holding up the black box from *Brahma*. "I've got something."

At the sound of Makali's voice, Zack stirred, blinking.

Valya never moved. In their time together, Dale had learned that his Russian lover possessed the valuable ability to sleep deeply anywhere, any place. Had she been dozing on a couch when the Bangalore vesicle struck, it was likely she would have awakened in space.

"Good," Zack said. "Can we see?"

Makali displayed the open black box for him— apparently never thinking to offer Dale a look.

Zack blinked. "It's just data."

"Wait for it."

Lack of an invitation never kept Dale Scott from getting what he wanted. He shifted ever so slightly, so he could see over Zack's shoulder.

Yes, *data*. The black box display was actually four displays: one showing the information on the control panel, a second showing data from the Bangalore Control Center. A third display was a camera view of the empty *Brahma* cabin, and the fourth an external shot.

The external camera was aimed at the *Venture* lander, visible like a silvery thumb on the horizon. Makali hit the fast-forward pad, which caused the numbers in the data displays to cycle.

Back to real time . . . the *Venture* lander ignited in a ball of white light. Within seconds, the *Brahma* data display froze, the BCC feed went black . . . and the internal camera tilted as the *Brahma* cabin was knocked on its side. (Knowing how fixed that camera was, Dale shuddered at the hammer blow that must have rocked *Brahma*'s cabin hard enough to move it.)

"Shit," Zack said.

"That's not the worst of it," Makali said. More

fast-forwarding. By now, Valya had stirred, though she couldn't possibly see the tiny black box screen.

Makali had to stop and start several times. The interior camera simply showed a darkened cabin on its side.

Until a face appeared.

"Jesus!" Dale said. It was there, then it wasn't . . . and then a shape could be seen moving around the cabin.

"Freeze that and play it back slowly," Zack told Makali, entirely unnecessarily.

Stopped, the face was blurry . . . but there was enough resolution to see that it wasn't human or Sentry. To Dale, it had a snout and two eyes, giving it some vague resemblance to an Earth-based animal like a greyhound. "Is that an Architect?" Makali said.

"Nope."

"It was big, whatever it was," Dale said, pointing to the way it took up volume in the *Brahma* cabin. "Lots of legs."

"Long ones," Zack said.

"Is it an organic being," Dale said, "or a machine? It seemed to have edges and angles."

"Maybe both," Makali said. "It's mechanical enough to survive in vacuum." She showed the playback to Valya, who clapped her hand over her mouth in shock and horror.

"You know who might be helpful here," Dale said, throwing out the latest in a series of suggestions likely to be ignored. "Dash."

"Excellent idea," Zack said. He glanced around. "How long before we make landfall?" he said.

"I make it another hour at least," Makali said.

"Then let's not wait."

It took some rearranging of bodies to get Zack to the rear of the raft, where he could signal Dash.

Dale was left hanging on to the front and looking down. What he saw there made him hiss, "Zack, freeze!"

"What *now*?" Zack said. He was suspended in a ridiculous posture, holding the black box out in front of him.

"Look down, and keep quiet!"

Zack handed the black box back to Makali, then flattened out to peer over the side of the raft into the water below.

Two meters down, no more, lay a pod of sleeping Sentries!

Makali saw them, too. Then Valya, who barely stifled a scream.

As one, the humans clustered in the center of the raft. "How many were there?" Makali said.

"Two dozen at least," Dale said. It looked as though an army platoon had decided to curl up together and take a nap . . . underwater.

"Can he be quieter?" Valya said, nodding to Dash. Each of the Sentry's regular nudges of the raft resulted in a splashing sound.

"Why don't *you* give our big friend that message?" Dale said.

"Why don't we all just sit still and trust that Dash knows what it's doing," Zack said. "For all we know, they could have been down there the whole time!" He handed the black box back to Makali. "That can wait."

Dale turned to look ahead at the south wall, where

the fog had lifted a bit. "Not to add to the general pessimism, but I don't see an exit of any kind."

"We're still too far away," Makali said. "And we can't
see everything."

It was true that there were structures at the south end,
as well as stands of vegetation. But it looked to Dale as
though the surface behind both obstructions was still
smooth and solid.

"How much longer?" Valya said.

Makali snapped, "An hour minus five minutes."

Zack said, "Hey, Dale, you're closest . . . see if we're
still sailing over those guys."

Dale edged back to the front of the raft. Not only
were they still passing over a herd of sleeping Sentries,
they seemed to be closer. "Still there, and not as deep as
they were."

"We're getting into the shallows, I bet," Makali said.

Dale lowered his head, which turned out to be a mistake. The chain holding his Hulk medallion around his
neck simply parted.

The shiny golden disk gently fluttered down, down
into the water, landing squarely on the sleeping face of
the nearest submerged Sentry.

Which opened its eyes.

"We've been spotted—" Dale said. He never finished
the warning. The raft rose out of the water, tilting to one
side. Dale had time to see Makali clutching the black box
to her chest . . . Valya scrabbling at the surface of the
raft . . . and Zack going into the water . . . and then he
was in the water, too.

It was warm, smelly, briny, and in his mouth. Everything around him was churning, as if whales were at war. Something hit him, spun him around.

He tried to swim, to reach the surface at least. He thought of not only angry Sentries, but also the flying piranha—

He felt himself grabbed from behind. He kicked out, got grabbed around the neck, broke that hold, and was able to surface.

He was looking back the way they'd come. The raft was visible, though upended. He saw Makali's head . . she was swimming toward him. No Zack, no Valya.

Or not in front of him, anyway. What drew his attention was the sight of a Sentry—Dash, he realized, since the creature was wearing the translator around its neck— half out of the water and beating the daylights out of another Sentry. The snarls and groaning were loud and ugly, like two warring walruses.

"Dale!" Zack's voice from behind him, tugging him by the shoulder.

He turned and started swimming. Valya was ahead of all of them, half-stumbling.

Dale's legs collided with something solid, like the wall of a pool. He realized he was in shallow water now and was able to stand.

Zack, too. Then Makali. "Keep going, everyone!" Zack said.

The order was unnecessary. Dale wanted as much distance between him and the warring Sentries as he could get, as quickly as possible.

The four of them emerged from the water onto another beach, in the shadows of a Sentry village. "Which way?" Dale shouted.

"Get to the wall!" Zack said, sounding confident even if, like Dale, he had no idea where to go.

They stumbled between the two nearest buildings. Dale realized that the grunting battle had stopped. He looked back . . . Dash was out of the water now, too, dripping, its greater arms red with what had to be blood. The Sentry headed directly for them. "No!" it said. "That way, that way!" Dash pointed to their left.

"You heard the man," Zack said. They formed a ragged, wet line, Valya behind Dash, Makali behind her, Zack, then Dale.

Dash seemed to be following a trail . . . there was a worn-down dirt path between the village and the wall. Bizarre trees with orange-colored leaves formed an archway over the path . . . they were low enough that Dash had to duck. The humans were able to go upright.

They entered an opening where the dirt path submerged itself in a narrow inlet. "I think we can get through that," Zack said.

But as he made the first splash, a silvery thing leaped out of the water, snarling and flashing its teeth. Without thinking, Dale executed a soccer-style midflight kick, nailing the creature and sending it across the inlet.

The flying piranha flopped and sputtered. Nasty as it was, it turned out to be two hands wide. "Do we kill it?" Dale said, hoping the answer was no, because he knew it meant stomping the vicious thing with his bare feet.

"Why waste time and energy?" Zack said. "Everyone across, now!"

They returned to dry land, shadows, and buildings.

Suddenly they not only slowed, they halted. Dash was standing in front of a cave opening very much like the entrance to the Beehive in the human habitat . . . only walled in with chunks of rock and mortar.

A long time ago.

"It's not here," the Sentry said.

"This isn't the exit?" Zack said.

"It was," Dash said. "Before my imprisonment. As a halfling, I played here."

"How long ago was this?" Makali said.

"It's not important," Zack said. "This isn't a way out." He glanced back at the water. "Are we going to be pursued? Are they specifically after us, or did we just disturb them?"

"We woke them," Dash said. "Yes, now they will pursue."

Dale said, "How many of them are there?"

"A lot," Makali said, pointing. On the water, three Sentries broke the surface and began swimming toward them with great purpose and speed. Four or five others emerged after the first three.

Zack sighed. "Are they a danger to us?"

"Extreme."

"Is there another way out of the habitat?"

"There were several. This one I knew best."

"Jesus," Dale said, losing patience. Couldn't they all see that they needed to be *moving*? "How far to the next one?"

Dash answered with nonsense syllables, another failing of the translation for units of distance. "Can you point in the right direction, at least?" Dale said, helpfully demonstrating the action.

Dash used its greater arms to point both left and right. "It could be either direction," it said.

Zack suddenly tilted his head back, looking up at the orange trees. Then he turned to Dash. "Can you lift me up?"

It was no surprise, really, that it took Dash several moments to grasp the concept. It took several seconds for English speaker Dale Scott to understand what Zack meant.

Zack was going to climb the tree. And with the giant Sentry grasping him and raising him like the Statue of Liberty torch, he was easily able to reach the lower branches of the nearest tree . . . and begin scrambling higher. "Watch for more Sentries!" Makali said.

"Absolutely!"

Zack reached his lookout spot—at least, the highest he could safely climb—and turned himself one way, then the other. "Can't see Sentry pursuit yet," he said. He was out of breath from the climb. "But there are buildings in the way. . . ."

Then, apparently satisfied, he began climbing down, a process that went quickly, even with an awkward landing. "Would the exit be inside a building?" he asked Dash.

"No, would be a stupid idea," the Sentry said.

"Then we keep going forward," Zack said. "There's

no open space back the way we came . . . it's all structures or the west wall of the habitat."

If they needed further prompting, it came in the form of a crunching sound in the opposite direction. Sentry pursuit.

With Dash in the lead, and Dale again bringing up the rear, they resumed their sprint to some kind of exit.

They reached a stretch of open beach—so open that Dale feared to cross it, since anyone within a couple of hundred meters would see them. Dash was plunging right ahead, its big head swiveling right and left.

Then the Sentry stopped. The south wall of the habitat here was dense with multicolored brush. The big alien plunged into it like a rhino fleeing a lion, leaving the humans panting and exposed on the beach.

"Do we follow him?" Valya said.

Zack was pointing farther down the beach, where what appeared to be a tidal wave of Sentries was now in pursuit. "Yes, for God's sake!" Zack yelled.

Deeper into the "forest," they found Dash ripping brush away from a smaller cave mouth. "This is it," it said.

Without waiting for further discussion, the Sentry grabbed Valya and threw her into the opening. Makali was quicker, and dived through. Zack, too.

Dale didn't need the assist but received one, anyway. The Sentry's hands were like vise grips, leaving certain bruises on his arm and leg.

Being tumbled into a disused cave mouth, its floor littered with rubble from an ancient fall or construction, left another set of bruises, but the lower gravity allowed Dale and the others to tumble like socks in a dryer.

As Dale lay on his side, catching his breath, he saw Dash squeeze through the opening, then immediately begin pulling rocks from the floor. "Work!" the Sentry commanded. He stuffed several into the passage.

"Come on, everybody, you heard the request," Zack said. In slow motion, as if battered by the fall, Makali and Valya began reaching for rocks.

What Dale heard was something entirely different, and substantially more disturbing: horrific scrabbling, grunting, and other nasty sounds from just beyond the opening.

The pursuing Sentries were here!

He rose and picked up the largest rock he could carry. With his hip, he shoved Valya aside and jammed the rock into the mouth. Combined with the earlier efforts, the opening was now half the size it had been—

And just in time. The mouth darkened as the big Sentries arrived.

A Sentry arm shot through the opening, the clawed hand slashing violently. Valya screamed. Even Makali looked startled. "More!" Dash said, continuing to stuff rocks into the mouth.

Seeing the value of this—the Sentries on the other side were pushing the rocks aside—Dale added more debris. "Zack," he said, "brace me!" He dropped to his back and used his feet to wedge the rocks more tightly. This did his feet no good at all, but he would rather limp on bloody soles than be captured by angry Sentries.

"I think that's as good as we get," Zack said, breathing hard and looking worn.

Dash seemed to agree; the opening was now small enough that a cat would have a hard time squeezing through. But it was large enough to allow one of the Sentries to reach inside again.

And this time the Sentry spoke. Its original voice was a raging growl that reminded Dale of an angry bear. But he could hear words, too: "Return!" "Savage!" "Traitor!" "Die!"

Dale realized that Dash's translator was picking up the Sentry's tirade, and transmitting pieces of it.

"Go!" Dash said, roughly shoving the humans farther down the tunnel.

Dale needed no encouragement to get as far from the angry Sentries as possible. Behind him, he heard the sudden crash of rocks falling. For a moment, he feared it meant the pursuing Sentries had broken through . . . but he realized that Dash had caused a cave-in near the mouth.

In a few moments, they were all in near-darkness, Makali and Valya walking a slow, unsteady point . . . Dale with Zack and, finally, Dash.

"They don't seem happy that you got away," Dale said to the Sentry.

Zack gave him his exasperated look. "You think it's going to respond to a statement like that?"

"Never know till you try."

"That was DSZ," Dash said.

"Your connate?" Zack said.

"Yes."

Dash took a moment to glance back at the opening . . . and DSZ's arm, still waving.

Before they had gone very far, Makali switched on the black box display. "Why now?" Dale said.

Makali held up the unit. "It's the only light we have."

He felt stupid, but to his amazement, Zack said, "I didn't realize it, either." Then he added, "Since you've got it running, why not show Dash?"

When Makali did so, the Sentry snatched it out of her hands with eager curiosity—or so it seemed to Dale. He was afraid the Sentry would smash the unit against the tunnel wall, dooming them to a dark passage.

Instead, the Sentry handed the black box back to Makali. "Do you know that creature?" Zack said. Receiving no answer, he turned to Valya. "What do you think?"

"I think he heard and understood you," Valya said.

Dash was already walking away, making long strides into the dark tunnel. He seemed not to require the sad little light the humans found so necessary.

They had to hurry to catch up. It was especially annoying for Dale; his feet hurt. He was probably leaving bloody footprints now.

Zack wasn't ready to give up the interrogation. "If you know what that creature is, tell us."

Dash kept walking, with Zack pursuing him like a puppy. "Is that the enemy? Is that what the Architects are afraid of? If so, I can understand your fear. . . ."

"Jesus Christ," Dale said, "how can you understand *anything* about this character!"

"Goddammit," Zack said, turning back and heading straight for him. He actually poked him in the chest. "I don't assume a fucking thing. I just want a *response*, okay?"

Dale didn't want a fight. "Well, I don't think you're getting one."

Makali stepped between them. "Both of you, stop this. We're losing Dash."

When they closed in, Zack tried again, but with a change of subject. "Now that we're out of your old habitat, where are you taking us?"

This time the Sentry answered. "Control," it said. "Vessel." Then, clearly unwilling to waste one more second communicating with humans, it ran on ahead.

Nevertheless, those were magic words, even to Dale. He wouldn't mind having control over this vessel at all. He had just about concluded that for the rest of his life he was going to have to give up the dream that he would ever have a clear idea what he was doing, or why. It was as if he had left motivation or reason behind on Earth.

And he no longer had his Hulk medallion for protection.

Some time later, Dash stopped and began clawing at what looked to Dale like another pile of rubble. "What now?" Valya said. She had been so silent during the hike that Dale had thought to stop and search for her . . . she had always been following, but slowly and painfully.

"I think it's another habitat," Zack said.

With five creatures and eleven hands (Dale saw that Dash was still protecting its number three arm and hand), this cave mouth was cleared quickly.

They were able to pass through without difficulty, though Dale noticed that the air was stale, burned, almost dead. He had to take several breaths to assure himself that he was still taking in oxygen.

Dash seemed to be laboring.

"Well, good news," Makali said. "We won't have to paddle across this one."

She was correct. This habitat was a giant void . . . a huge space lit only by scattered, yellowed glowworms that showed a barren, lifeless, blasted landscape.

RACHEL

Run.

Rachel Stewart's entire existence, her fourteen years of life, all her dreams, hopes, fantasies, accomplishments, disappointments, everything she owned, all that she had heard and seen, all reduced to one concept.

Run!

She was fast. Rather, playing soccer, with rest and food, she was faster than most girls her age. Was she faster than this Long Legs?

Or, as one of her father's oft-repeated jokes suggested, was she faster than one of the other potential victims? Faster than Cowboy?

She didn't know. She couldn't do anything about it, anyway—

But *run*!

Yvonne was the closest thing to a local guide. She had led them downstairs and out of the Museum of Lost Aliens and across "town," toward the far side of the habitat. Rachel had wondered why she was going so fast. Even Cowboy had seemed unwilling to keep up with her. The dog kept stopping every few meters and sitting down.

"What was that thing?" Pav said, walking as quickly

as he could while still looking over his shoulder. Rachel wanted to grab him and scream, *Run!*

"'Long Legs,'" Yvonne said. "But the name . . . whenever I think it, it makes me feel scared and sick."

"We already suspected it might not be friendly," Zhao said.

"What would it want with us?" Pav said. "I didn't think aliens ate humans."

"No," Yvonne said, "but it might want something we carry or have. Water. Energy. Matter."

"Can't we slow down?" Rachel said. "It was seriously messed up."

Yvonne looked at her with pity. "Oh, girl, it's probably put itself back together already."

"How is that possible?" Zhao said. "It just fell off a three-story building!"

"It's . . . it's partly machine. You saw it . . . reassemble itself."

"So you're not taking us someplace safe," Rachel said. "You're just—"

"—Getting you the hell away from the Long Legs."

At that moment, they heard an anguished howl from Cowboy. "What is it?" Pav said.

Looking around, Rachel could see no obvious threat . . . but, surrounded as they were by buildings, she couldn't actually see very far.

"Up," Zhao said, pointing.

The Long Legs—its upper torso still incompletely assembled—had apparently just leaped to the top of a building not fifty meters behind them.

"Run!" Yvonne said.

They were now in a panting, side-aching world of twists, veers down what appeared to be dead-end alleys that turned out to have narrow passages, sprints across open plazas, and near-dunkings in pools of colored goo.

It took only minutes before Zhao said, "We can't keep running like this. We have to kill that thing."

"With our bare hands?" Pav said.

"No," Zhao said. "We need a weapon. A gun."

Rachel didn't believe a gun would be useful against the Long Legs.

"No!" Yvonne said. She stopped; they all did, even the dog. Yvonne looked frantic, confused. "I meant, no, we don't use bare hands or guns. That thing is . . . it's an electrical field that holds it together, puts it back together. Overload it and we kill it." Yvonne closed her eyes, like a contestant on a game show trying, trying to remember some simple fact. "There are . . . God, the word . . . duplicators?"

"Plates?" Rachel said.

"Yes! That duplicating process requires huge amounts of power, so the plates are like . . . nodes. We need to find a plate." When the others stared at her, waiting for more, she said. "To electrocute the son of a bitch."

"And the on switch," Zhao said. "Don't forget the on switch."

Yvonne led them quickly through one last cluster of squat, ugly structures. Cowboy kept racing ahead, and Rachel felt compelled to call him back.

"Why don't you let him run?" Pav said. "He's a

Revenant. He may know more than we do." Rachel was ashamed that she hadn't thought of that. She kept treating Cowboy like, well, an ordinary dog, even though she suspected that, in his canine fashion, he could be channeling the Architects.

"City limits," Zhao said. He was right; they were out of the mass of buildings and alleys now . . . hard up against the looming, curving wall of the habitat.

The smooth quasi-concrete ground surface gave way to raw, packed-down earth. There were even patches of greenery and some trees . . . everything looking old.

This wasn't a walkway. Every few meters lay a cluster of pipes or other impediments.

"Which way?" Rachel said.

Yvonne had stopped and, eyes closed, arms outstretched, was turning in a slow circle.

"Great," Pav said, "now she's an antenna . . ."

This struck Rachel as both funny and true.

Yvonne stopped her turn with her arm pointed toward the south end of the habitat. "Somewhere along there," she said.

"Question," Rachel said, finding it difficult to talk with the endless exertion. "How do we get the Long Legs on the plate?"

"Bait," Zhao said. "One of us has to be on the plate, I think. To make the Long Legs attack."

"Zhao, I volunteer you," Pav said. He was working his way under, then over, the pipes.

"I'll do it," Rachel said. It wasn't nobility or the desire to sacrifice herself. One of them needed to be bait. She was smaller and quicker than the others. And it would spare her the agony of *watching*—

Then the Long Legs emerged from an alley—it was now *between* them and the plate.

Cowboy ran toward the Long Legs, barking furiously. Rachel was amused to note that the Long Legs treated the dog as a threat . . . backing away and moving to one side.

But they were still unable to reach the plate.

"Sorry, Rach, I don't think we're going to be able to use you as bait," Pav said.

"Yvonne," Zhao said. "What are you doing?"

The Revenant astronaut had her hands up against the nearest wall, running them slowly along it, as if searching for a minute crack in the surface.

"Time is our enemy, Yvonne," Zhao said, his voice growing more agitated.

"I'm looking for the controls, all right?" she said. "The voices are telling me, controls are everywhere . . . just got to—" She smiled. "Got 'em."

Rachel couldn't see anything different. "It's just a *wall.*"

Yvonne used her right index finger to draw a big rectangle on the wall . . . it was like dragging an image on a Slate screen.

But then half a dozen different colored boxes appeared inside the larger box Yvonne had sketched. Each one was marked with symbols.

Rachel could see the Long Legs approaching now, as if moving in for the kill. What would it feel like, she wondered? Would she be ripped into pieces? Or would her death be even creepier . . . being absorbed somehow? Sucked dry?

Closer and closer . . .

"Got it!" Yvonne shouted.

"What?"

"Just . . . everybody hold on! Seriously, I mean."

Rachel looked at Pav. She could hear the scraping, skittering sound of the Long Legs approaching. What? "Grab the pipe," Pav said. They all did.

With her arm hooked around an alien tube, Yvonne brushed her hand across the panel.

Rachel immediately felt her vision distorting, whether due to her eyeball changing shape, or the habitat itself, she couldn't say.

It was as if a gravity wave passed through them, simultaneously stretching the buildings, walls, and ground around them, squashing them . . . and dragging them toward the Long Legs and the plate.

But Rachel and the others held fast.

The Long Legs was slammed into the wall behind it, not hard enough to damage it . . . just to pin it.

"Here goes," Yvonne said. With difficulty, as if she were being pulled toward the plate herself, she touched the panel that activated the duplicator.

The Long Legs twitched, then froze as a massive electric jolt surged through it. Then it began to smoke and melt, matter dripping down the creature's sides as it began to shrink. Rachel wanted to look away but couldn't. She wanted this thing gone; if this was how it had to happen, too bad.

In less than a minute, the Long Legs was gone. Yvonne shut off the power.

"How did you do that?" Zhao said.

Yvonne seemed surprised. "I guess I accessed the gravity controls."

"The what?" Pav said.

"The whole NEO is, ah, filled with clumps of super-dense matter. There's a . . . a system of magnets that moves them around, which is why we have Earth-like gravity even though we should be bouncing like balloons." She blinked, confused. "I can't believe I know all that, some-how. It makes my head hurt and my stomach ache."

Zhao turned to Pav and Rachel. "The cat's-eyes, you called them. They can be controlled."

"Great," Pav said. He had knelt to hold on to Cow-boy. The dog seemed eager to sniff the remains of the Long Legs, and Pav was holding him back.

Zhao was taking a moment to be an engineer again. "Gravity. Nanotech plasm. 3-D printing. Morphogenetic mapping and retrieval. I'd love to see the main computer and power station for these things."

"Soon," Yvonne said, tapping her temple. She looked tired, but satisfied somehow. "We're on our way to some answers, I think."

Rachel was still distracted by the awful, gagging smell of the electrocuted Long Legs. It was like burned plastic times ten.

As for the Long Legs itself . . . there was sizzling black matter spattered all over the plate.

"Is it dead?" she said.

"For the moment," Yvonne said. "You can never really kill these things." Incredibly, as Rachel looked on, several puddles of former Long Legs goo began to shape themselves into squares, as if forming up for battle. "Oh my God, Yvonne, look."

"That's what I mean," Yvonne said. "We've got to go."

She made several additional passes at the control panel, which then, magically, closed itself down and vanished, leaving the wall as blank as it had been when Rachel first saw it.

There was a portal not far from them, large and, to Rachel's mind, industrial; it was worn and stained from the passage of God knew how many tons of goo or other fluids. There was a spillway of sorts, and channels leading from that to pools in the "city."

It also smelled bad, exactly like a sewer. Rachel's overwhelming impression of Keanu, at least the parts she had seen since leaving the human habitat, was of nasty odors. "Are you sure we should go through here?" she said to Yvonne.

"My voices are telling me it's not the best route, but it is the most direct."

"Are we going to have to walk much farther?" Pav said.

"I'll show you." She led them through the portal, striding purposefully now, like a woman with a mission. For a moment, Yvonne reminded Rachel of Megan going shopping. Her mother often said she did not possess the woman's shopping gene, the one that apparently allowed you to visit any store for infinite amounts of time, lingering and looking. Megan Stewart walked into a store with a list and walked out with an item soon after.

Rachel, too. She wanted to walk in and out of this store.

They wound up in a tunnel much like the one they had walked through earlier . . . old, still used, lit by some faint glowing element in the walls themselves.

"Now what?" Zhao said. "We're close to collapse. I don't think we have another multikilometer hike in us."

"Wait," Yvonne said. Rachel could hear a faint rumbling from down the tunnel. She immediately thought, *Not another cat's-eye!*

"Ah, everybody stand back. . . ." That was all the suggestion they needed. Rachel grabbed Cowboy and joined Pav and Zhao and Yvonne against the tunnel wall.

With a notable gust of wind—air being pushed through the tunnel—and a throbbing roar, a module slid in front of them and stopped.

The "car" was open on the side facing them—the interior was featureless and appeared to be designed to transfer goods as well as passengers.

As for the passengers—the car would have easily held a creature as wide as an elephant or as tall as a giraffe. Rachel found what might have been a restraint strap positioned above eye level. But when she touched it, the material crumbled.

Yvonne noticed. "I don't know how long it's been since this has been used."

"We're in no position to argue," Zhao said. "How do you make it go?"

XAVIER

"Where's Zack Stewart?" Brent Bynum said. He was sitting on the floor of the Temple, the tipped-over Woggle-Bug terrarium in front of him . . . together with its smear of roiling, growing bugs. Weldon was with him; so was Harley Drake.

Gabriel Jones was asleep or unconscious a few meters away.

Xavier Toutant heard Bynum's question as he hurried down from upstairs with food. Jaidev and his Bangalore guys were hard at work on . . . something. It had taken Xavier quite some time to get them to whip up some "fruit" juice and stew.

Xavier liked the fact that he had somehow become important to Jaidev and Nayar, and especially to Mr. Drake and Mr. Weldon. It reminded him of his first weeks at the restaurant, when Chef Charles realized that he wasn't all thumbs and could be entrusted with independent tasks, and spent time talking to him during his cigarette breaks about cheap-ass Le Roi and the stupid customers. All that had ended when Xavier got busted, of course.

But so far, during his days on Keanu, he had felt that

way again. As if he had a job, and that people trusted him to do it.

Even though he was hungry and tired, and more than a little worried about the Woggle-Bug deal, and about Chitran coming back and saying Camilla had been the one who killed her . . . and about Camilla, who seemed to have vanished . . . being sent to find Mr. Weldon had made Xavier almost unspeakably happy.

Right up to the moment when he found him with the one they called Bynum. Xavier had been surprised to find that being on the inside wasn't fun all the time, and this was one of them. If he hadn't already dealt with the monkey, or with Chitran, he would surely have run away in fright. But he remembered the man from the RV! Knew he had been gunned down by the Chinese fellow.

So now he had become another of these Revenants, struggling to cope with being alive again—what did they see during the time they were dead, he wondered?— while peeling off the coating they woke up wearing, like foil on a tamale.

And now he was back at the Temple, fetching food and water for the latest Revenant. Who didn't thank him or even acknowledge him as he placed the items in his hands. Well, maybe he was still in shock. Being dead would probably do that to a man.

"Zack's gone," Harley said.

Before Bynum could ask whether that meant *absent* or *dead*, Weldon said, "He and Williams, Makali, Valya, and Scott were checking out the vesicle port, then the

Beehive. They never came back. It's going on its second day."

"And the Chinese guy with the gun," Bynum said, obviously struggling with the memory. "Where is he?"

Xavier caught the warning look Weldon shot at Harley. Bynum's voice was calm, if incredibly tired . . . but it didn't hide the anger.

Which was quite understandable. Who wouldn't be angry with the man who killed you?

"He's also absent," Harley said. "We sent him after Zack's daughter and Taj's kid when they ran off."

It seemed to Xavier that Bynum was considering this—or that he had lapsed into unconsciousness. "You *trust* that guy?"

"It seemed like the right move," Weldon said. "We've had a murder—"

"Besides yours," Harley added.

Bynum stared at his food. Xavier imagined that it would require a mental adjustment to hear and accept phrases like *your murder.*

Weldon continued his update. "Some things are much better. We've made a lot of progress figuring out how to make the habitat sit up and beg." He indicated the food in Bynum's hands. "We can eat and drink for a while, we think. Nayar's people are already doing some pretty advanced . . . manufacturing or processing. But that murder . . . it seems to be tied to Camilla, the Brazilian girl—"

Bynum sat straight up. "Where is she?"

Harley looked at Weldon. Both men seemed reluctant to share additional information with Bynum. Well,

Xavier thought, he was a Revenant . . . like Camilla. Who knew what side any of them favored?

Finally Harley said, "We don't know where she is."

"I don't see Jones anywhere. . . ."

Weldon nodded toward a darker corner of the Temple. "Look for yourself."

The JSC director, formerly such a vital man, was little more than a shrunken husk dumped in the corner. "What happened to him?" Bynum said.

"Turned out he was suffering from kidney disease."

"And is now four hundred thousand miles from the nearest dialysis machine."

Xavier realized that Gabriel Jones was conscious. He had apparently heard what Weldon and Bynum had said about him, too. Which struck Xavier as rude and unthinking, not that any of the others noticed or cared.

"Okay, look," Bynum said, "whatever, whoever . . . I've been given a second chance." He looked directly at Harley, then said, "I don't know how long this will last, but the fact that it happened at all . . . okay, miracle, right? And, hell, how many people ever have the chance to know what their purpose in life is? Even a second life?"

"Brent, what are you talking about?"

"Before . . . even in Houston, I was fucking up. Out of my depth. Then, when the . . . what did you call it, vesicle? That big blob sitting there near the center, when that thing grabbed us, something went wrong. I just plain lost it. I paid for that breakdown, okay? Getting shot will put you straight, let me tell you."

"Isn't it more being brought back to life that gets you straight?" Harley said.

Bynum smiled and took another bite of the stew. This time he blinked, looked around, and found Xavier. "Hey, thanks, man. I keep running into you in some very strange places, don't I?"

"Well, we're glad you're better," Weldon said. "And that you have a purpose. Which is . . ."

Mouth full, Bynum gestured with the spoon, as if to say, *Exactly.* "I'm here as a messenger." Then he smiled. "John the Baptist, maybe! Being reborn here has connected me to Keanu and a ton of really interesting stuff . . . once I figure out how to approach it systematically. Right now, though, I believe that I'm here to tell you—"

The subject was tabled for the moment, as Vikram Nayar arrived. With him was a slim, smug-looking Hindu . . . Jaidev. Nayar looked fretful, as Xavier's momma would have put it.

If the Bangalore mission director was startled by Bynum's presence, he showed no sign of it. Perhaps he'd been warned. "Did you find Camilla?" Harley said.

"No."

"Do you know where she went?" Weldon said, losing patience. "It's sort of important."

"New kinds of hell are breaking loose," Nayar said.

Jaidev had a Tik-Talk, which, on Nayar's orders, he switched on, making Xavier wonder just how long the unit's batteries were going to last. "My people are telling me disturbing things," Nayar said. "The bugs aren't just here at the Temple. They have appeared at least three other places." Now he nodded in Bynum's direction as he took the Tik-Talk from Jaidev.

Nayar's hands were trembling, which greatly disturbed Xavier. Vikram Nayar was the most serene human Xavier had ever met—if he was freaking out, everyone should be freaking out.

Xavier was not one of the inner circle and had no obvious right to see what was on the Tik-Talk . . . but he felt, as an HB, that he was entitled. Also, by standing directly behind Harley Drake in his wheelchair, he was pretty much able to see what Harley saw.

Which was a series of cell-phone camera stills showing black Woggle-Bug growths on the shores of Lake Ganges, at the entrance to the Beehive, and at least three other places Xavier couldn't identify. Then there was a video showing a bizarre, augerlike thing grinding its way from underground to daylight with no apparent difficulty.

"What's that?" Weldon said, pointing to the auger.

"Another type of bug, it seems. Or at least an agglomeration of them," Nayar said. "They have the same coloring and texture. They even share the fractal structure." Seeing the lack of comprehension on at least two faces around him, he added, "I mean, the regular edges. As we look closer and closer, we just see more and more edges."

"Shit," Harley said. "We're dealing with an infestation."

"It's far worse than that," Nayar said, making Xavier even more unhappy.

The next still showed a black auger that seemed to have burrowed into the HB habitat from below. "What the hell?" Harley said.

"At least four of these drilling creatures broke ground just south of the Temple within the last hour. They've given us a clue to the Woggle-Bugs, if, as we think, they're related; these creatures are like termites, absorbing and eating, processing raw material, then growing and reproducing."

"Shit," Weldon said, rubbing his eyes.

"It gets worse," Nayar said. "Next video."

This one showed a winged creature—not big. There was a Bangalore woman in the shot, ducking away from a black dragonfly that was maybe a third of a meter long, with a comparable wingspan.

"This may be a third type. But we've only seen one of them so far. And this," Nayar said, calling up a final video. "This one was seen north of the Temple, and somebody said it appeared to have emerged from where the vesicles were."

"Zack said that was closed off," Weldon said.

"Maybe Zack was wrong," Harley said. "Or maybe things have changed. Things do seem to change around here."

The fourth creature was taller, larger, long-legged. To Xavier, it looked like a big black anteater.

"Have any of these things attacked humans yet?" Harley said.

Nayar gestured with the Tik-Talk. "One of the winged things buzzed that woman. But no, no one's been bitten."

Everyone was silent for several moments, trying to understand what they had seen, and what it meant.

Then Bynum spoke. Xavier had been watching the

Revenant; eyes closed, still subdued, he had been watching the others until now, when he seemed to summon energy from within. "Is that it?" he asked. His voice almost sounded like it had before his death.

"You need more?" Weldon snapped.

Bynum turned to Harley. "The word you need, Drake, isn't *infestation*. You could probably deal with that. The word is *invasion*."

Bynum turned to Nayar. "Your intuition was correct. All three of the new things you saw are just different forms of these bugs. More complex . . . templates." He seemed confused for a moment. "Yes, *templates* is the word in my head."

"The important question," Nayar said, "is whether these templates pose a threat."

"They do," Bynum said. "They're what everyone is fighting."

"Who's everyone?" Harley said. Exactly what Xavier wanted to know, too.

"The Architects," Bynum said. "And, essentially, every other race on the NEO. They have been fighting a war against these things for a seriously long time." He hesitated and seemed to check out, reminding Xavier of a sideline reporter at a football game listening to new information in his earpiece. "They're called the Gatherers, the Ravagers." He smiled, reminding Xavier of a quiz show contestant who had hit on just the right answer. "Reivers. They're the Reivers."

Weldon said, "Have we somehow been enlisted in a centuries-long interstellar war against . . . bugs and anteaters?"

"You're not getting this, are you?" Bynum said, as if talking to a dim child. "I've been sent to tell you this basic information: Unless we stop them here, the Reivers are going to suck up every bit of life and energy any of us have, just to make more of them. That's what they do wherever they go."

"Sounds efficient and focused," Weldon said.

Bynum turned to Harley. "What do I have to do to convince you that this"—he pointed at the Woggle-Bug smear—"is a real enemy?"

To Xavier, Harley seemed ready to believe Bynum. But he also deferred, as always, to Weldon. "Tell you what," he said to Bynum. "Go with Vikram and his team. Tell them everything you know, especially how to defend against the Reivers. That way, once we know what our next step is . . . we'll be ready."

It seemed logical to Xavier, but Bynum laughed. "Typical NASA. You guys bitch about the White House and everyone else, but when it comes to putting off painful decisions, you could give lessons."

He leaned down, putting himself nose to nose with Harley. "Every minute, every second you waste, you make this harder. Wait too long, and there won't be anything you can do about it, except watch the entire NEO be infected.

"And then, of course, there's Earth. These things love mineral-rich, wet environments that have lots of sun. That will be their ultimate target."

"Talk to Nayar," Harley said.

As Bynum began sharing his Keanu knowledge with Nayar and Jaidev—it seemed to Xavier that he was almost barraging the Bangalore men—Weldon leaned over to Harley and said, "This resurrection stuff raises a lot of shameful temptations," Weldon said.

"What are you talking about?" Harley answered.

"As big a pain in the ass as Bynum was in Houston, he's far worse now. He could be dangerous as shit, too."

"Agreed. So what?"

"Knowing that death isn't permanent anymore . . . aren't you just a little tempted to ice this guy again?"

Harley just shook his head and, perhaps realizing that Xavier could hear them, said, "Roll with me."

Weldon pushed Harley off toward the entrance.

The NASA man's suggestion disturbed Xavier. He had tried to imagine what Earth would be like if everyone knew for sure that death wasn't the end . . . that some part of them, some electrical memory, got uploaded to the universe . . . and, with the right technology, could be downloaded again into a new body. Take Momma . . . dying of cancer, going through all kinds of hell with chemo and radiation, having parts of her cut away.

If the Revenant technology existed on Earth, why, wouldn't you just skip all that pain and horror? Wouldn't you just go see a Dr. Death and be done with it, after arranging to be brought back, better, with no cancer?

And that was just good people like Momma. Look at Mr. Weldon—he wasn't a criminal or a murderer. But knowing that death was temporary . . . he was talking about killing Mr. Bynum just to solve a problem.

How many people would feel the same way?

Xavier wasn't sure he wanted to live in a world with Revenant technology.

But then, it didn't appear that that was an option. Not with this Reivers threat.

Xavier appreciated Bynum's energy and certainty. He was like a TV evangelist, the kind who had you convinced that angels were real . . . until five minutes after you changed to a different channel.

On the subject of a war, Xavier was leaning toward Shane Weldon's point of view. Bugs were a problem; Xavier hated most of them.

But how could the Architects, people who could build Keanu, travel between the stars, who held the power of life and death . . . how the hell could they be seriously threatened by termites?

The twilight landscape of the habitat certainly appeared calm. Xavier had already made some nice friends among the HBs. He would hate to think of them dying, even if they could be reborn.

Harley and Weldon rolled back to the group. "Okay," Harley said, "a mayoral decision. Vikram and Bynum, get to work eradicating these bugs. I don't care what chemical you have to develop, just do it ASAP."

"Fine," Nayar said. "Then what?"

"Then we work on defending the Temple. It's our major source of food and water now, and it's the only place where we have access to weapons and high tech."

"So you're not going to be proactive," Bynum said. "The Reivers will have this place overrun in two days. And they're not nice about it. Everyone out there will be dead."

Before Harley could offer an argument, three strange things happened very quickly.

First, a voice behind Xavier said, "Hey, people!" Gabriel Jones was not only standing, he almost looked like his old self. "Am I the only one around here with eyes?"

He pointed to the Temple opening, which was the second strange thing:

Sasha Blaine was there. With her was Camilla, her eyes wide with fear.

The third thing was a scream from somewhere far out in the habitat.

Part Six

Not sure I'm digging the space exploration experience. Used to think it might be cool, even after my dad got involved in it (though not so much from that point on, because your parents' work, no matter how cool, is NEVER cool).

What's the point? The ride doesn't look to be that much fun, unless you like crazy roller coasters. The voyage makes you ache and throw up, usually. And when you get to some new planet, you have to carry your air and water and tools—or hope to make them there. Yeah, that's a strategy: Let's replicate a few hundred or thousand years of human history this afternoon.

And, what happens if you run into somebody that doesn't want you there?

KEANU-PEDIA BY PAV, ENTRY #5

THE PRISONER

The former Prisoner now had companions. Or enemies.

Or food creatures.

Life on the home world was seven times seven times seven cycles in the far past. To the Prisoner, that life was a myth filled with improbable vistas and ridiculous activities. Imagine being able to swim in a straight line for more than a seventh of a cycle! Or to dive to a depth greater than the height of seven of the People!

Nevertheless, for all its skepticism, the Prisoner spoke the language of its ancestors, using the same terms. It was disconcerting to be confronted with situations for which it had no words.

As in this case: There were no other intelligent races on the home world, only the People; other ambulatory beings were divided into food creatures of the sea and enemies from the land.

Which category were the Prisoner's new companions to be? They were land creatures, and land was traditionally the home of the People's enemies. But the habitat was not the traditional environment.

Were the land creatures food? Their smell was neutral; their size was acceptable (the Prisoner could easily subdue, then rend one of them). Yet they had provided medical assistance and, far more important, had effectuated an end to imprisonment; social norms required the Prisoner to respond in kind, helping them to communicate, for example.

Attacking and eating them would simply be wrong, especially when the Prisoner still possessed a food source.

The problem remained. The Prisoner was forced to reach into an unused part of its vocabulary to class the companions with smaller, sleeker creatures from the home world that frequently accompanied individual members of the People on food-gathering swims, feasting on creatures the People did not eat.

From a distance, the creatures could have passed for smaller members of the People, except that they possessed only two arms.

That was it: Two Arms.

The encounter with these Two Arms had been troubling for other reasons. First, their speed was exhausting. Second, their anomalous presence; the Prisoner believed it knew all of the races resident in this world, outside the People's habitat. It and the Connate had been told the stories and shown the images for close to seven different types, from the Air Creatures to the Mud Crawlers.

What was the Two Arms' relationship to the People? Clearly they knew of them—and showed no overt hostility or fear.

Of course, given the Prisoner's hostile relationship with its own People, that was hardly to the Two Arms' credit. The Prisoner was prepared to believe, however, that the Two Arms possessed no detailed knowledge of the People's activities or conflicts. Likely they had no idea of the Prisoner's existence until their meeting.

Well, now they did. And the Prisoner was bound to them.

But beyond politeness, the key factor in determining the nature and tenure of the relationship was this:

Did the Two Arms know of the Ravagers? If not, they would soon. Best to act as if they did. It would be best to assume they did.

The vital question was this: Which side would the Two Arms choose? If they chose to be allies, all would be good.

If they chose to be enemies, well, then, with looming regret for the rudeness of repaying kindness with violence, the Two Arms might have to be eliminated and even consumed.

The Prisoner regretted the option, but actions taken by the Connate and the People made such violence inevitable.

The Prisoner's own relationship with the Ravagers was fraught; it had changed twice, and, given imprisonment and lack of contact, might be non-existent.

No matter. The Prisoner was still forced to act as if nothing had changed during the imprisonment. Understandings had been reached. Courses of action had been decided.

The first required action had been to gain control of the warship. That, however, would have required time and lack of pursuit.

The Connate and others knew of the Prisoner's escape and were on the trail already. Reaching the control habitat was no longer possible.

The Prisoner knew that the Ravagers' ultimate goal was not control of the warship. That was merely the means.

The Ravagers wanted to activate, then use, the external transport system, to expand their influence and field of operations.

So the plan must be changed.

It was not an easy thing for one of the People. But it was necessary for the Prisoner.

First, the dead habitat must be crossed, a challenge for any member of the People given the lack of water, elements in the atmosphere, and temperatures.

Then contact must be made with the nearest neighbors, the Air Creatures that guarded access to the warship's most vital systems.

The Air Creatures were not allies of the People nor of the Ravagers, but the Prisoner might be able to use that hostility to its advantage.

That action was moot until the habitat had been crossed.

And the Two Arms dealt with.

VALYA

"Where is this thing taking us?"

Valya, Dale, Makali, and Zack had followed Dash into the heart of the dead habitat for half an hour—sufficient time to cross at least two kilometers, maybe more—before Makali dropped back to ask the question. Sunk into a zone of sullen petulance, Dale kept close to Dash . . . conveniently leaving himself isolated from Valya and the others, who trailed at a distance of thirty meters.

Zack said, "I don't know." He smiled. "To the other side."

The other side couldn't come soon enough for Valya. This habitat was a landscape out of a cold war nightmare.

First they had traversed the open, shattered, scorched remains of a Beehive . . . though it was so distressed that none of them realized that until Makali pointed it out.

Then it was onto a surface that was nothing but gray, hard-packed ash. Occasionally they passed hillocks that seemed to cover structures that had been blasted or crushed. The weird twilight, approximately half the light found in the human or Sentry habitats, with a nasty bluish tint (based on the type of star that warmed the deceased inhabitants' home planet?), made it downright eerie. As a girl, Valya had enjoyed more than her share of monster and nuclear disaster movies. Now she half-expected to be confronted by a team of post-apocalypse vigilantes in black leather, or a swarm of fast-moving zombies.

So far, however, there had been nothing at all. No movement, no color, no life, no *sign* that life had ever existed here. Just the settled ash of a nuclear winter.

"Look at that," Makali said.

She had stopped in front of a good-sized boulder with fairly smooth sides. On it was the shadow of a creature that immediately struck Zack as crablike. It was wider than it was tall and seemed to be reaching out with flattened claws. "The former inhabitants, do you suppose?"

"Probably," Zack said. "It reminds me of images from Hiroshima." He trotted forward, catching up with Dash and Dale, and forcing Makali and Valya to do the same.

"Dash," he said, "a question: What happened here? In this habitat?"

"Sanitary procedure," the Sentry said.

"What needed to be sanitized?" Zack said. Valya wondered, had the crab creatures on the stone been the infection? Or the infected? Had the Architects—assuming they were the ones doing the sanitizing—destroyed a habitat in order to save it?

"Apostates," Dash said. That was the way it was translated, anyway.

Zack looked at Valya, who shook her head. "Non-believers?"

"Beings that refused to take part," Dash said.

"In what?"

"Corrective actions."

"Against whom?"

There was an uncommonly long pause. "Creatures called Ravagers."

"I don't know that term," Zack said, growing impatient. "We've got Architects and Sentries and Apostates and now Ravagers. What are the relationships?"

"Architects and Ravagers are at war."

"So whoever lived here—they were the Ravagers?"

"No," Dash said, and moved off so swiftly, with its long, relentless strides, that further interrogation was impossible. Dale hurried after the Sentry, leaving Valya with Zack and Makali.

All three were struggling with the lack of air. Valya wanted to prolong the restful moment as long as possible. She pointed back the way they had come, saying, "Whatever was detonated in that war must have been located behind us."

"Maybe they grew a nuke in their Beehive," Makali said.

"Don't assume it's a nuke," Zack said. "There are other kinds of weapons. Energy, microwave, plus things more advanced races could develop."

"The results are the same, aren't they?" Makali said. "Total destruction. So what difference does it make?"

It made this difference to Valya: She realized that the Architects weren't as advanced as she had hoped. And that nothing was as good as she wanted it to be.

———————

Valya, Zack, and Makali had to hurry to catch up, essentially having to take two steps for each one of the alien's, like children struggling to keep pace with their parents.

"About time," Dale said when they caught him. "Do you really want to linger here?" he said.

Valya was willing to concede that Dale had a valid point; the less time they spent here, the quicker they would reach the control center or power core, wherever the Sentry was leading them.

She was tired beyond belief, panting with every step. Hungry. Thirsty. So afraid that she was growing numb to fear.

And she hated everyone now. The stupid, unhelpful alien Dash. Dale, of course. And now even Makali and Zack.

The only encouraging thing about knowing she was likely to die . . . was that they would all die, too.

Zack hustled forward, closing to within earshot of Dash. Valya, Makali, and Dale did, too, even though it almost killed Valya to expend the extra energy. In fact, she lagged, and earned this: "Goddammit, Valya, will you fucking try to keep up?" Zack said. "I really need you."

So she closed on the leader, even though she wanted to either kill him or die . . . or kill him, *then* die.

"When we emerge," she heard him ask the Sentry, "where do we go next? And how far is it?" He smiled unsympathetically at Valya, as if to say, *Feel free to answer, too.*

"Exit habitat," Dash said.

"I understand," Zack said. "But where are we then? Which way do we go? Where is the control center?"

"Goals remain the same," the Sentry said.

"Can we fly Keanu?" Dale said. "Whatever he calls it, the 'warship'?"

"Control means control," Dash said.

"So we could turn it around and head back to Earth," Dale said, as irritating as he was persistent.

"Yes," the Sentry said, its translator voice neutral.

"Why didn't you do that?" Zack said to Dash. "Why didn't your people head home?"

Dash never broke stride. "No control," it said. "Before I was born."

They were three quarters of the way across the dead habitat now. Valya searched for their way out the other end as she considered the possibilities.

While the translator offered the same words and phrases as before, there was something in Dash's manner—the Sentry's posture, even the pitch of its real voice—that had changed somehow.

Of course, Valya knew that the Sentry, communicating in a vastly different language, with its own matrix of habits and assumptions, might very well kick into a second mode when revisiting the same subject at a later time. That was certainly a possibility—

Before Zack could probe further, Valya stumbled and sprawled face-first in the dirt.

It was her feet; she had been barefoot so long that her feet were raw and numb. Makali was first to offer a hand. "How is it?"

In her former life, Valya had had a propensity for collecting foot injuries. Stubbed and broken toes, ripped-off nails; if it could be done, she'd done it repeatedly.

And her usual method of dealing with it was to delay looking at the damage as long as possible, in the silly hope that it would be less than feared.

That was where she was now, turning over her blackened feet and seeing that she had worn the skin off the soles.

"Oh, shit," Makali said.

"We're all this way, aren't we?"

"Not all of us," Dale said.

Makali was wearing the kind of durable footgear an experienced hiker or climber wore under boots. Zack had the soiled and torn footwear of his EVA undergarment. "I wish I had something for you," Makali said.

"Help me get her up," Makali said. Zack was still closely following the Sentry.

"Fucking leave her," Dale said.

"What are you talking about?" Makali said. "We don't leave people."

"She's been dragging us down ever since we got out of Dash's prison."

Valya sat on the hard-packed ground, its texture like asbestos, and listened to this exchange with little interest. Even though she found Dale's attitude unfriendly and even infuriating, she wasn't sure she *could* get up and walk again.

But she was growing less happy with Makali, too, in spite of the fact that the woman was trying to help her. Why wouldn't she just let her be!

And as for Zack . . . what had possessed him to go to the Beehive—

Valya stopped. "Zack," she said, her voice a croak. "Zack!" she called.

But Zack had already turned back. "What is it *now*?" he said. In his impatience, Zack sounded just like Dale—or Zack talking to Dale. Which was exactly Valya's worry. "How are you feeling?"

"Awful," she said.

"Come on, Valya, Dale," Makali said. "Can we just keep moving? Why does everything have to be a debate?" She, too, was uncharacteristically impatient.

"Listen to yourselves," Valya said. "We're all on edge."

"Don't we have every right to be on edge?" Dale said. God, he was annoying. She fought the urge to slap him—

Steady; remember your discovery. "This environment is doing it," she said. "At best we're starving for oxygen. At worst, poisoned."

Zack, thank God, was quick to make the adjustment. "You're right: I've been out of breath since we entered. And I've been . . . really, really angry and suspicious. I thought I was just worn out."

"You are," Valya said. "We all are."

"Then it's more important than ever that we get through this," Makali said. She and Zack helped Valya to her feet. . . .

Her feet were numb and aching. She felt that every step scraped more flesh from the soles. But she realized the truth of Makali's statement. She had no choice but to go forward, as they had done ever since leaving the human habitat. . . .

The forced march resumed, though it was more of a shamble. This end of the destroyed habitat was a mess, reminding Valya of Japan or Bangladesh after the big tsunamis of the past decade, where entire cities had been scraped off the face of the Earth, scrambled into tiny pieces, then crushed into a lumpy field of junk. There was nothing recognizable—not that Valya expected to recognize anything.

But it was still a horrifying reminder of the destructive power of whatever had wiped out this habitat.

Just as they closed in on Dash, the Sentry suddenly veered off to the right side, likely in search of the exit.

Valya was turned toward Makali when her peripheral vision lit up with a flash. A moment later, he and the others heard a cracking honk.

A ball of light rose to the high ceiling and floated there. The center of the habitat looked as though day had broken . . . revealing even more devastation than Valya had realized.

The improved lighting also revealed that some structures were intact here, rounded, irregular domes like termite mounds three or four stories tall.

"A flare," Dale said. "Someone's looking for someone."

"Connate," Dash said. "My pursuers."

Zack could see big, mobile Sentry-like shapes at the north wall of the habitat.

"Shit," Scott said, "we should have realized they'd get through that passage."

Now the Sentry kicked into a higher gear, literally running away from Valya and the others, disappearing between the two nearest termite mounds.

"Why is it leaving us behind?" Dale said.

"Maybe Valya was right," Makali said. "We got him out; he doesn't need us anymore."

"Let's not get lost," Zack said, though the exertion was wearing on him; his voice was growing weaker.

It had been painful for Valya to walk at a steady pace. Running was agony. She quickly lost the others as they entered the shadowy, debris-strewn alleys between the termite mounds.

Even though she tried to keep up with the others—and Makali, in particular, kept looking back for her—because of the lack of light, the rough surface, and the tight clearances between the structures, Valya found herself alone.

She stopped. *They're only a few meters away,* she told herself. "Zack!" she shouted. "Makali!"

Her voice was weaker than Zack's . . . the sound seemed muffled, inaudible, as if she'd been shouting inside a recording studio—

Then she heard a clear fluttering sound as the light changed, growing even darker.

She barely had time to look up as a shadow fell on her, ending her pain and curiosity.

PAV

"What's Keanu's diameter?" Zhao said.

Yvonne Hall looked up. "Ninety to a hundred kilometers, uncertainty due to its shape."

"You mean, it isn't round?" Rachel said.

"Not remotely," the Revenant astronaut said. "More like an egg."

"Like the Earth," Pav said. He had heard his father talk about things like this for years. He still didn't know why it mattered. Earth wasn't perfectly round; big deal. It had never affected him when he lived there.

And Keanu was even less perfectly round. Again . . . *what does it mean to me, Pav, right now?*

"Correct," Yvonne told him, then turned to Zhao. "Why do you ask?"

All four humans were sitting on the floor of the railcar, which had been moving smoothly, and at a steady rate, through a whole series of tunnels for the past hour. Rachel was next to Pav, resting her head on his shoulder and holding the Slate.

Cowboy was curled up at their feet. Zhao and Yvonne sat across from them . . . a considerable distance, given the size of the railcar.

"If we've been traveling for an hour, and our speed is

thirty kilometers per hour, which is likely a low estimate, we should have traversed a third of the NEO, am I correct?"

"If we traveled in a straight line, sure," Yvonne said. "But . . . have you ever been in any big metro? New York, London, Moscow—?"

"I've been in Moscow," Pav said, not sure why he had to contribute to the conversation. It was either talk, or doze off.

"And I've been in Paris, London, New York, Beijing," Zhao said. "What's your point?"

"These aren't necessarily linear systems."

"You're applying human reasoning to alien engineering."

"Come on, there are certain concepts that are universal. These people are seriously more advanced than we are in almost every field . . . but look at this thing." She waved a hand at the ceiling. "Call it a module or an alien transport vehicle or whatever you want . . . it's a subway car."

"Yes, and it's moving through an alien subway system toward a habitat—"

"—We hope," Yvonne said.

"You're in touch with the whole system," Rachel said, rousing herself and looking alarmed. "Don't you *know*?"

"Everything shut down when the car started moving," Yvonne said. "It was kind of a relief, I have to say. Like having the noisy folks next door turning off the loud music."

"It leaves us blind, however." Zhao said. "Or, rather . . . deaf."

"Maybe it will start up when we get wherever this is going," Pav said. He sure hoped so. For a moment, he imagined them simply ping-ponging through the interior of Keanu forever . . . or until they starved or died of thirst.

"Look, everyone, the voices told me to get in the railcar, go with it. It's taking us somewhere—"

Zhao gestured to Pav and to Rachel. *"Why aren't you taking us back to our habitat?"*

Yvonne blinked, like a student facing a surprise question on an exam. "Because the voices said to take you to the control center. Not back where you came from."

"But what are *we* supposed to do *there*?" Rachel said.

"That isn't clear," Yvonne said. "I realize that's . . . not satisfying. I don't like it, either. But there's a job you and I and maybe even Cowboy have to do once we arrive."

The dog whimpered. Pav doubted he was responding to the sound of his name, because he seemed to be asleep. Pav wondered . . . what kinds of dreams did dogs have? All about chasing animals? Eating?

What kinds of dreams did Revenant dogs have?

Thoughts of eating prompted Pav to ask Yvonne, "Will there be food when we get to the control center?"

She smiled. "I hope so. I haven't eaten since I got killed."

"That's so weird," Pav said.

"Tell me about it," Yvonne said.

"Why are you doing this? Helping us. Finding the control center, all of that. If I'd been dead and brought back, I'd still be trying to figure it all out."

She gave a snorting laugh. "I'd like nothing better." Then she grew quiet for a moment. "I screwed up," she said. "About as big a screwup as anyone ever made—"

"My dad says it was Houston and Washington's fault—"

"But I was the one *there*," Yvonne said. "I was the one who . . . got scared and set off the bomb. So this is a way for me to put things right." There was a faraway look in her eyes that made Pav uncomfortable, as if he were looking at a ghost.

Then she said, "I just wish I knew what made Pogo go so crazy."

"I have no idea," Pav said. He only knew what had happened, that Pogo Downey, one of the four American astronauts, had been killed, then turned into a Revenant. And that he had tried to go aboard the *Venture* lander.

"It's not like I've had time to think it over," Yvonne said, shaking her head at the sheer mystery of the experience. "To me, it all happened, like, half an hour before I met you guys. I thought he was trying to take over the lander. Take off with it and fly it back to *Destiny* and not only leave everyone behind, but become some nasty kind of alien invader on Earth. But, you know, second thought? I wonder if he was trying to provoke me—provoke NASA or the White House—to set off that nuke and keep Keanu beings from reaching Earth."

"Could he do that?" Pav said. "I mean, aren't you . . . under control?"

Yvonne laughed. "Well, hell, I suppose I wouldn't really know, would I? But what I think, right now, is this: We're messengers or facilitators. We're supposed to be a link between the Architects and you. We have information, but we're not puppets."

Then Rachel stirred and shifted, distracting Pav. Yvonne reached for the dog, too, and the magical moment was over.

Pav was okay with that. He was feeling the way he had when his father talked to him about business or politics, where his lack of even basic information made him feel stupid. He didn't like that feeling.

Rachel automatically opened the Slate in her lap, calling up the image of her mother, Megan. "You mind?" she said.

"It's okay," he told her. Even though he wore the Slate on a strap, even though it had the same mass as a print magazine, he was tired of lugging it through tunnels and while running for his life from hostile Long Legs.

Tired of worrying about losing it. Not that the unit was going to be much use when its battery died . . . tomorrow or next week, what difference did it make?

Oops, he was back to thinking about death. *Stop it. Think about this control center Yvonne promised. Where you can fly the starship . . . access the other habitats . . .*

Pav looked at the inkings on his arm. He remembered being obsessed with getting one. It was the one thing the vyomanaut's kid could do to make himself momentarily cool, to remove himself from the science geek world and put him firmly into music. He wished he had a pen right now. There was a perfect spot to draw something . . . Captain of Keanu would be good. Or Long Legs Killer.

Rachel sniffed. Yvonne and Zhao were too far away to see, or pretended not to, but the girl was *crying*.

It was just one more annoying thing, from being angry all the time or weepy half the time, or too smart-ass or too needy or not fast enough or too young or whatever . . . he wasn't sure he liked this girl at all.

But he would have been pissed if she'd been leaning on Zhao or Yvonne instead of him—

The railcar simply stopped.

And the lights died.

"Please tell me this is normal," Rachel said.

"Did your voices tell you about this?" Zhao said to Yvonne.

Yvonne's body language was all the answer Pav needed. She slowly pushed up against the wall behind her, shaking her head slowly. *Trying to tune in?* Pav wondered.

Cowboy got to his four feet.

The only light was from the screen of the Slate.

"Can anyone hear ventilation?" Zhao said.

"We're still breathing," Yvonne said. She worked her way to the open side of the car and looked out. "Hey, I see something ahead of us."

And she clambered down and out.

Cowboy followed her as if commanded.

"Well," Zhao said, "do as our Revenants do."

They were a hundred meters short of an opening. With Yvonne eagerly leading the way, Cowboy dogging her heels, Pav, Rachel, and Zhao followed.

"Is your Wi-Fi working again?" Pav called. He had the Slate slung over his shoulder again. He wished he had his own Wi-Fi—or some way to contact Nayar and the others in the human habitat. They must believe them all dead by now.

Suddenly the lights and power returned. As one, the humans and the dog all looked back at the railcar, which was making lively sounds again. "Is that going to move?" Zhao said.

"Let's not find out," Yvonne said. "Besides, we've arrived."

The transition was quick . . . up a set of broad, slightly too-tall steps (Pav had to help Rachel), across an aged and faded tile surface, then through another tunnel much like the one that first gave them access to the human habitat.

The interior of the control habitat was so bright it hurt Pav's eyes. Blinking, he was able to see a brilliant, gridlike set of structures stretching to the far side of the habitat . . . which appeared to be smaller than the human one. It was like looking at a circuit board the size of a city . . . from the inside.

"You know, Yvonne," Zhao said behind Pav, "I'm very glad you have that guidance in your head. I can't imagine what task we're supposed to be accomplishing . . . or where we would start."

"So where *do* we go?" Rachel said. She was sounding more and more impatient.

Yvonne looked from side to side. "We're meeting someone."

"Who?" Zhao said.

Yvonne smiled. "Our guide, okay? Things are a bit confused. There should be a Beehive somewhere along here. . . . Everyone split up and see if you can find—"

"You've got to be kidding," Pav said. "We split up and we'll never find each other again."

"We don't split up and we may never find the thing we're supposed to meet."

"Fine," Zhao said. "Rachel and the dog and I will take this direction, along the wall. A hundred meters, and then we return to this place. You and Pav do the same the other direction. If we don't find our mystery alien, we do another search."

Rachel was about to protest, but Yvonne simply said, "Back in a few." And took off.

As Pav hurried to catch up, he wondered why Zhao had teamed them the way he had. An adult in each team, probably. It would have made more sense to put Rachel with Yvonne, but Pav could tell that Zhao didn't like him. He really didn't seem to like Indians, period.

Suddenly the lights in the habitat died, leaving them in the most total darkness Pav had ever experienced. The drone of machines, the whisper of wind or airflow . . . sounds Pav hadn't consciously noted, those were gone, too.

"Uh, here we go again?"

"My voices just went silent, too," Yvonne said.

"What do we do?"

"Well, the last time the power went out—" Before she finished the statement, the lights and power resumed, though not without a disturbing shower of sparks arcing from somewhere nearby.

"Yvonne, is this place falling apart?" Pav had a tough time thinking of a millennium-old alien starship as needing maintenance . . . but on further consideration, why not?

"There," she said.

A giant creature, easily twice the size of a human being, like some kind of ancient knight, but with four arms, sat on a bench like an old man in a park.

She sent Pav back to the rendezvous point to meet Rachel and Zhao. "We found him."

"Found what?" Zhao said.

"An Architect."

For a young man who never expected to ever meet an alien creature, two in one day was almost too many for Pav. Even so, trying to be calm and grown-up . . . Pav thought Yvonne and the Architect seemed like an unhappy couple. The alien was still slumped, almost immobile, its two legs sticking out like logs, its four arms limp like spaghetti . . . while Yvonne stood directly in front of him. She looked like a pilgrim making an offering to a badly designed stone god.

Zhao approached Yvonne, speaking so softly that Pav and Rachel, left behind, couldn't hear. Cowboy simply flopped on the ground, happier than he'd been in a while, apparently willing to see what these creatures got up to.

Only now did Pav notice that the Architect was partly covered in the same coating as the earlier Revenants. "I think he's just come back from the dead," he whispered to Rachel.

"That's not good."

"Why?"

"Because all the Revenants take a while to boot up."

That had certainly been the case with Yvonne. And, judging from the Architect, here, too.

Yvonne turned away from the alien and walked toward Pav and Rachel. "God, this is so frustrating."

"What's wrong?" Pav said, suddenly alarmed. "Isn't he the one you've been hearing in your head all along?"

"No! At least, I don't think so. I think he was just reborn like me."

"My dad said my mother could speak directly to her Architect."

"I can speak to him," Yvonne said. "I'm just not getting much back."

"How much speaking did you do when you were just . . . alive again?" Pav said, looking at Rachel, as if to say, *Shouldn't we ask this?*

Yvonne frowned. "Good point. But we don't have all the time in the world." She tapped her head. "My Wi-Fi was pretty clear on that."

"Yvonne, come back here!" Zhao said. "Bring Rachel, too!"

Zhao had stayed with the Architect, essentially keeping the giant alien company. As he and the others approached, Pav saw Zhao stand on tiptoes to touch one of the Architect's "hands"—which flexed, then folded up, as if the alien were doing a curl.

"What the hell are you doing?" Yvonne said.

"Just testing our friend," Zhao said. "He seems to be in distress."

"Noted," Yvonne said. "Now what?"

Zhao pointed at Rachel. "I heard her talk about her mother. And it occurs to me that the Architect might know about her and about Zack Stewart, too—"

The mention of Zack's name caused the Architect to stir and stand up to its complete, towering height. For Pav it was like watching a building being erected . . . and took a considerable amount of time. *They're* slow, he realized.

"He's trying to tell me something," Yvonne said. She put her hands to her head and groaned. "God, it's just so . . . noisy!"

Zhao put his hands on Yvonne's shoulders, rubbing them like a trainer with a boxer. "Relax, find the message . . . he obviously wants to communicate with us. You just have to allow it."

Yvonne's tortured expression suddenly relaxed. To Pav, it was as if the woman had just found the right channel on a radio. "He says, 'I am the Builders or the Designers or Architects.' Plural."

"Is there more than one of them in there?" Pav said. The creature was big enough to hold multiple personalities.

"It says, 'We have no time for debates or education.'" Yvonne looked at Rachel. "'We knew your parent.'"

"Which one?" Rachel said. "My mother? My father?"

"'Both!' and he's quite emphatic about that." She closed her eyes for a moment. There were tears now. "He just gave me a blast of imagery and . . . God, emotion about your mother. God, Rachel, I'm so sorry . . . I had no idea."

Pav tried to keep his mouth from simply falling open. Only on Keanu would a woman who had been brought back from the dead be expressing sympathies to a girl who had lost her mother—or was it because she had been brought back to life only to lose it a second time?

"Does he know my mother? Can he talk to her?"

The Architect made a gesture with all four arms, as if embracing all of them. It was so fast and large that it caused the dog to bark.

The Architect bent down to look at the dog, which only increased the barking. "Dammit, control that animal!" Zhao said, amusing Pav, who had no control over Cowboy.

But he did kneel and try to soothe the dog, a move that put him squarely in the shadow of the giant Architect. No wonder the dog was tense.

"What happened to my mother?" Rachel said. She was almost frantic. "What happened to her?"

"'She died.'"

"I know that! I saw her body! But how?"

"'Conflict with the Race of Guards,'" Yvonne said.

"The Sentries?" Rachel said. "Yes, my father said she had been killed by a Sentry—"

"Just like Pogo Downey," Yvonne said. "The first time."

Rachel was practically jumping up and down.

"'Your father is alive. He is a prisoner of the Sentries.'"

That news hit them hard. "How could that happen?"

Zhao said. "Have the Sentries invaded the human habitat?"

"'Your parent left the habitat,'" Yvonne said. "'He is fighting the same war we are.'"

"What war?" Pav said. He couldn't just stand to one side trying to keep the dog quiet.

"'The war we are losing.'"

Zhao was growing impatient, and for once Pav agreed with the Chinese agent. "Who are we supposed to be fighting, and why?"

"'I or we have contained the Reivers,' whoever they are, though the emotion associated with the word is incredible fear and loathing," Yvonne said. "'You let them loose inside us,' he says." She added, "I'm not sure I know what he's talking about."

Zhao replied, "I don't see how humans could have released or unleashed these Reivers, no matter who or what they are. We've only been present a couple of days. We were barely surviving—"

"And until the dog fell down the hole, we were trapped in that habitat," Rachel said.

Yvonne was shaking her head. "Our friend is quite certain of this. 'Your people,' meaning you and me, 'gave them access.'"

"Fine, we screwed up, though I still don't see how, or what difference it makes," Pav said. "I want to get back to the others."

"'You can't,'" Yvonne said, "'the return route is already infected. The Reivers must be contained, and their access to—'" She frowned. "I'm getting the image of a big white blob of some kind, something called a 'vesicle.' Ah, 'their access to the vesicle has to be prevented.'"

It took a moment for Zhao to convince Yvonne that what the Architect meant was the same type of vehicle that had brought the Houston and Bangalore groups to Keanu. "Why would these Reivers want or need a vesicle?"

"To get off this ship?" Rachel said.

"'To invade and infect,'" Yvonne said. "And the image was Earth. These Reivers want to take over Keanu, then use a vesicle to invade and infect Earth."

"We still don't know what these things *are*!" Pav said. He was getting a headache, almost certainly from hunger . . . and from being chased and pushed and terrified for the entire past day, or four days.

Zhao was more deliberate. To Yvonne he said, "When the Architect says 'Reivers,' what do you see?"

"Really? Bugs, at first. Nasty black-colored bugs, only edged . . . like Legos. But they . . . build up, assemble, aggregate into . . ." She closed her eyes for a moment. "Oh, shit, that explains it. The Reivers aren't bugs, just tiny, machine-based life. And they serve as building blocks for all kinds of other, more complex and capable creatures. We've already run into one. That Long Legs anteater thing was a Reiver assembly."

"Where do they come from?" Zhao said. "Did they grow here?"

"'No,'" Yvonne said, still using that distant tone that suggested she was directly channeling the Architect. "'They were . . . not scooped up. They invaded. They . . . can live almost anywhere, high pressure, vacuum. They attached themselves to another race, were hidden in them.'"

"All right then," Zhao said. "We seem to have some idea of the problem. What can we possibly do to help? This is the control center, correct? You wanted us here?"

"'Having you here was logical before the infection and invasion. System is already corrupted, failing. There is only one race that might provide assistance . . . their name is Skyphoi.'"

"Who are they? Yvonne, you were in the museum, too—"

"Yes, we saw them: the big gasbag jellyfish things—"

"And where are they?"

"'The next habitat.'"

"Let's go, then," Zhao said. "Is the transport system still safe?"

"'No system is uncorrupted,'" Yvonne said, "but I'm getting the clear impression we're using the railcar."

"We?" Pav said.

Before Yvonne could answer, the giant Architect began to move.

"Yes, we're all going, and right now."

"While we're doing that," Rachel said, "if you don't mind, can you tell everyone back in the habitat that we're alive and what we're doing?"

GABRIEL

"I just don't know what to do with her," Harley Drake said, his voice tired, his eyes red with fatigue.

What passed for a Houston-Bangalore Council had gathered on the ground floor of the Temple. Harley Drake, Shane Weldon, Vikram Nayar, and Gabriel Jones were there with Sasha Blaine and the accused, Camilla.

To Gabriel, Harley, the crippled former astronaut and new mayor of HB, seemed worn and distracted, brightening only when turning to Sasha Blaine, who was sitting with Camilla, offering comfort while asking the girl a few gentle questions.

Neither activity was producing results. The only thing Camilla seemed capable of doing was reciting a few lines of doggerel in Portuguese.

Gabriel and Bynum excluded, all three adult males had taken turns trying to interrogate Camilla. . . . Had she "hurt" Chitran? Had she let the bugs into the habitat? If yes to either, *why*?

It had not gone well. Camilla seemed feverish, certainly skittish, understandably so. And, while Gabriel had been an inattentive and largely absent father, even his limited experience with his daughter, Yvonne, had educated him to the impossibility of getting a girl to do anything she didn't want to do.

Also present, the Revenant Brent Bynum, largely silent, though Gabriel had watched him clutching himself, his head moving ever so slightly from side to side, as if engaged in an important internal conversation.

Which was likely.

Matters were complicated by a "war room" mood, too. Drake had dispatched Xavier Toutant and several other HBs to find out what the hell was going on elsewhere in the habitat. (It looked to Gabriel as though there were several fires.) They had not yet returned, adding to the general frustration.

The moment Harley Drake gave voice to his exasperation, Brent Bynum stood up. "You're wasting your time with the girl," he said. "I can tell you everything she knows."

"Except what she did and why!" Drake snapped.

"I can tell you that these Reivers are the greatest threat we face," Bynum said, persisting. "Not just to humans here in the habitat, but to the Architects and, frankly, everything we know in the universe."

"Jesus Christ, Brent," Harley Drake said. "I can see where they'd be *pests*. Maybe even a danger to our . . . fragile situation here. But a threat to the *entire universe*? I have a hard time with that."

"That's because you're not allowing yourself to think on the proper scale, Drake. You've only interfaced with their most basic, but still lethal mode . . . They have several other modes, each one bigger, more capable, much nastier . . . right up to an aggregate the size of this planetoid. The universe is a strange place, or do you need further evidence? Look," Bynum said, "think of the Reivers as intergalactic locusts, consuming all energy, useful matter, and information in their path. They leave nothing behind. They can be any size, almost any form."

"Von Neumann machines?" Nayar said. In case the others didn't know, he added, "They act like self-replicating nanoprobes."

"Which are completely theoretical," Harley said.

As always, Weldon spoke to the practical matter. "Well, they're here now. Can they be killed?"

"Since you think she knows, ask her!" Bynum pointed to Camilla.

"Hey, listen," Sasha said, "we have a limited ability to communicate with this girl. I mean, I don't give a shit if what you say is filling her head. . . . If she can't tell us in our limited German, it's useless. Second, she's nine years old. She's been through an incredible trauma—"

"I have *some* idea what it's like," Bynum said.

"You were an *adult*," Sasha said. "And you woke up in a world where you already had some idea what had happened to you, where people spoke your language—" For a moment, Gabriel thought that the tall redhead was going to punch the newly reborn White House man.

But, Revenant or not, Brent Bynum still possessed the ability to read a situation, then adapt. "You're right," he said. "I apologize. I just . . . have this information boiling inside me. It's like I have to tell you and right now, or I'll just explode. And you're supposed to act on it, too."

"We are acting," Weldon said. "In a few minutes, we're

going to eradicate those bugs," he said, pointing out the front of the Temple. "Then we'll get to dealing with the, ah, what did you call them? Larger aggregates?"

Harley turned to Nayar and Gabriel. "Could you gentlemen find out where our weapons program is?"

They headed for the ramp.

Gabriel Jones didn't believe in magic. ESP, Tarot, or his particular bugaboo—astrology—none of those subjects had ever impressed him as worth a moment's thought.

Not that he didn't appreciate wonder, not that, in spite of a hard-won stone-cold atheism, he didn't subscribe to the biblical preaching that there are "many mansions," that there were things human beings did not know or understand about the universe—and maybe never would.

The real problem was that all these systems seemed too easy. Think it, do it. Turn over the right card and you know the future. Speak a few words and a woman falls in love with you.

Really? How? With no cost? No use of energy?

Nevertheless, like anyone who was fascinated by the universe as it existed, who had watched *Star Trek*, he had an appreciation for Arthur C. Clarke's statement that "any sufficiently advanced technology is indistinguishable from magic."

By that standard, after a few hours' exposure to the wonders of the Temple, Gabriel Jones was now an official believer in magic.

Just a few hours ago, he had been so out of it—so

close to death—that he had no memory of how he had moved from his lonely corner of the first floor of the Temple to this third-story marvel . . . what now looked like a state-of-the-art chemical laboratory.

"We carried you," Vikram Nayar told him.

He returned to wakefulness there, lying on a composite slab of some kind, one plasticlike tube sucking blood out of him, another feeding it back in, Jaidev Mahabala perched on the stool.

"Don't tell me Bangalore had this stashed away," he said, happy to be able to offer a lame but spirited joke.

Jaidev was the engineer in charge, busy continuing his exploration of the various panels. He took Gabriel's remark seriously. "Of course not. The Temple system constructed it. And if you look closely, you'll realize it looks nothing like a dialysis machine. But it does seem to be making you better, correct?"

"Feels good, I'll say that." Gabriel had had only a handful of encounters with such machines, so he had no real idea of what older or foreign models might look like. And in truth, most of this one was hidden inside the "cabinets."

Nevertheless, with every few heartbeats—or, more likely, every few cubic centimeters of cleansed blood—Gabriel could feel his strength returning. "With all the things the group needs, this really wasn't a priority—"

"In one sense," said one of Jaidev's colleagues, "this was a good test, to see if we could progress beyond the replication of food, water, and basic tools to more complex items."

"I'm glad you did."

Jaidev shook his head as he continued to uncover various screens on the panel, and screens within them. He reminded Gabriel of a teenage boy scope-locked on a video game. "First, you're going to need this again. Second, we could reprogram the machine into something entirely different." The engineer rapped his knuckle on the countertop. "Everything apparently starts as plasm. And with the proper commands, it can be reshaped into extremely complex devices."

"I wonder what goodies you can make that we don't know about," Gabriel said, suddenly seeing possibilities. "Okay, it's 3-D printing to the nth degree. I just don't really understand it—"

Jaidev smiled. "When we first got here, we found walls, surfaces, blank panels. We simply started touching them to see what would happen. We got light. We got . . . these command panels."

The second engineer chimed in with enthusiasm. "They don't have words, but they have symbols and figures."

"The Architects seem to organize data and functions from the top down . . . from simple to less simple to complex."

"It's quite a leap from a Crock-Pot to even a coffeemaker."

"Remember," Jaidev said, "this habitat was designed to adapt to whatever beings enter it. *Something* is scanning us for body mass, temperature, chemical composition, then rearranging everything, from soil to air to plants and structures, to match those needs. So the system is preloaded for human beings. It was really just waiting for us to—"

"—to start touching things."

"Still," Gabriel said. He obviously had the evidence sticking into his arm, but he was curious as to how passionate, and informed, Jaidev was on this subject. He was, after all, the human race's only expert on Keanu design and fabrication.

The other, older engineer—Daksha was his name—was, if possible, even more enthusiastic. "Look, Dr. Jones, we had no ability to design a dialysis machine. We simply entered commands in the medical area of the panels . . . essentially telling the system, do things that people here need. The system recognized your problem and adapted. We have other devices here now, too, and we don't really know what they're for, or for whom!"

"Sounds like ESP," Gabriel said.

"We don't understand what part of the electromagnetic spectrum they're using," Jaidev said.

"—Or even if it's electromagnetic."

"I think we've already seen that the Architects have access to . . . information in states that we do not." He smiled. "But, truly, it was almost like typing two letters on your computer, and having it finish the word for you."

Scratch that disdain for ESP or telepathy.

"Remind me, I have something to show you," Nayar said, the moment their feet hit the ramp.

"What is it?"

"I'm not sure yet, but—"

They were already emerging on the second floor, where they found Jaidev and Daksha as busy as fry cooks in a fast-food joint. They were checking on various assistants who came down from the floor above carrying containers and what looked to Gabriel like pesticide sprayers. Weapons for use against the Reivers.

Then they sent them below.

"How's it coming along?" Gabriel said, one of those fatuous-but-necessary phrases people in his job had to use.

"We'll know soon," Jaidev said. "Meanwhile, let me show you this."

He motioned Nayar and Gabriel to a panel. "We've located some kind of system status repository. It appears we have access to a multidimensional map of Keanu and its interior, showing various tunnels and passages and what appears to be a transport system . . ." As Jaidev spoke and touched, Gabriel watched the screens. Yes, the roundish thing that was Keanu . . . honeycombed with cylindrical structures radiating from a cylindrical central core. There were eight of them, and Gabriel didn't need Bynum or Jaidev to tell them these were the habitats.

Toward the bottom of that core, a spherical chamber . . . all of them connected by a network of lines and links that reminded Gabriel of a 3-D spiderweb.

Off to one side, near the surface of Keanu, was another chamber . . . smaller than the habitats or that core, oddly shaped, its purpose even less clear than that of the other structures.

Being tactile engineers, of course, Jaidev and Daksha

kept changing the screens. The global map was replaced by close-in images, individual tunnels, different habitats (what had to be the human one flashed by), other hollow places.

Then an exterior showing Keanu moving in a cloud of some kind of particles or gas, like a multi-lobed comet. The cloud was so pervasive and tenuous, it was difficult to determine where it ended and empty space began.

"Is there an exterior that shows Earth?" Gabriel said. How far had they come in a week? How fast was Keanu going? How much acceleration? They likely weren't as far as the orbit of Mars—

"We assume so," Daksha said. "But we haven't found the space-tracking area yet."

"Anything is better than what we had," Gabriel said. "Means we don't have to depend on Brent Bynum."

"I don't know," Jaidev said. "It was Bynum who pointed us to this area, including the medical section."

Which was the main reason Gabriel kept his mouth shut when Bynum began to be annoying: He owed the man his life.

"Speaking of the Reivers," Nayar said, "Bynum helped us understand some of the information the database has on these things." He nodded to Jaidev.

"It's almost as if they are the perfect evolutionary response to the conditions of the universe," Jaidev said, unable to hide the excitement in his voice. "They can be micro- or macrobeings. They assemble into aggregates that allow them to scale up to any mass required. And all because they are pure processors, taking in energy, using it."

"They are essentially information," Daksha said.

Just then Xavier Toutant rushed up the ramp. He was out of breath and his face was sweaty, as if he'd just made a long run.

"We tried all the poisons," he said. "Both chemicals. We tried fire."

"Slow down," Nayar said.

"Some of the stuff just rolled off them. We were the only ones getting poisoned!"

"What do you mean?" Jaidev said. He took the news personally. *Like a good general,* Gabriel thought.

"It was like pouring gasoline on a fire. . . . There were more bugs afterward than when we started!"

Nayar was holding up his hand. "Nothing has worked, is that what you're saying?"

"That's impossible!" Jaidev said. He headed for the ramp, as if determined to check out this ridiculous story for himself.

Nayar said, "If he says our weapons failed, they failed! The intelligent option is to find better ones."

"And quickly," Gabriel added. He smiled. "How do you kill . . . what did you say the Reivers were? 'Pure information'? How do you kill that?"

"With different information," Jaidev said, almost grumbling. But Daksha touched him on the arm, as if to say, *Let's think about this.*

The two immediately moved off to confer.

"I have a lot of confidence in your team, Vikram."

"I hope it's not misplaced."

"They've worked wonders so far," he said, his tone far

lighter than his mood. "As we were coming up here, you said you had something important to show me?"

Nayar immediately walked up to the panel showing the Keanu schematic. He tapped on the screen, zooming in for a closer view of one of the passages between two habitats.

There were six indicators in the passage, all clumped together, four small, one very small, and one large.

"We've located Rachel, Pav, and Zhao," Vikram Nayar announced. "At least, we're fairly sure this is them. We have some ability to roll back the image, and were able to walk these indicators back through that habitat"—he pointed at the one invaded by Reivers—"then back, back, back to what appears to be ours."

He traced his finger through a series of turns and twists that covered a third of the distance across the NEO.

"Wow. They've gone a long way," Gabriel said. "How did you hear from them? Direct voice?"

"Close-up imagery."

"Security camera?"

"A system that compares to our security cameras the way this"—Nayar pointed to the cabinets and their mysterious readouts and equipment—"compares to a nineteenth-century factory."

"Can't wait to talk to them. I hope they're safe."

"It appears so," Nayar said, "to the extent that any of us are safe." Having grown more at home with the displays—or tired of Jaidev's super-fast changes, like a deranged husband with a TV remote—Nayar began to manipulate the images on the screen, bringing up a new version of the Keanu interior.

As Nayar's finger slid over the various habitats, each exploded into a larger view that showed hundreds, likely thousands of small indicators, most of them in motion.

"Notice this discoloration? You saw it in tunnels and habitats."

There were smears of a different color through one entire habitat, effectively eliminating any individual Markers, at spots in several others, and through a good percentage of the tunnel and passage network.

"Alien graffiti."

"Reiver infection," Nayar said. "It's not just their presence. It's interference. We're suffering from it, too. We lost all data for several minutes. And the interruptions are coming more frequently."

"Well, we know we have to eradicate them. That's what we're doing, right?" Gabriel tried to sound cheery; it was one of the handiest items in his managerial toolbox. But he felt sick, because he knew that scrubbing the bugs from the human habitat was a small step.

"They seem to be on the march," Nayar said, "the infection spreading toward one particular zone."

"It's not a habitat?"

"It's got a different shape, and it's closer to the surface. We just don't know."

"But you figure it can't be good."

"There's another thrust toward the core," Nayar said. "Which we know to be the power sources."

"Okay, sum up for me, in case I have to explain it to Drake and Weldon—"

"The Reivers are close to taking over the entire NEO."

Gabriel closed his eyes. None of this was exactly a surprise—the moment he had seen the Reiver infection on the Keanu map he had realized it was a serious problem. It was still troubling to hear it stated.

Then he looked at the indicators. "Why are there six? It was only Rachel, Taj's boy, and Zhao who went out."

Jaidev and Daksha returned and heard Gabriel's question. As if testing his knowledge, Nayar said, "Two are nonhuman. One is the dog. But the other . . ." He indicated the various colors and displays. "Body temperature, size, mass, even speed of movement—"

"The kinds of data Keanu routinely collects on every being here," Jaidev added.

"—are all different."

"Okay, then, there's one alien, a dog, and four humans. Who's the fourth?"

"Uh, the message," Jaidev said, "indicated it was your daughter, Yvonne."

DALE

"Double back," Zack told them.

They had just snaked their way through the collection of rounded structures that Dale Scott immediately thought of as Crapville, right to the point where they could see Dash ahead of them . . . and a clear Beehive-like opening in front of him.

Zack, Makali, and Dale. No Valya.

"God, she was right behind me," Makali said.

"Good, then she won't be far."

He didn't wait or issue orders, but simply shot back the way he had come, taking the left of a pair of routes. Makali looked at Dale. "You and he were both ahead of me on that path. If he's taking the left, we should take the right." There were really only two pathways through the rubble of Crapville.

The last thing Dale Scott wanted to do was to lose sight of the Sentry and turn away from the possible exit. He could feel himself on the verge of passing out, knowing that if he did, it would be the end.

But, fine, one more try.

He followed Makali through the debris, unable to see much. The flare of the pursuing Sentries had died out, leaving the humans to stumble around in the darkness like children in an unlit basement.

He wondered briefly how close the pursuers were. And if they caught the humans, what would they do? And what difference would it make?

"Dale!" Makali was somewhere in front of him, huffing and puffing. "Two paths again . . . go right, hear me?"

"Right, got it!"

A shadow passed over him, something silent, swift. Looking up, he saw what appeared to be a red balloon— not a Sentry in some kind of aircraft, thank God. The object disappeared from sight quickly, which was fine for Dale. He needed to watch his footing.

The right path suddenly appeared as a slightly less dark area in front of Dale. It was so clogged with debris that he had to drop to hands and knees to crawl over it . . . he immediately knew that, in her present condition, Valya had never reached it.

Which didn't mean, of course, that she wasn't still in front of him.

He slid down the far side of the mound of debris and almost pitched forward onto his face. He was walking on something slippery . . . fresh fluid of some kind.

He smelled something new, fresh, and nasty, too.

Oh shit! Around the nearest turn was a body, human, literally cut in two from top to bottom. One half had been scattered—Dale had been walking on the remains— while the other lay in a crumpled, bloody heap.

Valya.

"Over here!" Dale said. It started as a shout but ended

as a sob. *Oh fuck*. He took a breath, steadied himself against the nearest wall. "I . . . found . . . her!"

Yes, they had been poisoned, suffering from who knew what kind of oxygen deprivation and nasty trace element overload, all of it contributing to evil thoughts.

But Dale Scott had never wanted to see Valya truly dead. She was a friend—had been his lover—was part of the team!

Makali was first to arrive. She shrieked and turned away. Turning back, she shoved Dale. "What did you do?" she screamed. She actually began hitting him.

It was relatively easy to grab her fists and force them down. "What the fuck are you doing?"

Zack arrived then, clambering over the same pile of debris as Dale, and slipping, too. Then he stopped dead, as if punched. "God," was all he said.

Makali was in Dale's face. "You hated her!"

"Me?" he said. "You think I would or could do *this*?"

"Stop it," Zack said. "We're oxygen-starved and poisoned." He rubbed his face. "Well, there's nothing we can do for her." He held his right hand over the remains, as if offering a blessing. Dale wished he had thought of that.

Meanwhile, Makali knelt by the body. "Where's her bag?"

"What difference does it make?" Dale said. *Jesus, women*.

"It had the Tik-Talk, for one thing," Zack said. "But I don't see it anywhere."

"Sorry to hear it," Dale said. "It hasn't exactly been useful."

"Guess we'll never know now," Zack said. He seemed quite angry about it.

"Zack," Makali said, "who did this?"

"Dash's connate, maybe?" He looked in the general direction of the habitat. "I have no idea how fast Sentries can move. Maybe they caught up to us."

Dale thought that was silly. He had watched the pursuing Sentries long enough to see that they were at least half an hour behind the humans. "And maybe there's something else around here," Dale said. "These Reiver things, maybe?"

"Killers were Skyphoi," an electronic voice said behind them.

Dash was there—for how long? Dale wondered. The Sentry looked slumped, as defeated as any of the bedraggled humans. "And who are the Skyphoi?" Zack said. "And why would they want to kill Valya?"

"Skyphoi inhabit the next habitat. They are a newer race, our enemies."

"What are they doing here? Is this their habitat?"

"No. But they were the race that caused this," Dash said.

"They've got nukes?" Makali said.

"They worked with Architects on the sanitization. They have unusual destructive devices."

"What can we do?" Zack said. "What do they look like? How do we fight them?"

"They are air creatures," Dash said, which told Dale very little that was useful. "Come now," the Sentry said. "They will see the connate and my people—there will be war between them. We can escape." Without waiting for further questions, or offering further information, the Sentry turned and began to walk away.

Zack, Makali, and Dale looked at each other.

"If we don't reach that control center soon . . ." Makali said, and was unable to finish.

For once, Dale sympathized. "How many enemies does this guy have?" Dale said.

"I don't know," Zack said. "I just wish they all didn't turn out to be our enemies, too."

ZHAO

It was an article of faith among Zhao's instructors in Guoanbu that no assignment was like any other, that no amount of training or imagination would be sufficient to prepare an agent for unexpected occurrences . . . for the weather that prevented a pickup, for the domestic problems that caused an agent to turn, for the sports team that unexpectedly made the playoffs, filling and then emptying a stadium and causing a drunk, violent traffic jam at just the wrong hour. . . .

Colonel Dao, the most consistent proponent of this chaos theory, even had a name for such events, calling them "Zoo Animals," a term Zhao had always found as inappropriate (what did confined creatures have to do with chaotic mishaps?) as it was unforgettable.

Zhao had been living through a gigantic series of Zoo Animals.

As he swayed and lurched in response to the actions of the giant railcar—which had stopped and started twice because of total blackouts—he pondered what appeared to be a literal representation: two children of space travelers, one a girl obsessively and selfishly using up the last dregs of power in their only Slate in order to stare at images of her mother and father, the other a callow, impulsive, surly, uncooperative teen male.

Then there was the alive-again American astronaut Yvonne Hall. In Zhao's pre–*Destiny* and *Brahma* mission briefings, the African American woman had been described as equal parts intelligence and resentment, a potentially explosive combination that was, the material said, "likely to result in poor operational decision making." Such as setting off a suitcase nuclear device during humanity's first interplanetary mission? Talk about a Zoo Animal.

Her behavior since reappearing among the living had redeemed her somewhat. In Zhao's judgment, Yvonne had served as an adequate link to the intelligences that controlled the Near-Earth Object Keanu. Not a perfect link—he still seethed with anger and frustration at Yvonne's initial inability to relay any information of real or timely use. Had she been able to tune into the "voices in her head" earlier, for example, they might have been spared that terrifying encounter in that Museum of Lost Aliens.

But that had improved. She had managed to contact—indeed, to summon forth, like an ancient wizard—an actual Architect, and to bring him on their latest, hopefully final journey. The giant Zoo Animal now sprawled across the railcar from Zhao, Pav, and Rachel, patiently answering questions from Yvonne—or so it seemed. The Revenant astronaut was making gestures and looking quizzically at the Architect. Zhao hoped the alien was responding.

And, finally, the closest thing to an actual Zoo

Animal . . . the dog. The golden-Lab mix seemed to have made the smoothest adjustment to the strange environment. Certainly Cowboy had continued to act like a dog, barking at the threatening and sniffing at the interesting and unusual. When not so engaged, he simply kept company with the humans, as he did now, resting with head on forepaws and waiting patiently for the next event.

Of course, Zhao's experience with dogs was limited. He might be missing obvious signs of canine distress and dysfunction.

"Okay," Yvonne said, "we're almost there."

"I hope so," Pav said. "I don't want to be stuck here if the power goes out for good."

"It shouldn't," Yvonne said. "Though that is a sign of problems with the power core."

"Which someone is trying to repair, I hope," Zhao said.

"To be continued," Yvonne said. "When we arrive, we will let the Architect communicate with the Skyphoi—"

"Why?" Pav said, in that sneering voice Zhao had grown to hate. "Don't they speak one of our languages? What kind of advanced race are they?"

Yvonne, obviously familiar with teen sarcasm, remained patient. "They don't actually speak. They are basically like jellyfish, only they live in the air. They communicate by changing color. They're chromatophores."

Rachel stirred at this, closing down the Slate. "That might be cool to see."

Cool to see. The trio of Pav, Rachel, and Zhao had seen enough wonders and marvels for the population of

Guangdong for an entire century. Zhao wanted no more . . . cool things to see.

"Fine," Zhao said, "we'll stay in the hallway. What will our big friend be trying to do?"

"He wants to be sure that the vesicle is secure . . ."

"The what?" Pav said.

"The blob that brought us here," Rachel said. Then she turned to Yvonne. "And might be able to take us home."

"In theory," Yvonne said, glancing at the Architect for confirmation. Zhao didn't like the sound of that. Hadn't the Architect already told them humans were needed in a war? A war taking place some ungodly number of light-years away? They weren't going to help humans go back to Earth!

Yvonne was saying, "The important thing is that no one else takes it. Another one would take years to grow."

"What about the blackouts we're having?" Zhao said. Forget the mythical voyage home; concentrate on day-to-day survival right here.

"Part of the same process. Without steady power, there is no ability to control the vesicle—"

"—Or anything else, I would imagine," Zhao said.

Yvonne ignored that. "And the Architect believes the power core may need to be rebooted."

Zhao felt as though he'd been stabbed. Yvonne's casual tone, the single sentence, neither was sufficient to convey the impact of that concept. "And how," he said carefully, trying to keep his voice even, "does something like that happen?"

Yvonne gestured in the manner that Zhao had begun

to loathe, flapping her hands in front of her face. She might as well have said *I just don't know* aloud. "I have images of something I'll just have to call a starter kit. The Skyphoi have it."

"And these Skyphoi . . . they're quite powerful?" Zhao wished he could just ask the Architect directly. Given the being's height, it was difficult to see its face, much less judge its engagement or indifference.

Fortunately, Yvonne continued to relay information. "The Skyphoi are fierce and independent. They came the closest, the Architect says, to being the allies they wanted in the fight against the Reivers."

"But they still failed."

"Only because they are too limited; they can inhabit only a narrow range of environments, planets with low density and thick atmospheres."

"The Architects should have known that, shouldn't they?" Perhaps by challenging these statements, he could make the responses more useful.

"The Reivers spread to new environments faster than expected. This took place over . . . several thousand years."

Zhao shook his head. Too much, too weird. It was like the first time, at age fifteen, he had been able to bypass his country's filters to gain free access to the Internet. Naturally he had begun surfing pornography . . . clicking through one link after another, always chasing, never finding, never reaching the point where you think you'd found it, whatever it was.

"Who is this guy?" he said, not really intending it as a question.

"Oh," Yvonne said, "didn't I tell you? He's a Revenant, just like me."

"No, somehow you failed to let that slip," Zhao said.

"I know I said something."

Zhao was mortally sure Yvonne had never mentioned it. Besides, they'd been in the presence of the Architect for only a couple of hours. But why argue? "When did he die?"

"Long ago," Yvonne said. "Very long ago. The figure comes into my head as a hundred million years. Give or take a decimal point."

Zhao sat up. "That's an impressive figure," he said. "I'd always assumed that Keanu itself was on the order of several thousand years old . . . but you're talking a hundred times that—"

"A thousand times," Pav said. "Maybe a million." He and Rachel were paying attention now, having stirred from their reveries.

"It's like this," Yvonne said. "He's not really a person as we understand it," she said.

Before Zhao could process that bizarre notion, the railcar began to slow . . . a nice change from the sudden lurches Zhao and the others had experienced, especially on this trip with its blackouts. "Are we here?" he asked.

"I think so," Yvonne said. "I've got to tell you, I'm really tired of this. I don't understand two thirds of what's in my head. I just want to get something to eat and lie down and enjoy what time I have left."

"What do you mean?" Zhao said.

"Revenants don't last long," she said. "We're tools.

We're here to communicate, then . . . wear out." She blinked back tears.

"That seems cruel," Zhao said. "And horribly inefficient."

"Well, yeah!" Yvonne said, forcing a laugh. "I think they'd be happy to have us stick around longer, you know, just in case anybody had a question a month from now. But this whole apparatus"—she indicated her body—"is fragile and wears out in a hurry. I'm not complaining, mind you. I mean, given what happened . . . I know that souls survive, which is probably the most important thing anyone's ever learned, right? So even though I don't know what's next . . . I know there's *something*."

Zhao was not a toucher, but he couldn't help reaching for Yvonne's hand.

Then he forced himself to stand up, addressing the Architect directly. "Who are you?" he said. "Can you understand me?" He said it in English, in Mandarin, in Hindi.

"Lighten up," Pav said. He had likely understood two of Zhao's three statements. "He already said."

"*She* said, you mean." Rachel pointed at Yvonne.

Zhao was about to repeat his demand in French, when Yvonne went rigid and started to rise. She looked fearful. "He says that he can't engage on a verbal level, even with the proper translation device. Says it's a scaling problem—"

"Whatever that means," Zhao said.

"His processes are . . . slower?" Yvonne seemed to be

having a conversation with herself. Then she laughed out loud. "Okay, yes." She turned to Zhao, Pav, and Rachel. "If you need to use a name, call him 'Keanu.'"

"But that's the NEO," Rachel said.

"I think that's what Keanu is trying to tell us," Yvonne said. "This body is just a way for Keanu to communicate—"

The railcar came to a gentle stop.

"Everybody out," Yvonne said. "Hurry."

They emerged into another tunnel much like those they had visited earlier . . . during what was proving to be a day without end.

Beyond the railcar, however, the tunnel opened into what, on Earth, would have been a giant underground station worthy of the Paris or Moscow metros. And covering one wall of the station . . . a shimmering curtain of bubbles. "What on Earth is that?" Zhao said, pointing to the curtain.

"The way into the Skyphoi habitat," Yvonne said. And just like that, the former order was restored: Zhao would question, Yvonne would answer for the Architect.

Yvonne turned to Rachel. "Your father called it a Membrane, I think."

"My father."

Zhao found that revelation interesting. "Did our friend Keanu tell you that?"

"No. During the first EVA, Zack sent video of something that looked just like that, only smaller, when he and Pogo and the others made that first ingress." Zhao noticed that Yvonne was again blinking away tears. "God, that was only a week ago."

"Or another lifetime," Zhao said.

He and Pav and Rachel were following Yvonne and the Architect. The giant lumbered along like the drunks Zhao remembered seeing in the streets of Guangdong, though a more charitable explanation might be that its head kept brushing the top of the tunnel . . . and its legs appeared to be unsteady.

The dog trotted along happily, flanking them while taking momentary detours.

Zhao was fascinated by this big Membrane. "What's on the other side?" he asked.

"The Skyphoi habitat."

"So you said. Are we going in there?"

The lag between question and response was longer than expected. "No," Yvonne said. "Keanu says you wouldn't like it."

"Can we be the judge of that?"

"He means, it will kill you. Atmospheric pressure too high, too toxic."

"Is he going in?" Pav said.

"No," Yvonne said. Before she could say anything more, the Architect slowed to a stop.

They were looking at what appeared to be an accident scene at a balloon festival . . . if you allowed for the fact that the festival was taking place indoors.

Three large spherical objects floated in the "station" area, occasionally bumping up against the Membrane. They were mostly blue in color, ranging from desert sky to almost aquamarine, with flickers of other shades, too.

The creatures weren't perfectly spherical; their shapes kept changing with a regular rhythm. *It's as if they're breathing,* Zhao thought—and why wouldn't they?

The trio hovered over a fourth balloon, this one crimson in color, that lay half-deflated on the ground, emitting clouds of nasty-smelling gas.

"Are these the Skyphoi?" Rachel said.

"Yes," Yvonne said, "and that one is badly injured."

Keanu the Architect approached the scene, stopping some distance away and freezing into near-immobility. Zhao caught Yvonne a handful of meters from the Architect, with Pav and Rachel and Cowboy joining, too. He hoped this was a respectful distance.

He also hoped something would happen, because he felt even more paralyzed and helpless than at any time since being sluiced through the tunnels.

As they watched, the three Skyphoi barraged the Architect with colors. "They're talking to him," Yvonne said, "but he doesn't understand. He needs a Skyphoi Revenant."

Pav pointed to the dying Skyphoi. "What about that one?"

"That was the Skyphoi Revenant," Yvonne said quietly. "We didn't get here in time."

The dog suddenly began barking furiously, startling the Architect and causing the Skyphoi to rise and bump against each other.

"What is it?" Pav asked.

Cowboy took off down the tunnel beyond the accident scene.

"God, I don't like this," Rachel said. Pav put his arm

around her, a gesture Zhao appreciated. Even Yvonne seemed apprehensive.

Four figures emerged into the faint light of the "station," one notably taller than the others and looking like an image from a dark ages nightmare.

The other three, however, were undeniably human, though as ragged as refugees. Zhao squinted. . . . Who were they? And what was that thing they were with?

Rachel Stewart suddenly broke free from Pav and ran toward them, screaming, "Daddy! Daddy!"

Part Seven

Second thoughts: Okay, voyages of exploration usually suck, at least for most of the voyagers. For every Columbus or Admiral Zheng He who gets his name in the history books, there are a few dozen or a few hundred people who die along the way, and nobody thinks about them.

I guess that's how it goes.

On the plus side . . . you do get to see shit you'd never see if you stayed home. And meet some interesting people, depending on what you mean by people.

KEANU-PEDIA BY PAV, ENTRY #6

THE PRISONER

For many cycles, the Prisoner's only wish was to escape from its chamber, and to somehow shame its Connate. With the small aid of the Two Arms, that task had been accomplished.

But what shocking surprises awaited it! The changes in the habitat, the disappearance of its former allies!

The relentless pressure from the Two Arms to move, and to consider—much less act in support of—their petty goals.

The moment had been supremely disorienting, a reminder of the horror the Prisoner had felt when first locked away in the annex to the Beehive.

With no contact with its allies, hampered by these new companions, its only option now was to return to the original goal from many cycles back . . . the original mission that had been the cause of its downfall.

It seemed so far in the past—seven plus seven cycles—that the Prisoner and its Connate had plotted to turn the Small Ones' powers against them, creating their own assemblies that would fight, then absorb the others, giving the People final control of all habitats and the warship itself!

But then . . . to be betrayed by one's Connate! To have been forced to make the Small Ones his allies against the People!

Now the Prisoner's mission was clear: Locate its former manufacturing gear, and help the allies to shame and destroy the Connate.

Then . . . deal with the allies.

Help the allies. Shame and destroy its Connate.

Then, apparently, die.

Unless it found something new to live for.

MAKALI

Makali Pillay had endured many shocks and surprises since being scooped up in the Bangalore vesicle. But nothing prepared her for the sight of a teary teenage American girl running toward them. What was Rachel Stewart doing here? The last she knew, Zack's daughter was in the human habitat with 180-plus others!

And Pav was with her. And the Chinese spy, Zhao.

And the dog!

And a human woman she recognized as Yvonne Hall, the dead *Destiny* astronaut.

Followed by the Architect, and three giant jellyfish creatures.

It was good that she'd barely eaten or slept in the past forty hours. Emotional numbness and nearly paralyzing fatigue allowed her to be objective. This wasn't happening to her, this was some kind of lucid dream, one in which she knew what was happening, but was powerless to change it.

She feared for Zack Stewart's mental health. He had been reunited not only with his daughter—he hadn't even known she was missing!—but with Yvonne Hall. He was openly weeping, visibly confused, thoroughly shaken.

She realized that she was crying, too.

And so was Dale Scott. To Makali's astonishment, he slid an arm around her and pulled her close. She could feel him trembling. "God," he said. "We'd better get it together."

Makali agreed, because they weren't the only actors on this stage.

The Skyphoi had surrounded Dash. The Sentry stood impassive, almost immobile, as the giant balloon creatures bumped and floated above him, their colors flickering through the visible spectrum in what had to be deliberate patterns. "What do you suppose they're saying?" Makali said.

The three-way reunion between Zack and Rachel and Yvonne had settled down to the point where Makali felt she and Dale could join in. Rachel did the introductions, ending with the giant creature that could have knocked Dash the Sentry over: "This is the Architect."

"You mean, an Architect," Zack said.

"Aren't they the same?" Rachel said. Zack's tired nod confirmed it.

Makali noted the *Destiny* commander's body language: tense and wary. He had one hand on Rachel's shoulder, the other on Yvonne's. Now he subtly pushed his former crew member forward. "Does he remember me?"

"Yes," Yvonne said.

"And my wife?" Zack said.

"Yes."

"Why did she die again? Can he answer that?"

"I can," Yvonne said. "Because the stress of being

reborn, becoming a Revenant, is so great that adult bodies often don't last long. They are created to serve as bridges between two races . . . once communion and understanding is established, they begin to fail." A look passed between Yvonne and Zack, who was about to offer consolation or commiseration, Makali felt. But Yvonne stopped him. "Information persists," she said. "Take that for what it's worth. . . . If you're asking me, I don't know that I'd *want* to go through this again. . . . Remember what I'm looking forward to: dying for the second time. It wasn't that much fun the first time through."

"It seems really mean," Rachel said.

"Maybe," Yvonne said. "But I don't think they know. Or care." She considered it further. "They're really not like us."

Makali looked at Dale, who simply stared at the hard-packed ground. She felt that she was eavesdropping on a moment of great intimacy, like a confession to a priest. Of course, there was no intimacy. There were other creatures and other activities all around them.

But the idea of confession suddenly caused her to wonder, perhaps stupidly, what a priest would make of this Revenant business, or how certain knowledge of life after death would affect religious thought—

At that moment the power died again, the *thrum* of the railcar—which Makali had been hearing without recognizing the source—died, and so did the lighting in the tunnel.

The only illumination was from the three Skyphoi, lit

up like lanterns with their own power . . . and now showing impressive collections of internal organs.

Before Makali could make sense of what she was seeing, Dash joined them, the Sentry almost a ghostly voice in the dark. It said, "If my people emerge and find us, there will be casualties." It wasn't clear to Makali whether Dash was addressing the Architect or Zack.

"More casualties, you mean," Dale said. "Who killed Valya?"

"The Skyphoi have a history of conflict," the Sentry said.

"Not with us," Dale said.

"The Skyphoi detected me," Dash said, "and judged me to be hostile. You were with me."

"There's no point to a postmortem now," Zack said. "The question remains: How do we get to the vesicle?" He turned to the Architect. "That's the mission right now, isn't it? For everyone? Get to the vesicle before these Reivers do?"

"And stop the Reiver infection," Yvonne said.

Makali was torn between hoping to observe the Architect and these Skyphoi—and the now-familiar Sentry in its interactions with the other aliens—and wanting to simply help Zack and get on with the work.

She wanted to go *home*. During their few free moments in the march across the blasted habitat, Zack had begun to enthuse about the possibilities. "You guys rode a vesicle here. There's no reason we can't ride a vesicle back to Earth."

But that had been an hour ago, before Valya was killed. Before this . . . insane rendezvous.

The various parties quickly established that the vesicle pod was adjacent to, but on the other side of, the Skyphoi habitat. "Can we go through?" Zack asked.

"No," Yvonne said, channeling the Architect. "Too dangerous for you."

"How come these guys can come into our habitat, but we can't handle theirs?" Dale said. "The atmospheres have to be pretty good matches."

"There's no surface," Yvonne said.

"There's *got* to be a surface of some kind!"

"I think what she means," Zack said, "is that the Skyphoi are creatures of the air . . . their habitat is filled with oxygen and other elements, but is really a giant cylinder."

"Imagine the human habitat with no floor," Makali said.

"It would be like trying to walk across the Grand Canyon," Yvonne said, speaking more for herself, Makali realized. "You could do it, but it would take you a long time. And the Skyphoi aren't strong enough to carry you.

"We have to use the transports." She nodded at the waiting railcar farther down the tunnel.

Now Zhao pointed to the Skyphoi. "It's *their* habitat. Can they get there more quickly?"

"Of course," Yvonne said. "But they will be unable to do much if they do reach the vesicle. The Reivers have already . . . evolved ways to kill the Skyphoi."

Even now one of the Skyphoi, its color a sickly pink, had to slide back through the Membrane.

"Then what fucking use are they?" Dale Scott muttered. Makali thought she was the only one who heard him, but apparently the Architect had better ears than the humans.

"You should hope that you never need to know," Yvonne said.

"Assuming we reach the vesicle in time," Zack said, "we're still facing these Reivers. We don't even know what they look like, much less how to fight them."

Zhao and Pav and Yvonne explained. The thought of microscopic nanotemplates was bad enough; Makali had spent much of her life in tropical or subtropical regions. The bugs in Houston annoyed her, especially when she stepped on them barefoot.

The idea of bugs that were not only intelligent as a group, but capable of assembling themselves into creatures on any scale . . .

"They're vulnerable to heat," Yvonne said. "And energy, though only in high, concentrated doses. The best weapon is speed. We have to beat them to the vesicle."

With no further discussion, the group—including the Architect—turned as one and headed directly for the railcar. Only Dash seemed to lag, a fact Dale Scott commemorated by saying, "Move it or lose it, big boy."

The Sentry gave no sign that it heard or understood.

Before they reached the railcar, Makali heard Rachel say to Zack, "Daddy, what if the power goes out while we're on the way?"

Makali didn't hear Zack's answer. Was he still feeling like the glass was half full? She hoped so, for everyone's sake.

Makali had judged the railcar to be far larger than needed, the size of a semitrailer. But with the entire group crammed into it—Zack holding Rachel by the hand, Zhao, Pav, the dog, Dale, Yvonne, Makali, the Architect, and the Sentry—Makali felt as though she were back in Bangalore, crammed into public transport.

It was an impression rather than a fact; the Architect placed itself at one end of the car, the humans clustered in the middle, while Dash the Sentry hunkered at the other end, its many arms busy with objects it was removing from its vest.

The first motion was a violent lurch. "Wow," Zack said, "just like liftoff!"

Makali asked Zhao, "Is that normal?"

"No," he said.

"Should I be worried?"

The Chinese spy smiled. "If it will make dying easier."

Makali couldn't help asking, "What makes this thing go? Is it electric?"

"Driven by super-dense mass," Zhao said. "Cat's-eyes, like really, really tiny marbles."

"But electricity must drive them," she said, happy to be thinking about alien transport technology rather than improbable and likely non-existent weapons.

"Yes," Yvonne said, "the warship contains a network of power and fluid conduits."

"Which means this whole system is subject to blackout?"

"There are backup systems," Yvonne said, but only that much. Her sudden shifts between disinterest and engagement were starting to bother Makali.

"Well, that's reassuring," Makali said, unable to hide the sarcasm. She turned to Zhao. "Are you reassured?"

"I'm pondering the weapon we can use against the Reivers," he said. "Along with wondering how they got to the NEO in the first place, and what they really want."

Yvonne turned to them. "'They came,'" she said, with the familiar channeling-Keanu tone, "'as unwanted passengers on an arriving spacecraft. Like mice on a sailing ship. We thought we had exterminated them,'" she continued, totally given over to her avatar mode now. "'But one race deliberately hid a colony, which then reestablished itself.'"

Now she shuddered, and seemed to wake up. "What they want is to suck every one of us dry, take all our energy and life to make more of them. Apply that to maybe the entire galaxy. Their goal is to . . . transform everything into their kind of being or matter."

Makali grinned at Zhao, who seemed stunned to disbelief. "So, what have you got? A paper clip in your pocket?" She nodded at Pav, who cradled a Slate in his lap. "We could boot that up and dazzle them with graphics or pound them with loud music." She patted her pocket. "I've got a Tik-Talk. Maybe I could throw it at them—"

Yvonne sat up straight. "Use the Tik-Talk," she said.

Zack heard her, too. "For what?"

"Contact with the habitat!" Rachel said.

"How would that even work?" Makali said.

Yvonne looked happy for the first time since Makali had met her. "Signals have a tough time going through habitats, but these tunnels not only conduct mass, they conduct energy and radiation—"

"Got it," Makali said, thumbing the power button. She was pleased to note that the battery indicator was, appropriately, half full. Then she offered the Tik-Talk to Zack. "Your call, boss."

"You go ahead."

She needed no further encouragement. "Hello, Temple. Hello, Temple, this is Makali Pillay. Anybody home?"

They all waited. Thirty seconds passed. "For God's sake, keep trying," Dale said. "It's standard operating procedure."

"I'm hardly a standard operator," she snapped. But she repeated the call.

Then waited. Still nothing.

"Are we sure it's working?" Rachel said.

"You can hear the carrier wave," Pav said. He slid forward, assuming a praying posture in front of Makali and the Tik-Talk. "Come on, somebody!"

"While this would be great," Dale said, "it doesn't change our situation." He looked at Yvonne, then at Zack. "We've still got to get to the vesicle. The Temple people aren't going to be able to help—"

"Hello!" A voice spoke from the Tik-Talk. "Who is this? Where are you?"

Harley Drake. Makali handed the Tik-Talk to Zack.

There wasn't time for a long chat. And from what Makali heard about the situation in the human habitat, only a long chat would be sufficient to catch them up. The infestation was bad news, certainly. Camilla's strange behavior—also bad.

But the wonderful things being whipped up by Nayar's team in the Temple? Not only tools, but food, water, clothing, medical equipment?

Weapons?

Still, in spite of what Makali was hearing from Harley on the speaker, Dale's point was sound: There wasn't anything the Temple team could do to help them against the Reivers. Not yet, anyway.

She actually moved away. It was too painful to listen. She preferred instead to watch Yvonne and the Architect, both of them in silent communion for the entire conversation between Zack and Harley.

Then there was Dash the Sentry, alone with its alien thoughts. As she looked, something about the Sentry's appearance troubled Makali.

Makali turned back to the conversation in time to hear Zhao say, "I don't know how to fight the Reivers face-to-face, but I've been trained in asymmetric or cyberwar methods."

She sat down next to Dale, who had been paying closer attention. "What is he talking about?"

"A weapon to use against the Reivers."

"Oh, really?"

"If you have a life form that is pure information, the weapon to use is—"

"A lie?" Makali said.

"Well, corrupt information. Or corrupt information that keeps on corrupting."

"What does that mean in practical terms?"

"Damned if I know," Dale said. "But I think we're into biological warfare. Bug on bug, something that will turn their strengths against them."

She let her head loll back. Among the many drawbacks of living on adrenaline for forty hours straight was the need to sit down and effectively shut down more often and more completely. She felt that now . . . a bone-deep weariness that made her question every decision, every hope.

Nothing looked good right now. "I was just thinking," she said to Dale, on the chance that stirring herself for a new conversation would restart her motor. "Why were the Skyphoi in the dead habitat to begin with?"

"What do you mean?"

"Were they there to help Dash, or catch him?"

"I assume it was to help him . . . they were vectored there by whatever voices they hear."

"But what if they were trying to catch Dash instead? Or even kill him?"

"Well, okay, but they haven't said anything—"

"They can't say shit that we understand! Maybe all those freaky colors have been the Skyphoi saying, 'The Sentry is a murderer!'"

She suddenly turned to look at Dash again.

There was an item on the Sentry's left lower arm. That was what she had been recording without actually seeing.

It looked like a piece of fabric.

"You've seen how difficult it is to communicate from one habitat to another, or from one race to another! And their Revenant or communicator is dead."

"I think you've gone without food or sleep for too long."

She nudged Dale. "Okay, check out the Sentry's arm. Any idea what that is?"

Dale stiffened. "It's from Valya's bag," he said.

"Ask yourself what he's doing with it."

"I don't have to," he said. "The Skyphoi didn't kill Valya—fucking Dash did!"

Dale was already in motion. Makali put her hand on his arm. "What do you think you're doing?"

"Good question." That was Zack Stewart from across the railcar. He had handed the Tik-Talk off to Zhao and had been watching Makali and Dale.

Makali saw no way to tell Zack of their suspicions without alerting Dash, who remained busy and apparently oblivious four meters away.

Not secretly, of course. But who needed secrets? "We were just talking some Earth history."

Zack knew that wasn't true, that they were hiding something. "Okay . . ."

"About Americans' involvement in various conflicts going back a century . . . and how we frequently discovered we had been slow to recognize the threat of fascism."

"Yeah," Zack said. Rachel and Pav were looking at each other. Yvonne was staring straight at Makali.

"Like Hitler," Dale said. "Americans were slow to realize what a danger Hitler was—" And here Dale glanced toward Dash.

Moving with a speed Makali found surprising and alarming, the Sentry pushed itself away from the wall, pulled itself toward the open side of the railcar, and jumped out.

Rachel screamed. The dog barked and jumped out, too.

"What's going on?" Yvonne said. She pointed to the Architect, who was otherwise impassive. "He's very confused."

"Dash is working for the other side," Dale said. "It killed Valya and the Skyphoi Revenant—"

The railcar rattled to a violent stop, throwing everyone forward.

"Now what?" Dale said. "Another blackout?"

"He stopped us," Yvonne said.

"Well, make him start us again," Zhao said. "We can't waste more time."

"What about Cowboy?" Rachel said.

"We're not stopping for a dog," Zack said. "But we're stopped, right?" Yvonne nodded.

"Let's find the son of a bitch before he does something else to us."

He headed for the hatch and jumped into the dark tunnel.

Rachel Stewart started to follow her father out of the railcar, but Makali got in her way. "You stay." She turned to Pav. "Keep her here."

Pav grabbed for Rachel's arm.

Now Zhao was up. "What are you going to do?"

"I'm going to kill that thing," Dale said, "even if I have to use bare hands."

"Unlikely," Zhao said.

"First we're going to catch him and make him talk," Makali said. "Yvonne, if you think your link with the Architect will work at a distance, you should come with us."

The astronaut headed for the open hatch. The Architect didn't move.

Zack was already fifteen meters ahead of them, running after Dash. But the *Destiny* commander's feet were obviously hindering him; Makali saw him slow, hop in pain, then try to get going again.

She and Dale quickly caught up with him. Yvonne was close behind. "Hey, Dash!" Dale shouted.

The Sentry ignored him. But the alien couldn't ignore Cowboy. The dog was the fastest being in the tunnel—with a snarling yelp, he caught the Sentry and began tugging at its garments.

The Sentry actually stopped. As it struggled with the dog, it faced the approaching humans. Now what? Makali wondered. She well remembered the story of Pogo Downey's ill-fated encounter with a hostile Sentry.

But she didn't need a plan of action after all; Dale simply rushed the Sentry like a football linebacker, slamming the alien between knees and waist.

The Sentry was staggered, but not felled—until Zack

Stewart hit him, too. Dash hit the wall, then stumbled sideways.

With the dog barking and looking for an opening, Dale and Zack, working together for the first time, tried to pin the Sentry.

It's come to this, Makali realized. Two weeks ago she could only fantasize about discovering hard evidence of alien life. Now they were tackling a genuine alien being. If it weren't so tragic, it would be hilarious.

"We *saved* you," Zack yelled at Dash.

"I . . . expressed gratitude." It was strange hearing a calm, monotonic voice emerge from the translation unit when the Sentry was clearly struggling.

"Didn't last long."

"I had my mission."

"I don't understand your mission. Or anything you've done."

"We are bred to fight, even our own kind. It's in our water—"

Before Yvonne or Makali could add their weight, Dash flung them aside as if they were angry cats. Dale landed on Cowboy, who squealed in pain.

With impressive speed and determination, Dash was off again, soon with four humans and a dog in ragged pursuit.

Within moments Dash had passed through a T-junction in the tunnel. As Makali, Zack, Dale, and Yvonne huffed and puffed in the Sentry's wake, Zack said, "We're never going to catch him again."

"Maybe we should let him go," Makali said, mindful of Zhao's urging about their mission to the power core.

"No. He's killed humans and he's involved with the Reivers. We need what he knows."

"No we don't," Yvonne said. "We need to . . ."

She turned back and looked at the railcar a hundred meters away.

It was moving *toward them*.

"We need to get out of the way," she said. "This way!" She pushed or dragged the other three into the side tunnel. Cowboy was faster than all of them.

They had barely exited the main passage before the railcar flashed past them like a whisper. Makali felt the explosion of displaced air and a disturbing rippling sensation, as if her entire body had been stretched wide, then allowed to snap back to its original state.

"What the hell was that?" Dale said.

"Cat's-eye passing," Yvonne said, as if that explained anything.

The railcar had stopped a few meters away. Zhao, Pav, and Rachel were emerging slowly, like accident victims. "Who did that?" Zhao said.

"Keanu did it," Yvonne said simply.

Dash lay on the floor of the tunnel in front of the railcar. The impact had been horrific; flattened on one side, oozing internal fluid, the Sentry looked as though it had been dropped from a ten-story building. The dog sniffed at the remains and didn't much like what it smelled.

Zack knelt to examine the body. After a moment, he simply sat back. "I've got to tell you, I'm getting tired of finding these things dead." He slowly rose. "That makes three."

Only now did he realize that his fourteen-year-old

daughter was standing two meters away, taking in the entire gruesome scene. "Rachel," he said.

"Don't worry, Daddy. After the things I've seen . . ."

Makali noted that Pav was holding her hand. And that the Architect had emerged from the railcar. The silent giant moved like an old man with arthritis.

Then the power died again. Unlike the previous momentary blackouts Makali had experienced, this was accompanied by a sound that might have been a distant explosion. The entire tunnel—indeed, all of Keanu—seemed to shudder.

"Tell me that was another cat's-eye," Makali said.

"Sorry," Yvonne said, nodding to the Architect, who now appeared hunched over. "That was the vesicle being launched with Reivers on board."

"We're too late. It's going to Earth."

"The son of a bitch suckered us," Dale said.

"What are you talking about?" Zack said. The power returned but immediately went off again. The whole system seemed to be sputtering.

"He stalled us just long enough!" Dale laughed. "He literally threw himself under the bus so these Reivers could get to the vesicle first!"

"Does that mean we're screwed?" Pav said. "We can't go home?"

"I'm more worried about whether Keanu will survive," Zhao said. "The power's not steady."

Zack turned to Yvonne. "This is the Architect's world," he said. "What can we do?"

"Go to the Skyphoi," Yvonne said. "They're our only hope now."

HARLEY

"It's a form of the disease that afflicts Dr. Jones," Jaidev said. "His attacks the organs from within. This attacks the brain and central nervous system." He was holding a crude-looking injector filled with a milky fluid.

"But it kills the host," Harley Drake said.

"Yes." The serious-minded Indian engineer looked at Harley as if he were an idiot. And not for the first time. "How else would it do the job?"

Shane Weldon sat down next to Harley. They were at the worktable in the second-floor "kitchen" of the Temple. The light was so low it was like camping out. The sounds of the habitat—a distant drone, the whisper of a faint breeze, and what Harley now realized was a creaking sound he associated with spacecraft expanding and contracting—had all died away as the power dropped to a minimum.

The only sounds were footsteps of HBs running up and down the ramps, as Harley and Nayar gathered their "war council."

That, and Gabriel Jones's broken voice. A few steps away, he was using the Tik-Talk to converse with his daughter, Yvonne, who had been killed in the horrific and misguided detonation of the baby nuke during the first exploration of Keanu.

Had been killed. Alive again. Harley Drake kept thinking about that idea.

Well, he was just grateful that the Tik-Talk still worked, and that they'd been able to locate Zack Stewart and the others. They knew that the Reivers had launched the vesicle toward Earth and essentially shut down Keanu's power core.

Not that any of this was especially comforting. If the power core didn't get rebooted, they were likely all dead, and with Keanu dead, not likely to become Revenants.

But the information had allowed them to come up with plans: Zack and his team would attempt to deal with the core while the Temple would stage a counterattack against these Reivers, the cause of all the problems. Jaidev and his magicians had seized on a suggestion by Zhao and had managed to produce one dosage of this brain-attacking horror before every system shut down. Their bioweapon was based on samples from Gabriel Jones. Harley wasn't quite sure how or why, but biochemistry had never been his field. Or close to it.

"The Reivers reproduce quickly and efficiently," Jaidev said. "They pass information and apparently genetic material from one aggregate to another . . . anything poisonous or damaging that hits one in its information-processing center, also known as its brain, will hit them all."

"I still don't get how we get it to them," Weldon said. "The Reivers have totally corrupted and infested the

Keanu system. What is the actual vector? You don't just jam that injector into the nearest pile of Reiver goo."

"It goes into a human host," Harley said.

There was another interruption caused by a group of people descending from the third floor as another individual tried to reach the second. It was Xavier Toutant, with this sad message: "Mr. Bynum is dead."

There was an additional bit of data for Harley's consideration: the apparent sell-by date for the Keanu Revenants. It was as if they were brought back to perform a single function, then tossed aside.

Not every Revenant, of course, and certainly not at the same rate. Look at Camilla. Also, animals from cows to cats and birds to bats had been emerging from the Beehive for the past several days. None of the HBs had been able to figure out a pattern—assuming there was one—but one thing was clear: None of the animals displayed the types of wear and tear that affected Revenants Camilla and then Chitran and now, finally, Brent Bynum. They had probably been deemed too lacking.

"Is that the bug zapper?" Xavier said, pointing to the injector.

"Not to go all operational security at this late date," Weldon said, "but aren't we afraid they might hear what we're planning?"

"The Reivers?" Nayar said, standing up for his team. "If they are literally bugging us, then they know all our moves and we are wasting our time. Let's remember that while they've corrupted Keanu's systems, they are still quasi-organic beings with their own vulnerabilities and limitations. Which we will exploit."

"By injecting someone with the . . . the bug zapper?" Weldon said.

"No, Shane," Harley said. "By infecting *someone* with a fast-moving fatal disease that will kill *him*, and by killing him and putting his personality matrix, or whatever it is Keanu is able to isolate and reuse, into the Revenant system." He had been reluctant to say it aloud, he realized, because that someone was going to have to be Mayor Harley Drake.

So he would get stuck with the bug zapper. He would be the one to quickly plunge into a feverish coma and death. It would be his poisoned and corrupted morpho-genetic data that would be absorbed into the Keanu system, and quickly into the Reivers . . . where it would burn them all.

"Oh." Weldon looked at the injector. "So I guess the question is—"

"Who," Nayar said. "Not when. This has to happen immediately."

"There's no point waiting," Harley said. "It's my job." He had hoped that saying it aloud would make it seem easier, somehow. So far . . . no.

Then Sasha Blaine came hurrying up the steps, all red hair and inescapably impressive figure in a tank top. *Great*, Harley thought, *let your last conscious thoughts be lustful.*

That surge of inappropriate interest passed quickly, because even in the faint light, Sasha was clearly distraught. "What's wrong?" Harley said, as if there was anything else that could possibly go wrong.

"Camilla left."

"She was curled up in a ball in the corner," Weldon said. "Just like Bynum."

Sasha turned to him. "Oh, she was. I thought she had gone completely catatonic, and was just talking to her in German. Nothing, nothing, nothing. Then I started repeating her little ditty about '*ratos*' and she sat right up. And just ran away."

"Then forget her," Nayar said. "I know she's a child, I know she's not responsible, but we have larger problems." He pointed to the injector. "We need to make our move now to have any chance."

He slid it toward Harley.

Sasha intercepted it. "Oh, no," she said.

"Yes," Harley said.

"Why you?"

"It has to be one of us," Weldon said.

Sasha turned to him again. "Except 'us' has turned into 'Harley.'"

"I'm the leader," Harley said.

"I'm the leader, too," a voice said behind them.

It was Gabriel Jones, his eyes still red and face still shining from a very emotional conversation. "These people were my responsibility from the beginning. The weapon uses my . . . tissue. If anyone should make the sacrifice, it should be me."

"You need to see Yvonne face-to-face again," Harley said.

"Oh, Harley, she's wearing out. Dying like Bynum." He forced a smile. "She seems okay with it . . . says she fulfilled her mission, redeemed herself. But she won't last."

"Actually," Shane Weldon said, "none of us will last if the core isn't rebooted and the Reivers eliminated."

Jones pointed at Weldon. "Exactly. And I'm the biggest medical burden. I'm past my sell-by date. Give *me* the zapper."

For one selfish moment, Harley felt a flood of relief. Gabriel Jones *was* the most logical victim.

And yet . . . Harley was in charge. If there was one lesson he had learned in life, one thing he believed in without question, it was this: The guy in charge makes the big decisions. The captain goes down with the ship. "Sorry, Gabe," he said, and reached for the injector.

Then Xavier Toutant stepped forward, snatched up the injector—and handed it to Jones! Before any of them could stop him, the JSC director touched it to his arm and triggered it.

He seemed about to say something . . . but failed, as his eyes rolled up in his head and he fainted.

Nayar and Jaidev caught him and gently lowered him to the floor. "For God's sake," Harley said, "make him comfortable." *As he dies.*

"God, that was brave," Sasha said.

"Let's hope it wasn't for nothing," Shane Weldon said.

ZACK

The encounter with the Skyphoi had been strange even by Zack Stewart's improved and expanded scale of strangeness.

The survivors of the Dash treachery had returned to the "station" in the railcar, bumping along on low power, like a golf cart with a dying battery. A pair of the giant balloon creatures had been waiting, both flashing chromatophores in patterns the humans could not and would likely never understand.

The failing state of the railcar matched that of the Architect. It seemed to be declining into immobility and likely death at the same rate as the entire NEO. When Zack said as much, Rachel announced, "That's because he is Keanu." Zack would have loved to pursue that, but the Architect went into terminal failure at that instant, slumping to one side and almost crushing Zhao. "Daddy!" Rachel shouted.

Zack and Dale reached for the Architect, their hands failing to find purchase on the creature's garments. But sheer muscle power allowed them to extricate Zhao.

As the Chinese spy slid out from under the Architect, he said, "Should I try some kind of resuscitation?"

"Where the hell would you start?" Dale said.

"It doesn't matter," Yvonne said. "He's gone."

Zack didn't like the way Yvonne looked: gray and list-less. "How are you doing?" Had she been linked, some-how, to the Architect as the alien died? And how did the death of this creature relate to the possible death of Keanu itself? Was the Near-Earth Object itself dead already? How would you be able to tell?

"As okay as I'm going to be," she said. "For the first time since . . . coming back, I feel like myself. No more voices in my head." She managed a smile, one that was so familiar to Zack from their time as astronauts that it brought tears to his eyes.

Well, hell, everything was bringing tears to his eyes right now.

"Last things," she said. "Think of the Skyphoi as cus-todians or caretakers. They live a long time by our stan-dards. They aren't truly individuals, or not all the time, so there's a lot of continuity over generations. They're masters of the systems, though. They devise repairs, and other races, with hands, do the dirty work."

"So that's us," Makali said. "Hands."

"For a vessel like this, yes," Yvonne said. "The Sky-phoi wouldn't have built anything like Keanu."

"What do they have?" Zack said.

"A trigger to restart the power core."

"Won't that be . . . very large?" Dale said. "I mean, the power core has got to be massive."

"It will be powerful but appropriately sized," Yvonne said. "Our job is to deliver it and activate it."

"Then what?" Zack said. "The lights come back on, we find our way back to the habitat, great. But the Reivers are still running loose, right?"

"Correct," Yvonne said. "But with Keanu's systems up and running again, there will be . . . sanitary measures."

Zack recognized the words. Dash had used them to describe the blasted habitat of the crab creatures. Dale caught it, too. "Okay, note to the Skyphoi: We have a say in sanitary measures. No zapping of the human habitat."

But he seemed too tired to say more, and Zack, realizing there would be more and trickier work after a reboot, felt the same.

He reminded himself of his NASA training. Follow the checklist, one step at a time. The reboot would be a big one.

He had handed Yvonne the Tik-Talk at that point. Then, with some distance yet to travel, seeing that Dale and Makali were sunk in one corner, Rachel and Pav clinging to each other and holding hands, the dog resting its head on its paws, and Yvonne tearfully talking to her father . . . all of his charges accounted for . . . Zack allowed himself to close his eyes.

And fell into the deepest sleep he had known in days, since before the arrival of the vesicle Objects . . . likely before his launch from Earth on *Destiny-7*.

He was in a crowded bus or a subway car much like this railcar . . . in his dream, he was aware of the similarity . . . but pressed up against him was Megan. She looked younger, as she had when they first met and fell in love, long before the astronaut or journalist or parental years.

And they kissed, lips on lips, his hand sliding into her

shirt . . . again, as he and she and they often had, falling
into a sweet surging stupor that he wanted to last and last
and last and—

He woke. No one was moving except the door. The
railcar had stopped. The interior was dark, the only illumination a series of flickering lights from somewhere
outside.

And he felt . . . elated. Not aroused, though there was
a bit of that, just happy for once. He was a bit rested, that
was good.

It was like the early weeks of his first space station
mission, once he'd passed that crucial thirty-day point,
becoming not only physically acclimated to life in microgravity, but at home with the long days, the isolation, the
small joys of making an experiment work, or just creating
a meal.

It was a mind-set suited to life off Earth . . . life on
Keanu, perhaps.

"Everybody out," he said, "end of the line."

A pair of Skyphoi were waiting. As Zack and the others
approached, one of them extruded a silvery package,
which clattered to the ground.

Zack was distracted by the swirling gasbags as they
kept shifting positions, and by the look on Rachel's face,
which varied from wonder to terror.

But now he finally focused on the package . . . a silvery
suitcase that looked a lot like the Personal Preference
Kits astronauts carried on missions—the containers for
personal items, patches, photographs, school pennants.

He wondered why the Skyphoi had used it, but only for a moment. He touched Yvonne's shoulder and said, quietly, "Is that where they put the nuke on *Venture*? In one of the PPKs?"

She nodded. "The Skyphoi like to use templates that we would recognize. That way they know what we can carry."

"I wish they'd picked something else," he said.

Now one of the Skyphoi started moving away, farther up the tunnel. "Where do you suppose he's going?" Makali said.

They found an answer with the second Skyphoi, which dropped behind them and, strangely, began to expand, like an inflating balloon. "I think we're being herded," Zhao said.

"No," Makali said. "Defended."

Zack heard a growling buzz from somewhere down the tunnel . . . through the semitransparent body of the second Skyphoi, he could see swiftly moving shapes. "What the hell is that?"

"Oh, God, Daddy, it's a Long Legs."

Before he could ask for clarification, Pav said, "A type of Reiver."

"Commander," Dale said, "we've gotta go."

Zack picked up the case. It was so light he wondered if it actually held anything useful. What did you use to reignite the power core of a starship? Well, Dr. Stewart, that depends on the nature of the core—anti-matter? Or something even more exotic?

He didn't need to know. He just needed to make it work.

As the second Skyphoi fought its rearguard action, the humans followed the first creature up the tunnel . . . Zack, Rachel, and Yvonne in the lead, Zhao and Pav and Cowboy right behind . . . Makali and Dale at the rear.

"So the plan," Zack said, huffing and puffing, "is this: Enter the core, place the unit within, get out. How long do I have?"

"I don't know," Yvonne said. "I really, really wish I could tell you, but I'm out of info." She nodded at the floating Skyphoi. "They control the ignition. They'll know."

Zack wanted to scream with laughter. All the decisions he had made, from the crazy gravity gauge trick on *Brahma* to throwing the rover off the side of Vesuvius Vent, to confronting the first Architect to going overland from the shattered Beehive to the Sentry habitat . . . each one had been his to make, his to live with.

Now he was a courier for implacable, uncommunicative, unknowable aliens.

And not only his life, but the lives of every human on Keanu—and very possibly the lives of the entire human race—depended on them.

There was a universal lesson in that somewhere. But he was too tired and frustrated to appreciate it.

The Skyphoi brought them to a side shaft and a Membrane. "This is the core?" Pav said.

"Might be the entrance to another shaft," Dale said. He turned to Zack. "Okay, Commander, hand it over."

"It's my job, Dale."

Dale nodded toward Rachel. "Your daughter disagrees."

"He's right, Daddy," Rachel said. "Let someone else do this. Please!"

Zack looked at her dirty, pretty, exhausted, distraught face, seeing traces of her mother. "I'd draw straws, but we don't have any," he said. That wasn't enough, for either of them.

He took his daughter's hand and led her away, to where they were directly under the floating, flashing Sky-phoi . . . the closest thing to a zone of privacy. "I love you, Rachel—"

"Don't say that! It means you think you're never going to see me again."

"I am going to see you again. In a few minutes, the moment I drop this thing off."

"I'm afraid," she said. "Mom went away, then she came back, then . . ." She collapsed against him, sobbing.

He couldn't allow himself to do the same. *Be a father. Be a leader.*

"Look, honey, baby girl." He kissed her. "Look!" He finally got her attention. "We're all . . . information. That's what the universe is. And it never really dies, okay? But it has to keep changing. That's why the Reivers are bad—they're frozen, they don't get worse and they never get better. We may have to die or go away or change state to get better."

"I hate that."

"Don't hate it. It's the most miraculous thing humans have ever discovered."

Saying it aloud, he almost convinced himself. But all

around them, the air began to grow stagnant. Temperatures were dropping.

There was an ominous rumbling, as if Keanu were suffering death throes. *Maybe that's what a NEO's death is like,* Zack thought; *it breaks up, scattering itself across space....*

He had to act now. One last hug, one last kiss. "I'll see you in a little while. Go with Makali."

He turned to the others. He was almost shouting. "This isn't a suicide mission. I'll meet you guys right here once I've got this bad boy working again."

He never let go of the unit. If he did, he'd never pick it up again.

He pointed to the Tik-Talk, which was now in Zhao's hands. "Tell Harley that I expect a decent meal for the first time. Something in a steak should do it."

Then, picking up the package, he stepped into the Membrane, and fell into darkness.

There was almost no gravity in the shaft. Zack was barely aware that he was falling.

The landing was soft, featherlike, so gentle that he was able to tuck his knees up—just like living in microgravity aboard the International Space Station—and land on both feet.

He wasn't steady; the entire chamber continued to rock, like Los Angeles with aftershocks. It made every movement more difficult, more urgent—

He ended up in another ancient stone-tile chamber,

with five shafts leading in different directions. Before he had to confront the decision of which to take, he saw that he wasn't alone.

The Revenant girl Camilla waited for him. She had been sitting in the darkness. Now she rose.

Odd how this child seemed to haunt these moments.

Even odder that he kept having them.

"Everyone back at the Temple is wondering what happened to you," he said, knowing she wouldn't understand.

To his shock, she said, in English, "Regrettable. I became infected. I became an instrument of the enemy. It was like a fever—I could only sing this little song from my childhood about '*ratos*.' I was warning you—"

"About the Reivers."

"Yes."

"But you're no longer constrained."

"Oh, no. I'm destroyed," Camilla said. "But the infection is contained within me. When I die, it dies, too."

For the first time since reconnecting with Rachel, Zack grew alarmed. *This isn't right.* But the only comment he could offer was, "I'm sorry." Then, feeling that to be inadequate, added, "Your communication skills have improved."

"We are able to work more efficiently with young subjects," she said. "I speak for the Architect."

"I figured." He looked around. "Do you know the way to the core?"

She immediately turned to the shaft across from them and pointed. "Okay," he said. "Are you coming with me?"

"The effort is straining my body," she said. "I have very little time."

What did that mean? Was she going to sit down and die here? He held out his hand. "I'll help."

And, stumbling as another quake jolted them, she took Zack's hand.

Steadying himself as best he could, he slung the kit over his shoulder.

It was like walking into the first few meters of the Beehive, though longer and straighter. Zack was grateful for the distance, since it allowed him to ask, "Do you take messages to the Architect, too? To Keanu itself?"

"That is the nature of communication. We hear you."

"That's good," he said. They passed through another Membrane, the curtain shimmering in response to the quaking and shuddering. "Because this reboot and saving you, the ship, is only half the battle."

"What else do you want?"

"To save Earth," he said, surprised to hear those words come out of his mouth. "I want to keep that vesicle from reaching my home planet. Nothing else matters." He imagined the Reiver vesicle splashing down in the ocean, or touching down in some remote forest or mountain range. How long would it take for the nasty little creatures, exposed to sunlight, awash in oxygen and soil and hydrogen, to start reproducing at some fantastic rate?

He pictured the beautiful blue-and-white sphere of

Earth, as he had seen it close up from the space station, and far away from *Destiny*. Now add a black spot of contagion in the middle of the USA. How quickly would it spread? How long before the entire North American continent was that horrible color, awash with Reiver templates?

The world?

And what would it mean? Would people die? Quite likely, just as swiftly and horribly as they would if a mutated Ebola virus struck.

Or would Earth and humanity be transformed into something mean, ugly, Reiver-like.

"The war isn't on your planet," Camilla said. "The battlefield is elsewhere."

"I think the battlefield is everywhere," he said. "The sooner you realize that, the sooner you'll start to win."

She was silent for several moments. Then: "We were unsuited to fighting the Reivers. Too old, too fragile, too large scale."

"Too large scale?"

"Our reactions, our thought processes—they are simply too slow. We can't compete against creatures who live in fractions of fractions of a moment. They can make a million decisions in the time it takes us to make one. And there are other flaws, too."

Zack said, "So consider this: We're a few hundred humans in a ten-thousand-year-old ship. We might be able to help you with one battle when Keanu gets wherever it's going, but if I were you, I'd want seven billion weapons—I'd want the entire population of Earth working as a team."

"You can't promise that, and mobilizing your entire

population is impossible. We had a difficult time collecting two hundred, and you are still not a fighting unit."

"That may be our strength," Zack said, afraid he was losing the most important argument in human history. "Think of us as bridging the gap between you and the Reivers. We're smaller, faster, capable of operating in discrete units. But we are still individuals. We'll never act as a bloc, the way they do."

Then she said, "We are still suspicious. Consider your actions here."

"Individuals make mistakes. Groups of individuals make bigger ones. It's how we learn and change."

A long silence. Finally she said, "If you accomplish the restart, we will consider turning the vessel around and returning to Earth."

That would have to do. He hugged the girl, a bit of a trick with the rattling and shaking all around them. He wanted to laugh out loud. He thought of his friends and surviving family members—his poor parents and the hell they must have gone through these past two weeks—and all the workers in the space community, not to mention the astronomers who had discovered the NEO in the first place . . . the look on their faces when they realized that Keanu was heading back!

Assuming, of course, that he succeeded—

They stumbled into a vast brilliant cylinder tens of kilometers tall. Zack felt like a microbe at the focus of a telescope.

High above them, what appeared to be a brown dwarf star floated . . . fading even as Zack watched.

"We have little time," Camilla said.

"What do I do with this unit?" Zack said. "Is there a switch or a trigger?"

"Oh," she said, "you triggered it by carrying it through the last Membrane. Drop it there."

Zack did as Camilla directed. Before the unit left his hand, it began to throb, grow warm, grow *heavy*.

The girl drifted forward, deeper into the cylinder. "Not that way," he said. "Let's get out of here."

Camilla stopped, spread her arms as if in benediction. Then turned to Zack with a smile.

Zack didn't need to ask the next question. Camilla's posture told him everything. "We aren't getting out, are we?"

"If the device is used properly, we have no chance of survival."

Oh God, he thought. He exhaled once, twice, three times. With the rocking and rolling motion of the NEO interior, he felt like a captain on a sinking ship.

There was the case, glowing with a white-hot brilliance, like a doorway opening to heaven—

Sadness hit him like a hammer. Good-bye Earth and friends and NASA and Michigan and Mom and Dad and strawberries and clean sheets and sunrises and the stars and kisses and music and Rachel and Megan and—

Holding hands, he and Camilla walked into the holy light.

Epilogue

And there was war in heaven: Michael and his angels fought against the dragon; and the dragon fought and his angels, And prevailed not; neither was their place found any more in heaven.
REVELATION 12:7–8

We're still here.
KEANU-PEDIA BY PAV, MUCH LATER ENTRY

RACHEL

Rachel was shocked at how much the gravesite had changed since her last visit. But then, she wasn't in the habit of visiting. There was always too much to do. And the memory of her parents was still strong. She still thought of them every day.

Even after twenty-one years.

Besides, while the remains of her mother's second body were buried here, there was only a stone to Zachary Stewart's memory. He had never returned from the power core.

She had often relived her last conversation with Yvonne, who died less than a day after Zack entered the shaft that dropped him into Keanu's power core. Yvonne had clearly wanted to comfort Rachel on her loss, even as she was dying.

"Why are the Reivers so bad?" she remembered asking Yvonne. "Couldn't we find a way to work with them? Aren't they just information arranged differently?"

"Exactly," Yvonne said. "They are perfect machines for the collection of energy and its use. Their only purpose seems to be replication."

"Isn't that what we do?"

"No," Yvonne said. "We have love and free will, and our information grows and changes . . ."

"The Reivers are where information goes to die."

And if we don't stop them, Rachel had concluded, *that's what the universe becomes. Dead.*

Her deputy mayor got her attention. "Do you wish to remain in private?"

Sentries were always so deferential, a state that would have startled any of the Houston Bangalores in their early encounters with the aquatic race. Their motives, their incomprehensible savagery, all combined to make them unwelcome crewmates. But years of negotiation and, frankly, mutual evolution had not only resulted in a truce—they had created a kinder, gentler type of Sentry. If they were going to be useful in a war on Earth, they would have to step out of their comfort zone.

Sentries would have to be the warriors they once were. Because that was what they were facing.

When the Reivers launched the vesicle, they also commanded Keanu's propulsion system to fire a long, sustained burst, not only accelerating the NEO to its greatest speed, but depleting its onboard fuel supply so thoroughly that it took years—decades—to replenish.

One of the side effects of this fuel starvation and system crash had been the elimination of the Revenant function. No human had been reborn since the day of the power core restart, though some HBs continued to try. No animals beyond the dozen that had been released. It was only after Beehive technology was imported to the Temple system that experiments in 3-D manufacturing and plasm manipulation created a permanent animal population, though not without much pain and loss.

All the while, Keanu was moving farther and farther from Earth.

It had been difficult . . . not just eradicating the Reivers. The Gabriel Jones–delivered information virus, aka the bug zapper, had done most of the work, causing the machinelike beings to evolve themselves into unstable and unsurvivable forms that then crashed, collapsed, and died. All of them, from tiny bugs to Long Legs and other forms.

But it had taken years before humans were certain that there were no Reiver colonies anywhere on the interior or surface of Keanu.

Rachel was in her early twenties when the HBs, then numbering more than three hundred and living in two habitats, were able to fire Keanu's engines again, braking the trajectory (which took five years) and firing the vessel back toward Earth.

With limited fuel, however, Keanu was never able to reach the same velocity . . . the flight "home" took three times as long as the flight out. Until recently, there had been no communication with Earth. It had taken years of experimentation with Keanu's systems to develop such a system—and more years until the vessel was within range.

Then there had been a long series of debates—what do we know about Earth? If the Reivers reached it, the entire planet might be infected, enemy territory.

So we wait, Rachel thought. Until today.

Pav Radhakrishnan, her longtime lover and confidant,

approached, edging in front of the Sentry. "Madame Mayor," Pav said, relishing the term because he knew it irritated Rachel, "what are your orders? Do we answer Earth, do we stay silent and fly on by, or—?"

She rose. As she did, she happened to glance back across the habitat to the original Temple, now surrounded by Keanu-grown apartments and fabrication facilities. There were fields, roads, passages that connected to other habitats. The HB population now stood at close to one thousand.

So different from those first days.

Rachel turned to face Pav, and DSA, connate of DSZ, her best friend among the Sentries and her functioning first mate. "We're not going to fly on by," she said.

"I know," Pav said. "But you always like to hear all the options."

"And we can't remain silent much longer," DSA said through its translator. "There is no evidence that we've been tracked, but we are detectable by telescopes that existed a human century ago."

It was not going to be easy. In fact, if the Reivers had indeed reached Earth, Rachel and Pav and all the HBs were facing a continuation of the ugly little war her father had fought and won twenty-one years ago.

What would Zack Stewart say? Or Megan?

"Let's go get 'em."

BLIND TRANSMISSION RECEIVED ABOARD KEANU:

Greetings!

Colin Edgely here . . . discoverer of Keanu back in 2016, transmitting from an undisclosed location.

It's twenty-one years to the day since the *Venture* and *Brahma* crews landed on Keanu, twenty-one years to the week that 187 humans were taken there by means unknown. Some of us have watched you fly away from Earth and the solar system.

Some fewer have watched you fly back.

We hope you can read this or understand it:

DON'T

[Message corrupted.]

Acknowledgments

An SF trilogy, especially an epic SF trilogy of which *Heaven's War* is the middle chapter, takes time. We've been working on this since January 2007 and have a bit of road ahead of us.

So, first, thanks are due our wives, Marina Black and Cindy Cassutt, and the children, Milo, Sayle, Ryan, and Alexandra.

At Ace Books, Ginjer Buchanan, Kat Sherbo, and Rosanne Romanello. At Pan Macmillan, Julie Crisp and Bella Pagan.

Simon Lipskar at Writers House.

A special shout-out to those who supported *Heaven's Shadow*: Rick Kleffel, Lou Anders, and Paul Cornell.

And double thanks to those who are continuing on Keanu's journey.

D.S.G. & M.C.
Los Angeles, December 2011

FROM AUTHORS
DAVID S. GOYER &
MICHAEL CASSUTT

HEAVEN'S
SHADOW

An immense object is approaching Earth. Two manned vehicles race through space to land first on its frozen, desolate surface: one launched by NASA, the other representing the Russian-Indian-Brazilian Coalition. Both crews have orders to do whatever it takes to claim it as their own.

But the entity is not simply a rock hurtling through the blackness. It has been sent to Earth for a reason. A vastly more intelligent race is desperately attempting to communicate with our primitive species. And its interstellar courier carries a message that the very core of humanity has responded to since time began.

Help us...

PRAISE FOR *HEAVEN'S SHADOW*

"[A] trippy, pulse-pounding tale."
—Guillermo del Toro, creator of *Pan's Labyrinth* and *New York Times* bestselling coauthor of *The Night Eternal*

"Cassutt and Goyer give Arthur C. Clarke a run for his money."
—Robert J. Sawyer, Hugo and Nebula award–winning author of *Red Planet Blues*

facebook.com/HeavensShadowtheTrilogy
facebook.com/AceRocBooks
penguin.com

M1272T0213

THE ULTIMATE WRITERS OF
SCIENCE FICTION